FYRE FLY

Book 2 of Friendly Fyre

Kia Leep

Pulsar Publishing

BOOK I RECAP

After dying from a heart attack on Earth, Fyre is reincarnated in a fantasy world to find she's now in the body of a flightless harpy—and a woman. Magic is a difficult concept for her to swallow, given her previous career as an aeronautical engineer, but she's fascinated to learn whatever she can about these new laws of physics. Forming a pact with a gemstone with a voracious appetite for rocks, the so-called Dungeon Core digs Fyre from her frozen cave and helps guide her to another resident of the cave system.

Mirzayael, an arachnoid, is half-spider-half-woman and head guard of Fyreneth's Keep. Despite her suspicions with Fyre's unexpected arrival, she takes her back to her underground kingdom.

In the midst of questioning her gender, Fyre is thrown into a much stranger identity crisis as the residents of the Keep draw parallels between her and their ancient ruler, a harpy named Fyreneth. Their founder had also wielded a powerful artifact capable of shaping the earth itself, and she died burying their kingdom beneath the arctic to protect her people from hostile gods and their ardent devotees, the Kingdom of Jorria. Fyre finds this association doubly concerning considering the Role this world's magic system has given her: The Dark Lord.

Focusing on survival and determined to subvert the implications of her Role, Fyre uses the Dungeon Core and her newfound fire-wielding abilities to bring warmth to the Fyrethians' city. While in the process of exploring the nearby caverns, she also discovers a giant ice dragon, trapped in a cave far beneath the surface. After freeing him, the beast is revealed to be a seven-year-old child named Ollie, and just like Fyre, he's another soul from Earth that's been reincarnated on this world. Fyre begins to wonder how many more transplanted people from Earth there might be.

As Fyre and Mirzayael begin restoring Fyreneth's underground castle, Ollie's conspicuous flights attract the attention of an old Fyrethian colony that had fled the collapse of their kingdom hundreds of years prior. Now reunited, Fyreneth's people begin to thrive once more.

Unfortunately, their activity also draws the attention of their ancient foes, the Jorrians. The kingdom launches a siege against Fyreneth's Fortress, with the intention of burying them for good.

But the Fyrethians refuse to go down without a fight. Using the Dungeon Core's stone-altering abilities, Fyre is able to put her aerodynamics expertise to use by raising the Fortress as a giant floating city. From the sky, they are able to destroy the Jorrian army with ease. With the shadow of her Role looming over her, however, Fyre chooses to spare the now-defenseless Jorrian kingdom. With the battle over, Fyre sets sail for the horizon, in search of a home for her new family and friends where they can live in peace once and for all.

Chapter One

THE SKY'S THE LIMIT

"*COME ON, FYRE!*" Ollie calls. The white dragon vanishes in a swirl of mist as he plunges into a nearby cloud. "*RACE YOU!*"

"*I am slightly preoccupied at the moment,*" I mentally reply. "*We can play after I finish taking these measurements.*"

"*BOOOO, MEASUREMENTS,*" Ollie says. He reappears as he tears out the opposite side of the cloud, dispersing it entirely with a few flaps of his enormous wings. He does a couple of loop-de-loops after that, and his delight echoes down our mental connection as clearly as if he were the seven-year-old human he'd been born as, giggling in my arms.

"Fyre?" Dizzi prompts me. The harpy is hovering nearby, her wind affinity allowing her to levitate in the air rather than needing to fly tight laps, as classical aerodynamics would require from such physiology. "I asked what distance we're at now."

"Sorry," I call back. "Ollie was asking to play. Let me check."

I myself am also hovering in the sky, using a Jet spell to gimbal five magical fires lit beneath my talons, wings, and one of my hands. In my other hand I'm holding a rock. It's entirely unremarkable, except that it belongs to the Dungeon Core, a fact that the Dungeon Core won't let me forget.

Even though the Core is physically back in Fyreneth's Fortress, securely attached to the throne, it shifts nervously in my mind as I access its interface.

It urges me to be careful with its rock. Now that we are in the sky, there are no more nearby rocks—except for what's already in its fortress—so it would be very sad if I dropped and lost this one.

I won't drop it, I assure the Dungeon Core. And even if I did, I'm sure Dizzi or Ollie would be delighted to plunge through the sky after it to try and catch it before it hit the ocean, thousands of meters below.

The Dungeon Core catches this last thought and is extremely un-reassured!

It's been like this ever since we took to the sky. The air is very much not the Dungeon Core's element, which has resulted in it acting protective of its dirt. I've reiterated that our flight is only a temporary state, since the wind arcana in the cloudstone won't last forever. We'll settle back on land again, when we can find somewhere with a natural source of arcana that can keep the palace powered.

Unsurprisingly, these assurances do little to placate the Dungeon Core.

In its interface, I Check several characteristics of the rock I'm currently holding.

[Dolomite,] Echo reports. [Hardness: 3.6. Mass: 2.5 kilograms. Distance: 1481 meters.]

"About a kilometer and a half," I tell Dizzi.

She frowns, looking back to Fyreneth's Fortress. "That can't be right. We're way closer than that."

"The distance is measured from the city's center of mass, not its outer walls," I tell her. "So a lot of the range falls within the city."

Hesitantly, I drift a few more feet away from the city. It only takes Echo a couple seconds to speak up.

[Role Requirement,] she says as the Sanity stat in the corner of my vision flips from 100% to 99%. [The Dark Lord must protect her kingdom.]

And by this, what Echo really means is that I need to stay close enough to the city that it's deemed "protected." Unfortunately, I haven't been able to get her to give me the specific parameters she uses to determine these metrics.

Which is why I've decided to reverse engineer them.

"*FYRE*," Ollie abruptly speaks up, alarmed. "*ARE YOU OKAY?*"

At the same time, Mirzayael mentally reaches out. "*Something feels wrong. Are you injured?*"

"*I'm fine,*" I tell them both. I retreat a few meters back toward the Fortress until Echo's warnings vanish and my Sanity returns to 100%. "*It's just the Role Requirement experiment I told you guys about. Sorry, I didn't realize you'd also be able to sense its effect on me.*"

At 99% it was little more than a faint static, but even that minor stat change was enough to induce a flicker of anxiety in me. The first time I broke the requirements, the pain had become so overwhelming I'd eventually lost consciousness.

"*Please do not attempt anything rash,*" Mirzayael says sternly, though I can feel her relief.

Ollie loops back toward me, and I have to gimbal my flames against the wind of his approach to keep from being blown back. "*IS THERE ANYTHING I CAN DO TO HELP?*"

I frown. "*Is this triggering your Role Requirement, Ollie?*" His Role, The Dragon, requires him to protect me when I'm in danger. I'm not wild about this Role Requirement either, but I am hesitant to test its limits in search of a loophole, lest I cause any harm to Ollie.

"*NO,*" he says to my relief. "*I'M JUST BORED.*"

"Fyre?" Dizzi once again prompts.

I shake my head. "Sorry. Mirzayael and Ollie were worried when the Role Requirement activated."

Dizzi's eyes dance in amusement. "You've got a whole village in that head of yours."

With the Dungeon Core integrated into the entire city-castle of Fyreneth's Fortress, that's more accurate than she thinks.

"One-thousand, four-hundred, and eighty-two meters is the limit," I tell Dizzi. "Let's record that as our baseline."

"It's a shame you didn't record the distance the first time the Role Requirement kicked in," Dizzi remarks. "We could have used that to determine if these Levels of yours influence your range at all."

It is a possible factor to consider, though Leveling up a couple kilometers above sea-level is easier said than done. The metrics which seem to affect my Level are dealing damage (not an option), taking damage (not a preferable option), and performing magic. This, of course, is the most viable route, however it only counts if I am doing my own magic, like the Jet spells I'm using to keep myself aloft. Anything through the Dungeon Core's interface tragically does not count.

"I'll check next time I get a level up," I tell my apprentice. "Though I wonder if protecting the Kingdom is more dependent on the security of the Fortress than my individual powerset."

"I'm more than happy to dig into the Fortress's weapons systems." Dizzi rubs her hands together excitedly. "I haven't fully deciphered the spell circuits in the watch towers, but from what I can read, there's some pretty awesome spells still buried in the Fortress's walls."

The suggestion leaves me feeling uneasy. It's hard to forget the horns of Jorria blaring faintly in warning from below as we sailed over their city. There would have been nothing they could have done to stop us. If the Fortress is equipped with weapons, and if those fell into the wrong hands...

"Let's continue to focus on excavating the defensive spell networks first," I tell her.

It wasn't until we'd taken to the air that additional features of the Fortress had revealed themselves. During its initial ascension, one of the city's five watch towers was damaged, and when some teens later explored the abandoned structure, they discovered an ancient network of spell circles.

Each of the four remaining watch towers houses one enormously complex spell circle. Dizzi thinks some are defensive and some are offensive: I've only had a brief opportunity to investigate them myself, which led to me discovering even more sections of the castle that were disconnected from the throne room, which itself serves as a sort of magical central hub to the Fortress. These capabilities would have been invaluable when the Jorrians initially attacked. But I hadn't had time to explore every inch of Fyreneth's Fortress before, and I have even less time now, given I've been busy with, well. Everything.

Which is why I'm currently leaving the investigation to Dizzi. *Delegate*, I can hear Mirzayael telling me. *You can't do everything yourself.*

"*You're thinking about me*," Mirzayael says. "*I can feel it.*"

I smile. "*They're good thoughts, I promise.*"

"*I wouldn't expect anything less.*"

I chuckle. Mirzayael's humor is so dry, you'd think she grew up in a desert. But since we established a Psionic Link, the amusement she feels, even when delivering a joke with an entirely straight face, has provided a useful tell for determining which remarks are made in jest.

"You talking to Mirzayael again?" Dizzi asks, arching a mischievous eyebrow.

I look at her in surprise. "How did you know?"

"You get this small smile when you do." She grins herself, and despite the chill of the wind, I can feel heat rising up the back of my neck.

"*IS IT TIME TO PLAY YET?*" Ollie asks.

I mentally check my agenda: Mirzayael and I aren't scheduled for our daily report for another thirty minutes. "*Alright,*" I agree. "*Just let me put the Dungeon Core's rock away before it has a panic attack.*"

"*OH, I CAN TAKE IT BACK,*" Ollie volunteers, forgetting that I can simply add it to the Core's Inventory.

But the Dungeon Core hears Ollie's suggestion and is relieved anyway. Yes, please! Finally! It cannot afford to lose any more rocks.

"*IF I SEE ANY MORE ISLANDS I'LL GRAB YOU SOME MORE,*" Ollie tells the Dungeon Core, which vibrates with excitement.

The Core's anxiety ratcheted up the first few days we were in the air, until Ollie noticed a small rocky island not much larger than himself and retrieved a few clawfuls of rocks to bring back to the Fortress. Ever since then, the Core has thought very highly of Ollie, and the boy is absolutely delighted to be the rock's favorite. As far as I can tell, Ollie views the Dungeon Core like some kind of pet, and takes every opportunity available to make it happy.

Ollie flips over mid-flight and heads toward me. When he's close, I toss the rock his way, and he catches it in his mouth. As he whips past us, on the way to the Fortress, the vortices of his wake fling Dizzi and I into a tumble. Dizzi shrieks in delight, and my stomach lurches into my throat, but we both recover without incident as the dragon disappears back within the Fortress.

Above the city, the silhouettes of other harpies dot the sky. In the sunlight, from this distance, Fyreneth's Fortress indeed looks like a city that spent several hundred years in a grimy cave. While the rooftops are made from stone the color of flames, the tiles are worn from a million drips of calcium enriched water. The white walls of buildings are stained with grey and black streaks. Cracks run up many of the walls, where water and ice seeped in over hundreds of years.

But every day it looks more refined than the last. Every time I look back, it seems to have changed in some subtle way, like a flower slowly blooming. It's only been a week since we left the arctic behind, but the enthusiasm which infects the city is palpable. Someone finds something that needs doing and starts the work before it's even made it up the chain to Mirzayael and I. My heart aches for how much I love this city and its people.

"Beautiful, isn't it?" Dizzi remarks, watching the Fortress beside me. "Those rudders were a stroke of genius."

I chuckle. I should have suspected it was the technological aspects she finds beautiful, not that I can blame her. "It wasn't my genius," I say. "I just implemented the findings of the scientists and inventors who came before me. Though I suspect they never anticipated an application quite like this."

Dizzi laughs. "I doubt even Fyreneth imagined something like this. But doesn't that make it more exciting? We're doing something the world has never seen! I can't wait to see their reaction."

I'm somewhat more hesitant to encounter our first city that isn't Jorria. Will they treat us the same as the Jorrians did? Will they be willing to keep open hearts and open minds? I know so little about this planet, and since the Fyrethians have spent hundreds of years in the arctic disconnected from the rest of society, their knowledge is based on a world that existed hundreds of years ago. Anything might have changed in that time.

At least we're all in the dark together.

"We've much to tidy up before we're ready for any company," I say.

Dizzi grimaces. "Cleaning isn't *nearly* as fun as inventing."

"Well luckily for you, I'm the one stuck on maintenance while you get to be on science duty," I tease. As we chat, Ollie's silhouette reappears over the Fortress. I'd caught flickers of the mental exchange between Ollie and the Dungeon Core in the back of my mind; Ollie likely spat the rock out in the throne room, whereupon the Core added it back to its Inventory. An entirely pointless exchange, given I could have simply added the stone back to its Inventory out here and avoided the inevitable pool of dragon saliva that will need to be cleaned up before (another) resident slips in it.

But at least they're having fun. In the midst of all this maintenance and repair, taking time for joy is equally important. I should talk to Mirzayael about that later. We've been in work mode ever since the Fortress lifted into the air; we could all use a break.

A gust of wind hits Dizzi and I as Ollie whips past, giggling in my head. I correct my tumble with a laugh, then launch myself after him.

"You won't get away that easily," I call.

Ollie shrieks in delight—and lets out a significantly more menacing roar—as he dives into a cloudbank. I fly after, the wind rustling through my feathers and the sun warm against my back.

Chapter Two

Aircraft Maintenance 101

By the time I need to return to my duties in the fortress, one of the younger harpies, Meritis, arrives to play with Ollie in my stead. Though he's barely a teenager himself, he'd helped in the battle against Jorria and has become rather fond of Ollie ever since. (Although, to be fair, pretty much everyone is fond of Ollie.) Unlike other male harpies, who have colorful plumage in a variety of blue, green, and purple hues, Meritis is brown and grey, similar to most female harpies. A tailor family of dwarves are working with him on feather dye that won't affect his flight, I've heard.

The dyes are also being used in textiles and paint. It takes a little time out of my day any time a group of workers asks me (or rather, the Dungeon Core) to synthesize more materials from the Core's catalog, but the results speak for themselves. Newly painted houses, colorful clothing and pottery—the high spirits of the Fyrethians have quickly become reflected in the vibrance of the furnishings that fill the halls.

Well, most of the halls.

"Where are we at with water collecting?" I ask Dizzi as she leads me into the main bathhouse. The expansive collection of rooms, once covered in bright mosaics, is now faded and yet to be restored. Instead, the bathhouse has been converted into a water storage facility. Without the natural springs to provide us with water, all we have is what we were able to take with us when we launched the Fortress—and what we've been able to collect from the skies ever since.

Several dracid are fast at work, including Sora, Nek's wife, and Torim, the unofficial voice of the Fyrethian colony who joined us. Most dracid have a water affinity, which is why they've become the go-to workers for developing the water collection and purification system, but Dizzi's also been assisting with the spell circles, given her background in artificing.

"It's coming along," she tells me as we walk around an empty basin that several dracid are working in, busy creating a spell circle at its bottom. "I think we'll have all the kinks worked out before we run out of drinking water."

"Let's hope that 'I think' turns into an 'I'm certain' here in the next couple of days," I say.

Torim catches sight of us and nods in greeting. After excusing himself from the other workers, he makes his way over.

"Lord Fyre. Dizzinir," he says. Dizzi makes a face. "Is everything well?"

"As well as can be expected, given all the excitement." I share a weary smile with him. "I realized it had been a few days since I last visited and I thought I'd have a look around."

He nods, turning back to examine the room. "We've completed all the purification spells. The spring water is entirely potable now, so we no longer need to rely on you to clean the water."

That's a relief. I'd spent hours adding volumes of water into the Dungeon Core's inventory (a task it was not very thrilled to participate in) so I could strip out enough contaminants and minerals to turn it into drinking water. Now that the dracid have that aspect covered, I can devote my time to other tasks.

"We've added a few water collection spells to the roof of the palace," Torim continues, "and that will work well to siphon any rain water we get into this storage facility, but it's dependent entirely on rainfall. For something sustainable, we need to complete the spell circuit that will pull humidity from the air."

"Is there anything I can do to help?" I ask. Using the bathhouse as the water storage facility is only a temporary solution. Dizzi and Torim are in the process of designing underground storage tanks, but perfecting the collection and purification aspects are of higher importance.

Torim shakes his head. "We'll need your help when we are ready to create the permanent storage tanks, connect them to the plumbing network, and transfer this store of water to them. But in the meantime, we are able to do the work ourselves. If all goes smoothly, we might finish in another week."

"I'm glad to hear it," I say. "Please let me know if there's anything you need. I'm sure everyone will be happy once the bathhouses can be used for baths again."

"I didn't even get a chance to use them when they were connected to the hot spring," Dizzi says with a dejected sigh.

I can relate. They had been operable for about two weeks before the Jorrians' attack, but Dizzi and I had been too busy excitedly sharing our information on airfoils, chemistry, and artificing to take advantage of them. And in the few days running up to the battle, I doubt anyone had time to stop by.

Torim gives another respectful bow of his head as he returns to his work, and Dizzi and I move on.

"I'm going to head back to the workshop," Dizzi says. "Work on my spell designs. You want to come?"

I shake my head. "I should do a lap to check up on the Fortress's circles, then I'll be tagging up with Mirzayael for the daily briefing."

Dizzi wrinkles her nose. "Sure glad I don't have your job. Daily briefings sound miserable."

A necessary evil for which my previous life as a corporate drone has prepared me depressingly well.

Maybe the truly Dark work of a Dark Lord is daily stand-ups.

"Have fun doing science," I tell her. "Don't blow anything up."

"But you told me to have fun!" Dizzi laughs, then a flap of her wings and a gust of wind carry her away.

Ahh, to be young and blinded by the veil of perceived indestructibility.

In truth, however, I quite like my morning rounds. I could deduce most of the information from the Dungeon Core's interface, but nothing quite beats visual inspection. Besides, I'll never pass up an opportunity to stretch my wings outside and soak up the sun.

Flying just outside the city walls, I check the air pressure spell circuit inscribed on its outer surface, first. The chain encompasses the Fortress like a great necklace. Dizzi and the other harpies helped me set it up on the third day of flight, after just about everyone except the harpies started to come down with a bad case of altitude sickness. The spell keeps the pressure within the Fortress similar to that of sea level. Radiating outward from the walls, the air pressure gradually decreases to that of the ambient atmosphere, so the harpies (and Ollie) who fly outside the Fortress don't experience an abrupt and unpleasant ear-pop each time they pass through the spell. Since this is a wind spell, we had to wire it into the cloudstones at the Fortress's base to gain enough air arcana to keep the spell network powered. It won't significantly diminish our supply, but it might reduce the time we are capable of staying aloft from six months to something like five.

The looming deadline for finding a place to settle is always in the back of my mind, and grows more pressing by the day. Right now, however, with the ocean beneath us and the more immediate needs of food, water, and climate to address, research on a suitable landing spot will have to wait.

I pause once or twice to examine portions of the wall and have the Dungeon Core repair or strengthen any sections that look like they might be in danger of crumbling, but otherwise all is in order.

One happy consequence of increasing the air pressure within the boundaries of the Fortress is that it also increases the air temperature—thank you, Boyle's Law. By tweaking the volume and pressure that we allow inside the range, we can control the ambient temperature almost as precisely as a thermostat. We honestly lucked out there, because with the loss of the hot springs, things would have gotten pretty cold pretty fast. Of course, Fyrethians are no stranger to cold weather, but insulation is much more difficult out here in the open air than it had been in the caves.

The bubble of warmth also keeps the Fortress's rudders and control surfaces from icing over. What I wouldn't have given for something like this back on Earth.

As I fly back up to the palace, I can make out areas of the city that are being utilized for agriculture. Crops and livestock are far outside my wheelhouse, and we have an exceptionally small variety of plants and creatures to cultivate, but the Fyrethians seem to be making do. I look forward to the day when we pass over green islands and the harpies are able to retrieve more fruits and vegetables to add to our diet.

When I arrive in the throne room, I find it empty (save a giant puddle of dragon spit near the balcony entrance). There are two thrones in the room now. One that the Dungeon Core is happily nestled inside, and a second seated next to it, this one adapted to arachnoid physiology.

We've used the thrones exactly once, and even then only briefly and uncomfortably at the insistence of others during an awkward coronation ceremony. Most of our time in the palace is spent in one of the two smaller and more cozy rooms connected to the throne room: my workshop, on the south side, or the war room, on the north side. Since the battle with the Jorrians, the latter has been converted into an office, which Mirzayael and I use to pore over reports, requests, and logistics of every conceivable variety. Due to the color of the cozy furniture that's been added, we've started to call it "the red room."

This is also where we typically meet for our morning brief, though when I step inside, I find the office empty.

I turn my mind toward Mirzayael and feel a faint thrum of concern. I frown at that. Mirzayael takes everything seriously, but typically she faces obstacles with determination rather than worry. I suspect I know what this is about.

"*Where are you?*" I ask, mentally reaching out.

She doesn't immediately reply, so she must be talking with someone. Over the time I used it with Ollie and the Dungeon Core, the Psionic Link spell eventually leveled up enough that I now have the ability to go prying in the heads of those I was connected to, should I so choose. I have not chosen to, given I believe this to be a gross invasion of privacy, but it can be hard not to accidentally catch peripheral thoughts and emotions when they're felt loud enough.

Finally, Mirzayael responds. "*It's the prisoners,*" she says. "*One of them isn't doing well. They are still refusing healing.*"

My stomach sours. Despite all our achievements, this remains the one point of contention within the Fortress. A continuing source of hurt and anger and fear that festers at us.

I quickly turn for our makeshift prison. *"I'm on my way."*

Though we hadn't realized it at the time, in the chaos of the fight, Fyrethians weren't the only people present within the Fortress when it took flight. Three still-living Jorrians were later found to have become trapped within our walls when the city took to the sky.

One of them is a human named Ragna. She had been one of the Jorrians to venture into the cave systems and lay siege to the Fortress's main gates. She had even managed to breach it, along with a handful of her fellow soldiers. All her allies had either been slain or forced out when the Fortress took flight. Ragna had been knocked unconscious in the conflict and went overlooked until she woke the next day.

The other two Jorrian prisoners are felis named Ylva and Gardi. From what I saw of the Jorrian army, and from what the Fyrethians have told me, the majority of Jorrians are human, though there are a smaller percentage of felis and dwarves in their ranks as well. These two felis are Jorrians who had been on the surface when the Fortress broke through, and fell into the city when the ground beneath them vanished. The Jorrians who had been above the Fortress perished in the fall, and the Dungeon Core had consumed them the moment they were no longer classified as "alive." (Which itself is as disturbing as it was a blessing, as it prevented anyone from having to encounter the remains.)

All perished, I should say, save the two felis. I wonder if it was simply incredible luck, or if the reflexes of their species had anything to do with their survival. Either way, it only helped them to an extent; both are in very bad shape.

I find Mirzayael along with Nek and a young dwarf named Opal at our makeshift prison. We don't have a dungeon in the Fortress, at least not that I've been able to locate, so the structure I now stand before is the best we could come up with on short notice.

It's a small unused room beneath the palace, far enough away from any of the inhabited houses to be out of sight and out of mind. Beneath much of the city is an entire network of derelict buildings, in fact. I had the Dungeon Core secure this one by closing off all doors but one; the guards then fitted a cross bar and bolt to the outside.

The group is standing a healthy distance from the prison, likely so they aren't overheard. Nek is comforting the dwarf girl, who's fidgeting and nervous. They both turn to look at me when I arrive, their expressions grim.

Opal shakes her head. "I'm sorry. I know you asked me to heal them, but they wouldn't let me do it."

"You've nothing to apologize for," I say. "We can't make them agree, only try to convince them it's in their best interest. Surely they'll change their tune when they realize the alternative is death."

Nek gives me a tired look. "I'm afraid it seems not. Ylva is dead."

Chapter Three

THE PRISONERS

I pinch the bridge of my nose. I can already feel a headache coming on. "When did she pass?"

"Just a few minutes ago," Opal says, lowering her voice. "I'm not sure if the other prisoners are even aware yet. I could feel her fading so I tried to help again, but the other two attacked Nek when he opened the door."

I look at Nek skeptically. "Aren't they secured?"

"Yes," Mirzayael interrupts. "However I have ordered my guards to leave at the slightest provocation. The health of the prisoners is not worth risking the lives of our people."

"But they pose no actual threat?" I press. I can understand her stance, but if we had the capacity to save a life, and only did nothing because of Mirzayael's orders... Honestly, I'm not sure what the solution is here. I just don't like it.

"No," Mirzayael says cooly.

I sigh. "I will go speak with them. Opal, do you still feel comfortable offering healing if they are willing?"

There's fear in her eyes, and her hands are clenched in a worried knot, but she nods anyway.

"Thank you," I say, and I truly am thankful for her help. We only have a handful of healers in the Fortress to begin with, and even fewer who were willing to offer their services to the enemy. Beryl's retirement certainly hasn't helped things, but she's more than earned it. Opal was one of her understudies, so this will have to do.

Mirzayael just frowns at my suggestion, and I can feel her distaste like bitterness on the back of my tongue. When we first discovered the Jorrians, she had suggested we let them die—or, in the case of those healthy enough to recover, simply toss them overboard. "It would make our lives easier," she said.

I can't even disagree. The prisoners are a source of growing tension within the Fortress. No one wants them here, not even me. But I refused to commit war crimes when we flew over Jorria, and I'm not about to start now.

I head over to the prison's door, and Nek opens it for me. Inside, the room is dark, save for faintly glowing runes on the ceiling and walls which create an artificial twilight. Staying in the doorway, I touch a hand to the wall, pressing some of my mana into the spell circuit, and the room brightens.

It's a single room with no furnishings. The Jorrians are each secured to a different corner, where a few sheets of cloth serve as makeshift beds. They each have a bowl for water, a bowl for food, and a hole in the floor for waste.

Ragna, the human Jorrian, growls at the light and leaps to her feet. The shackle around her wrist, fixed to the floor on a short chain, doesn't even let her stand all the way straight. Her other arm is secured across her chest in a makeshift sling she hasn't allowed any of the healers to address. It will heal wrong if she waits much longer. Her broken arm and a large scab across her forehead are her only wounds.

Gardi, the felis, is slumped against the wall. They use a set of pronouns that aren't used for men or women, which is a concept I was vaguely familiar with on Earth but hadn't personally encountered. Luckily, Echo provides pronouns along with an individual's stats, so it's only been a minor adjustment for me to make.

Unlike Nek, who has the patterns of a snow leopard, Gardi is tan and brown, similar to the coat of a mountain lion. They narrow their eyes at me, but remain still.

I doubt they could stand even if they wanted to. They have bones broken in both legs, their tail, one arm, and their ribs. The healers have told me there's internal injuries as well, though they can't get more precise than that without a closer examination.

"You," Ragna spits, jerking against her manacle. "You're their leader."

"Co-leader, actually." I look at the last corner of the room, where the felis Ylva lays motionless. I step toward her.

Ragna drops to the floor and kicks her legs out at my feet. Given it's her wrist that's secured to the chain, this actually provides her with substantial reach. I side-step her attempt to sweep my legs out from under me, which moves me closer to Gardi. They exhale a quick breath, and white frost blows away from their mouth, swirling toward me.

[Blaze activated.]

Fire erupts around me, evaporating whatever ice-based attack the Jorrian had been trying to launch. Ragna and Gardi flinch away from the heat.

[3 points of Burn damage dealt.]

Whoops—that's enough of that. I let the spell go out.

"*Are you alright?*" Mirzayael mentally asks.

I appreciate that she's keeping the conversation private, so the Jorrians remain unaware of her concern. "*I'm fine,*" I assure her. "*Just a bit of theatrics.*"

Aloud, I say, "I'm starting to understand why none of the healers have been able to help you."

Ragna scoffs. "As if you'd heal any of us. We know the offer is merely a trick."

I meet her gaze, disappointed. She returns the look, eyes burning with hatred. "It's not a trick," I tell her. "What would we have to gain from that?"

"To play with us," she says. "To torture us, before you kill us."

"If we wanted you dead, you already would be," I say. "Though your stubbornness may have achieved that already." I kneel by Ylva's body.

"Don't touch her," Gardi growls. It's the first thing they've said, and even that much sounds like an effort. Their voice is weak and wet.

I lay a hand on Ylva's wrist. Her fur is so soft. Beneath it, however, I can find no pulse, and when I hold a hand to her mouth, I can feel no breath. The body isn't even cold yet. I Check her just to be certain: [Deceased]

"I'm sorry," I tell them. "If our healer had been able to get to her sooner..."

"What?" Ragna cries. "No. You're lying. She was just awake! She was just breathing. She..."

Gardi watches Ylva's body for a moment longer, then they lean their head back against the wall with a weary sigh.

"You will die next if we can't treat your wounds," I tell Gardi. "I suspect you already know this."

Gardi says nothing. I turn to Ragna. "That arm will be permanently maimed if it isn't set."

"Why do you care?" Her voice is shaking as she tears her gaze away from Ylva, but her eyes are dry. "You're the enemy."

It strikes me at that moment how young they are. They're both barely into their twenties, I think. Soldiers shouldn't be that young.

"Enemy or not, I don't want anyone to suffer," I tell her. "And we don't have to remain adversaries. I'd like to think that we can find common ground."

Ragna's expression hardens, and she spits at the ground. "There is no common ground to be found with those forsaken by the gods."

I shake my head. "To punish children for your hate of their parents hardly seems righteous to me. Even if the Fyrethian ancestors were forsaken by the gods, that doesn't justify your treatment of our people today."

Ragna only glowers at me. "If you did not want us to treat you as Fyreneth, then why do you pretend to be her reborn?"

I can't help but laugh at that, which shakes surprised looks out of both Ragna and Gardi. I guess that hadn't been the reaction they were expecting. "I don't. I'm not Fyreneth, have no desire to be her, and you can ask anyone in this kingdom to confirm that I've done everything in my power to dissuade people of that notion."

For once, the Jorrians don't seem to know what to say. Clearly, they'd been told a different story.

"I will be back to visit tomorrow," I promise them, turning back to Ylva's body. "I would again encourage you to consider accepting the healing we're offering you. But if you hurt my healers, then I'm afraid there will have to be repercussions, so I would dissuade you from any more futile attempts to attack your guards." I rest a hand on Ylva's chest.

"What are you doing?" Ragna demands.

"She's dead," I say. "I need to remove her body before she begins to decay."

"No!" Ragna strains against her cuff. "Leave her! She needs a warrior's ceremony. You heathens would not give her the honor she deserves!"

I clench my jaw and blow a measured breath out my nose. "You're making it very difficult to foster empathy for you, do you realize?"

"Please," Gardi breathes. "We will take care of her."

"You're in no condition to do anything," I tell them. "You want to give her a proper ceremony? Fine. Get better first. I will store the body for now."

I nudge the Dungeon Core, directing its attention to Ylva. *Don't digest it,* I warn the Core. *We're just putting it in your Inventory.*

Swallowing things whole isn't nearly as tasty as chewing them, but the Dungeon Core agrees, happy to have anything to consume.

Ylva's body vanishes, and Ragna gasps. Gardi might have, too, if they weren't struggling to simply breathe.

And then something strange happens. I notice a shift on the Dungeon Core's Map interface. Usually, I keep the Interface bare, just providing me with a three-dimensional display of the Fortress and all the stone beneath. I mainly use this to visualize the layout of the castle and keep tabs on the spell networks and the flight dynamics and control structures. However, that's really just a simplified version of what I could display.

As long as the Dungeon Core has consumed a substance, and it falls within the Dungeon Core's range, it can appear on its Map interface. This includes all sorts of things besides just rocks: bowls, pots, tools, even textiles (after the Core ate a blanket, once). Populating my mental map with all these things is extreme overkill, however, and it only serves to clutter the interface, so I keep most of these things from displaying. But I discovered another thing that could be displayed on the Map: living things.

Although the Core isn't capable of adding living things to its Inventory, it is fully capable of consuming the remains of dead plants and animals. I had noticed, once, after the Core ate some dead mushrooms and moss, that the living equivalents had appeared as options to display on the Map.

And now the option "Felis" has appeared.

In fact, as I'm looking through the list of displayable artifacts, I find that Human is also already on the list.

"Okay."

The word pulls me out of my most recent and disturbing revelation.

Gardi closes their eyes, resting against the wall. "The healer. Please."

"What?" Ragna hisses. "Gardi, no! They can't be trusted."

They don't respond. I leave to go get Opal; she's still willing to help, so she and Nek head back into the cell while Mirzayael and I wait outside. She regards me for a long moment.

"Out with it, already," I say with a sigh.

"They could just be accepting help to better fight us," Mirzayael says.

"They could be," I agree. "But I don't think they are."

"They're not going to become a friend just because we stopped them from dying," she continues.

I rub my forehead. "I know."

"And we can't hold a ceremony for Jorrian dead," she says firmly. "Do you know how that would look?"

I grimace. She's right, of course. I didn't mean to lie to them. It had just seemed like the right thing to do. I would have wanted the opportunity to bury my friends, in their shoes. "I'll figure something out."

Mirzayael's scowl breaks into weariness. "Kindness won't win every battle for you. It didn't with Jorria. And while we may never have to deal with them again, we're likely to run into other people who will be equally hostile. What will you do when that day comes? Are you prepared to fight again?"

"I am," I assure her. "I'll do everything in my power to stop that from happening. But if we do find ourselves facing another foe, and if there's truly no common ground that can be reached, this city comes first. It always will."

Mirzayael breathes out a faint laugh. "Even in your hypothetical you're looking for common ground."

"It will be a difficult world to navigate without," I say.

Nek and Opal step back outside the cell, and Nek secures the door.

"Well?" I ask as they join us.

"I repaired the internal damage in the felis," Opal says. "I don't have enough mana to heal all their wounds. I partially healed the bones in their arm and chest. I'll need to return for at least three more sessions to address everything else."

"Thank you," I say. "And Ragna?"

"She refused," Nek grumbles. "Again."

I hadn't really expected anything less. But Gardi accepting healing is progress, at least. "I'd like to return again during your next healing session," I tell Opal.

"Please do," she says, looking quite relieved. "I'd feel better with you there."

Opal leaves and Nek returns to guard duty as Mirzayael and I head back up toward the palace.

"About protecting the Fortress." I mentally dip back into the Dungeon Core interface while we walk. "I've just discovered something of interest."

While I explain the Map options to her, and what happened when the Dungeon Core took the dead felis into its Inventory, I mentally activate the Human and Felis options on the Map. The Fortress immediately lights up with hundreds of tiny dots. While the dots don't provide any information other than "Felis" when examined, it still strikes me as a powerful tool. I can track the location and movement of every felis—and the one human—within the Core's range.

Mirzayael listens intently while I lay all this out. "That is unsettling," she remarks, echoing my own thoughts. "But useful. I would feel better about engaging with outsiders if I knew their movements could be tracked, and if I knew we could keep track of our own."

"Only if they're felis or human," I say. "Any other species would be invisible to the Map Interface."

Mirzayael regards me thoughtfully.

"I don't like that look," I say.

Mirzayael smiles. "I wish to try an experiment."

She could knock me over with a feather. "You *what?*"

"Come." She turns down a side passage, taking us away from the throne room and toward the wing that had become devoted to personal chambers. Mentally, I feel her probing the Dungeon Core. "*I have something I'd like for you to eat.*"

The Dungeon Core hums happily in our minds. Oh, good! It really loves eating. Eating is its favorite thing!

Has it mentioned that?

CHAPTER FOUR

A LIGHT SNACK

Mirzayael leads me back to her chambers, increasingly ratcheting up my confusion.

"What could you possibly have in here that you want the Dungeon Core to eat?" I ask. One of her weapons, so those could be tracked on the interface? That wouldn't surprise me, but she would have taken me to the (admittedly meager) armory instead.

Mirzayael's room is sparse, though it's accumulated a couple trinkets since we moved into the palace. In addition to her bed, clothes chest, and weapons and armor display, she now has a handful of items on her otherwise empty stone shelves, including an antler given to her by Ollie. (He had deemed it 'too pretty to eat.')

Mirzayael begins digging through her clothes chest. Given her vanishingly few sets of clothes, it only takes her a moment to produce a long black stick. She turns back to me, holding it out.

It's as long as her arm, wider at one end and narrow at the other, with a very faint sheen. The wide end appears cracked and cratered. It takes me a moment to contextualize what I'm looking at.

"Oh my god." I take a step back. "Why do you still have that?"

Mirzayael shrugs. "Beryl asked if I wanted to keep it. I said yes. I don't believe in waste."

"You kept it in with your clothes?" I ask, slightly horrified.

Mirzayael seems perplexed. "I cleaned it first."

"That's not the issue." I laugh out of bafflement. "Mirzayael, that's your *leg*."

She raises an eyebrow. "Yes, I am aware. Do you think if the Dungeon Core consumed it, arachnoids would populate on your Map interface?"

I shake my head. I'm all for practicality, but sometimes Mirzayael's bluntness catches even me off guard. "Are you sure?"

"I'm not using it," she says. "And it's not as though a healer could reattach it anyway. This may put it to good use."

Most people wouldn't so easily offer up a part of their body for a ravenous and inhuman creature to consume. But Mirzayael is not most people.

"Alright," I agree. "If you're comfortable with it, then we can see if the Dungeon Core will take it."

We both know the Core will be all too happy to accept.

When I still hesitate, Mirzayael mentally reaches out to Core. "*Here*," she says, drawing its attention to the carapace of her severed leg. "*Eat this.*"

The Dungeon Core curiously looks at the leg. Oh, something new! It looks tasty. Okay!

And Mirzayael's severed leg vanishes from her hands. I wince as the Dungeon Core makes crunching noises in our head, like someone scarfing down a carrot. I probably should have specified for the Core to swallow the leg whole, instead of disincorporating it, in case Mirzayael wanted it back, but she doesn't even blink.

"Well?" she asks.

I check the Map interface and sort for living creatures. At the very top, above Felis and Human, now sits Arachnoid.

"Good lord," I murmur.

"It worked, then?" she asks.

"It did."

She brightens. "Good! This is useful. I am starting to understand the appeal of your experiments. We can ask other species to donate limbs in order to complete the catalog."

I look at her in horror. "We absolutely will not!"

"Fyre, you yourself pointed out the usefulness of this feature for keeping the Fortress's inhabitants safe." Mirzayael returns to her chest to refold and pack away the clothes she had removed. "I wonder, too, if this might affect the range of your Role Requirement. Would being able to account for all the people within your domain not classify it as more secure and protected?"

This is a good point, actually. I should re-measure the range of my Role Requirement to see if anything has changed after these new additions to the Map's interface.

"If it does impact how 'secure' the System deems the Fortress, then you may be onto something," I say. "However until I can prove that, I am begging you to not go around the castle asking for inhabitants to donate a limb or two."

Mirzayael finally cracks a smile. "Don't be absurd, Fyre. I'd ask for families to donate their deceased."

Ah. That is far less objectionable. Still, though, it's an incredibly sensitive request. "We can discuss that option *if* your hypothesis is correct," I say. "But please allow me to confirm the range before you begin spreading this request."

"That is acceptable," Mirzayael says, still smiling faintly. I suspect she enjoys causing me discomfort.

I let out a breath, sitting down heavily on the edge of Mirzayael's bed. I mentally run through everything else I need to do today and when I might have time to head back out to re-check my Role Requirement's range. So many developments, and it's not even lunch. What a way to start the day.

Mirzayael sits down beside me. "We never did get to our daily briefing."

I chuckle. "I suspect daily events will increasingly get in the way of daily briefings."

"It only seems to be getting busier around here," Mirzayael agrees.

I lean to the side until my shoulder bumps lightly into her arm. She stays still, not leaning into me, but not leaning away, either. "I'm sorry about telling the Jorrians they could have a ceremony for their dead," I say. "I know that was naive of me. I know how that would hurt everyone, in the wake of the people we've lost."

"You have already apologized," Mirzayael says.

"I know. But we're a team, and I should have conferred with you, first."

"Conference is appreciated," Mirzayael says. "But we need to be able to act independently, too, and trust each other to make appropriate judgement calls. If we stop to talk through every decision, we'll never get anything done."

"Fair point." I chew on this. "About ceremonies. Or rather, celebrations. I was thinking we were overdue for one ourselves."

Mirzayael hums in consideration. "To celebrate the victory? Or the city's ascension?"

"Both," I say. "And to celebrate everyone who fought for this city. A celebration to take pride in what we've achieved, against the odds, against those who believed we couldn't. Too much energy is being wasted dwelling on the Jorrians when we could instead be spending it on ourselves."

"It won't resolve the prisoner issue," Mirzayael says. She pauses a moment. "But I don't think it would hurt anything either. You're right; we deserve something constructive to focus on. What do you have in mind for this celebration?"

I shrug. "I've never been much of a party person. What would you do?"

Mirzayael looks down at me with an incredulous laugh. "And you think I am?"

I can't help but laugh along with her. "What a pair we make! We'll end up establishing the most lackluster kingdom in the world if we don't find someone to intervene. Let's put out a call for external input, then. This is a task to be outsourced."

"I'm more than happy to let others plan festivities," Mirzayael agrees.

"Great. Who should we ask?"

We're both silent for a moment.

"Nek?" Mirzayael suggests.

"Dizzi?" I wonder. We desperately need to broaden our friend circles.

Mirzayael snorts. "That girl has far too high of an interest in explosives. I don't know what sort of festivities she'd come up with, but they would be liable to blow us all up."

The joke tickles something in the back of my mind. "Explosives..."

"What?" Mirzayael says. "No, no explosives. How are bombs festive?"

I leap to my feet. "They're exactly what we need. You're a genius, Mir!" I throw my arms around her.

Mirzayael stiffens beneath my hug. "Fyre, what are you talking about?"

"I'll show you." I let go, grinning at her baffled expression. "Just give me a day to work out the kinks. It'll be fun!" I dash for the door, excited to try something new. Maybe I needed a break from everything, too.

"Explosives are not fun," Mirzayael calls after.

I'm already hurrying down the hall. "*These ones are!*" I mentally reply.

"*Dizzi is a bad influence on you,*" Mirzayael says, but I can feel her amusement and curiosity.

Despite my eagerness to create some basic fireworks, I first perform the responsible action of flying out to test my Role Requirement range. (Besides, I can mentally sift through the chemicals available to me in the Dungeon Core's interface while I fly.)

I highly doubt I'm the first person in this world to create firecrackers, given their extensive history on Earth, but I've yet to see the technology used by Fyrethians—or Jorrians for that matter. It makes sense if most people from the arctic don't have fire affinities; they'd focus their technology on that which could be powered by types of magic they specialize in. Not to mention, the Fyrethians were underground, so explosives that shot into the air would have been highly inadvisable. But now that we're in the sky and living in a city of stone, such creations would be much more safe to play with.

[Role Requirement,] Echo warns, and I stop my flight. I pull a rock from the Dungeon Core's Inventory (it grumbles mildly) and I Check the distance from the city's center of mass.

[Distance: 1623 meters.]

My heart leaps. Mirzayael was right. More situational awareness of the Fortress classifies it as "better protected" to this system.

Echo, I think. *Is there a way to quantify how 'protected' the Kingdom is?*

[Bounds undefined,] Echo says.

I try a different approach. *Can you associate a Stat with the distance I am able to move from the kingdom's center of mass without activating the Role Requirement warnings?*

[Affirmative,] Echo says. [Stat defined. Role Range: 1.62 kilometers]

Excellent. Now perhaps I won't have to go flying around and pushing the boundaries of my Role each time I want to check if the range has increased.

"You were right," I report to Mirzayael as I head back to the palace. *"Adding more species to the Core's list counts as fortifying the security of the Fortress. My range has increased as a result."*

"I'm glad it allotted you more freedom," Mirzayael replies. *"Though I care very little about what this System of yours classifies as secure or not. Even if it hadn't increased your range, it still would have been to our advantage to add species to your Map. Things can be useful to us, even if your System doesn't deem it so."*

It's true; the System can be fairly arbitrary at times. And while the way it quantifies and restricts things can feel artificial, that doesn't negate the value of things it overlooks.

"You still wish to ask Fyrethians to add their deceased to the Core's Inventory?" I asked.

"I do," she says. *"And if you do not feel comfortable doing so, then I can make the request in your stead."*

"Let's just keep it quiet and respectful," I say. *"I don't want to make a general announcement. Only speak to families who have lost members on an individual basis."*

"Understood."

I still can't say I'm wild about the idea. But Mirzayael feels this is important, and it can't be denied that it will help us if and when we encounter land and other people. If we are going to lead together effectively, then compromise is something both of us must be willing to engage in.

When I make it back to my workshop, I find Dizzi already inside, doing some artificing work on a piece of cloudstone. A layout of runes and spell circle sketches are stretched across the surface before her, which she pauses to check as she carefully etches a design into a smooth face of the rock. It might be the only time she's careful about anything.

She looks up after a moment. "Oh, hey! Thought I heard someone come in." She lifts the stone and her engraver. "I'm making a toy. Want to help?"

I eye the stone in amusement. "Hard at work on the plumbing designs, I see."

"Hey, I gotta do something creative *some time* or I'd lose my mind." Dizzi sets her work down and scrunches her face in disgust. "Plumbing is boring."

"Well I've got something more interesting than plumbing you could help me with," I offer.

Dizzi eyes me skeptically. "That's a low bar."

"It involves controlled explosions."

Dizzi slams her hands down on the workbench. "Tell me every-thing."

CHAPTER FIVE

NEVER GOING BACK

Opal is relieved when we finally reach the Jorrian's fourth and final healing session later that week. While I've been present, at least, neither of them have tried to attack us again, but I can't blame Opal for wanting to be done with them. Of course, Ragna still hasn't allowed us to heal her arm. After Gardi's session the previous night, Opal took me aside to inform me that if she wasn't allowed access to the woman's arm in the next few days, they might need to re-break the bone to set it properly. I'm sure Ragna would just love that.

Gardi sits with their back to Opal as she works—the vulnerability of the position does not escape me. Opal's hands glow with a golden hue as she gently presses at their tail and back; Ragna watches with unconcealed disdain.

After a few more minutes of work, Opal stops, lowering her hands. "That should fix the worst of it."

Gardi begins to turn around and Opal scrambles to her feet, hurrying over to my side. But the felis makes no move to pursue her, instead rolling their neck and shoulders, as much as their bindings allow.

They tip their head to Opal. "Thank you." For a moment, my heart swells. They thanked her! This is progress. But before I'm given much of a chance to revel in the success, they continue. "I am glad I will have the chance to be at peak health when I am put to death. I will be able to stand with my head held high when the axe falls."

I gape at them, momentarily too stunned to think of a response.

Gardi looks at Ragna. "You should accept healing, too."

She scoffs. "I don't need my arm to stand proudly."

I shake myself out of my shock. "Opal, thank you for your assistance. You may leave now if you like."

She nervously bobs her head. "Thank you, Lord Fyre," she mumbles as she hurries from the cell.

I look between the two Jorrians, baffled and disappointed. "Why do you think we're going to execute you?"

Gardi tips their head, cat ears flicking. "Why else heal me but to make me presentable in public? At first, I didn't believe you when you said you didn't wish me dead. But then I realized that allowing me to expire in a cell, away from the public eye, would be a lost opportunity when you could otherwise use me for a public execution. Making an example of a weak and broken enemy carries less weight than putting down one who is strong and defiant."

I stare at them. "No! No, that's not what I want at all! Can you really not conceive that I don't want to kill either of you?"

The Jorrians exchange a skeptical look.

"Then why heal us?" Gardi asks.

"Because it's the right thing to do," I say, exasperated. I sit down so I'm at eye level with them. "Is that so hard to believe?"

"I mean, yeah," Ragna says. "We're the enemy. Of course you'd want us put to death."

I rest my hands on my knees, letting out a frustrated sigh. "Look, I won't lie to you. There are many people here who would rather see you dead. They are hurting. *You* hurt them. But the battle is over, and killing you now would achieve nothing."

"Then what do you want from us?" Ragna demands.

"Nothing," I say truthfully. "Keeping you here is more trouble than it's worth; I'm still trying to figure out what to do with you."

"Release us, then," Gardi says. "If you don't intend to kill us, and you don't wish to keep us, then let us go home."

I grimace. "I'm afraid that's not possible at this time."

"Why not?" Gardi asks.

It slowly dawns on me. Ragna had been knocked out in the midst of the fight. Gardi had similarly lost consciousness during their fall. *They don't know.*

"Where do you think we are right now?" I carefully ask.

Ragna frowns. "A terribly designed prison in your Fortress."

Gardi shrugs in agreement.

"We don't have prisons," I feel obligated to explain. "This was the best we could come up with on short notice. But where *specifically* do you think we are?"

"I don't understand what you're getting at," Gardi says.

I massage a temple, closing an eye as I consult the Dungeon Core's Map. The 'prison' is in an underground portion of the castle. The backside of the room leads into solid rock. There are a couple bath pipes on the other side, along with literal tons of rock. We're about half a kilometer from the edge of the Fortress.

"I'm going to show you something," I decide. "Because you won't believe me if I only tell you."

I tap the Dungeon Core and let it know I've got a new job for it. The Core brightens at my suggestion; it hasn't gotten to move a lot of rocks in forever!

It's not even been two weeks since we launched, I remind it. *You did plenty of rock moving then.*

The Core didn't know that forever meant two weeks.

That's not what I... I stop myself from going down that rabbit hole. *Ready to get to work?*

The Core happily takes a bite out of the back wall, and a hole two meters across instantly appears in the stone.

Ragna jerks back, hitting the end of her manacle and knocking her head against the wall. Gardi also startles.

"Don't worry," I tell them, attempting to hold back a smile. "It only likes eating rocks."

"What in Heaven's name is this?" Gardi asks, voice quiet and awed.

"It's the work of the Dungeon Core," I tell them, climbing to my feet. "It's what helped us... well, you'll see." Next, I have the Core carve out the anchors where Gardi and Ragna's chains are fixed to the floor. If the Jorrians were to stand, they'd now be dragging a chunk of stone on a chain behind them like some kind of prison ball.

Well. I guess it's exactly a prison ball.

Ragna stares at her loose shackle.

"Please do not use this opportunity in an attempt to flee or attack me," I warn them. I flick a hand in gesture, and the Core grabs the stone at the end of their chains and slams them back into the ground. With another gesture, the Core digs them up again. It finds these instructions very amusing, and is about to repeat the demonstration before I stop it.

"If I'm forced to restrain you while you're standing, it might do some damage to your shoulders, and I'd rather not have to call Opal back for more healing. Now." I gesture for them to stand. "You could use an opportunity to stretch your legs."

After a moment, the Jorrians hesitantly push themselves to their feet. Ragna slowly stands, the rock at the end of her manacle scraping heavily across the ground and pulling her into a slouch. Gardi stands more slowly, but still staggers into the wall. They stay there for a moment, pausing to rotate each ankle. I guess it *has* been some time since they've been able to move.

I hold up a hand, activating a Spark above my palm so we'll have a source of light.

"Go on," I tell Ragna and Gardi, nodding toward the tunnel. "You two first."

Neither look like they particularly want to head into the pitch-black tunnel that abruptly appeared in the wall of their room, and certainly not with me at their backs. But after a long stretch of hesitation, Gardi grunts, picks up the stone-end of their chain, and steps forward. Ragna does the same, holding her anchor under her arm with her good hand. They step into the tunnel.

The Dungeon Core burrows ahead of us, clearing a mostly straight path around some pipes. The Jorrians walk in silence, my fire casting their shadows out before them. I watch carefully for any sign that they might turn on me, but Gardi appears too weary, frequently scuffing their feet as they walk, and Ragna's hands are full. A small light appears ahead of us. In a few short minutes, we reach the end.

"Be careful not to get too close to the edge," I warn them. "If you fall, I doubt anyone will be able to catch you in time."

I snuff out my Spark as the ambient light takes over. Gardi and Ragna edge closer, blinking and squinting against the sunlight.

The ocean sparkles with refracting waves, stretching to the horizon. Clouds skim over the world, some of them floating beneath us. A faint wind, dulled by the atmospheric spell, blows into our tunnel.

Gardi lunges toward me. I summon fire to my hands as I pivot away, already reaching for the Dungeon Core—

They hit the ground, scrambling away from the ledge. Their pupils are blown wide, all their hair standing on end. They push themself away until their back presses against the tunnel wall, where they remain, breathing hard and trembling.

They weren't attacking me; they were scrambling to get away from the ledge. They'd been so stoic before now that it didn't even occur to me they might panic at the sight of the drop off.

But they fell through the ice. I should have realized there might be some associated trauma there. I grimace. Unsure how to address it, I turn back to Ragna.

If she noticed Gardi's panic attack, she isn't showing it. She's still standing at the opening, as still as a statue, looking out over the waves.

"I don't understand," she finally croaks. "Where are we? How did this happen?"

"We decided we weren't interested in sticking around for your people to continuously assault," I say. "So, we left. I rerouted the cloud-stone in nearby caverns to be used as a source of lift. With its mana, Fyreneth's ingenious spellwork, and the Dungeon Core's control, we turned the city into a floating fortress and left the arctic behind."

Ragna slowly sinks to her knees. Gardi's breathing gradually levels, but they don't lift their gaze from the solid stone beneath them.

"This is why I can't take you back to Jorria," I finally say as the silence stretches. "We're never going back."

"Then what will you do with us?" Ragna asks, looking up at me. None of her previous animosity is present in her expression. She's too shaken for anything other than shock right now.

"When we reach land, we can let you go," I say. "What you do from there is up to you. Perhaps you can find someone who will sail you back home."

Ragna slowly shakes her head, her voice faint. "I don't even know which way that is."

Neither speak again after that. As I wait for them to recover, I watch them pityingly. These two waged war on our home. They hate us and everything we stand for. Yet I can't find it in myself to feel satisfaction at their pain. I regret everything that led to this—that they are even here at all.

Finally, Ragna stirs. She pushes herself to her feet with a pained groan, letting her stone anchor scrape across the ground behind her. She doesn't look at me as she stops at Gardi's side, putting a hand on their shoulder. They flinch, then blink, eyes refocusing as they look up at her.

"We should head back," I tell them.

Neither respond, but Gardi climbs to their feet as well. Heads bowed, the Jorrians trudge back down the tunnel. I have the Dungeon Core re-seal the stone behind us as we return to their cell. The Core secures their shackles to the floor once more, and I'm turning to leave when Ragna makes a noise.

"I'll take the healing," she says, quickly glancing away when we make eye contact. She glares at a spot on the ground. "If it's still an offer."

"I'll let Opal know," I say. My gaze wanders over to Gardi, who still appears shell shocked. I don't know what to say to them. It feels strange to want to comfort someone who would kill me in other circumstances. This entire situation is far too messy for my liking.

Before I leave, I have the Core shift their chain's anchors, moving them closer so the two Jorrians are no longer kept separated on opposite ends of the small room. As I shut the door behind me, I hear Ragna shuffle over to Gardi.

Outside, Nek is waiting for me. He locks the door, then gives me a regarding look.

"I know," I say. "I know. Do you think I'm being foolish?"

"I think you are being you," he says with a faint smile.

I exhale a laugh through my nose. "That sounds about right. I don't know what else to do. I just... I wish I could make everyone happy."

Nek grumbles thoughtfully at that. "I don't think that should be the goal. You can keep everyone safe. And that will mean making some people unhappy."

Hopefully not a type of safety that manifests in 'the Dark Lord enforcing her will over everyone' variety.

"I'll do my best," I promise him. "I'll do everything I can."

He chuckles. "It's okay to not always be at your best. And you can't do everything yourself. That's what the rest of us are here for."

Between the Jorrians and this, my emotional bandwidth feels about wrung dry. "You're right. I just don't want to overburden others, so I'm never sure what work is appropriate to offload."

"In this case?" Nek looks at me critically. "It looks like you could offload some of that stress. Would you like a hug?"

He always knows what to say. "Yes, please."

Nek opens his arms, and I wrap him in an embrace, burying my face in his fur.

He pats my back as I lean against him, and my shoulders sag as they let go of an unrealized tension I'd been carrying.

The embrace is warm and comforting, and it causes my mind to drift to someone else I'd like to hug, too.

CHAPTER SIX

SOMETHING IN THE WATER

"The water system is nearly complete," Torim reports during the morning brief that we're still desperately struggling to normalize within our ever-shifting schedules.

We're all huddled in the red room. What had once been the war table has been pushed to the far wall and now acts as a desk, presently overflowing with slates spelled with various record-keeping metrics. A handful of chairs line the walls, and rolls of vellum are stuffed into the corners.

"We'll be ready to connect to the plumbing system within the next two days," the dracid continues. "Assuming the underground tanks are complete."

I glance at Dizzi, who's perched on a chair and busy etching runes into a stone.

"Dizzinir," Mirzayael snaps, and the harpy jumps.

"What?" She looks around to find all eyes on her. "Oh. Sorry. Yeah, the tank plans are basically done. Just need some finishing touches. And then Fyre can whip the structures up in a snap, right?"

"Finishing touches?" I press.

"Okay so I've been a little distracted with the fireworks," Dizzi admits, grinning. "They're just so much fun! I found a way to spell a delay into the explosives so we can time them better. Do you think you could refine some more potassium nitrate for me? I'm almost out."

Mirzayael gives me a flat look. "*Why must you encourage her?*" she thinks at me privately.

I force myself to keep a straight face. "*Celebration preparations are important, too!*" Honestly, though, I delight in learning artificing from Dizzi just as much as she delights in learning chemistry and aerodynamics from me. The applications of fusing both skillsets are undeniably entertaining. As Dizzi said; if I didn't have some form of creative outlet, I'd lose my mind.

"I'll produce more of the compound once the plumbing designs are complete," I tell Dizzi. I can feel Mirzayael's satisfaction even as Dizzi wrinkles her nose.

"I'll get it done by the end of the day," she promises with a sigh.

"Speaking of celebration preparations," I say, turning to Nek, "what do our food stores look like? How feasible is our schedule?"

He folds his arms, leaning against the wall as his tail swishes lazily behind his legs. "Agate says we can make it work. If we can spare more water from the supply, we can focus on soups, stews, and spiced drinks, which would stretch our food stores much further."

"That shouldn't be a problem," Torim says.

Mirzayael nods appreciatively. "Any other immediate concerns?"

Nek's tail stops.

"Yes?" I prompt.

"It's not a concern, exactly," he says. He looks at Mirzayael when he answers. "But the scouts are starting to grumble about guard duty with the Jorrians."

I grimace. This isn't exactly a surprise.

"Do you foresee any conflicts?" Mirzayael asks.

Nek grimaces. "Not immediately, but... Well, the uncertainty around the Jorrians' fate isn't helping anything. How long will they be here? There may only be two of them, but we're all on rations, so of course some guards are complaining about any amount of food being handed over to the prisoners. Several guards have also voiced that they feel the activity is a waste of time. They'd rather be helping with preparations for the festival, or working with Agate's agriculture team, or even volunteering with the textile group."

"They don't feel productive," I surmise. And if they're turning their frustration on the Jorrians, that could be problematic. We need to give them something to do that makes them feel like they're contributing.

Mirzayael looks at me. "We've discussed expanding their training previously. I think it's time to explore that option."

We have, though briefly. In the immediate aftermath of the Fortress's ascension, Mirzayael expressed frustration at the disorganization she and Torim had witnessed in their guards and scouts during the Jorrian attack. Fyrethians are not trained soldiers. Most only have enough weapons training to hunt arctic prey. Mirzayael worries that next time, against a different threat, they might face higher losses. I like to hope there won't be a next time. But I can't stake the future of this kingdom on a wish.

"What do you have in mind?" I ask her.

"Formal training and scheduled drills," she says. "I've been working on a plan with Nek and Torim. Right now our groups of scouts are disjointed, each still largely gravitating toward those they were familiar with before our colonies joined. We need to split them into integrated squads and set up a rigid training structure to develop better cohesion."

"I didn't realize that was an issue," I admit.

"It's not a serious problem," Torim chimes in, "but it's clear the underground Fyrethians are not used to working alongside harpies, for instance, which has exposed gaps in coordinated training capabilities. More formalized training would not only help with this, but would improve overall morale, I think. It feels good to feel competent."

"Can we afford to spare the workforce?" I ask the others. "Nek, you mentioned many of the scouts were splitting their time by helping with other groups. Would creating a dedicated guard negatively impact our overall productivity?"

"We've fifty-four individuals who currently act as part of the guard," Nek says. "If we turn it into a dedicated full-time position, that number might drop slightly. That's less than two percent of the total population."

"We can afford it," Mirzayael assures me. "And by the time we interact with other nations, we'll want to have something formal and effective. If for no other reason than to ensure everyone feels safe when outsiders are walking through our streets."

"*Not to mention,*" she adds privately, "*this might help with your Role Range.*"

I'm sure it would. But she's right that Fyrethians simply *feeling* safe is valuable by itself. When people are nervous, they're also more likely to do something dangerous or rash.

"I defer to your expertise," I say.

"Good." Mirzayael turns to Torim. "When your work is done with the water system, we would appreciate your leadership back within the Guard."

He tips his head. "I would be honored."

The meeting finishes up a few minutes later. There are always knots we have to work through, but to be honest, I'm surprised things are progressing as smoothly as they are. Shelter has long since been established. Water is nearly taken care of. Our food supply is still in a tenuous position, but approaching stability. Once we reach land, the harpies can help make up any deficit by collecting food from below—not to mention, there's been talk about attempting to fish, though the logistics of that are still being worked out. Altogether, we're in a good position to start focusing on security and morale. Not to mention, finding a place for us to land before the city runs out of mana.

Once the Jorrians are dropped off, I'll feel like I can finally sigh a breath of relief.

"Have you thought about what we should do next?" I ask Mirzayael as the meeting disperses and everyone begins to trickle away.

She raises an eyebrow at me. "Next after what?"

I splay my hands around us. "After all this. Once all the emergencies are dealt with and everything's become routine."

"I'm not sure this will ever feel routine," Mirzayael says. "There will always be something to preoccupy us."

Probably more true than I would like. "Okay then. In the midst of dealing with our non-routine, what do you think we should be working on next?"

Mirzayael purses her lips in thought. "I would like to increase the security of the Fortress. Not from a training and guard standpoint, but by exploring more of the Fortress's capabilities. You've told me there's much buried in these walls we still don't yet understand."

Of course she'd go right back to security. "We can investigate the defensive spell circles in the watchtowers if you like." At least it would be nice to spend some time working with her one-on-one again, instead of how we're currently forced to divide and conquer the never-ending to-do list.

"I think we should also investigate the offensive capabilities," Mirzayael says.

My heart sinks at the suggestion, and I know she can feel it.

"There is no shame in being able to fight back," Mirzayael says. "Once we run out of wind arcana and this castle lands, we won't be able to so easily pick it up again and flee the next army that marches on our doors. We'll need to be capable of putting up a fight."

"I know," I say. "That doesn't mean I have to like it." I spend a moment attempting to sort through my feelings on the matter, and Mirzayael graciously waits for me.

"Alright," I say. "But I propose a compromise. If these systems will be operated by guards, then we'll need more than just you and me—and possibly Dizzi—to work through them. Let's assemble a small team of artificers and commanders to decipher and practice operating the spell network. We'll start with defensive capabilities only. Once we've a good understanding of the spells, and we've created a system for safely training guards on their use, I'll feel comfortable moving to the offensive capabilities."

Mirzayael is already nodding along. "But," I add, "I want to treat the offensive research more discriminately. We should use the defensive research phase to determine those responsible enough to be brought into the offensive research phase. I don't want everyone in this castle to have the knowledge and capability of activating some death ray on a whim."

Mirzayael folds her arms, drumming her fingers against herself. "In a scenario where the only ones familiar with the weapons become injured, it would cripple our weapons systems. Common knowledge of how to operate them would be safer."

"If their operation is common knowledge, that could also lead to outsiders easily learning to wield them against us," I counter. "I would rather have potential enemies underestimate our offensive potential than view us as a flying war machine." Not to mention, entering into relations with outside communities will certainly be easier if they don't start off assuming we're dangerous.

"Hmm." Mirzayael frowns at me, but it's a thoughtful look rather than one of distaste. "That is a fair point. Fyrethians are all too familiar with being underestimated, but it is tactically a good position to be in. They won't prepare appropriately if they don't know what we're capable of." She nods curtly. "Alright, I can agree to this compromise. Defense systems first, then handle the weapons systems with more discretion."

As I understand it, since neither of us find this plan ideal, that must make it a good compromise.

"What about you?" Mirzayael suddenly asks. "What had you wanted to work on next?"

"Oh," I say. "Well, I was just thinking I never had the chance to use the bathhouse before we repurposed it as our water facility. It would be nice to get that up and running again."

Mirzayael stares at me for a moment. Then she bursts into a laugh. "I ask for a city-wide weapons system and you want a bath."

I smile sheepishly. "I don't think I properly defined the scope of my original question."

"No," she laughs. "You didn't."

I'm out in the lowest tier of the city, working with a dwarf named Agate who's heading our agriculture efforts, when Ollie reaches out to me.

"*FYRE?*" He always asks, like he's calling on a phone and I might not answer.

Agate gestures to the moss and mushroom fields, which are positioned vertically against the shade of the wall. "We could use more phosphorus for these," he says. "Their growth is a bit stunted, and I suspect the soil is to blame."

"I'll get some more processed," I promise.

"*Hey, Ollie,*" I mentally reply. "*What's up?*"

"*MERITIS SAYS THERE'S SOMETHING IN THE WATER.*"

I tip my head. "*What kind of something?*"

"*HE DIDN'T SAY. I WISH I COULD ASK HIM!*"

Poor kid. He and the young harpy Meritis are quickly becoming fast friends, as much as they can when the communication is one sided. After getting over his initial awe of being in my presence, Meritus increasingly shows up to ask me to act as interpreter between him and Ollie.

"*I'll be there in a moment,*" I tell him.

I excuse myself from Agate and head a safe distance away from the crops before activating a Jet (a lesson learned at the expense of a small crop of button mushrooms the previous week). My stomach flutters with the thrill of flight as I blast into the sky—a thrill I hope I'll never grow tired of. Details of the Fortress shrink from view as I circle around the city, finding Ollie in the sky to the northwest. I nudge his mind to get his attention, and he flips back around to fly back to me. Meritis is riding on his neck.

"*IT'S OVER HERE,*" Ollie tells me, gesturing for me to follow.

"I can't go too far from the Fortress," I say aloud for Meritis as well.

"It's not far," Meritis promises. "It's just beneath that cloud over there. If we dip beneath the city you can see it from here."

I gesture for them to show me. "Lead the way."

Mirzayael notices the mental chatter. Ollie and I weren't intentionally broadcasting our conversation to her, but Ollie isn't terribly well practiced with restraining his thoughts, either.

"*What's going on?*" she asks.

"*Not sure,*" I reply. "*Something in the water, it seems. I'll let you know.*"

We coast downward until the Fortress is a looming shadow overhead.

"*THERE IT IS,*" Ollie says, at the same time Meritis points. "See?"

From this distance, it's hard to make out against the glare of sunlight on the water. But after a moment of searching, I find what it was they saw. My heart lurches up into my throat. I didn't think it would happen so quickly. I thought we'd have more time to settle in, first.

"What is it?" Meritis asks.

I watch it a moment longer to be sure. "It's a ship," I finally say, letting Mirzayael know as well. "It seems we've reached the coast."

CHAPTER SEVEN

AN INCH OF PROGRESS

We talk it over and eventually decide not to send harpies down to speak with the ship. We don't know how they would react to a flock of strangers descending on them from a giant floating city, and none of us want to risk the safety of a few of our scouts when we'd have no way to help or retrieve them should something happen. Besides, if there's one ship out here, there are bound to be more.

And there are. The next day we spot two of them. Ollie and Meritis also discover a flock of gulls (which they disperse, to their extreme enjoyment and no doubt the birds' abject terror). We must be close to land now.

Mirzayael and I visit the Jorrians the following day, as much as she loathes seeing them. Now that they're healed, Mirzayael is worried they'll make an escape attempt. Even though they're without weapons, they're still capable of using magic, and there's nothing we can do to stop them from wielding that.

I've taken time to Check both of them already. Gardi is a level 24 felis floe mason, while Ragna is a level 27 human frost hunter. Gardi has a mana pool of 320, rivaling my own mana reserves of 500, but Ragna only has 20, a number that I've found consistent in people who aren't magically inclined. While Ragna's class sounds more dangerous than Gardi's, the latter poses a larger threat for a potential break-out.

"Good news," I tell the Jorrians as Mirzayael ducks inside behind me. "We should be reaching land soon. Once we find a way to get you down, we never have to see each other again."

Neither appear particularly thrilled by this.

"You're just going to dump us on the first scrap of rock you find?" Ragna scoffs.

"Of course not," I say. "We've passed several small islets already." In fact, Mirzayael had been very tempted to put them down there, but I leave that part out. "Once we find a town or city, we'll drop you off there."

"You could be leaving us with enemies," Gardi remarks.

Mirzayael barks out a laugh, and I raise an eyebrow. Of course the Jorrians have more enemies than just the Fyrethians. Why am I not surprised?

"If you'd rather be dropped into the ocean, that can be arranged," Mirzayael says.

They both glare at her. But Mirzayael isn't being antagonistic because of her distaste for the Jorrians (well, not *just* because of that,) but because she wants to provoke them. If they're hiding some magic abilities that they might use to try to break out, it's best if both of us are here to assess the danger they pose—and stop them.

"The point is, you have vanishingly few options," I say. "If you don't want to be released near civilization, are you implying you'd rather stay here?"

"Of course not." Ragna's glare returns to me. "We want to go home!"

"Home?" Mirzayael scoffs. "You're lucky you're not being put to death. You're in no position to be making demands."

"She's right," I add. "You know returning to Jorria is not an option. Even if we were capable of turning this city around, we have no incentive to. So if you don't want to stay here, and you don't want to be dropped off, you're in quite the dilemma."

"You might as well be sentencing us to death," Ragna continues to protest. "We won't have any food or money. We won't even know where we are. How do you expect us to get home?"

Reasoning with these two can make the Dungeon Core seem judicious.

"I fail to see how any of that is our problem," Mirzayael says.

"And I have complete faith in your resourcefulness," I add, managing to not sound sardonic. "You'll be in a city, so I highly doubt you'll starve. Perhaps you could put your skills to use to earn some extra coin."

"What, sword fighting?" Ragna asks. "And with no sword of our own? We'll be next to useless."

Mirzayael snorts. "I imagine in the last few decades you two developed *some* productive skills outside of pillaging and killing before deciding to invade our home."

Ragna bares her teeth, but to Gardi's merit, they lower their gaze.

"No?" I ask. "Well, there will be no better time to learn."

The Jorrians remain silent and steaming.

"If you decide you'd rather be imprisoned indefinitely, be sure to let us know," Mirzayael says. "I'm sure we can find a way to make that work."

Ragna spits at the ground, but neither seem like they're provoked enough to try anything. Honestly, I'm a bit relieved. But as Mirzayael and I turn to leave, Gardi speaks up.

"I'm an architect," they say. I stop, looking back at them. Their tail twitches in agitation. "Or, I was studying to be one, anyway. Apprenticing to fix houses with my ice affinity. I was brought to the battle to ensure the ice on the surface remained stable." Their gaze lingers on an empty corner of the room. "Ylva was an ice weaver, too."

"Excellent," Mirzayael says, her voice brittle. "Perhaps you can find work in town cooling people's drinks."

But I hesitate. "What do you mean you were brought? Were you not a soldier?"

Gardi shrugs. "Technically. Everyone serves for two years when they reach adulthood. I'd delayed mine for the apprenticeship but was drafted for the Fyrethian incursion."

Ragna hisses at them. "What are you doing? Providing intel to the enemy—"

Gardi looks at her flatly. "I hardly see how any of that could be used against us. Besides, you heard them." They settle back against the wall, closing their eyes. "We're not going home."

Neither respond to us after that, so Mirzayael and I depart.

"What do you make of that?" I ask as we head back up to the main palace.

Mirzayael shrugs. "I wasn't expecting them to fall over themselves thanking us for our mercifulness."

"I meant about Gardi," I say. "They seem to have been bothered by the idea of being lumped in with the other soldiers."

"Pity," she says dryly. Mirzayael glances down at me. "Where are you going with this?"

"I don't know," I admit. "Just reflecting, I guess. It seemed Gardi might be willing to talk."

Mirzayael groans. "Please don't tell me you think you can rehabilitate them."

"No," I object. Mirzayael snorts, because she knows that's exactly what I was thinking. "But what do you think about something like a learning exchange? This could be a good opportunity to learn from each other. Not out of the goodness of my heart!" I quickly add when I can feel Mirzayael's already forming objection. "But as a way to learn more about Jorria. How they operate. What they might know about us, the gods, and the rest of the world. Not to mention, we need to find somewhere to land in the next few months; they might know something that could help us."

"I know your real intentions," Mirzayael teases. "Despite how much you're trying to make this sound reasonable." Even so, she considers it. "I do like the sound of interrogating them. If you can get them to talk, there's valuable information we could stand to gain. They mentioned having other enemies—those have the potential to be allies for us."

"Will you allow me to try, then?" I ask.

Mirzayael faintly smiles. "I doubt I could stop you, even if I wanted to. Just, be careful," she adds. "I know you believe these individuals deserve a chance at redemption. You may be right, but that doesn't mean they're willing to change. Don't stake too much hope on them. They'll hurt you, if you let them."

"I can protect myself," I object. "And with the Dungeon Core, I won't be in any danger."

Mirzayael stops, and I pause as well, turning to her questioningly.

She taps my chest, just above my heart. "They'll hurt you, if you let them."

Ah. "I'll be careful," I promise.

I can feel Mirzayael's doubt at these words, but it's also accompanied by fondness. She views my misguided trust in others as a weakness and a strength.

"It's not misguided," I object.

Mirzayael chuckles as she turns away.

A guard opens the cell door for me as I squeeze through with an armful of blankets. The Jorrians look up in surprise.

"Hello!" I greet them, dropping the blankets to the floor. "I've returned with bribery."

Gardi gives me a disbelieving look. "You're openly acknowledging that?"

"I figured it would expedite the conversation," I say, sitting across from them as I shrug off my bag and begin unpacking its supplies. "You would have accused me of it regardless. This way we can cut to the chase." I spread the leather over the ground between us; it's a very rough map of the world. "I can make your lives more comfortable while you are here. You can provide me information about the areas we'll be flying over. We all benefit."

"Information that can be used against us is not worth a few scraps of cloth," Ragna scoffs.

"How would we use this against you?" I ask. "You don't want to be dropped off in enemy lands; now is your opportunity to tell us which lands those are and where *you* want to be dropped off." I tap the icy continent at the bottom of the map. "This is where Jorria is, correct?" I trace my finger an inch to the northeast. "This is where we think we are now. We're getting close to the southern tip of this other continent. Do you know what it's called?"

Neither Jorrian speaks.

I sigh. "I know you don't trust me. I'm one of the enemy rulers, right?" I pause, and neither reply. "That may be true, but I never pursued this position. I have no skill in politics or public speaking. In fact, I am a scientist by trade. Buried in a book is my preferred place to be. But I stumbled into a source of great power, and so now it is my moral obligation to use that power to help people. I want you to believe me when I tell you this."

Gardi eyes me doubtfully. "Why does it matter to you what we believe?"

"Belief is its own kind of power," I say. "It can formulate and drive one's actions. Belief has as much power to do good as to cause harm. If you're willing to trust me, we can find a solution that will do the most amount of good by all of us."

"Trust," Ragna spits. "How could we trust anything that comes from the mouth of a Forsaken?"

I look at her sadly and sigh. "Why do you hate us so much? What have any of us living done to draw such ire?"

"You defy the will of the gods," she says.

I rub a temple. "That doesn't answer my question. You hate us for the supposed actions of ancient predecessors. Explain to me why such hatred of them should extend to us today?"

"You impersonate their fallen leader," Ragna says, leaning forward, eyes flashing with anger. "You carry her legacy forward. You continue to stand against everything the gods stand for!"

I gesture to the empty room around us. "If what you say is true, then why are we still here? If the gods took issue with our existence, where are they?"

Ragna falters at this. "They will come," she says a moment later. "They will deliver justice."

"Justice," I sigh. Perhaps Mirzayael was right about the foolishness of this endeavor. "What justice exists in murder? Do you know how many kids we have in this city? If the gods come, as you say, and they deliver retribution onto all our children—is that just?" Even the thought stirs anger in me. "When we sailed over Jorria, weapons at the ready, distant horns blaring in warning, would raining down vengeance on your streets have been just?"

Ragna pales, and Gardi stirs. "You didn't."

I hold their looks for a moment. "No," I say. "We didn't. I suppose that makes us more just than those you worship."

I start to pack my map supplies away once more. "It is a shame. I had hoped we could find common ground. But rest assured, I won't return to bother you further until we've found suitable land for your release."

As I'm reaching out to grab the map, however, Ragna places a hand on it as well, stopping me.

"This is Valenia," she says, pointing to one of the continents. She drags her finger over to another. "And this is Dunmora." She taps at a spot on the south point of Dunmora. "It would be better to leave us in Dunmora than Valenia. There's a string of islands that are used as a trade route and could take us back home."

I'm surprised Ragna was the one to speak up. I'd thought if anyone, it would have come from Gardi.

"Thank you," I say, settling back down. "Though based on our current location, we may already be too far east of the island chain you use. It will take a while to come back around again."

"We can wait," Gardi says, folding their arms as they regard the map. "We've nothing better to do."

I squint at them. Was that a joke?

"Your map is shit," Ragna says, glaring at it. I suppose that's an improvement over glaring at me. "You don't even have Mount Shale."

I push the map her way, along with a piece of charcoal. "For a people who've spent hundreds of years underground, I was actually impressed we were able to come up with a map at all. If you'd like to garnish it with more details, be my guest."

Ragna hesitates, looking at Gardi.

"We are not cartographers," they say. "We can make some guesses."

"Can I come back for it tomorrow?" I ask. I wonder if they'll actually label things correctly, or if they'll use this to try to mislead me.

Ragna snorts. "Why are you asking us for permission?"

"Trust," I say with a smile.

I leave the blankets along with the map.

CHAPTER EIGHT

A ROCKY PROPOSAL

"So what do you think?" I ask the next day. I spread the Jorrians' map out over the red room's main table. Torim brings over his own map that he'd sketched out in advance, setting it next to the Jorrians'. He pores over the markings on both.

"As far as I can tell, it's largely accurate," the dracid says. He taps his claw on a few cities at the south end of Valenia. "I think these cities might be incorrect. But it was rare our scouts encountered foreign ships, so our knowledge of the area is also limited. And the Jorrians mostly trade with Dunmora, so it could be an honest mistake."

"What about the cities farther north?" I ask. "They only put three on the map."

Torim shrugs. "I don't know many cities in the northern hemisphere either. I couldn't confirm or deny."

"We'll be fleshing out our maps soon enough," Mirzayael remarks. "We passed more islands earlier this morning."

We believe we're travelling almost parallel to the coast, which is why it's taking longer to reach the mainland than we first expected. But given the number of islands and shoals we're passing over, it should be any day now.

My stomach flutters in anticipation. "Are we ready?"

Torim and Mirzayael exchange a thoughtful look.

"The guards are falling into a routine," Mirzayael says. "They're as ready for outsiders as they can be, given what little time we've had to train them."

"We've started to transition our water stores over to the tanks," Torim adds. "I don't know that we will have enough to support many visitors, but food is the more pressing issue."

"Hopefully resolved once we have access to land and can begin to trade," I say.

What will other cities be like, I wonder? The Jorrians and Fyrethians are both such hard, stoic people. Was it the environment that made them that way, or is much of the rest of the world similarly suspicious and isolated?

There are so many unknown variables to try to prepare for.

A knock comes at the door.

"Enter," Mirzayael calls.

Nek steps inside. "Forgive me for interrupting," he says. His gaze shifts over to me. "I don't know if now is a good time, but..."

"Nek, it's *us*," Mirzayael says, exasperated. "Just because I'm queen now doesn't mean our relationship has changed. Spit it out."

Nek dips his head apologetically. "You wanted me to report if there have been any deaths. An elderly dwarf from the Frostone family just passed."

My heart sinks. "I'm so sorry. Please pass on our condolences."

"Actually," Mirzayael says, "we should give them in person." Mentally, she adds to me, *"We should speak with them about using the Dungeon Core to dispose of the body."*

My heart sinks even lower. I knew this day would come, but I haven't prepared for it. I don't even know what I should say to them.

"I can do the talking," Mirzayael offers, catching my hesitation.

"Alright," I say, not liking any of it. But I've already agreed to this; I can't back out now. I turn to Nek. "Would you be able to ask when is a good time for us to visit?"

"Of course," he says. "I'll return shortly."

I continue to watch the door after he's left. Mirzayael puts a light hand on my shoulder. "Even you can't stop death."

"I know." I lean against her side. Her shell is cool and soothing against my shoulder.

The rest of the morning passes in an ever-present flurry of things in need of fixing: Some of the crops aren't doing well, so we need to try changing the composition of the soil. Dizzi manages to explode a set of fireworks in the lab without killing anyone. The kitchen crew and the water purification team are having a disagreement on how much water can be used for the celebration. Ollie pops in to show me a pretty shell he found on an islet we passed over.

The shell itself was too small for Ollie to carry, but Meritis was happy to show it off for him. The pair brought back extra for the Dungeon Core to eat, and it excitedly did so, snapping up the shells like potato chips.

Eventually, the time comes for us to visit the Frostone family.

"Is there appropriate attire we should wear?" I ask Mirzayael as we head to our quarters to freshen up first. "Where I'm from, wearing black was common in such circumstances."

"Do you have a black set of clothing?" she asks me.

"Well, no," I admit.

She chuckles.

"That was just an example!" I object. "I wasn't sure what the customs around death are like here."

"Your normal clothes are fine," she assures me. "I'll meet you back here in a moment."

Even so, when Mirzayael returns, she's no longer wearing her armor, instead simply dressed in street attire; or the closest approximation she has to that. Her clothes are practical, form fitting, and plain. She still manages to look quite striking. The silver and tan of her clothes stand out starkly against the black of her shell, which shines as if it's been polished. My bright, fiery plumage feels like such an absurd contrast next to her.

"I suspect our death customs will be changing," Mirzayael says to me, picking up where we left off as we head to meet up with Nek. "Previously we would hold a ceremony and bury the dead in the moss fields, allowing them to feed the plants that helped sustain us. It was circular. I've heard the lost colony, meanwhile, performed an air burial, allowing wild birds to be nurtured off the dead. In this floating castle of ours, we may need to find a temporary solution, at least until we land."

"You mean, assuming we don't use the Dungeon Core as a way to dispose of the dead," I say.

She dips her head in agreement.

"We could still hold the ceremony aspect," I say. "What is typically involved in that?"

"It is usually a private affair," Mirzayael says. "The family and perhaps a few close friends of the deceased would spend a night together, telling stories of the loved one, and sharing good food and drink—if any is available. What the Frostone family decides to do will not be of our concern."

"I see." A private celebration of life, it sounds like. I wonder if anything like that was held for me back on Earth after I died. "Every day it feels like I'm learning new things I should have already known. Sometimes I think I'll never catch up."

"No one knows everything," Mirzayael teases. "Though I doubt that will stop you from trying."

I chuckle. "It probably won't."

We meet up with Nek at the entrance to the palace, and he guides us through the nearby streets. The highest tiers of the city are populated now, and while all of them are fleshed out on the Dungeon Core's Map interface, I haven't had much time to explore the area in person. Nek leads us to an area of interconnected homes mostly populated by dwarves, arachnoids, and felis.

The inhabitants of Fyreneth's keep have unfortunately established semi-segregated living arrangements based on the needs of each species; the dracid, for instance, need homes that are sufficiently heated, and without the hot springs to provide natural warmth, most of those families have migrated to heated rooms within the palace. Meanwhile, the harpies prefer tiered houses with balconies where they can stretch their wings, and many have taken up residence in the palace's spires. Dwarves and arachnoids, on the other hand, seem to prefer the cooler, darker network of homes beneath the palace that remind me of the caves we left behind. I intend to create suitable accommodations to diversify these living arrangements when I have time, but... well, I nearly never have time.

The house Nek leads us to is a multigenerational home with at least twenty inhabitants. Most are dwarves, but there are a couple of arachnoids and felis in the family as well. I would assume they married in, but given Nek and Sora have kids that are a dracid and felis... Honestly, I'm still not sure how all that works.

The Frostones greet us with smiles, but their eyes are weary.

"Lord Mirzayael. Lord Fyre." One of the dwarves steps up, dipping his head in greeting. "We're honored by your visit." His face is wrinkled, and his beard is wispy and white. Echo identifies him as Mica.

"I'm sorry for your loss," I say. "I wish he could have seen the rest of the world."

"Carnelian lived long enough to see our people take flight, and that itself is more than most." Mica beckons for us to follow him inside. "Please, come in."

The dwarf leads us further into the house, though Mirzayael and I have to pause consistently to greet other members of the family. As we wind our way back, we pass by an open door from which a bright light is shining. I curiously glance in as we pass, wondering if it's some sort of amplified Glow spell, but instead I catch sight of a brightly glowing orb nestled atop a pillow. I'm unable to Check it before we've already passed, but my interest is piqued. Perhaps I'll ask on the way back.

Mica stops outside a door. "He's just inside. We haven't decided what we'll do with his body yet. It's just been..." His eyes mist up.

"I'm so sorry." I hold out my hands in offering, and he beckons me in. I kneel down to give him a hug.

When I'm done, we step into the room, and Mirzayael closes it behind us. "What to do with him is what we'd like to speak with you about, actually," she says. "We have a proposal to make."

Mica wipes a thumb at the corner of each eye, then frowns in question at Mirzayael. "What proposal, my lords?"

"It's to do with Fyreneth's crown," I say before Mirzayael can continue. I know she offered to speak on my behalf, but I feel like this is a question I should pose myself.

Besides, Mirzayael would be unlikely to ask with much tact.

"We recently discovered a new capability," I continue. "One that will help fortify the security of the Fortress."

I explain our request as delicately as I can. I know it is no small ask. But Mica listens the whole way through, never once interrupting. When I finish, my stomach is filled with butterflies. Who am I to ask for such an intimate sacrifice?

"His body would be incorporated into Fyreneth's crown?" Mica asks.

"Yes," Mirzayael says. "Although, we would not require the entire body, if you would prefer to hold a traditional ceremony. Just a limb would suffice."

I look at her in horror.

She raises an eyebrow at me. "*What?*" she mentally asks. "*It's true.*"

Mica is shaking his head. "I don't know what to say. That even in death he could be used to help our kingdom—that would be an incredible honor. I'm sure he would have wanted it, if he could tell you himself." He swipes at his eyes again. "What do you need from us?"

"Nothing," I say. "It would only take a moment." Yet, I hesitate. "Would the rest of your family like to say their goodbyes, first?"

Mica leaves to speak with the rest of the house, and as it turns out, they all are *quite* interested in witnessing Fyreneth's Crown work its magic. The actual Dungeon Core is still in the throne room (or, its Lair, as the Dungeon Core prefers to call it,) but its reach encompasses the whole kingdom. The Frostone family crowds around us as Mirzayael and I settle at the bedside of Carnelian's body.

I look around the room. "If you'd like to say any words…"

"We've already made our peace, Lord Fyre," Mica says. He pats the edge of the bed, looking at Carnelian with a sad smile. "We're ready."

Mirzayael's mind bumps up against my own, radiating comfort and encouragement like the warmth of a sun.

I set a hand over the dwarf's body and tap into the Dungeon Core, telling it what I'd like for it to do. Blissfully unaware of the emotionally heavy atmosphere of the room, the Core happily agrees, pulling Carnelian's body into its inventory and disassembling his remains. Beneath my hand, the body vanishes, clothes and all.

Several of the family members gasp and murmur. Mirzayael moves to speak with Mica and the others. In my Interface, I note hundreds of new dots populate the Map. Now the list of species include:

- Human

- Felis

- Arachnoid

- Dwarf

Only harpy and dracid are unaccounted for.

And dragon, I suppose, but I doubt I'll get one of those to add to the Core's Inventory anytime soon.

I check my Role Range stat next: 2.38 kilometers. Still not enough to reach the ground, but I'm getting close. It also appears that this increased my range more than the last species I added to the Dungeon Core's list. It must not be a linear relationship, then. That's good; if harpy and dracid are added, my range might increase substantially.

Although my enthusiasm for this is significantly dampened by what would be required for the final two species to be accounted for.

Mirzayael and I linger to speak with anyone who wishes to talk to us, and Beryl even shows up to say hello. She's been enjoying her retirement, it seems.

"Took long enough to dump the responsibility on some younger folk," she happily says.

After a time, the conversation winds down, and we make our way back toward the front of the house. On the way we pass by the room with the glowing orb I'd caught sight of earlier. I attempt to subtly Check it as we pass, though the direction of my gaze draws Mirzayael's attention, too.

"Ah, congratulations," Mirzayael remarks, glancing around the Frostones. "To whom should I pass on my blessings?"

I stare at the dialogue box Echo just created, unsure how to react.

"That would be Jasper, Zakaiya, and Rei," Mica says.

"Ah. Zakaiya and Rei are in the guard." Mirzayael frowns. "They should have told me. I can shift them to less mana-intensive activities."

"I'm sure that's not necessary," Mica insists. "They all seem happy with the rate of development so far."

"Please let them know they are free to approach me should anything change," Mirzayael says.

Mica bows his head in appreciation. "Of course. Thank you."

I distractedly mumble some sort of goodbye as we depart, my mind still spinning with questions. Mirzayael must be able to sense some of my bewilderment, as she gives me a curious look. "You've been quiet."

Even though there are very few others walking the streets, I still lower my voice when I reply, faintly embarrassed. "As I mentioned earlier, I am constantly encountering new topics I need to learn about," I tell her. "I have a long overdue question I would like to ask. It will sound silly, however."

She raises an intrigued eyebrow. "I can't wait to hear this."

I can still hear Echo's voice in my head when I had her investigate the glowing sphere. [Check: Gestating Soul.]

"Mirzayael," I say haltingly, heat creeping up the back of my neck. "How are children conceived?"

Mirzayael blinks at the question. Then she throws her head back and laughs, long and loud.

CHAPTER NINE

THE EQUATION OF A SOUL

It takes a while for Mirzayael to stop laughing.

My cheeks burn fiercely the whole time, but it's all I can do to wait until she's done, wiping the tears from her eyes. On the bright side, I suppose, that's the most I've ever seen her laugh.

"Fyre, you can't mean to tell me you don't know how *babies* are made," she says, still chuckling. She gestures for me to follow as we talk, and we begin our trek back to the palace.

At least this way I won't have to maintain eye contact the entire conversation. "I suspect the mechanics might be significantly different from what I'm accustomed to in my world."

"Well, what do you want to know?" Mirzayael asks.

Her amusement is still dancing through my thoughts. I take a moment to ensure that our minds are quarantined from anything Ollie might accidentally overhear. "This feels like something we should be discussing in private," I say, glancing around self-consciously. As usual, however, the streets are largely empty.

"What, are you afraid someone might discover your lack of knowledge about procreation?" Mirzayael teases.

My blush deepens. "I am quite familiar with intercourse, thank you. I did have a child back on my world, after all."

Mirzayael's smile fades, looking down at me. "You didn't tell me that."

I blink. "I didn't?" I suppose not. Caroline is a beautiful memory as much as she is a painful one. This world has been an opportunity for me to start over in more ways than one. "Right. Well. I suppose that is a subject we could discuss later. What I really mean is, are you sure it's appropriate to talk about such things in public?"

"Why wouldn't it be?" she asks.

I fidget, picking at a loose feather on my wrist. "Well, where I'm from, it's a rather private matter. But I'm beginning to gather you don't have the same social stigmas attached."

"It sounds as though we don't," Mirzayael agrees. "The birth of a soul is the most natural thing. Why would it be stigmatized?"

"That is a complex topic of conversation," I admit. "But I'm glad to hear it's different here."

Mirzayael tips her head. "What is it exactly that you want to know? You had a kid yourself, so..."

"Well." I know this topic of conversation isn't embarrassing for Mirzayael, but it's still exceptionally uncomfortable for me. "On my world, we didn't have magic. Souls were a concept some believed in, but there was nothing concrete—nothing observable. Our method of procreation involved, um, the physical compatibility of a set of organs..."

"Sex," Mirzayael says bluntly.

"Right." I briefly consider having the Dungeon Core open a hole up beneath my feet so the ground can swallow me whole. "Sex. Yes."

"Obviously, we have that, too," Mirzayael says. "Though it's rather limited, isn't it? Different species can't procreate via intercourse, and even if the partners are the same species, most of the same gender and many of differing genders still won't be able to conceive a child via sex for one reason or another. It's a rather outdated form of procreation. I'd say most partners engage in it recreationally rather than with the intention of conceiving."

I cannot express how deeply unbearable this entire conversation is for me. But I'm already this far in, so I might as well see it to the end.

"Where I'm from, that's the only way to conceive," I say. Well, not accounting for modern technological advancements, though bringing that up now would only muddy the waters.

Mirzayael appears surprised. "No magical conception? But what about those who could not conceive biologically?"

"Then they weren't able to conceive at all," I say. "Adoption was an option for some."

Mirzayael's face falls. "How sad."

"We didn't have any other choice." I shrug. "This magical conception you mentioned. I am assuming that is how many here are conceived?"

"It is," she says. "Not only many, but most. I'd say less than one in ten children are born biologically. Depending on the species, birth can be an intense physical strain on the parent. Soul gestation is more controlled and safe. The tradeoff is that it can magically drain the parents and take much longer."

We're finally veering out of death-by-mortification territory. "How does soul gestation work?" I ask.

Mirzayael casually shrugs. "It's not a complicated process. The partners in question donate their mana to a shared pool to start the process. When enough magic has accumulated, it coalesces into a proto-soul. From there, the parents must continuously feed more magic into it. If it is too little, the proto-soul will shrink and eventually disperse. The more magic the parents have to offer, the faster the soul can form and grow. A truly powerful mage could make one on their own. For those with less magic, it can help to pair up with more individuals so each parent would need to contribute less mana overall. And once enough magic has accumulated, the proto-soul becomes a true soul. After the soul gestates for long enough, its body will form around it."

I frown at that. "Spontaneously?"

Mirzayael shakes her head. "It can take as long for the soul to form its body as it did for the proto-soul to become a gestating soul. Perhaps as fast as one month, or as long as several years, depending on how much mana the parents are able to donate. It's very magic intensive. But separate from parental mana donation rates, different species also form faster or slower than others. It's at that time the parents will learn what species the child will be."

My mind is whirling with more questions. "They don't know the species of their child until that point?"

"It could be the species of any of the parents who donated magic," Mirzayael says. "Some say that whichever parent donated the most magic is most likely to pass on their species to the child, but this claim is often debated. However, it is usually true that physical traits of parents who donate magic often show up in their children. Certain coat patterns; relative heights, and so on."

I wish I remembered more about genetics than how to make a Punnett square, because magical phenotypes sound like a captivating subject unto itself.

"You said some species are faster or slower to form than others," I say, backtracking. "Is this related to the size of the species the soul ends up becoming?"

"Typically, yes," Mirzayael acknowledges. "Dracid, arachnoid, and harpies all conceive eggs. Felis, humans, and dwarves have live births. Eggs are smaller, so these bodies tend to form around the souls much more quickly, though they require additional time and attention even after the soul gestation is complete; the eggs still need to develop and hatch. Meanwhile, felis, human, and dwarf infants will take longer for their bodies to form, but when they do, their births are complete."

"So it takes more magic for felis, human, and dwarf souls to form bodies," I surmise. "Are these species innately more magical than the others?"

"No," Mirzayael says. "It's actually more likely to be the reverse."

"Then this sounds like a case of conservation of energy," I muse. "The magic is being converted into matter. The more matter the final product has, the more magic is required as an input."

Mirzayael shrugs. "I suppose so."

This concept is fascinating, especially in how simultaneously different and familiar this is to scientific principles I'm already familiar with.

It's almost how the Core's Inventory works, to a degree. It costs magic to break things down and build things up. But what goes into the Inventory isn't converted to pure magic: it's more like the object is temporarily moved somewhere else, and for a small magical fee can be retrieved again. None of this contradicts my own understanding of conservation of mass and energy.

It also potentially provides an answer to a question I've long wondered about: Where did my body come from?

It's doubtful that my soul came to inhabit an already living (or even recently deceased) corpse, given the remote location in which I appeared. Which means my body must have spontaneously formed when my soul coalesced in this world. However I arrived in a fully adult body rather than a child's (or, god forbid, inside an egg). I can only imagine how much magic it must have taken to create this body.

"Intriguing," I mutter. "Do you think…" I trail off, unsure if I should even voice the spontaneous thought.

"Might as well ask it," Mirzayael says. "It will only eat you up if you don't."

She really has come to know me well, hasn't she?

"You said that traits of the child can be inherited by the parents who donated magic to the new soul," I start.

"Yes." She raises a questioning eyebrow.

I'm back to fidgeting again, thinking back on the room full of bones. "Well, there's been certain similarities drawn between my appearance and Fyreneth. Do you suppose… given the location where I was found… potentially some of her physical remains were incorporated into my manifestation?"

Mirzayael stares at me.

"That was probably a silly speculation," I hurriedly say.

"Perhaps." Mirzayael's look turns thoughtful. "Perhaps not. I don't know. I've never heard of such a thing happening… but you weren't the only one to appear in such a way. And Ollie's body would have required far more matter or magic than yours, so it's not impossible. I wonder… Perhaps there were dragon bones buried where Ollie appeared. It's been a long time since anyone has seen a living ice dragon."

"Then you really think it's possible?" I run a hand down my feathered arm. "This body might have used Fyreneth as a sort of… template?"

Mirzayael shakes her head. "I'm beginning to learn that anything's possible with you. Though if this does have something to do with your manifestation here, it leads to the question: Who or what donated the magic that formed your new body?"

I'd been wondering the same thing. I have faint memories of something that transpired between Earth and this world. What was it? There was a fight of some sort. There were other presences there in the dark. Had those been more souls, like me and Ollie? I try to approximate how many I had sensed, but everything had been so abstract and so much time has passed since that day that the details of the memory have faded. There's not enough there for me to take anything useful.

I can only shake my head at Mirzayael's question. "That's something I may never learn the answer to." I brighten. "But this has been a delightful subject to learn about. It gives me hope for Ollie's future."

Mirzayael blinks. "Ollie? What does he have to do with this?"

"Well, perhaps this is preemptive of me," I say. "He's still a child; when he's an adult, maybe he won't even be interested in starting a family. But trying to imagine what his future might look like has always made me a bit somber. It seems other dragons in this world are animalistic, while Ollie is intelligent. Couple that with his inability to speak, and I was concerned he was doomed to a life of solitude. It's encouraging to know he could one day start his own family, if he wanted to."

"A life of solitude?" Mirzayael repeats. "He has us to speak to."

"He does," I agree. "Though you, me, and the Dungeon Core... that feels a bit restrictive, don't you think?"

Mirzayael sighs wistfully.

I raise a bemused eyebrow.

"I was just thinking how nice it would be if I only ever had to speak to three people," she says.

I playfully elbow her.

"But there might be other ways for him to achieve speech so he's not only reliant on your telepathy," Mirzayael considers. "Depending on how flexible his talons are, there's always Common Signs. And I'm sure there are fields of magic that might be able to help. I'm not sure anyone within Fyreneth's Fortress has expertise in either of those areas, but if we speak to outsiders about the issue..."

"What's this?" I tease. "*You* suggesting we talk to outsiders?"

"Yes," Mirzayael deadpans. "You've made me intolerably soft."

I smile. "It's a good idea. I'll look into it when we have the opportunity."

Both of us pause then as a small white spider made of silk scuttles down the hallway toward us. Mirzayael stoops to the ground, extending her hand. The construct scurries up onto her palm.

"Land in sight," the spider says in Torim's voice when Mirzayael taps a rune on its back. "The harpies are reporting a coastline. North by north-east. We'll be upon it by the end of the day."

Mirzayael lowers the messenger spider, looking at me. "Well. It seems that opportunity has arrived."

CHAPTER TEN

GO FISH

What was originally a nondescript smudge on the horizon—and then obscured by low clouds the following day—abruptly resolves into a coastline. Just about everyone in Fyreneth's Fortress migrates from the city center to the outer walls to look down on the approaching land. The water turns sapphire blue as it approaches the mainland.

Boats speckle the water, though I can't make out a port. It can't be far, though, given so many indications of civilization.

After finishing my daily lap around the city to check on the spell network, I land on the wall near Mirzayael, Nek, Torim, and Dizzi, cutting off my Jet. They're all craning over the parapet, looking down on the ten thousand-foot drop with varying levels of unease. Or in Dizzi's case, giddy excitement.

"Do you think we should try to make contact this time?" I ask them. "They might be able to point us to the nearest city."

"Would we even be able to do anything with that information?" Torim asks.

I waffle my hand while Dizzi shakes her head.

"We can technically nudge the Fortress in whatever direction we like," I explain, "though doing so drains the cloudstone."

"We're more at the whims of the wind than anything," Dizzi adds.

"We could at least get confirmation of our maps," Torim considers. There's an unspoken 'but' at the end of his comment.

"Would the risk to the harpies we send down be worth it?" Mirzayael wonders.

"We'll have to make that leap at *some* point or another." I hesitate. "I wouldn't want to seem aggressive, but..."

Mirzayael grins. "This I have to hear."

"What if we sent them down with a deterrent?" I say. "Something that might make the boats think twice about attacking us."

"What sort of deterrent are you thinking?" Nek asks.

A shadow flickers over us, blotting out the sun as Ollie circles and lands on a wide stretch of wall nearby. The stone beneath our feet shakes as he sets down.

"*FYRE!*" He turns to me with a terrifying grin. "*LOOK WHAT MERITIS AND I FOUND!*"

The harpy hops from his back, holding up something slimy and writhing. "Look what Ollie found!"

"What in the Abyss is that?" Mirzayael demands, taking the words right out of my mouth.

"*ECHO SAYS IT'S A STRIPED EEL,*" Ollie says, while Meritis says, "I dunno, but Ollie ate a lot of them!"

Mirzayael puts a hand on my arm as my alarm spikes.

"Are they safe to eat?" I cry.

[Check: Striped eel,] Echo pipes up. [These predators are known for luring birds and wyverns in by swimming near the surface, only to use water arcana to knock the flying creatures from the sky and drown them beneath the waves.]

I guess that didn't work out in their favor when they lured in a dragon.

But are they toxic? I ask Echo.

[Negative.]

Thank god.

"I'm sure the kitchen will be... surprised to work with this," I say. "Meritis, would you mind taking that up to the palace?"

"Sure! Bye, Ollie!" He waves the eel around as he jumps back into the air and spirals off toward the palace.

"*THEY'RE REALLY TASTY,*" Ollie says as he watches the harpy leave. "*LIKE FISH STICKS.*"

"Perhaps you can lead some fishing excursions," I tell him. "But first, I've got a different task I'd like to ask you to help with."

Nek's eyes widen. "Well, he'll certainly act as a deterrent, that's for sure."

"Or his presence will instigate a fight," Torim remarks. "I don't know many who will take a look at him and feel more at ease."

"We don't need them to feel at ease," Mirzayael says. "We need them to think twice about attacking our scouts."

"It's not a perfect plan," I admit. "But since Ollie and I are connected, I'll be able to see through his eyes and hear through his ears. I can keep tabs on what's happening and notify others if we need to send backup." I turn to Ollie. "But the decision is not up to us, it's up to you. Would you like to accompany some of the scouts down to greet the ships?"

"*OH, YES!*" Ollie cries. "*THAT SOUNDS FUN. I'VE WANTED TO SAY HI TO THE BOATS, BUT MERITIS TOLD ME WE PROBABLY SHOULDN'T WHENEVER I GOT TOO CLOSE.*"

"*Remind me to give Meritis a hug later,*" I privately remark to Mirzayael. Her mouth twitches in the ghost of a smile.

"Let's organize a party." Mirzayael nods to Nek and Dizzi. "Nek, bring all our harpy scouts to the wall. Dizzi, any harpy volunteers you can find. Eighteen or older."

"Aye, Captain!" Dizzi says with a mock salute, then jumps from the wall. Nek departs with a more formal bow.

I regard Ollie as we wait for the others to return. He has a small saddle that was made for me before I learned how to fly, though I haven't needed to use it since then. When Meritis rides on Ollie's neck, he just slots himself between a few spines and loosely holds on with his arms and legs; falling off isn't a great risk when he can just spread his wings and fly on his own.

"Ollie, what do you think about other people riding on your back?" I ask him. "Would that be okay with you?"

He's flopped over on his side while we're waiting for the others to return, eyes half closed and tail draped over the wall like a cat lounging in the sun. He tips his head at my question.

"*UM, SURE, I GUESS,*" he says. "*WHICH ONES?*"

"Anyone who can't fly," I say. "We could make a much larger saddle to put on your back so you could help take people like Mirzayael or Nek down to the surface. They wouldn't have any other way to get down." At least, not yet.

"*OH, OKAY!*" Ollie stretches, a low yawn rumbling down his throat. "*NOT BEING ABLE TO FLY WOULD BE SO SAD. I LOVE FLYING!*"

I chuckle, patting his snout. "Me too."

I can feel a mental objection surfacing from Mirzayael, but whatever she'd been thinking, she doesn't voice it.

"We could perhaps fit up to ten passengers on his back," Mirzayael says instead, looking him over thoughtfully.

"I was thinking closer to twenty," I say. "More, maybe, if you add riders along the neck spines."

Mirzayael shakes her head. "That might restrict his mobility. And we will want to save room for storage space."

"Oh, good point," I agree. "When we start participating in trade, we'll need ways to secure cargo of various shapes and sizes." I frown. "Though Ollie can't be our only source of transportation. That will significantly limit our capabilities."

Mirzayael raises an eyebrow. "Just how much trade do you think we will be engaging in?"

"As much as we can, I suppose." But the question is, how? I don't want Ollie to become a pack mule, but harpies are lightweight and can't carry much on their own. We'll need to make some form of carrier that can rise and descend. Already a couple ideas are percolating in the back of my head; I'll need to discuss them later with Dizzi.

"In the meantime," I say, pulling my attention back to the present, "what can we bring for today's encounter?"

"What do you mean?" Mirzayael asks.

I splay my hands. "We can't have a dragon and small platoon of armed harpies drop down on them and have nothing to show for a peace offering. We want to start off on the right foot."

"A gift?" Mirzayael makes a face. "We already have scarcely little to give away."

"Something to trade," I counter. "Perhaps they'll have something that could benefit us."

"I don't know what we can afford to lose," Mirzayael says.

She has a point there. We can't give up any of our food or crops, and we're not prosperous enough yet to have made much beyond the essentials.

I could offer up some of the fireworks Dizzi and I have been working on. (Okay, mostly Dizzi, after I showed her the basics.) I could create things from the material that's still stored in the Dungeon Core's Inventory, though mostly all I have to offer are different types of stone. Perhaps some of that would be valuable for building material, but it would be far too heavy for harpies to carry. What do we have to offer *today?* Something lightweight. Something disposable. Is there anything we needed when we were in the arctic that isn't as necessary now?

"What about winter gear?" I ask, turning to Torim. "Some felis and arachnoid families were working on heavy blankets, weren't they?"

"They made a few blankets and coats before the Fortress took flight," Torim says. "But once the climate spell took hold, they shifted to warm weather garb."

"Do we still have those?" I ask. "If they're not in use, that could be something we can stand to trade for something more valuable."

Mirzayael nods appreciatively. "I like this idea. Yes, let's investigate if the textile group has anything in storage they are willing to share."

"Of course." Torim steps away to speak with an arachnoid guard, who hurries off to deliver the message. While harpies are the fastest species in Fyreneth's Fortress, arachnoids are a close second, and perhaps even exceed harpies when navigating streets and indoor buildings.

Nek's harpy guards are the first to return, followed a few minutes later by a handful of volunteers Dizzi was able to gather. Altogether we have nineteen harpies who volunteer to fly down and greet the ships with Ollie.

"Should Dizzi be in charge?" I privately ask Mirzayael. *"She **is** the Royal Scientist, so she has seniority."*

Mirzayael doesn't attempt to hide the face she makes. *"She's likely to get us into a geopolitical conflict."*

I rub my nose, hiding my smile. *"Disarming friendliness may play to our advantage. Are there any acceptable alternatives?"*

Mirzayael looks over the harpies. *"Salvia is my best guard. They're Hetlanir's child."* My heart sinks at the reminder; Hetlanir had been the lost colony's leader before he died saving Beryl from the Jorrians' attack. *"However, they won't turn twenty for another two months. They are intelligent and perceptive, but young and lack experience."* She hesitates. *"And I think you're right that someone stiff and rigid is not who we need in this situation."*

I raise an amused eyebrow at her. *"What's this? You're recommending we put someone excitable and friendly in charge?"*

Her lips pull in the faintest of smiles. *"Only in this specific instance."*

"Alright, you two love birds," Dizzi says, landing on the wall near us. "You're doing that thing again where you go all silent and make eyes at each other. What's going on?"

Warmth colors my cheeks, and Mirzayael scowls, turning to Dizzi. "We were discussing if you were the optimal candidate to lead this mission. I am having second thoughts."

Dizzi grins. "It's my winning personality, isn't it?"

"Actually, yes," I say before Mirzayael can completely rescind her decision. "We want to start off on the right foot. Which means your personability will work in our favor—and we would also like to request that you refrain from engaging in any talk about bomb making, explosives, or any weaponry for that matter." She opens her mouth. "No matter how conversation-relevant it might be."

"Awww," Dizzi sighs. "Well, alright, you guys are the boss. Bosses. Queens."

Mirzayael's eye twitches.

I pull Dizzi aside to give Mirzayael a break as I deliver the rest of the brief. "There will be a few goals to this encounter," I tell her. "First of course, is to establish friendly relations and gather more information about our location. If we can obtain a world map, or even a local map, so much the better. Anything that can help us research potential landing sites will be crucial. And if you have the opportunity, we're also open to engaging in trade..."

Despite Dizzi's excitable nature, she really is sharp as a razor and quickly picks up on what we're asking her to do. By the end of the hour, Torim's scout returns with some textile workers, showing us some of the frankly stunning silk blankets and fur coats they'd produced. I'm hesitant to give them up, in fact, but the weavers seem very excited to have their work offered as our city's first official attempt at trade. Whatever we get in return, I'm going to make sure they're greatly compensated for their generosity.

The heavy blankets and winter coats also end up being too heavy for many of the harpies to fly with, so in the end we bundle it all together and secure them high on Ollie's neck. Having witnessed Ollie's water landings before—and his aversion to any form of caution—we decide the goods will be safer higher up.

He wiggles his neck as they're fixed in place. "*IT ITCHES*," he complains, scratching at his neck just below the ties.

"Careful!" I say. "If you snag them, it will all come apart." I pull his massive claws away and dig my fingers into his scales, scratching as hard as I can under and around the ropes. He rumbles happily, tipping his head back. "It will just be for a little bit, too. We'll try to get them off as soon as we can. And we'll work on something that feels better for next time."

"*FIIIIINE,*" he sighs, giving a disappointed grumble when I stop scratching. He flutters his wings. "*THEN LET'S HURRY UP AND DO IT!*"

"Let's," I agree.

Mirzayael is already in the midst of doling out final orders to her scouts; the volunteer harpies attempt to look sufficiently professional as she does.

I activate Psionic Senses, and feel the mental connection to Ollie snap into focus. Suddenly our surroundings sound louder and echoey, and I'm presented with double-vision as I look through Ollie's eyes back down at us all gathered around him. I close one eye to help separate my vision from his. We really do look small from his perspective.

"*I'll be with you the whole time,*" I tell him, sending a wave of reassurance along with the thought.

Ollie, who likely doesn't even recognize the potential danger of any of this, happily beams in my head. "*OKAY!*"

"Alright then." I look back over the wall. I want so badly to go with them. My range is almost, *almost* enough to accompany them. Maybe I can expedite my research into the Fortress's defense systems, which I've admittedly been neglecting. But for today, there's nothing I can do but watch.

"*Ready?*" Mirzayael mentally nudges.

I nod.

Mirzayael turns back to the harpies. "Ready?" I can feel anticipation humming through Ollie. "Launch!"

Ollie lets out an excited trill as he dives off the wall, and the flock of harpies descend after him.

CHAPTER ELEVEN

YOUR TYPICAL FLYING CITY

I have to close both eyes when Ollie drops toward the ocean and the double vision becomes too dizzying.

"You alright?" Mirzayael asks.

"Yes," I say. Ollie is laughing in my head as he plummets several hundred feet before snapping his wings open and slowing his descent. "Just keeping an eye on things."

"Keep me tied in," Mirzayael says. Her voice is tight, and I can feel her anxiety through our mental bond. Not that Mirzayael gets particularly anxious—at least, not in the way I feel it from Ollie or even the Dungeon Core. Her form of anxiety feels more like a mental tension; sharp, high vigilance, as if readying for an attack. I wonder what mine feels like to her? Not that anxiety is something I often experience.

Ollie flares his wings, banking toward the rapidly approaching ships, and my stomach flutters.

Okay, anxiety isn't something I *often* experience. Outside worrying about Ollie.

The ships themselves aren't particularly large—perhaps there's a ten-person crew on each one—though over the last hour they've all grouped up, likely in reaction to the appearance of a floating city hovering overhead. Dizzi flies out ahead of Ollie, turning back to him.

"I'll go first," she tells him. "You can land in the water over there." She points to an area that gives the ships a healthy buffer of distance (while still remaining within Ollie's Icebeam range.)

"*AWWW, I WANTED TO GET CLOSER,*" Ollie grumbles.

"*Listen to Dizzi,*" I tell him. "*You'll be able to swim over if it's safe.*"

He makes his pouting known, but complies, kicking up a spray of water as he flaps his wings just before dropping down into the sea.

"*AH,*" he sighs contentedly, shaking down his body like a dog. He nearly dips his head under, too, before Mirzayael catches the thought.

"*Keep the goods dry!*" she cries, and Ollie's head jerks back up in surprise.

"*SORRY,*" he says, embarrassed. "*I FORGOT.*"

Regret colors Mirzayael's mind, too. "*No, it's alright. I shouldn't have yelled.*"

Ollie is quickly distracted as a couple of harpies land on his back, and he concentrates very hard on not shaking them off. They tickle.

Ahead of him, Dizzi and the rest of the harpies are nearing the three ships. Their wind affinities allow them to almost hover in place, which is a small blessing; at least they can approach slowly and hopefully convey that they aren't a threat.

Unfortunately, they're slightly too far away for Ollie to hear any discussion that might be taking place between them.

"Can Ollie move closer?" I ask Mirzayael. I feel her lean forward next to me, likely looking down over the wall.

"How close does he need to get?"

"I can't accurately gauge his distance from here," I admit. "Would it be risky to close half the distance?"

Mirzayael is silent for a moment. "It might make them nervous. But I think it will be alright if he can do so gradually, without drawing much attention to himself."

Easier said than done with a dragon. But I can't be of any help if I can't hear what's being discussed.

"*Ollie?*" I prompt. "*Would you mind swimming a little closer? But do it slowly if you can. Like you're sneaking up on them.*"

Maybe not the best simile, but it gets the point across.

"*OH, YEAH!*" Ollie says. "*I'M GOOD AT SNEAKING. I'VE GOT A LOT OF FISH THAT WAY. LOOK, I CAN DO IT WITH-OUT EVEN MOVING MY LEGS!*"

Ollie is still watching the nearby ships, but I can feel his tail begin to gently wave back and forth. Sure enough, it propels him forward with barely a ripple. I'm not sure if the harpies on his back even notice they're drifting.

"*Great job,*" I tell him. He really is surprisingly good at sneaking, despite his thousands of kilograms of mass. "*I'll let you know where to stop. But if you hear anyone yell, or if anyone throws anything at you, stop right away.*"

Not that arrows have proven capable of doing any damage to Ollie in the past, and not that I can see any sort of cannons on the nearby ships, but I don't want to chance it.

Ollie, for his part, seems entirely unbothered by the warning. His mind is skipping around between all sorts of thoughts, from wanting to duck under the waves for a proper swim, to reminding himself not to knock off any of his harpy passengers like he did that one time with Meritis, to wondering if the boats would like to race later.

Dizzi and several harpies are hovering at deck-level before the nearest ship, still a healthy distance away. Good; them being so low might help them appear less intimidating. Ollie's distance is still far from ideal, but I can start to make out some of the conversation taking place.

"...don't even know what that is," Dizzi admits. "Our city is pretty new, actually."

The captain, a dracid, nervously glances toward me. Or, Ollie, rather.

"*That's enough,*" I tell him. "*Stop here.*"

"You understand our wariness, what with your beast nearby," she says. The dracid speaks with a strong, lyrical accent, barely hitting the hard sounds while leaning into the soft ones. I'd noticed the Jorrians had a faint accent, too, but not nearly as strong as this.

Ollie mentally laughs at being called a beast, and huffs out a frosty breath. I have to curb my own annoyance at the descriptor, but it's probably for the best that Ollie takes it as a compliment.

Dizzi holds up her hands. "Sorry. I can see how it looks. He's just here for our own protection. We didn't know who we'd end up talking to down here. If it helps, I can come aboard alone."

I tense up.

"What is it?" Mirzayael asks.

"Dizzi offered to board the ship by herself," I say. More than ever, I wish we had a better way to communicate. Mirzayael's spider constructs work well as recording devices, but what we really need are radios. My Psionic Link serves exactly such a purpose, however the spell is permanent, and bringing too many people into the network concerns me from a privacy standpoint.

Mirzayael swears. "I knew I should have put one of my guards in charge."

I chew on the inside of my cheek. "Nothing we can do about it now. It might be alright."

The dracid captain glances between Dizzi, Ollie, the other ships, and the rest of the harpies hovering nearby. Finally, she nods. "Alright. Just you for now."

"Ollie, can you get Echo to Check that person?" I ask him. *"Everyone else, too, but her first."*

"SURE!"

Dizzi alights on the rail of the fishing boat, which fills me with relief. She may be overly enthusiastic, at times, but she's not naive. Keeping to the rail gives her a quick escape route if needed, and prevents her from being surrounded. I relay everything I see and hear to Mirzayael. She doesn't respond, but her tension winds tighter.

Ollie starts reading off stats he's getting from Echo.

The captain is a Level 31 Dracid Navigator named Marina. That class sounds relatively benign, which I count as a good sign. Everyone else on her ship is lower level and also have classes related to fishing, sailing, or merchandising. Each level and class he reads off makes me feel a little bit better about the situation. No one seems to have a primary class in some field of combat, at least.

The ship also includes two new species of people. Echo had given me the names 'nereid' and 'lamia' before, but this is my first time seeing them. Nereids are aquatic looking people covered in scales and fins, with gills adorning their throats. They're mostly blue, green, and purple. Lamia, meanwhile, appear to have the torso of a human, but are snake from the waist down. The snake half comes in varying patterns of diamonds and stripes in just about every color imaginable.

"You're sure that's not the Drifting Isles?" Marina asks, glancing up at our city.

Curious, I ask Ollie to look up at us too. He cranes his head back toward the city.

I suck in a breath.

"Fyre?" Mirzayael asks, alarmed.

"It's okay," I say. "I just haven't seen the Fortress from the ground before. It's... it's something else."

Clouds swirl around the city, repelled by our atmospheric spell system, which creates a dramatic, almost hurricane-like effect. I had never considered how big the city would appear from the ground. For some reason, I thought it would look smaller or more distant. But there's no hiding this castle in the sky. It stretches wide overhead, and the underbelly of carved cloudstone and enormous rudders provides an imposing view. No wonder the ships were nervous. Ollie would be the least of their worries.

"No, sorry," Dizzi says. "Just your typical flying city. Actually, we were hoping to get some directions."

Marina snorts, giving Dizzi a skeptical but amused look. "Where to?"

"Well, where *are*, more like," Dizzi says. "Is this Dunmora?"

"Yes..." The captain pauses as if she's unsure if she should say more. Then she whistles for one of her crewmates, and a human hurries over to her side. Dizzi's wings give a small flap; she was startled by the human, but she plays it off like she's just adjusting her balance. Marina tells him to go retrieve one of her coastline maps, and the human runs off.

Dizzi nods to the other nearby ships, gradually drifting closer. "Friends of yours?"

"Competitors," Marina says. "We all fish the same waters. Though the arrival of your city somewhat overshadowed our rivalry, and we were about to speak when your flock arrived. There's been talk of the

Drifting Isles passing over the last few days. I suspect the sightings have actually been you."

"Guilty," Dizzi says with a grin. "And I know it sounds unlikely, but we really are just a recently-launched city trying to figure out where we are and where we'll be headed. So any information you can offer is helpful." She gestures back toward Ollie. "We've got a small store of supplies, too, that we can use in payment. If you're okay with it, I can have them bring some over."

Marina again gives Ollie a calculating look.

I mentally prod him. *"Can you show her the gifts you brought?"*

"SURE!" Ollie turns his head to the side so Dizzi and Marina have a better view of the bundle strapped to his neck.

The captain's eyebrows lift. "I've never seen a tame dragon before. At least, not one of this size."

"He's not tame, he's intelligent," Dizzi says. "Which is why he's no danger to you unless you're a danger to us. Right Ollie?"

Ollie proudly lifts his chin and gives a happy trill at being recognized. His Role means he has to protect me, but I can tell that he's tickled by the idea that everyone in the Fortress sees him as a sort of guardian. I'll have to be careful to not let that pride balloon out of proportion, no matter how much he's earned it.

"He's named Ollie?" Marina repeats dubiously.

"Yes, and it's a very good name," Dizzi insists. "Hey, would you mind passing on the message to the other ships that we're not here to cause any trouble? I'd like to send some of my flock to greet them, too, but it would help smooth things out if you could vouch for us."

Marina gives Dizzi a long, hard look, and I can't blame her. She doesn't know a thing about us yet. Vouching for us is a stretch. But Dizzi's question was made so casually and innocently, I think she understands there was no ill intent behind it.

"You may bring over the goods," Marina finally responds. "I wish to check the content. If it's as you say, I'll pass your message along."

Dizzi perks up. "Great! Thanks for giving us a chance." She waves for Ollie to swim over, and he's more than happy to do so. The ship's crew nervously backs away when Ollie rests his chin on the railing beside Dizzi and she scratches his muzzle in his favorite spot. Two of the harpies set to work untying the goods. To the captain's merit, she doesn't retreat, watching Ollie with an obvious mix of fear and awe.

The bundle of goods is unloaded, and Marina inspects the contents. Dizzi invites a couple more harpies on board—the volunteers, I notice, not any of Mirzayael's guards—and instigates lighthearted small talk with a couple of the crew. I recall Dizzi acting in a similar fashion when we first encountered her colony and both sides were tense and uncertain around each other. She was the first to jump in, the first to ask questions and chat openly. And just like back then, her carefree attitude is starting to warm both groups to each other. She's the oil in our machine, I realize. As much as she's happy to bury herself in artificing and research, it's her people skills we're going to need to make better use of going forward.

I smile to myself. I'm sure I'll never hear the end of it if I ask her to become an ambassador.

After another minute of talk, the captain heads to the bow of her ship. I can't really tell what she's doing from the way Ollie is angled, but he glances her way after the first flash of light bursts into the sky. He lifts his head, watching curiously.

Marina has one hand pressed to a spell circle carved into the bow of her ship, and her other hand is held before her, moving rapidly through different gestures. At the same time, large symbols appear in the air above her.

"OH!" Ollie says. *"ECHO SAYS 'FOREIGN LANGUAGE DE-TECTED.' SHOULD I TRANSLATE?"*

"Please do!" I say, fascinated by the display. The symbols overhead are fairly simple in design: a circle, or a cross, or a line. Shapes that could be easily distinguished from a large distance. They sometimes change color, too. That combination of shape and color could produce a multitude of meanings, I imagine. It's similar to signal lights we'd use at airports, but this version appears far more complex and seems to be derived from some sort of sign language.

Ollie begins to repeat the translations he receives from Echo. *"UM, IT'S KIND OF CONFUSING,"* he admits. *"THEY'RE NOT US-ING FULL SENTENCES. OKAY, SHE SAYS: ENCOUNTER POS-ITIVE UNCERTAIN. DANGER LOW UNCERTAIN. TRADE OFFER LINENS. REQUEST BOARDING. REQUEST HEAD-ING."* Ollie pauses when Marina stops signing and the last glowing symbol dies out. *"WHAT'S ALL THAT MEAN?"*

"I think she's saying they're still a little unsure about us, but are tentatively vouching for us," I reply, puzzling through the message myself. *"At least she passed along the message that we're just here to trade and get a map."*

"Hm." Mirzayael's skepticism permeates her reaction to Ollie's report. "The message does appear friendly, at least on the surface."

I chuckle. "You think there might be a hidden and malicious message somewhere in there?"

"It's entirely possible," she insists. But there's no fire behind her words. "Though, strange as it may seem, I suspect you are right in this instance."

I laugh. "Just in this instance."

The other ships respond a minute later, agreeing to boarding and trade. Marina gives the go-ahead for Dizzi to speak with the other ships, and she splits up the harpies, flitting around to introduce each group herself.

Over the next hour, the worry that had been distantly brewing inside me evaporates. The ships offer their maps for consultation, one trades us a copy, and as soon as one ship makes an offer on the fur coats and blankets, a bidding war between the vessels ensues.

The day grows long, and Ollie and the harpies eventually return to the city with a large store of fish and a handful of maps in tow. Everyone excitedly gathers around the spoils as they're laid out to be recorded. Mirzayael congratulates Dizzi on the "competent negotiations which exceeded her expectations," a level of praise which shocks Dizzi even more than it does me.

That night, I fall asleep smiling.

CHAPTER TWELVE

THE WATCHTOWER

The watchtower's floor is covered in dust and loose pebbles, which the Dungeon Core happily licks up as I point out new areas in need of tidying.

While the tower comfortably fits within the Core's area of influence, prior to today I'd only ever visited it through the Dungeon Core's interface. The stairs in this tower, along with the other four watchtowers, had partially or fully collapsed, so it hadn't been high on my to-do list before some harpies began investigating the open windows at the top. That was when the spell circles were discovered.

They'd slipped past my attention before now as all their spell circuits had been broken by cracks in the rock. I still have dozens of lines connected to the throne that lead nowhere, the veins of magically conductive ore terminating before they reach any spells. Since all of these broken lines are somewhere underground, the only way for me to find where the break is, and what it should be connected to, would be to use the Dungeon Core to mentally scour through the stone.

Repairing the lines themselves won't be much of an issue. However, I'd like to examine the spells they're designed to control first; I don't want to accidentally turn on any of the Fortress's functions before knowing what they're for. Especially given the city was never originally designed to float kilometers above the ground.

"The second landing is blocked," Mirzayael tells me from below. She'd probably have no problem scaling the tower from the outside herself, but she's accompanying the crew of researchers we've brought to start deciphering the spell circles.

"One moment." I direct the Dungeon Core to start rebuilding the staircase and fixing any other structural damage we can find. This task takes much of my oversight and concentration (the Core really has no concept of structural integrity) so I pause, closing my eyes, as I set about the task.

"This place is amazing!" Dizzi says. I can hear her running a hand over the floor, where the enormous, room-sized spell circle is inlaid. "Every day is something new! Do you suppose there's even more buried underground somewhere no one would ever see?"

"That sounds like a headache for future-me," I say. The Core has eaten all the rubble that was blocking the second landing, and now I'm getting it to reinforce the ceiling that had caved in. Switching to the Map interface, I can see seven markers on that floor begin to move up the steps: two arachnoids, three felis, and two dwarves. I know there should be at least two more dracid and one harpy joining us on this excavation, but none of them appear on my map. It's odd to know there's people there but not be able to see them. I smile faintly. Ghosts of the Map Interface.

"What's weird is that the spell circles in each tower don't appear to be the same," Dizzy continues. "At least, from what I can make out.

But why would all of them be different? You'd think you'd want the same functionality to be spread symmetrically around the city."

"Unless each is capable of acting over the entire city anyway," I say, still focusing on fixing the lower floors of the tower. "Maybe each one builds on the other in some way."

"That would kind of suck, given the tower we lost," Dizzi remarks.

Yes, it might pose an issue. We'd lost the fifth watchtower when the Fortress first ascended. Though without knowing what spell might have been carved there before it was reduced to rubble (and eaten by the Dungeon Core without my permission, I might add, preventing me from rebuilding it like a bunch of jigsaw pieces,) there's no sense in moaning about it. We've got four other towers to work through already.

It takes five minutes for me to finish repairing the tower, and another ten for the researchers to make it to the top. Everyone but Mirzayael and one of the harpies is breathing heavily by the time they reach the top floor. One of the dwarfs collapses against the wall.

"We're going to need to do something about that climb," a felis says between breaths.

The harpy who isn't catching their breath—or rather, doing a good job at disguising it—is Salvia, a young guard and the child of Hetlanir that Mirzayael had pointed out to me before. Their feathers are as white as snow, and their eyes an intense, bright blue, as if they were cut from an iceberg. Salvia catches my gaze and I smile. They return it with a curt nod, then turn away to survey the room, all business. I'm starting to understand why Mirzayael favors them.

"Alright!" Dizzi claps her hands, and one of the felis's ears flick in irritation. "Everyone excited to do some science?"

This is met with a varying chorus of affirmations and groans.

It's a patchwork crew. No one is technically a researcher, though I suppose Dizzi and I come closest. But the dwarf Chert has recently been volunteering assistance with Dizzi on her fireworks, since he has a stone affinity, and the two dracid worked under Torim to help build the temporary water holding system. I suspect these three would have flourished in some sort of academic environment. The rest are volunteers with at least a passing proficiency in the arcane, but I certainly don't hold their inexperience against them; their interest in helping already speaks to their potential.

Neither Fyreneth's Keep nor the Lost Colony had much documentation on spellwork—most of that knowledge had decayed in Fyreneth's library over the centuries—but between the two colonies, Dizzi was able to compile a fairly impressive list of known runes and their natures. I myself haven't had much of a chance to dig into rune theory, but as I understand it, the symbols can be combined in various ways to create spell circles from scratch. Or in this case, help determine what an already designed circle might have been meant for.

Conceptually, I'm enamored with this branch of magic. It reminds me very much of functions and code blocks. If I had more time to dedicate to the subject, I'm certain I'd have already lost weeks to its study. Maybe one day, when we're no longer rushing to do everything at once, I'll have an hour or two of free time in my days again. Isn't that a nice thought?

"Let's start with what we do know," I say, gesturing to the spell circle inscribed on the floor. There are dozens of cracks running through it, though otherwise it is largely intact. The spell circles we discovered in the other towers are more damaged, so this one will be good to start the researchers on. A practice excavation, if you will.

I crouch, tracing a finger over a line of runes. I recognize a couple from spell circles I excavated with Dizzi when we were preparing the

Fortress for its flight. Beckoning the researchers over to crowd around me, I gesture to a section of the floor. "Does anyone know the meaning of this? Besides Dizzi," I add as she eagerly opens her mouth to answer.

The room is silent for a moment, and I'm abruptly thrown back to similar onboarding meetings with new engineers too nervous or self-conscious to ask questions that might expose their ignorance.

"Or the meaning of any of the runes?" I amend. I tap one of the squiggles cut into the stone. "I'm still learning myself, so whatever insight you have is valuable to me. This one, I think, is a logic rune. It connects the meaning of nearby runes to one another."

"Ah..." Chert makes a noise like he'd like to say something, but he clearly lost his nerve.

I gesture to him anyway. "What can you tell me about it?"

The dwarf pales at being put on the spot, but Dizzi snorts at his hesitation. "Oh, come on, Chert! I know you know it. It's not like she's going to bite your head off."

Dizzi's helpful encouragement summons a deep shade of red to Chert's complexion. Goodness, he's the exact opposite of her, isn't he?

"It's called 'ko,'" Chert says, staring at the rune so as to avoid making eye contact with me. "And it does connect the meaning of adjacent runes. Specifically, it designates the function of the rune in the negative direction to the subject of the rune in the positive direction."

Positive and negative referring to counter-clockwise and clockwise, respectively, I'd been delighted to learn. It was rather like the terminology used in physics. Some concepts seem to be universal.

"Excellent," I say. "I didn't realize this rune was directional. That's good to know. How about this one?" I point to another rune, one I know I've seen before in the spell circles Torim helped work on for the water system.

On a hunch, I pick out one of the dracid. "What can you tell me about it?"

"That rune is called 'zie,'" she immediately replies. "It's used to specify an area of effect."

Aha, so they do know more than they're letting on.

A felis jumps in next, volunteering another rune without me having to prompt anyone for it, and with that the ice finally seems to shatter. The group crowds closer, anyone who recognizes anything pointing out the rune and sharing what they know about it. Excluding Dizzi, they can collectively identify about half the runes in the circle. At that point I was going to finally let Dizzi jump in, who I can tell is about ready to explode from being excluded for so long, but then something remarkable happens. They begin to guess at meanings of the unknown runes from the context of their surroundings.

That was precisely the next step I had been hoping to guide them to, and they'd gotten there on their own. I step back to watch the young researchers work, filled with pride. When you're a parent, your goal is to prepare your kid for the world well enough such that you become obsolete. It's a counterintuitive feeling for a mark of success to be that you're no longer needed.

Something about that idea snags on the back of my mind. It feels related to my Role Requirement, which is also contradictory, on the surface. The better I protect the kingdom, the further I'm able to go from it. But to leave it behind is to leave it more exposed, which should in turn make it less protected and reduce my range.

Which itself should be a self-defeating feedback loop. Yet, that doesn't seem right. I don't have the full picture. There's some other angle to this Role I haven't yet fully grasped.

After the group gets stuck on one section of the circle, I wave for Dizzi to join in.

"Finally!" she cries. "Okay, so, first you guys were wrong about this one. It's called 'petu' and you were close when you thought it was another connective rune, though it would be more accurate to say it's a modifier..."

I watch as Dizzi eagerly drowns the new recruits in a deluge of rune theory of which I'm sure they'll only be able to remember a fraction.

"It seems to be going well," Mirzayael notes as Dizzi continues her lecture.

"Better than I could have hoped," I agree. *"Solving this spell circle will boost their confidence going into the more damaged and difficult ones. At this rate, we might get all of them repaired before the week is out."*

"Will you know what all of them do at that time?" she asks.

"Theoretically," I say. *"It would be unwise to replace missing runes without knowing what should have been there in the first place. And to know what should have gone there in the first place, we need to understand what the circle was designed to do. We do that by reading the runes... many of which are damaged."*

"That sounds circular," Mirzayael remarks.

I smile. *"It is. But that's why we have all these people here to work through it together. Different perspectives, different ideas, tackling things from different angles..."* My mind drifts back to my Role Requirement.

"What is it?" she asks, noting my troubled thoughts.

"I wish I could say," I admit. *"It's this Role Requirement and the Role Range. Why have a requirement to keep something safe, but the reward is to allow me to leave the very thing I'm supposed to protect?"*

"Maybe it's not a reward," Mirzayael suggests. *"But rather a consequence."*

I glance up at her. *"What do you mean?"*

"You're not being rewarded with a greater distance the more the Fortress is protected," she says. *"The more the Fortress is protected, the further you can leave it while exposing it to the same level of threat."*

That's when it all clicks into place for me. *"Yes! Of course. You're a genius."*

Mirzayael snorts out loud, which causes one of the researchers to glance her way. *"That's a first."*

"But I believe you're right," I insist. *"The Range is a reflection of how well-protected the Fortress is. The more the Fortress becomes self-sufficient, the less this 'Needs Protection' factor is reliant on my proximity. So effectively, once the range has expanded so far as to encompass the world, my abilities will be a moot point because the city will have more power than anything I'm individually capable of."*

Though I wonder... Even if I'm able to make my protection factor inconsequential to the city's ability to protect itself, will my value ever reach zero, or just become very small? Because if it's non-zero, and the city ever *does* come under attack, then it might activate my Role Requirement and punishing Sanity Stat regardless.

Hmmm. A conundrum. But one I don't need to be puzzling over now. And indeed, I won't be able to answer this hypothetical without more data. For now, deciphering these spell circles and hooking them back up to the throne is more than enough to worry about.

Chapter Thirteen

ECONOMICS 101

When we finish deciphering the first watchtower spell circle, Dizzi and Mirzayael are both equally excited to try it out.

"I still need to hook it up to the network," I tell them. "And get these cracks fixed."

In the couple of places where cracks intersect the runes, Dizzi and some of the other researchers have already finished sketching out the correct symbol with chalk.

This is a rather delicate operation, I tell the Dungeon Core, drawing its attention to the circle. *We need to be careful to preserve the face of this rock when we seal the cracks. And see where the chalk is?*

Yes, the Dungeon Core likes chalk! It's soft and sweet and dissolves in just the best way.

Well I'm happy to inform you it's on the table, I say, smiling at the Core's enthusiasm, even for something this small. *But you'll need to eat the stone beneath it as well, to a depth of one centimeter.*

Yay! The Dungeon Core enjoys eating multiple rocks at the same time. Sometimes they taste better together! Can it do it now?

"Everyone ready?" I ask. The researchers have all retreated to the outskirts around the room, of which there's just enough space to stand without touching the spell circle.

"Ready!" Dizzi cries.

I repeat my instructions to the Dungeon Core two more times, just to make sure it understands how crucial it is to not destroy the circle itself, and then stand back to let it work.

With a sharp *crack,* the gaps in the floor snap closed, and a few of the researchers jump. The surface knits itself back together, smoothing any signs of the previous cracks away. Then the chalk hisses and sinks into the face of the stone, as if corroded by a layer of acid. In my head, I am presented with an impression of a massive tongue running across the floor, savoring every bit of crumbs it manages to lick away.

"*Well that's fairly disturbing,*" Mirzayael privately remarks.

I hold in a chuckle. "*At least it's not simulating chewing sounds. I don't even know where it learned that from.*"

It takes less than ten seconds to fix the spell circle.

"Is that it?" Chert asks.

"Dizzi, can you double check if all the runes look like they've been shaped correctly?" I ask her.

"Of course!" she beckons the others closer. "Come on, everyone, take a look. Even the smallest detail could screw up the whole spell. Let's go over them one by one."

As the researchers work their way around the room, I Check the spell circle. Previously, Echo had only been able to identify it as a [Damaged spell circle.] Now, however, she has a different message for me.

[Greater Shield Spell. Mana requirement: 100 mana per second.]

I rock back on my heels. Dizzi and the others had already deduced that the purpose of the spell was to cast a protective barrier over the city. It's good to get confirmation that they were correct. But it's the incredibly high mana requirement that surprises me.

I myself only have 500 base mana. Ollie has about double that amount. We could each only power the shield for a handful of seconds at most. Of course, from all the mana ore that was consumed before we raised the Fortress, the Dungeon Core and I have access to a pool of mana in the millions, but that's the same mana pool that is powering the Fortress and keeping the cloudstone buoyant. It should only be used under extreme circumstances, and even then we would need to ensure we don't consume enough mana to cause the Fortress to lose its flight capabilities.

"Looks good to us," Dizzi reports, even though I already knew that to be the case. I wasn't going to interrupt their investigation, however; I won't be able to oversee the research for each of the other spell circles, especially the more damaged ones, and this is good practice for them.

"Great," I say. "I'll link it back to the throne. What can you all tell me about the mana requirement?"

They all crowd around once more, and a couple reach out to touch the circle. I dip into the Dungeon Core's interface, allowing my mind to expand into the Core's senses and sink beneath the stone. I trace the spell circuit through the city, searching for the break in its line.

Dizzi makes an annoyed grumbling sound. "It doesn't have an affinity requirement, which is good. Anyone should be able to operate it. But the amount of mana to activate it... It's going to be a lot."

"I wouldn't be able to do it," one of the researchers admits.

"Me neither," says another.

I find the break in the spell circuit a hundred meters down the line and quickly repair it. Though the spell circle may be dormant, it's now connected back to the throne, which makes it connected to the Dungeon Core, which in turn means I can now remotely activate it.

"You're telling me this spell is inoperable?" Mirzayael asks.

"No." This is from Salvia. They've hardly said three words since they got here, instead sharply observing everything the others point out. From their mana levels and class, they're clearly a warrior, not a mage, but the fact that they're here to learn something outside their wheelhouse tells me they have an innate curiosity—or at the very least, ambition. Whatever the motive, I suspect they will become a valuable asset to the Fortress in some respect or another. Mirzayael is right; they may be young, but they're inevitable leadership material.

"We can use multiple mages," they say. "That's why it was designed to be so large, and with extra space around the edges of the room. You could have perhaps twenty people standing around the perimeter. They could then pool their mana resources together to activate the spell."

"Bingo," I say. A felis tips her head at the word. "I mean, precisely. I have some insight into how much mana it takes to power the spell. If I can document the mana reserves of all the guards and mages in the city—and anyone else who would volunteer to operate spell circles in a time of need—I should be able to quantify how many would be needed to power it, and for how long. But from my initial estimates, Ollie and I alone could only activate it for about fifteen seconds. A group of ten young mages could probably do the same."

"Fifteen seconds?" Mirzayael repeats.

Echo, can you begin to Check and compile a list of base Mana stores for all Fyrethians I encounter going forward?

[Affirmative.] Immediately, the names and base Mana stats of everyone in this room appear in a list at the side of my vision. That list will quickly get overwhelming the moment I step before a crowd. I sort it from highest to lowest mana, then dismiss it to review later.

"That hardly seems useful at all," Mirzayael continues.

"Depending on the timing of things, it could be critical," I say. "But you're right that it should be used judiciously. And if push comes to shove, we can use what the Dungeon Core has access to. Still, given this spell's mana consumption, I suspect the effect will be exceptionally strong—at least, while active."

Mirzayael blows out a breath. "It's more than we had before." She adds mentally, *"Does this affect your Role Range at all?"*

I pause to check. It has, minutely. The Role increased from 2.39 km to 2.50 km. That's interesting, because I would have thought such a hugely impactful spell would have a greater impact on my range. Perhaps this is because it's not currently in effect. As a test, I toggle off the ability to see species on the Dungeon Core's map, and the thousands of dots on the interface vanish. My hypothesis was right: the range decreases to 1.33 km. I quickly turn the capability back on.

"It boosts it a little," I tell Mirzayael. *"But I suspect while the spell is activated, my range will grow exponentially."*

"Good work," I say aloud to everyone else. "Dizzi, I leave it to you how you wish to tackle the other three towers, be it continuing to work as a group or divide and conquer."

"I'll do a preliminary assessment of each of the spell circles first and let you know," she says.

I've already spoken to her about the agreement I made with Mirzayael; we'll start working on the defensive spell circles first, then work on anything that might be designed as a weapon with a smaller, trusted team.

"I'll leave it to you," I say, stepping away. "Great job today."

As Dizzi excitedly speaks with the other researchers about their plan for the next week, Mirzayael and I depart. This was a nice break from my daily routine. It's delightfully refreshing to get back to a bit of science, and witness a younger generation's budding enthusiasm. But now it's done, and there's always something else for me to be doing, somewhere else for me to be.

The same goes for Mirzayael. Wordlessly, we each head in a different direction, already focused on our next task, yet with our minds close it feels like we're still walking side by side. I can faintly feel Mirzayael fretting about the boats we'd encountered the day before.

"Worried they'll swim up here without us knowing?" I tease.

"I'm worried about the next group," she says. The harbor for the fishing boats we'd traded with had been to the west, while our Fortress continues to drift east. From the maps they provided us with, we'll be approaching another city tomorrow. Our first city.

"What if they don't receive us as kindly as the last?" she wonders.

"It's always a possibility," I concede.

"And even if we do, what do we have to offer?"

Now that is a good question. We were able to scrounge together some unneeded coats and blankets the day before, but we don't have much in the way of trade supplies or exports at this time. The fish we'd traded for are an absolute boon to us, but would surely be mundane to a coastal town.

"We need to develop an economic plan," I realize. The Fyrethians operate on a communal system. Various groups have naturally arisen from this; Yequirael's tailors, Mirzayael's guards, Agate's agriculture team, Torim's water purification group. Many of these are divided along the affinities and skillsets of different species. People find where their skills are most needed and work there. The products of each group are distributed across the city evenly or, if there isn't enough to accommodate everyone (as is more often the case) to whomever needs it the most. Our population is still small enough that this system has posed no issues prior to now. But if we're going to engage in trade, we

need to shape this into a more concrete, efficient system, and begin to think long term.

Unfortunately, economics is something I know embarrassingly little about.

"You should speak with Nek," Mirzayael says. *"He's been tracking the city-wide inventory."*

"Good idea." Right, I don't have to know economics. I have others I can rely on who are or will become the experts in these fields for me. Maybe he'll have some ideas on where we are positioned to produce a surplus of some product.

But knowing what our own people are capable of is only half the equation. We can't produce an export no one is interested in importing. We know so little about the rest of the world. We need more information.

I find Nek back in the red room. He's speaking with the dwarf Agate.

"I'm not interrupting?" I ask.

Nek smiles wearily. "When there's always something to be doing, interruptions lose all meaning."

"You deserve a break," I tell him. We all do.

"The Festival will be a break," Nek says. "For one day, at least."

And yet, why do I suspect we'll all just be working overtime?

"Are we still on schedule?" I ask. The celebration is planned for one week from today, and I can already feel the mood in the Fortress begin to buzz with anticipation. There are no decorations yet—we don't have much materials or time to spend on that—but there are plenty of other things to look forward to.

The arachnoid family who had brewed libations for our previous feast, when our colonies had reunited, has joined forces with some water purification dracid and a farmer from the agriculture team to create a new type of drink that might taste better than gasoline this time.

The chefs were also delighted to be given the supply of fish to work with, and are experimenting with new dishes.

The water purification team is finishing moving our drinking water into the underground storage tanks, and talk has begun about starting to fill the bathhouse to be used again for its original purpose.

And rumors of Dizzi's fireworks have already spread through the city to the extent that I worry she won't be able to live up to their expectations.

"Ahead of schedule, actually," Nek happily reports. He sets aside the papers he was working on, and Agate bows his head to me as he departs. "The fish has helped a lot with that. We were going to have to spread the feast pretty thin before, but this is going to go a long way to make up for that."

"Do you suppose we've one or two fish to spare?" I ask him.

"I don't think that would be an issue." His ears flick. "What for?"

"Trade," I say. "Which is another thing I'd like to discuss with you." I gesture for him to follow. "Come. I'll explain while we walk."

Chapter Fourteen

MORE BRIBERY

Nek is not enthused by my plan.

"Fyre, forgive me for voicing my dissent," he says as we head down the tunnel, smoked fish in hand. "But I'm not convinced the prisoners deserve the mercy you're giving them."

"I know," I say. "And I understand the optics of offering Jorrians any degree of kindness. But I would be a hypocrite if I didn't believe in second chances. That isn't to say I trust them," I add, noting Nek's scowl and flattened ears. "And it's not to say I believe they will change their ways. But they deserve the chance, regardless of what they choose to do with it."

Nek sighs heavily, shaking his head, but doesn't argue the point. Mirzayael and I have already gone in circles around this anyway.

The cell guard nods to me and Nek, stepping aside to let us through. Ragna and Gardi look up as we duck inside. Both their gazes flicker over me—by now a familiar appearance—then quickly shift to Nek. I'm sure they've heard his voice outside before, but I don't know if he's ever spoken with them. In fact, it's likely none of the guards have.

They're huddled close to one another, as if they had been in the middle of talking, and they're sitting on one of the folded blankets I'd given them last time. I'm glad to see them actually using the blankets. I wasn't sure if they would snub the olive branch. And the one I've brought today will be far more tempting than the last.

"This is Nek," I tell the Jorrians. "He's accompanying me today because he's quickly and inadvertently becoming our Master Treasurer. I wanted to speak with you both about commerce."

Both the Jorrians seem caught off guard by today's topic of conversation.

"Commerce?" Ragna asks skeptically.

"Indeed." I sit down across from the Jorrians, gesturing for Nek to join me, and he reluctantly settles by my side. The floor is hard, cold, and more than a little dirty, but I ignore it. I set the small bundle of food between us.

"More bribery?" I think I can detect a note of humor in Gardi's voice.

"Think of it as a show of thanks," I say, pushing it forward. "We've recently been able to acquire official maps of the region. The ones you detailed for us were both helpful and accurate. I appreciate your assistance."

Ragna squints suspiciously at the bundle until Gardi leans forward to pull it back to them. They undo the twine, and Ragna leans over to look.

The smell of smoked fish fills the air between us, and my mouth waters. I haven't had any of the fish yet, myself, but I heard the chefs were planning to share a few of their new recipes tonight as a test for the upcoming Festival. These two pieces had been deemed a failed recipe and were going to be re-used in a stew until I intervened. I doubt the Jorrians would mind that it was butchered improperly by one of the young helpers.

"It must be poisoned," Ragna says. "This is a trick."

A low growl rumbles from Nek, and I put a hand on his knee, silencing him. Before I can reply, however, Gardi snorts.

"They wouldn't keep us around this long just to poison us now." They hook some of the meat with a claw and pull it from the bones, then pop it in their mouth. Gardi closes their eyes for a moment, letting out a small sigh. They pass it to Ragna next. "There. If I die, you'll know it's poison."

She glares at them for a moment, and it seems like she really is about to wait and see. The smell of the cooked meat is too much for her willpower to overcome, however. She lasts three seconds before hungrily digging in.

"Hopefully this is the beginning of better meals for all of us," I say as the two pass the fish back and forth. "I imagine at least as long as we drift along the coastline, seafood will become an abundant commodity. However, what we could use your help with is learning more about who we might encounter and what it is they might want."

I unroll a hastily drawn replica of one of the maps the fishing boats traded us. We didn't want to risk the original copy being damaged or destroyed, so it's still in the red room, but we already have a scribe working on several more copies to be safe.

I point out a spot on the map. "We are here. We believe we will come within range of this town tomorrow. Deltin. Do you know anything about it?"

Ragna glances at the map, then shrugs. "Haven't heard of it."

Gardi also shakes their head. "I'm also unfamiliar. Neither of us will likely know much about any of these cities."

"Of course," Nek says dryly. "They will accept our gifts but offer nothing in return. As to be expected from Jorrians."

"Nek," I start. Ragna jerks forward with a hiss, but her chain goes taut. Both Nek and Gardi's hair is on-end, their tails flicking back and forth.

"Enough," I snap at all of them. "This bickering gets none of us anywhere."

Everyone continues to stare at one another, and the air feels tense between us.

Nek is the first one to deflate. "My apologies, Lord Fyre." His hair settles back down a little, but not all the way. Gardi also leans back, arms folded, hair still partially puffed up. Ragna tears her gaze away from all of us, glaring at the wall instead.

"You're unfamiliar with this coast, correct?" I ask Gardi, as they seem the most likely to cooperate. "That's why you can't tell us much about these cities."

"Correct," they say stiffly.

"But not nothing." I wait.

They hold my gaze for a moment, then sigh, looking down at the map. "I don't know the names of any of the cities here. They're too small, and I didn't work in the trade business. All I know is that the foreign goods we received from Dunmora tended to be metal. Armor, weapons, tools."

"Spices," Ragna adds, glaring at the map. Glaring seems to have become her default expression. "Fruit and vegetables."

"Ah, right." Gardi nods. "I tried some of that 'cactus' once. Didn't much care for it. Too expensive, anyway. Probably the royals could afford better produce than the rest of us."

None of this is as illuminating as I had hoped. The real question is, what do the people of Dunmora want? What do we have that they might need?

"What did you trade in return?" I ask.

"I don't know," Ragna says. "We're not merchants."

Gardi shrugs in agreement. "Probably furs. Oilskins. Oh, Master Teloc sold spells to the traders, sometimes. Perhaps those were passed along."

I try not to show my excitement at this breadcrumb they just dropped for me. "You performed spells for them?"

"No, sold them," they repeat. "Small things, like freeze resistant spells for their ships. One time they asked Master Teloc to draw something for producing small blocks of ice." They pinch their fingers together. "It was so small it couldn't have been useful for much of anything. But they liked that one."

Drawing spells. They're talking about spell circles. But all the spell circles in Fyreneth's fortress are carved into the stone. How would one sell such a thing?

You draw it on something mobile. Like paper.

I want to smack myself in the forehead. Of course! It's obvious in retrospect. The Fyrethians didn't put their spells on paper because that was a scarce resource; stone, meanwhile, was in abundance. Even Dizzi etches all her work onto her artificing inventions. It's not that you can't do spell circles any other way, it's simply that carving the spells has historically been the most practical option for Fyrethians. I'd become so used to how they do things that I'd never even considered it was one application of a broader technique.

We don't have paper in the traditional sense—not made of wood and pulp. But we do have vellum made from thin, dried, animal skin, which is what we've been using for our maps.

Unfortunately, most of the parchment we have was made recently, in the weeks since we had begun hunting above ground. Though we have more now than we had in years prior, it's still a rare commodity and not nearly enough to act as a viable export. But we could trade for paper, turn them into spells, and trade them back.

Oh, Dizzi is going to love this.

I look to Nek. "Is there anything else you'd like to ask about?"

He's barely engaged in the conversation at all. Not that I had really expected any different. I can't fault him for the feelings he harbors toward the Jorrians.

But he surprises me.

"The merchants asked you for these spells directly?" Nek asks Gardi.

The two felis stare at each other for a moment, their tails flicking in agitation.

"We don't have to tell them anything," Ragna tells them.

This seems to break Gardi out of their thoughts. "No," they agree. "Though I don't see the harm in this, at least." They look back to Nek. "The dockmaster would create a list of desired commodities that the traders would bring back to the city. Sometimes they'd be posted so you could approach the traders and let them know you had what they were looking for. My master never sought them out; we had too much other work to do. But one day they found our shop, and since she was too busy, I did the spellwork for her on the side. The pay wasn't bad, I think."

Nek grunts, and his head twitches in the smallest fraction of a nod.

When Nek gives no further indication that he has more questions, I step in once more. "I think that's about all we wanted to talk with you about today. Thank you again for being so helpful. Oh," I add as I recall something. "Though I do have one last question before I leave.

Unrelated to all the trade discussion. Have either of you heard of the Drifting Isles?"

Both the Jorrians immediately sit up straight, tense and alarmed.

"Is it close?" Gardi asks.

"We're not going to hit it, are we?" Ragna asks.

I exchange a surprised and baffled look with Nek.

"No," he says. "We have never heard of such a place."

"One of the fishing boats mistook us for the Drifting Isles," I add. "No one I've spoken to has heard of it before."

Both Jorrians slump once more, clearly relieved. "It's a Ruin," Ragna said. "Dangerous. Shit... you better not run into it and get us killed."

"Run into it in the sky?" I clarify.

"It's a floating city," Gardi says. "Well, the remains of a city. Like Ragna said, it's dangerous. If you see it, steer clear."

I smile faintly. "I appreciate your concern."

"It's not concern for *you*," Ragna snaps. "It's cursed. It's said the Ruins were cities the gods destroyed."

I raise an eyebrow. "Like Fyreneth's Kingdom?" I can feel Nek tense beside me.

"Probably," Ragna says. "Whatever they did to draw the gods' ire, I'm sure they deserved it."

"Probably?" I continue to prod. "It doesn't seem like you know much about these ruins."

"It was a long time ago," Gardi says. "A thousand years before Fyreneth's Fall. There are no records for how the Ruins came to be. But intervention from the pantheon seems likely."

Interesting. A pattern in truth, or a pattern applied by the Jorrians to explain something they don't understand?

Echo, what can you tell me about these Ruins? I ask her.

[There are fifteen known Ruins across all of Lusio,] Echo says. [Each are the remains of an ancient civilization connected to an arcana source dimension, leaking ambient magic into the surrounding area. This magic has the potential to affect terrain, fauna, and flora alike.]

Intriguing. Though notably there is no explanation of how these Ruins came to be. *What led to the destruction of their civilization?* I ask.

[<ACCESS DENIED>]

I raise an eyebrow. The only other time Echo has responded to me this way was when I had tried to gather more information about the System, its users, and how it functioned. What would some ancient, magical ruins of an extinct civilization have to do with that? Or perhaps these are unrelated but equally confidential topics.

And who is the one with access to this classified information, I wonder?

More questions. Always more questions.

"Fyre?" Nek prompts.

I realize everyone is watching me. "Excuse me. I was lost in thought." I flash the group a smile. "Well, if there is nothing else, we'll be on our way. Thank you for indulging my questions."

Ragna and Gardi share a perplexed look as Nek and I stand to leave. Nek also seems curious.

"Is there something wrong?" he asks me after we leave.

"I'm not sure," I admit. "But I think I need to start asking more questions and digging for answers. Even if I hit a wall, at least that will start to give me an idea of the shape of the problem I am dealing with. Sometimes, what isn't said can be as revealing as what is."

"I... see," Nek says, clearly perplexed.

I chuckle, patting his arm. "Sorry. Just rambling out loud."

But I do think it's past time I dedicated a day or so to grilling Echo and researching deeper into the inner workings of this magic System Ollie and I are entwined in. I've just been taking every day as they come. I keep getting caught up in immediate needs and problems to fix. For a long while, I've been operating in survival mode.

But I don't have to do that anymore. I have Mirzayael to carry half the load, and we have our council to help delegate tasks and responsibilities. I can step back if I need to—for a little while, anyway—and focus on the longer term and bigger picture. We aren't in immediate danger. We can allow ourselves to breathe.

"So," I ask Nek, thinking back on our conversation with the Jorrians. "What did you learn from that exchange?"

Nek scowls. "They are arrogant people."

"I don't disagree," I say. "Ragna especially. But that doesn't mean we can't learn anything from them. Perhaps even things they didn't intend to reveal."

Nek's ears slowly rise back up. "What Gardi said about trade. It has me thinking about how we are currently handling logistics."

"Or not handling it," I tease.

He finally allows himself a small smile. "Yes. We need better organization. And not only should we be tracking what we produce, we should also be tracking needs. We distribute food based on what we have to spare, but this is not sustainable. We will be able to better focus our efforts if we track where we might be lagging."

"We should create a census," I agree. "Species, family sizes, what they are lacking, what they are producing. Specialties and skills. Currently we allow anyone to work in any group they please. But it is possible, for instance, we have an overabundance in textiles and are lacking hands in agriculture."

Nek frowns. "You think we should tell people where to work?"

"I think we should tell people where work is needed," I say. "I suspect many don't have strong feelings about where they work, and from what I know of Fyrethians, most are happy to offer their services where they can do the most good. But they can't do that if we don't know where the help is needed."

Nek thoughtfully nods at this. "Yes. This is a wise plan. I will begin to gather this information."

"Thank you," I say. "And Nek," I add, "the same goes to you. I know you've fallen into this role naturally because you are good at talking with people and eager to please, but you started as Mirzayael's second. If that's the work you prefer, and you'd rather move back to training the city guards, that can absolutely be arranged. I don't want you doing something you don't enjoy."

Nek grins down at me, revealing his feline canines. "On the contrary, Fyre. I think this position suits me much better. I'm very happy with where I'm at."

His words fill me with warm affection. "Me too."

Chapter Fifteen

Neutral Buoyancy Vessel

"I SEE IT," Ollie excitedly calls. *"I SEE IT! LOOK THERE!"*

None of the harpies have called anything out, though we're all watching. According to the maps, we should nearly be upon Deltin. I close my eyes and activate Psionic Sense to look through Ollie's instead.

At the edge of the horizon is a smudge of white against the green and blue coastline. An inlet where some of the forest has been cleared and the distant hints of civilization can just barely be made out.

A flutter of excitement goes through me. "You're right! Great eyes, Ollie."

Of all the species in our kingdom, harpies are thought to have the keenest vision, though it seems dragon eyes are sharper still.

"Where?" Mirzayael and Dizzi ask at the same time.

"Right where we thought it would be," I say, switching off Psionic Sense and moving back to my own vision. I can't make it out this way, either. "We're perhaps eighty kilometers out. We will nearly be on top of it this time tomorrow."

"So far?" Mirzayael asks, surprised.

"The horizon gets much farther away the higher you climb," I say. I can only imagine what it's like for Mirzayael and the others who spent their entire lives underground. They were just getting used to being able to see a mile or two across the arctic planes—and now look where we are.

Everything is changing so fast. I hope I can keep up.

I turn back to Mirzayael. "Ready for round two?"

"I hope it goes as smoothly as the first time," she says, "though I will not be counting on it."

I press my lips together in an attempt to hide my amusement. Mirzayael senses it anyway.

She scowls at me. "It is better to be cautious than surprised."

"I know," I say, my smile finally breaking through. "I can always count on you to prepare for the worst." This was not intended as a slight, and she doesn't take it that way.

"*Want to try your new harness?*" I ask Ollie.

He flips around from where he's circling in the nearby clouds and glides back to us.

"*ONLY IF IT DOESN'T ITCH THIS TIME,*" he says, landing on a nearby platform atop the city wall built specifically for him.

"I've been assured they're working hard to make it not itch." I catch Nek's eye and beckon him over. "Where are we at with the cargo carrier?"

"The team is still working on it," he says. "But it should be done this evening."

"And trade items?" Mirzayael asks.

Dizzi perks up. "I could throw together some of those spell circles Fyre asked for."

When I'd initially told her my plan for mobile spell circle designs, she'd bent over sideways from laughing so hard. Then she'd grabbed a slate, drawn a spell circle with a piece of chalk, and flourished her hand beneath it.

"You're not the first to think of alternatives to carving them," she teased.

I did feel rather silly once she pointed it out.

She ran her hand over the chalk, wiping half the spell circle away. "But a mobile version that can be packaged small, is lightweight, and resistant to damage would be very useful. We've got enough vellum to make a couple now. If you can get me more parchment, then we'll be talking."

It's one of the many items on the trade list Nek is compiling. We have one for exports and one for imports—the latter of which is more of a wish list than anything. Food and craftwork materials are both high in the ranking.

The city buzzes with activity as the day advances, everyone preparing for another trade attempt. Supplies are gathered near Ollie's platform, and Sora, Nek's wife, works on fitting the harness to Ollie, along with the rest of her team. They make continuous small adjustments as he complains about something pinching, or tickling, or itching. I suspect their efforts to eliminate all complaints are in vain.

Dizzi chats with the other harpies that will be heading down, and once again I desperately wish I could go with them. But I shouldn't complain too much; my Role Requirement is merely restricting me to what most of the city's inhabitants are restricted to, anyway. Until we have a reliable and safe method to come up and down, we'll all be stuck up here for a while.

Once the saddle is in place, Meritis flaps up to try it out. Though we don't know who or what we might face on the ground, no one objects to the young boy acting as a test subject for the harness. We need a harpy to try it out, in case anything fails or comes loose, and Ollie is most comfortable around Meritis. I covertly spoke with his parents when he first volunteered, but they didn't seem worried. I guess a two-hundred-ton dragon on his side helps to alleviate some fears.

"This is weird." Meritis laughs as Sora tightens some of the leather straps about his legs and adjusts a few spider silk ropes that are wrapped around Ollie's neck and shoulders. "Now you really won't be able to shake me off!"

Ollie emits a low grumble that resonates in my sternum, which I've come to learn is the dragon equivalent of a giggle.

"*WE'LL SEE ABOUT THAT*," he says.

"*No we won't!*" I object, alarmed. "*The goal is not to try to shake him off. You'll have cargo on your back, remember?*"

Ollie rolls his eyes and lets out a heavy sigh. "*FIIIIINE.*"

I squint at the boys suspiciously. "*Have* you been playing a game where you try to shake Meritis off?"

Both harpy and dragon suddenly seem to find something in the opposite direction very interesting.

I sigh. Far be it from me to put a damper on their friendship. And Meritis is older and a capable flier; I should trust him. "Just be careful," I tell them.

Gradually, the city on the horizon grows closer and bigger; we still haven't closed half the distance, but now it's within line of sight for even species with poorer eyesight. Holding my hand out at arm's length, it's almost the size of my talon.

Finally, a scout descends from the sky, sending up a gust of wind as they flap to slow their landing.

"Captain." Salvia bows their head to Mirzayael, and then to me. "There's been a sighting. At least one vessel is headed our way."

"Great. I'll tell Ollie." I turn to Mirzayael with nervous excitement. "Ready?"

"Yes," she says. "We have prepared as well as we could, and I've drilled the team on all possible scenarios and contingencies."

"Alright," I say. "Then let's—"

Salvia clears their throat. "Sorry, my lords. But I wasn't finished with the report. The vessel that's heading our way appears to be flying."

"What?" Mirzayael says.

It takes a moment for her words to sink in, then I let out a disbelieving laugh. "Every possible scenario and contingency, you said?"

Mirzayael scowls. "Where is it? How do you know?"

Salvia nods toward the city. "Come see for yourselves. We thought it was a boat at first; the perspective tricked our eyes. But it's getting bigger."

"Show us," Mirzayael says.

Salvia takes off, and I join them in the air while Mirzayael races atop the city wall. They take us part way around the Fortress before landing. Two other harpy scouts are already here, keeping tabs on the approaching vessel.

It's easy to pick out. A dot of red against the blue ocean. But I'm not entirely sure what I'm seeing. I can't make out masts or other ship-like features. It's just an oval-shaped red smudge.

We all stare at it in silence, equally puzzled. Salvia is right: it does seem to be getting bigger. It's rising to meet us.

Because it's a hot air balloon.

"Oh!" I say at the realization. No wonder I couldn't see any structures; they're obscured by the balloon. Or maybe it's more of a zeppelin, given its shape. Whatever it is, it's definitely heading our way.

"Change of plans," I say. "I'm going down with the greeting team. Ollie will stay here—there's nowhere for him to land and I don't want him blowing the ship away."

I can feel Mirzayael's instinctive objection to this, but a moment later, she nods. "I understand. Please be careful."

"I will." Mentally, I add, *"I'll stay in contact with you."*

This eases some of her concern, but not all of it.

Word of the airship spreads quickly, and the city soon dissolves into chaos. People eagerly hurry to the walls to look, even as Torim and Mirzayael try to direct them away. Nek is scrambling to figure out what goods are small enough to carry with us, since we won't be using Ollie, and Ollie himself won't stop pestering me.

"PLEAAAAASE," he begs again. *"I WANT TO GO SEE!"*

"No," I say, managing to keep my mounting irritation out of my voice. "As I said before, you might pose a threat to their ship. If they land on the shore or at sea, and I give the go-ahead, then you can join us. But until then you will need to stay here."

"WHAT IF YOU'RE IN DANGER?" he asks, still not ready to give it up.

"If your Role Requirement triggers, then of course you may come to my aid," I say. All the main leaders know about my and Ollie's Role Requirements, and they know to be on alert if Ollie ever springs into action. Both he and I would be able to tell Mirzayael if something was wrong, and she could relay the message to everyone else.

Hopefully, it will never come to that.

"*OKAY,*" he huffs, dragging the word out.

"There will be more trades than just today." Though I can tell that more than anything he's just disappointed he didn't get to try the harness out with Meritis.

He was *definitely* planning to try to shake the boy from his back.

I'll deal with that inevitable problem later.

"We're ready," Dizzi tells me. The other harpies are clustered at the edge of the wall, looking down. The ship is now the size of my fist held at arm's length. It's below the city, but doesn't appear to be getting any closer. They're waiting for us.

I grab one of the bags Nek put together and cinch it over my shoulders and around my torso. I pull the clasps tight, ensuring the bag doesn't interfere with my wings, which protrude from my lower back. Not that my wings are particularly necessary for the way I fly, but they're excellent stabilizers.

"Okay," I say, joining the others. "Everyone excited?"

I get a smattering of nervous smiles in return. Good enough. "Alright then. Let's fly."

"*Good luck,*" Mirzayael privately says as the harpies dive off the wall and I activate my Jets.

My stomach fills with butterflies the moment I move out into the open air, with nothing but ocean far, far beneath me. The harpies are flying ahead of me, since they can't risk getting too close to my open flames, but they're flying slow, almost gliding down toward the ship. We don't want our arrival to be misconstrued as an act of aggression.

As we approach the airship, details resolve across the structure, all of which fascinate me.

Some aspects are very similar to technology from Earth; it has a rudder, elevator flaps, and even two stubby little wings equipped with ailerons. They clearly have some knowledge of aerodynamics. But the familiar control surfaces are about where the similarities end.

A large deck, almost like a nautical ship, is suspended beneath the oblong balloon. There are several holes in the bottom of the balloon where open flames are heating the contained air, much like a hot air balloon. But the ratios are all off; there's no way a balloon that small could suspend such a huge wooden ship. I suspect the runes glowing along its hull have something to do with that.

The ship is slowly yawing so the long-side faces us. I hope that means they want to talk and aren't lining up to fire off cannon balls of some sort. The harpies hang back a respectful distance, so I move to the front of the group.

I glance toward Dizzi, and she gives me an encouraging thumbs up. Mirzayael says nothing, but I can feel her tension as she watches our interactions play out over the distance. Ollie is watching, too, though he feels more grumpy than worried. And the Dungeon Core...

The Core is blissfully unaware of all of this, its mind wandering around the kingdom and through the stone to happily gawk at any new pebble it finds.

Ah, to be a timeless inhuman entity without a care in the world.

I'm delaying.

Talking to a bunch of potentially hostile strangers while everyone watches me isn't going to start getting any less intimidating. Taming my nerves, I pitch forward and approach the airship.

Chapter Sixteen

Aircraft Maintenance

At least a dozen crewmembers on the airship are at the rail, watching me with various degrees of wariness and disbelief. I quickly have Echo scan them and read off their levels and classes. Most don't appear combat oriented, so I allow myself to slightly relax. A couple are also new species I haven't encountered before—great. More species Mirzayael will want me to add to the Dungeon Core's index.

"Hello," I call, slowly drifting forward. "I hope we didn't alarm you. We were hoping to speak with your captain and potentially trade some goods."

"See? I told you they weren't wyverns!"

I hadn't been able to overhear the first meeting with the fishing boats that well, as I was at a distance and listening through Ollie, but I thought I'd detected an accent before. It's very clear now. It's the same language, but the sounds feel more soft. Interestingly, I didn't perceive the Jorrians to have an accent too different from the Fyrethians.

"How's I supposed to know from that distance?" an elf objects, glaring at a nearby human. "It's the Drifting Isles! They's supposed to be wyverns!"

"Er, we're not the Drifting Isles, actually," I say. Mirzayael and I had discussed using the name as a cover after the last case of mistaken identity, but determined that had the potential to blow up in our faces when someone with more knowledge of the Ruin inevitably revealed us to be lying.

"We're the Flying Fortress," I say, leaving off Fyreneth's name. Even though we decided it would be better not to lie, this was one omission we thought it would be best to withhold until we learn more about how the rest of the world views Fyrethians—if they remember them at all. "We're fairly new to the whole flying thing, actually. As I said, we're merely interested in trade."

A different human steps forward, tall, muscular, and scarred. His skin is dark brown, and his black hair is worn in short twists. He's wearing a sleeveless shirt and a faint, confident smile. Echo identifies him as Marlowe; I can tell he's the captain before he even speaks.

"New to flying?" he repeats, a hint of amusement in his deep tone. "Then what did they call your city before? Just, Fortress?"

Cheeky. But it's exactly what I would have wondered from the outside. I grin. "You're not far off. May we come aboard to talk? I can't keep these flames up all day."

Technically I could use the mana the Dungeon Core has access to, but that's been set aside to keep the Fortress running—and flying—so I try to only rely on my own mana stores for personal use.

He eyes my Jets curiously. "Interesting technique, that. But I don't know we'll have much to offer if it's trade you're after. We were coming out here to capture some wyverns for ourselves, so our stores are light." Even so, he beckons me forward. "Well, no sense in wasting the trip.

You can come aboard if you're careful with those flames. But if you singe my ship, you'll pay for it."

I'm uncertain if he means that in a monetarily or metaphorically threatening way, but it's a reasonable stipulation regardless.

I turn back to Dizzi. "You're with me. The harpies with empty packs can head back. The ones carrying goods can come aboard. I don't want to crowd them."

"You got it!" Dizzi passes my message along as I reach out to Mirza-yael and relay the same.

The order makes her nervous. "*They could overpower you with so few of your guards around.*"

"*I don't think they'd try that.*" The crew is admittedly rougher look-ing than the fishing boats we'd run into before, but there's something about this captain I can't put my finger on that I like. "*All of us can fly, while they don't have any harpies on their crew. If it came to it, we could cut their balloon and jump off.*" Not that I particularly like the idea, but I'm sure it's something that's already crossed Marlowe's mind.

I can feel Mirzayael's approval of the slightly horrific contingency plan. "*Good. Alright. Still, be cautious.*"

"*I will,*" I promise, drifting closer to the airship.

Getting on, however, presents itself to be somewhat of an issue.

The moment I cut my flames, I'll begin to fall. This isn't an issue in the Fortress, because the ground is stone everywhere save the crop fields. But in this case, there's not enough room for me to comfortably hover under the balloon without my Jets scorching the wood deck below. Which means I'll need to cut my flames before I'm over the deck, and for that, I'll need a bit of help from momentum.

"If I could have some space, please," I say.

Captain Marlowe gestures for his crew to make room, watching with a curious, amused look to see what I'll do next. I really hope I've gauged the angles right and I'm not about to make a fool of myself.

Backing up and dropping slightly below the level of the main deck, I flare my Jets, firing myself up toward the ship. I cut the flames just about when I'm level with the rail. My stomach lurches, though my trajectory continues to take me up and over the side of the ship. Almost too far up—for a moment I'm terrified I'm about to crash into the balloon—then I reach the apex of my arc, and gravity pulls me down once more. I land hard on the wood, and go stumbling forward, flapping my wings to keep upright. Heart hammering in my chest, I straighten up and turn around, attempting to appear much more nonchalant than I feel. Dizzi and the other five harpies easily touch down after me with small gusts of wind.

Captain Marlowe rumbles with a laugh. "An impressive show. And not one wooden plank singed. Shame—I was hoping to squeeze some coins out of you to pay for some much-needed repairs."

"Sorry to disappoint," I say, tucking my wings in. "I doubt we have currency you would have been able to use, anyway."

"New to Dunmora?" he asks.

"You're the second group we've encountered," I admit.

The other harpies are keeping rather close to me, and the rest of Marlowe's crew is hanging back, uncertain. I was expecting Dizzi to break the ice, but even she seems a little reserved. I glance over the crew again, wondering if I've missed something. They're mostly humans and dracid, with a smattering of elves.

Ah.

Fyrethians are of course very familiar with dracid, what with the dragon-like people making up a sizable portion of our population. Elves, however, are new to me, and so I assume they're new to the

Fyrethians, too. And humans... Well, over half the Jorrian population were humans.

I recall Dizzi acting nervous on the fishing ship when a human had approached, and her reaction abruptly clicks into place.

But people from one country are not representative of people everywhere, which I am sure the Fyrethians understand, given the Jorrian dwarves and felis that also fought against us. If some have developed an unconscious bias or fear, I can't blame them; we'll work through it.

Branching out into this much larger world is going to be uncomfortable. We're going to be confronted with the unknown on a daily basis. But putting ourselves in these new, uncertain situations is the only way to grow used to it. And once such excursions start to feel commonplace, we'll surely become a force to be reckoned with.

"Your ship is amazing," I say, turning in a circle to take it all in. Mast-like pedestals are situated beneath each opening in the balloon, spell circles and runes carved in their surface; on top of each column is a live flame. "That can't be the only lift mechanism. You have small wings, too. How does it lift such heavy wood?"

The captain raises an amused eyebrow. "How does your stone city fly?"

"Cloudstone," I say. The implication in his question sparks my interest. "Is there wind arcana in the wood, too?"

"Nay, we aren't rich enough for cloudwood," Marlowe says. He raps a knuckle on the railing. "The spell circles keep us aloft. Wind and null."

I tip my head. "How does null arcana help?" I'd asked Echo about that field of magic before, but from what I can recall, it is mostly used in magical applications that involve summonings and bindings.

"It has spatial attributes," Dizzi jumps in before Marlowe can respond. "One application can be to alter gravity in an area. Very interesting. I didn't think to use it on this sort of scale. Though I'm not sure we have any null arcana mages among us, anyway."

Marlowe gives Dizzi an appraising look. "Mage?"

"Artificer," she says, puffing up proudly. "The best in the kingdom." It's good to see her warming up, now that she's back in her element.

Marlowe grunts, scratching at the stubble on his chin. "Perhaps there's trade we can do after all. We don't have much on us, save for some equipment and a week's worth of standard supplies, but I'll see what we can do. Tam." He beckons an elf over. "Go over the inventory with our guests."

I start to step toward the elf, but the captain shakes his head. "No, you and your artificer friend with me. I've got some spells I'd like looked at."

Dizzi looks at me questioningly, and I nod. "Let's see what we can do. Salvia," I say, turning to the harpy who's standing stoically with the rest. If they're bothered by the presence of the humans and elves, they're not showing it. "Are you comfortable handling the trade talks for a few minutes while we step away?"

"Of course, my lord," Salvia says. "I made myself familiar with our inventory before we departed."

"I'll leave it to you, then." It should be a good test of their leadership skills, which I'm sure Mirzayael would appreciate.

Dizzi and I follow Captain Marlowe to the helm of his ship.

"I didn't realize we were in such an esteemed presence as that of a lord," he says. His tone is flat, but I suspect there's a level of humor, or perhaps sarcasm, in the remark.

"I suspect the honorific is overstated," I say.

Dizzi snorts, undermining my remark. Thanks, Dizzi.

The captain doesn't comment on this. "I'm Marlowe, by the way." He offers his hand.

Oh, I'd completely forgotten introductions! Sometimes I lose track of what people have told me versus what Echo has told me. It's easy to take her insight for granted.

"Fyre," I say, clasping his hand. "And this is my science officer, Dizzi."

"A pleasure to meet you both," Captain Marlowe says. He leads us to the bow of the ship, where the main wheel and a variety of levers and spell circles are arrayed. This is interesting. I'd expect the helm to be located at the aft end of the ship, since it steers the rudder, as is the case with sail ships. However, the controls are instead at the forward end, more similar to aircraft. They must have a complex system of mechanisms in the ship's underbelly to control the rudder remotely.

Captain Marlowe swipes his hand over a spell circle, which illuminates.

On second thought, I suspect the rudder is more likely steered by magic.

"We've been having issues with the starboard aileron lately," he says. "Though we can find nothing wrong with the mechanisms or spells."

Dizzi leans excitedly over the control panel. "Wow! This network is amazing. I haven't seen some of these designs before." She traces a finger over the lines of a spell circle. "Hmm, but it's pretty rudimentary. Hey Fyre, do you remember that lift equation offhand?"

"Yes," I say, trying to decipher the runes. I can read a bit of it now, but I'm far from fluent. "What are you thinking?"

When we were designing the Fortress for flight, I had provided all of the aerodynamic knowledge I could recall off the top of my head, and re-derived a few more equations besides. I'd worked through the theory with Dizzi, and she'd been able to incorporate some of it into spell circles of her own design. There's so much more I can't remember—I'd kill for a Flight Dynamics textbook—but given enough time and experimentation, I'm sure I could recreate many more equations of importance.

Then again, if I taught Dizzi differential equations and linear algebra, I'm a little afraid how quickly I'd become obsolete.

"This spell isn't very efficient," she says, pointing to a circle. I can read enough of the runes to know that spell steers the ship. It's probably connected to the rudder in some way. "You can use the general lift spell on each of the wings instead. It's simpler, more controlled, easier to maintain, and saves mana. I bet I could work in one of those feedback loops you showed me..."

Ah, rolling to induce a yaw. She learns fast.

"I'll draw something up," she excitedly tells Captain Marlowe, producing a piece of chalk out of nowhere.

He eyes her skeptically. "Well that's much appreciated, but it doesn't explain the issue with the aileron."

"Oh." Dizzi absently taps one of the runes. "There's a hairline crack between *set* and *tab*. It's probably shorting intermittently and disrupting the circle's function."

The captain leans over the panel in surprise, and I chuckle.

"Perhaps we should leave her to it," I say, stepping aside. "She gets a bit sucked in with things like this." I was much the same when I was her age.

Though Mirzayael would insist I'm much the same now.

Captain Marlowe moves to the side with me, though he doesn't go far, positioning himself so he can keep a careful eye on the both of us while Dizzi sketches out a new design on the panel.

"You two are something else," he says. Do my ears deceive me, or does he sound impressed? "Can't say I was expecting this when we struck out this morning."

"Sorry we're not the wyverns you were seeking," I say.

Marlowe chuckles. "I think meeting a couple talented and beautiful harpies more than makes up for it."

An embarrassed heat flushes through me. What? Beautiful? He's not talking about me, is he? I've never been called beautiful in my life—not in this one, or my life previous. He must be talking about Dizzi and... and some of the other harpies.

"*Are you alright?*" Mirzayael asks. "*You feel... nervous?*"

Flustered, I try to stem my emotions and keep them from radiating back to Mirzayael. "*It's fine,*" I quickly reply.

"Fyre?" Captain Marlowe prompts.

I haven't said anything for a moment. "Sorry. Lost in thought. I, too, am glad we found your ship." I smooth the rest of my nerves out, focusing on business once more. (But in the back of my head, a small voice is still spinning on that thought. Beautiful. Am I beautiful?) "I was hoping you could tell me more about the town we're approaching. Are there more airships in Deltin?"

"Deltin? No, not likely," Marlowe says. He shifts his attention from Dizzi to the rest of his crew, who are speaking with our scouts. They've opened up their bags to share what they've brought, and another appears to have produced a list of his own he's sharing with Salvia.

"Deltin isn't very large," Marlowe continues. "We were only in the area to drop off a shipment. Then we heard rumors of a sighting of the Drifting Isles and came out to investigate. There's always something valuable you can scrounge from its passing, even if it's just capturing more wyverns for trade."

I ask Echo to tell me about wyverns as he talks, and I get a quick rundown. [Wyverns are a winged, bipedal, bird-sized reptile of the dracus family. Frequently captured and raised to be pets or carrier lizards, they are naturally found in the wild, and especially tend to gravitate to the Drifting Isles. The reason for this attraction is unknown, but speculated to do with the ambient storm arcana found in the Ruin.]

"Too bad," I say. "Dealing with more airships would be terribly convenient for us."

"Well, you don't have to worry about that," the captain says. "Three days beyond Deltin is our hometown, Mount Haze. It's South Dunmora's second largest sky dock. There will be plenty of ships there interested in your Fortress, I'm sure."

My heart skips. We'd spent all this time planning trips down to the surface, but I hadn't been expecting for our city to receive visitors—at least, not this soon.

Some of my emotions must have slipped through the cracks of my mind once more, for Mirzayael's presence resurfaces. "*What is it?*" she demands. "*Don't tell me it's fine again.*"

"*It's not a bad thing,*" I assure her. "*Just surprising. When do you think we'll be ready to accept visitors into our city?*"

"*I don't like this question,*" Mirzayael lets me know. "*But perhaps three weeks. Maybe four.*"

I smile nervously. "*How do you feel about four days?*"

Chapter Seventeen

TRADE TALKS

"I don't like this," Mirzayael thinks. *"We know nothing about them."*

"GUESTS?" Ollie repeats excitedly. "*ARE THEY BRINGING ANY TOYS?*"

The Dungeon Core notices the airship as it enters its range. Oh, it has not eaten these things before! Can it have a little taste? Just a nibble.

"No!" I cry.

Captain Marlowe raises an eyebrow at me. "Something the matter?"

"No," I repeat. I try to smooth out my expression, which undoubtedly was in some state of alarm. "Just thinking of something. I'm glad you accepted our invitation."

"Please, give me a few minutes," I tell my mental ensemble. *"I need a clear head."*

I tune out Mirzayael and Ollie's mental connections. I'd do the same with the Dungeon Core—if I trusted it to not eat any parts of the airship that just sailed into its range.

We ended up staying longer than planned, and by the time we were ready to depart, the sun was hanging low on the horizon. I asked if they'd prefer to dock at our city and spend the night, and after talking it over with his crew, Marlowe accepted.

It was only after I offered that I realized I hadn't asked Mirzayael if it would be alright. I do feel a bit guilty about that; we're supposed to be a team. But what's done is done, and Mirzayael *had* said I don't need to check with her on everything.

Besides, a trial run won't hurt anything.

"The air's growing warmer," Marlowe remarks as we ascend.

"Oh. Yes, that would be the atmospheric spell we have in effect around the Fortress," I say.

He raises his brows. "The entire city?"

"It helps with the altitude sickness, and keeps the city heated."

"It thickens the air," the captain surmises, adjusting some of the spells on his control panel.

"It does," I admit, a bit impressed. "I'm surprised you could tell."

"I know my ship," he says. Dizzi's new spell circles are sketched out in chalk on a blank portion of the panel, but they're currently inactive. Everyone agreed it would be best to switch flight controls over to the new spell circuit *after* the ship was safely grounded. "It's handling here how it usually handles at sea level."

"The spell gradually dissipates the further it gets from the Fortress, so there's no abrupt change in pressure," I explain.

Captain Marlowe chuckles, the sound rumbling and low. "Kind of you to be so considerate for us airships."

"It was designed for our harpies, admittedly," I say. "Though now I'm glad we have it."

As we come level with the city walls, Marlowe's crew gasps and murmurs. Much of the city was obscured from below. But up here, lit with the fiery colors of the sunset, it truly is a breathtaking sight.

I gradually tune myself back into Ollie and Mirzayael's mental frequencies.

Mirzayael is grumbling something to Ollie. "*...half a mind to let you do exactly that.*"

"*Do what?*" I ask, suspicious.

"*FYRE! MIRZAYAEL SAID I COULD COME GREET THE SHIP!*"

"*I did not,*" she objects.

"*Hold on, Ollie,*" I tell him, but the dragon has already taken flight from where he had been perched on a balcony high outside the palace, and I can see him coasting down toward us.

"We have a dragon and he's friendly," I quickly blurt out before anyone can panic. No one seems to have noticed the approaching—

Someone gives a startled shout. Okay, now they've noticed.

Ollie flaps his wings as he lands on the nearby city wall, his wind buffeting the ship. More people cry out in alarm.

Ollie giggles. "*IT LOOKS LIKE A TOY. LOOK, THE BALLOON IS JUST MY SIZE!*" He lets out an amused huff, and a cold puff of air rolls over us. Several of the crew draw weapons, but their captain stays them.

"Hold!" He gives me a sharp look.

For a moment, I catch a dangerous flicker in his eyes—something I'd feared to find when we first boarded his ship. Then it's gone, and he lets out an annoyed sigh.

"Anyone else, and I'd think this was some kind of set up," he says, risking a look back toward the dragon. "But you seem far too earnest for that. Mind telling me why you didn't inform me of your pet?"

"He's not a pet. He's..." What, a seven-year-old human child from another world transported into the body of a dragon? "...my familiar."

That's how everyone sees Ollie, anyway, and it's easier than trying to explain the truth.

"I'm sorry," I say. "I meant to ask him to stay back, but he's too curious for his own good."

"*Ollie, do not approach the ship,*" I mentally add. "*They're all a bit spooked.*"

Mirzayael laughs ruefully. "*At least now they'll think twice about trying to pull something.*"

Not helping, Mir.

"Familiar?" Captain Marlowe asks, watching Ollie in a mix of awe and caution. "You certainly picked a big one."

Ollie lays down, his tail draping over the wall like a lounging cat. Though he's still watching us, head tipped curiously, he at least appears a bit less threatening now. The crew continues to shoot him nervous glances, but the few who drew weapons sheath them once more.

It takes another ten minutes for the ship to maneuver into position and dock, anchoring to the city wall with dozens of ropes. As the crew prepares to disembark, I have all the harpies withdraw as well.

"I will speak with you again momentarily, captain," I say, respectfully bowing my head. "I wish to speak with the welcome party and ensure all arrangements are in order."

"I'll be seeing you shortly, then." Captain Marlowe turns back to his crew, surveying their preparations.

I hop over the ship's rail and activate a brief Jet to slow my fall. It's only a few feet down, but the crew is deploying a handful of ladders to close the gap.

Mirzayael is there waiting for me, along with most of her guard and the other council leaders. At some point before the airship docked, she managed to retrieve her spear and don some of her favorite armor.

She looks rather imposing—and not just because she's scowling—as I head her way. I attempt an apologetic smile.

"*We're not ready for this,*" she says, even though I'm within earshot. She must not want the other guards to hear her voice such doubts.

"*We'll need to be,*" I reply. "*If we're going to be passing by a city full of airships in less than a week, hosting guests will become inevitable. Better to get practice with this small group than to be unprepared and overwhelmed with the next.*"

"Guests," Mirzayael repeats with distaste. "*Our city was never meant to host...*"

She trails off, her thoughts turning uncertain. But of course, Fyreneth's kingdom *was* designed to host outsiders. It had once been a city open to anyone—that's what Beryl had said, anyway. Mirzayael, too, understands that Fyreneth would have wanted to see her vision fulfilled. Yet it's antithetical to everything Mirzayael has ever believed. Things have changed since Fyreneth's reign. I can feel her warring with these two opposing sets of values.

"One step at a time," I tell her, stopping at her side and patting her nearest leg. Her torso is too high, or I would have executed a more comforting gesture. Like... rub her back, perhaps. Or squeeze her shoulder. Or pull her into a hug.

Though it's hard to envision Mirzayael finding any of these acts reassuring, and I'm not particularly good at physical expressions of affection, anyway.

But to my surprise, she returns the gesture, resting a hand on my shoulder. The contact flushes me with warmth.

I keep careful hold of my thoughts.

Captain Marlowe and a portion of his crew descend from their ship to meet us on the wall. He looks between Mirzayael and I.

"Captain Marlowe," I say, "This is Lord Mirzayael, co-ruler of our Fortress."

His mouth twitches with a smile as he approaches and gives a respectful bow. "Pleased to make your acquaintance. My crew and I appreciate the spontaneous hospitality." His gaze goes back to me, eyes dancing with mischievous amusement. "An overstated honorific, you said?"

At the time, I hadn't expected them all to come back to the Fortress with us. "I'm sure you can understand the need to exercise prudence among strangers."

"Aye," he agrees. "Though I'd like to hope this will be the start of a fruitful relationship between us."

Mirzayael's grip briefly tightens on my shoulder before she lets go, beckoning the captain and his crew to follow. "We will show you to where you may room for the night, if it will not be on your ship. Then, we can speak more over supper."

Marlowe tips his head. "Much obliged."

Most of the houses in Fyreneth's Fortress are empty, so staking out a place for them to stay for the night is not difficult. The aviators look around the city in awe as we lead them up the winding streets of the city until we arrive at the palace entrance. To this day, we still have communal meals in the palace's great hall. I'm unsure what the room had been dedicated to originally, but it will forever forth be our dining room.

Marlowe's crew gawk as we lead them inside. The architecture really is stunning, especially now that most of the signs of age have been repaired. Spell circles light sconces in the walls, and a fire motif is apparent both in the color and design of arches that stretch far overhead. All the main chambers are large enough for harpies to comfortably fly in, and in fact many rooms are joined not only with doors at their base, but also with openings near the ceiling. Though it's still before sunset, some have already filed into the mess hall and started to eat.

Fyrethians generally sit in groups of five to ten, forming a circle around the shared food in the middle. Countless rings of cushions and furs are arranged around the hall for this purpose.

The one at the head of the room is where Mirzayael, the other council members, and I often sit. We invite Captain Marlowe to join us, and show his crew to nearby circles, already partly populated with early eaters. I make sure to keep at least two Fyrethians and two of Marlowe's crew together as I space them out, so no one feels threatened and alone, but also to encourage interactions between the two groups. When I sit down, I choose a direction facing the rest of the hall so I can keep an eye on things. Mirzayael sits to my right and Marlowe to my left, both also facing the mess hall.

"It's extraordinary," Marlowe says, his eyes wandering across the mosaics in the ceiling and walls. "I've never seen anything like it."

"It's beautiful," I agree, admiring the art.

"Did you have this done?" he wonders, likely drawing the connection between my plumage and the fiery harpy motifs throughout.

"No, everything you see here long predates us," I say, sharing a look with Mirzayael. "We just inherited it."

"I'm surprised I've never heard of this place before," Marlowe says. "Where did you come from?"

I hesitate. I wasn't expecting him to dig down to our roots so quickly. Mirzayael and I had agreed to leave Fyreneth's name out of any discussions with traders, but the more we interact with them, the more difficult that will become.

Mirzayael speaks up before I've decided what would be appropriate to say. "The arctic."

"*Is that alright to divulge?*" I mentally ask her.

"I wish to gauge his reaction and see what he knows about the place," Mirzayael replies. *"If he knows anything about us."*

Captain Marlowe frowns thoughtfully. "Not much familiar with those parts. Airships don't do well in such weather. Tough place to live, I imagine." He raises an eyebrow at us. "Is that why you left?"

"In part," I allow. "We are searching for a more hospitable place to set our kingdom down for good."

"Are you? That's a shame." Marlowe looks up when a few plates of food are laid between us. They're a few of the fish meals the chefs developed from the first ship we traded with. The new dishes have been an amazing change of pace. "A floating city is so much more interesting than a stationary one."

I laugh at that. "I'd tend to agree. But our cloudstone won't keep us aloft forever."

"Unfortunate," Marlowe says as I serve him a plate of the meal. "I can't imagine how much easier it would be to guard your borders. Not as many beasts to worry about up here, either."

"Not *as many*?" Mirzayael asks.

"Oh, sure," Captain Marlowe says. He gestures to one of his scars, a long gash that runs down his forearm. "A hippogriff gave me this one. The color of our ship is good to avoid air collisions at a port, but also good at attracting curious animals in the wild."

To my surprise, Mirzayael's interest actually seems to be piqued. "What other sort of animals have you run into?"

"In the air?" Marlowe asks. "Well, it depends on where you are. But we've had run-ins with griffins, lightning hawks, amphipteres..."

I'm starting to deduce where all the captain's scars came from.

I quietly remove myself from the conversation to allow Marlowe and Mirzayael to talk. It's rare she's interested in something like this, so I better leave her to it for as long as it lasts.

As the meal goes on, we each take turns fetching more dishes or drink from the kitchen. The Fyrethians and the aviators appear to be warming up to one another. Mirzayael's mind feels at ease. Well, her version of at ease, which is still a good deal more tense and vigilant than anyone else I've ever known. Eventually, conversation turns back to trade.

"I wish we had more to offer," the captain says, "but as we were flying out for a hunt, we didn't bring much with us."

"Actually, I have a strange request you might be able to help me with," I say to Captain Marlowe. "Please indulge me."

He crooks an eyebrow. "I'm indulging."

"I wonder if I could take shavings of material off your ship," I say. "It contains several alloys of metal that isn't yet in... ah, our archives. It wouldn't be much, or anywhere you'd miss it."

Marlowe blinks. "Can't say I was expecting that," he admits. "How would these shavings help your archives?"

The Dungeon Core's presence is one thing Mirzayael and I agreed should not be disseminated to any outside forces. The legends around Fyreneth indicate it was somehow entangled in the motives for the original fall of her empire, so the only thing we gain from revealing its presence is unwanted attention.

Luckily, Dizzi jumps in before I can come up with a good response. "We've got some material analysis spells," she says. "I use them in my artificing lab. There's still holes in my catalog of matter, and the more I fill in, the more complex inventions I can construct."

That's not even a lie, either. We've filled out quite a bit of the Periodic Table, which Dizzi eats up like... well I guess like the Dungeon Core eats up rocks.

Marlowe looks thoughtfully amused, but nods along to Dizzi's explanation. "How could I say no after you designed those new flight spells for us?" He looks back to Mirzayael and me. "Knowledge. That's the commodity you should be focused on trading."

We'd already spoken with him about how little we have to trade, and our concern about arriving at Mount Haze with little to offer.

"Most merchants might not see the value," he adds, "but if you could get some mages and scholars up here, they'd pay a pretty penny just to examine this atmospheric spell you have."

"People would pay for such knowledge?" Mirzayael asks skeptically.

I'm skeptical for a different reason. "Knowledge should be freely shared."

"That sort of reasoning will leave you poor," Captain Marlowe says to me. "But there's many ways you could do it. Trade some of your knowledge for some of theirs. Sell some of these flight spell circle designs—or even just the theory behind them. Sounds like you've got some kind of archives in the works; those don't fly over your city every day. Knowledge-share between the continents can take some time. Your city has the potential to be an imposing learning hub—possibly more so than the Athenaeum of Miasmere, given your mobility."

A flying Library of Alexandria? Now that is a dream I would love to manifest! If only we could stay aloft indefinitely to make that happen.

"And what do you stand to gain from all this?" Mirzayael asks. "As you said, you've little to offer by way of trade."

There's a mischievous curl to his smile. "Nothing but your good favor, I should hope."

Mirzayael gives him a hard look. "And I imagine this good favor would include certain trade privileges?"

He grins. "I wouldn't want to presume. But if you were to offer my crew priority in the trading of any commodities we procure, I certainly wouldn't object."

Mirzayael walked right into that one.

"I think we can work something out," I say before Mirzayael can respond with something prickly. "Of course, we could also benefit from a knowledgeable advisor who could help oversee initial trade opportunities while dealing with Mount Haze."

Marlowe's grin broadens. "I think that can be arranged."

Mirzayael is skeptical. "*You don't think he'll try to take advantage of us?*"

"*He might*," I admit. "*But we won't know until we try. It can't hurt to start making allies now; and if he is looking to swindle us, I've only established him as our go-between for Mount Haze, not anywhere else.*"

Mirzayael chews on this, then sends her approval. "*That's an acceptable plan. We'll see how he handles the first few trade discussions and can reevaluate from there.*"

I try to imagine the Mirzayael I first met agreeing to give a stranger a chance to prove their trustworthiness. A *human* stranger, no less. She's changed since then, even if the change is subtle. I wonder if I've changed in ways I might not be aware of, too?

I'm standing up to grab more water when I notice one of Mirzayael's small silk spiders scurry up to her. She pauses, then sweeps up the spell construct and pushes herself to her feet. Alarm swells within her mind.

"If you would excuse me," she says casually, betraying none of her inner turmoil. "I need to attend to something. I should be back before long."

She takes up her spear, calmly strolling toward the nearest doorway.

Without looking at me, she mentally says, "*The Jorrians' cell is open. The prisoners have escaped.*"

Chapter Eighteen

SCUFFLE

I freeze for a moment. "*What*?"

Mirzayael has already stepped out of the hall and is out of sight. Bringing up the Map Interface, I can see a dot labeled Arachnoid racing down the hall.

"Something the matter?" Captain Marlowe asks.

"*The Jorrians,*" Mirzayael repeats in my head. "*I set up a trigger so if their cell door opened unscheduled, I would be notified.*"

"I should probably go check," I say to the captain, hoping my face isn't betraying my concern. "Sorry to step out, Dizzi?"

"No problem," she says, happily waving to me. "We can talk about the airship spells!"

"*WHAT'S GOING ON?*" Ollie wonders. Mirzayael's messages had only been privately shared with me, but he must have picked up on our worry from one or both of us.

Our meal circle is at the end of the room, situated near an open wall and platform where Ollie is currently lounging. He curves his head around, watching me. "*WHERE DID MIRZAYAEL GO?*"

"*A problem with our prisoners,*" I tell him as I attempt to casually leave the room. The Jorrian cell is deep within the palace, nowhere

Ollie would be able to reach. *"Can you keep an eye on things while I'm gone?"* I ask him. *"I don't think it will be an issue, but let me know if our guests cause any trouble."*

"OH, UM, OKAY!" He sounds a little nervous, and my heart squeezes. I shouldn't be asking so much of a kid. Sometimes it's easy to forget he's so young. *"YOU'LL BE CAREFUL?"*

"Promise." As soon as I'm out the door, I activate my Jets, firing down the hall after Mirzayael.

"The outsiders must be behind this," Mirzayael growls. *"The timing is too convenient."*

"We don't know that yet," I say, watching her dot on my map. Even with my Jets activated, she's almost able to outrun me. I have to slow around corners and keep an eye out for any people dots on my map so I don't scorch anyone. Mirzayael, meanwhile, can run up walls, which helps significantly with maintaining her speed around tight passages.

I shift my view of the Map over to the cells where we're keeping the Jorrians.

"Two people," I tell her. *"Just human and felis."*

"The two Jorrians," Mirzayael says. *"No guard? That doesn't make any sense. How did they get out? Even if they got the door open, we had them manacled in place."*

I pause, consulting the Map again. The felis and human are still inside it. *"I don't know if they did,"* I say, perplexed. *"Are you sure they got out?"*

Mirzayael is tinged with uncertainty, too. *"The door is open, at least."*

I nudge the Dungeon Core, asking to borrow its senses. It's more than happy to let me dive into the rocks. It does this all the time!

I extend my consciousness toward the cell, first feeling for the manacles—the ground where they're attached seems undisturbed. But Mirzayael is right—the door is open.

My shoulder clips something hard, and pain and surprise jolt through me.

"*Fyre!*"

The contact spins me around and I go crashing into a wall.

[15 points of Bludgeoning damage self-inflicted,] Echo says.

I wrench my consciousness out of Dungeon Core, as I slump to the floor, head spinning. It takes me a moment to realize what happened.

I clipped a corner while my mind was elsewhere. I put a steadying hand to my head. I don't think I have a concussion, at least.

"Fyre!" Mirzayael reappears at the end of the hall, rushing back to me.

"No, I'm okay!" I call, waving for her to go back. "I was just a bit stupid. I should know better than to be on my phone while driving." I wince at my very poor joke.

Mirzayael rushes up to me anyway, grabbing the hand I was using to wave at her, and yanks me to my feet. A surprised squawk slips out of me.

"You're hurt!" Her face is pinched with concern. Her hand hovers over my arm.

My shoulder is throbbing and skinned from where I struck the wall; a few feathers are gone and some dots of blood are starting to bead.

"It will heal itself," I assure her. "Worry about me later. We have the Jorrians to worry about now."

She hesitates for a moment longer, clearly still concerned. Then, her face hardens. "Of course. Let's go."

"Right behind you."

I jump into the air after her, this time leaving the Dungeon Core's interface be. That was a lesson well learned. I've always known I sort of lose track of my body when I plunge too deep into the Core's consciousness, but I didn't think a quick look would do any harm. At least it was here, and the damage was minimal, rather than somewhere I could have gotten seriously injured.

"I think they're still in the cell," I tell Mirzayael. We're not far, now. "But you're right that the door *is* open. I don't understand what's happening."

"We'll find out soon," she says, raising her spear. "Guard up!"

Yelling echoes down the hall before we round the last corner. There are at least two people shouting, voices raised and dripping with anger. I have no idea what to think. We're missing something—

I round the corner, and the cell comes into view. The room is empty, and the cell door is open. But from the raised voices, people are definitely still inside it.

Mirzayael and I exchange a puzzled look. I shut off my Jets, skidding to a stop before the door.

Ice covers the floor and doorframe.

"Traitor!" someone screams. "You're a traitor to our home! You're a traitor to Lorata! You—"

"I'll kill you!" a second voice cries. "Murderer! Let me go! I'll kill you!"

Bewildered, I step into the room—and then it all makes sense.

Ragna is on her feet, fist raised, but her torso and a leg are encased in ice. It looks as though dozens of icicles sprung from the ground, pinning the human in place. She has one free hand, which she uses to beat and claw at the ice that's trapped her. "Traitor!" she screams again.

Across from her is Salvia. The young harpy has a spear in hand, and is also frozen. Their eyes are locked on Ragna, face contorted with rage, tears spilling down their cheeks. "Let me go!" they demand. "Murderers!"

Gardi is seated on the ground between them, staring down at their hands, not reacting to any of the words flung their way. I wouldn't even be sure if they were conscious if their ears hadn't flicked my way when Mirzayael and I entered.

"Oh, Salvia," I say, sadness welling up in me. "You didn't."

As the harpy catches sight of Mirzayael and I, all the fight goes out of them. They hang limply in their ice prison and begin to sob.

Mirzayael goes to their side. Ragna is still slinging insults, alternating between Salvia and Gardi. I try to ignore it, and crouch down in front of the felis.

"Gardi," I say.

They look up at me, expressionless.

"Can you release Salvia from the ice, please? We'll make sure she doesn't hurt you or Ragna."

They look back down at their hands. Without even moving, the ice around Salvia shatters and spills to the ground.

Salvia attempts to lunge forward, but Mirzayael grabs them. "They killed him!" they choke out. "My dad is dead because of them!"

Hetlanir. Of course.

"These two didn't kill your father," I say, standing back up.

"It doesn't matter," Salvia says, their face still contorted with hate, tears still streaming down their face. "He deserves justice!"

"And he's had it," Mirzayael says firmly. "I slew your father's killer with my own hands. Vengeance was served."

"No," Salvia chokes. Mirzayael firmly begins to guide them out of the cell. "No! But I have to... I need to... Dad. I miss my dad. I miss him."

Their sobs become more muted as they leave the room, and then all that is left is Ragna's hateful screams. I can't stand it for much longer. I tap the Dungeon Core for help and outline the section of space I'd like filled with stone. It happily obliges, slamming a wall of rock up from the floor in front of Ragna. This does get a reaction out of Gardi, and they flinch back, staring at the wall in shock, as Ragna's voice is cut off. I sigh at the blissful quiet that ensues. Distantly, I can hear Mirzayael and Salvia speaking outside.

"Is she..." It's the first thing Gardi's said since we arrived.

"I didn't hurt her," I assure them. "She's just on the other side of that wall. But I wanted to speak privately." I take their manacled wrists in my hands, and direct the Dungeon Core to remove them. It happily eats the cuff in three or four invisible bites, chewing on the pieces of metal that vanish back into its Inventory. Gardi stares at their wrist. The fur is pressed flat where the manacle had been.

"Come on." I stand, pausing before the door. "You can walk?"

Gardi blankly looks up at me. They look tired. Defeated. I half expect them to go back to staring at the floor, but after a moment they shakily push themself to their feet. Instead of leading them out into the other room with Salvia and Mirzayael, I have the Dungeon Core carve a hole in the back wall. Gardi wordlessly follows me inside.

Following my direction, the Dungeon Core eats a tunnel to a nearby chamber. I light a Spark in my hands as I guide Gardi through. This room, like all the rooms down here save for the impromptu jail, is empty. It's medium sized, and there's dark doorways leading to other rooms and halls in what was likely a house, once upon a time. I close the hole behind us, and seal the other entrances to this house that would lead back into the chamber with Mirzayael and Salvia.

"I believe I understand what transpired," I say to them. "But I'd like to hear the full story from you."

They gently rub their wrist where the cuff had been, massaging a thumb over their chafed skin.

"Why did you remove it?" they ask, voice hoarse.

"Because you're smart," I say. "You won't attempt to attack me—you understand there would be no point to it."

They don't reply.

"With that kind of magic at your disposal, if you'd wanted to, you could have broken out of that cell before now." I watch them carefully. "Why didn't you?"

"Because I'm smart." Their mouth almost twitches into a rueful smile. "Where would I go?"

"You could kill someone," I say. "Probably do a lot of damage before we captured you. Given the opportunity, that's what Ragna would have done."

They slowly shake their head. "I'm not a killer."

"I believe you," I say gently.

Gardi turns away, looking around the room. There's not much to see; if there was ever any furniture, it's long since gone, though the occasional gemstone or crystal vein built into the walls reflects my firelight.

"We heard a conversation outside." They trace one such sparkling vein down the wall with a claw. "They offered to take the other guard's position and give him a break. Only a few minutes later, the harpy came in." Gardi pauses. "How old are they?"

"Nineteen, I believe."

Gardi nods. "I thought it was something like that. The same age as my little sister."

My throat tightens. Somehow, before this point, I never actually paused to think about our prisoners' family. Who they might miss. Who might be grieving them as they're assumed dead.

They're still absently tapping at precious stones in the wall. I think the distraction is the only way they can bring themself to speak to me. They wouldn't be able to say all this to my face.

"I knew what they were there for the moment they stepped into the cell," Gardi finally continues. "I could see it in their eyes. Ragna didn't realize until the harpy lifted their spear. I froze them. Ragna saw the opportunity that presented. She would have killed them."

Gardi is silent again. I wait.

Their shoulders slump. "I could have let her do it. Some might say I *should* have. But I couldn't. I kept thinking of my sister..." They knock their forehead against the stone and leave it resting there. "She's right. I *am* a traitor."

How can I even reply to that? A reassurance from the enemy would only reinforce their self-flagellation. But they saved a life—possibly two. They did the right thing.

At least, from our perspective. But Ragna will hate them after this.

I sigh. "I'll relocate you to a different cell."

Gardi nods against the wall.

"*Fyre?*" Mirzayael reaches out. "*I've calmed Salvia down. Everything in order on your end?*"

"*As much as can be,*" I reply. "*Ragna's behind the wall in there. I'll take it down when we leave. I stepped away with Gardi to speak with them privately.*"

"*Salvia admitted they were going to use the dinner with the airship crew as a distraction,*" Mirzayael says. "*They convinced Xarius to go on*" *break and took up his position as guard. But when Salvia entered to slay the prisoners, the felis froze them before they could attack. Then they froze their own cellmate when she was going to retaliate."*

I sigh. *"That matches the account I've received here."*

"What should we do with them?" Mirzayael wonders. *"The Jorrians can be separated. But Salvia..."*

I don't know either. Should we punish them? They went behind our backs in an attempt to execute the Jorrians. They need to face consequences.

But I understand their rage and pain. Their father was killed by the Jorrians. Isn't that punishment enough? And they're still just a kid. They acted impulsively. Do they need discipline, or support? Or both?

I massage a temple. I'm not cut out for this. I'm not qualified to be handling these types of scenarios. Perhaps I was wrong to have made the choices that led to this scenario in the first place.

Should I have agreed to dispatch the two Jorrians when they were first discovered? It would have made all our lives easier. It would have reduced tensions within the guard and prevented altercations such as this. And what if Ragna had killed Salvia? How could I justify keeping two enemies alive at the cost of one of our own? For as long as they remain here, that will always be a risk.

I know something being easy doesn't make it right, but in this case, I'm not even sure what right is.

"I don't know," I wearily reply to Mirzayael. *"Let's discuss it later, after we've had time to process."*

"Thank you," I say to Gardi. "I know that's not what you want to hear—not from me. But thank you for saving them. You did the right thing, even if it doesn't feel like it."

When they don't reply, I gently take their arm and lead them away. Using the Dungeon Core, I adapt another room into a cell a few doors down from the original. Gardi lets me lead them into this one. The room is so bare. We've effectively relegated the Jorrians to solitary confinement, now.

"I'll have more blankets delivered shortly," I tell them.

They take a seat in the middle of the room and don't reply.

How much longer can we keep them like this? I promised we would release them back with people who trade with Jorria, who could possibly take them home, but now I don't know if we can wait for that.

"We'll be over a city in the next week," I tell them. "I'm told it has airships. We could see if any could arrange passage to somewhere that could take you home."

"I don't have a home," they say, their voice leaden. "Not when they learn what I did."

I open my mouth to respond with something comforting, but I can find nothing to say. When I leave, I don't put their shackle back on.

CHAPTER NINETEEN

MOVING FORWARD

Captain Marlowe departs the next morning, sailing ahead to inform the cities of our approach and peaceful intentions—and no doubt to establish himself as our emissary and ensure he's owed a cut of the profits. His advanced warning should make me feel better about the impending contact with nearby cities, but the previous night's conflict still weighs heavily on me.

There's no sort of community service we can put Salvia on—the city pretty much already operates communally—so we decide to temporarily remove them from guard duties and training. The harpy's anger has simmered down overnight, and now at least a hint of regret tinges their scowl. I'm not sure if the regret is for attacking the Jorrians, or for not succeeding in killing them.

But the event has me unsettled. I couldn't see Salvia on the Dungeon Core's Map Interface because I still don't have harpies added to the catalog. It highlights how exposed we could be to other types of sabotage once we start letting large numbers of strangers within the walls. Mirzayael is right; I need to prioritize completing that list.

"Have you started working on the spell circles in the other towers?" I ask Dizzi during our daily leadership meeting.

We're in the red room once more, along with all the council members. I've wearily collapsed into one of the room's chairs, while Mirzayael paces behind me in clear agitation.

"I've started working on all of them," Dizzi says. "But I've only brought the research team to two of the other towers. The third is definitely designed to be some sort of weapon. I've started a list of those I think are trustworthy enough to work on it."

"Is Salvia on it?" Mirzayael asks, pausing.

"They're on my maybe-list," Dizzi says.

"Remove them for now," I say. "We can reevaluate them later."

Dizzi cocks an eyebrow. "Is there a problem?"

I look at Mirzayael. Salvia is under her command. It's her call.

She grimaces. "There was an altercation last night..."

I watch Nek, Dizzi, and Torim's expressions as Mirzayael gives them the rundown of what happened. They vary between surprised, angry, and skeptical.

"I'll be doubling the guard shifts to avoid a repeat of the incident," Mirzayael says in closing.

"Wow." Dizzi leans back, interlocking her fingers behind her head. "I didn't think they had it in them."

"Hetlanir was an important figure in our community," Torim says, frowning. "Our colony has not forgotten his sacrifice. If this gets out, they will likely take Salvia's side."

I was afraid of that.

"Perhaps for your people." Nek's ears go flat. "But for our colony, they may be more upset that Salvia disobeyed direct orders from Fyre and Mirzayael."

"This has the potential to drive a wedge between our people," Mirzayael realizes.

"Then what is the solution?" Torim wonders. "Cover it up?"

Even the suggestion makes me grimace, but it might be our best path forward. "Only Salvia is aware of what has transpired, and they've agreed to be discreet about it."

"For now," Mirzayael grumbles. "But I'm more concerned about what to do with them."

We all consider this in silent contemplation for a moment. A punishment would be fitting; but we'd have to explain what the punishment is for, and Salvia isn't the only one who lost family to the Jorrians. Calling attention to the prisoners would only increase the friction between our people. Not to mention, Salvia is still young. They made a terrible mistake, motivated by heartache; I don't want to irreparably damage their standing in Fyrethian society if this is something they are willing to work past.

"Whatever is to be done with Salvia, the Jorrians need to go," Nek says with a rumbling sigh. "Their presence here will only tempt others to do the same."

He's right. But I think about Gardi and the empty tone in their voice when they said they no longer had a home.

"I'd like to drop Ragna off at one of the nearest cities," I say. "I told both of them we'd try to get them home. I was hoping for some change of heart, but after last night, I believe whatever progress we made has been shattered beyond repair. Ragna won't consider trusting us again. The sooner we release her, the sooner we reduce the likelihood of another conflict."

Everyone seems relieved by this suggestion.

"What about the other one?" Torim asks.

I hesitate, knowing people are going to like this suggestion significantly less. "I think they should be given the opportunity for rehabilitation."

"Absolutely not," Torim says.

"They're a danger," Nek agrees.

Even Dizzi looks skeptical. "Are you sure?"

Mirzayael just waits for me to explain my reasoning.

"I don't think they're a danger," I say, addressing Nek's concern. "First, they're not even a soldier; they were an ice worker conscripted to sturdy the ice on the surface when the assault first began. An ability they've clearly been hiding before now. They could have broken out any moment after they were healed, but they haven't.

"Second, Gardi spared Salvia's life. They were going to kill the Jorrians; Gardi had every reason to take their life, and given the magic they were capable of..." I meet Mirzayael's gaze. "You saw it. They easily could have killed the person they were targeting with those ice shards. But they didn't.

"And finally, they not only saved Salvia's life, but stopped their ally from doing what they could not. It would have been easy for them to only use the spell in their own self-defense and allow Ragna to dispatch of the indefensible Salvia. But they didn't. They stopped Ragna, too."

I blow out a breath. "They don't want any more death. That much is clear. And Ragna certainly won't see them as an ally anymore. So our options are to release Gardi, whereupon they'll be executed or exiled, or give them the opportunity for a second chance."

Nek is shaking his head.

Mirzayael also doesn't like this. "Even *if* they are able to reform, how could we ever trust them? They're an outsider."

"So was I," I counter. "So was Ollie."

"So were our ancestors," Torim adds with a sigh. "Were they not all strangers from different lands, carrying with them different values, brought together beneath Fyreneth's banner?"

I wasn't expecting to receive support from Torim. The dracid can be difficult to pin down.

This quiets Nek and Mirzayael's objections.

She shakes her head. "What do you have in mind?"

"Occasional supervised outings," I say. "Allow them to stretch their legs a little. See the sun. Witness what sort of people we really are. We can see what happens from there."

"Their presence will upset many Fyrethians," Nek points out. "Especially ones who have lost family members."

"Only Salvia and a few of our healers know what Gardi looks like," I say. "But we can wait until we make contact with the next city. Get people used to the idea of *any* outsiders walking through our streets first."

"Waiting's probably a good idea," Dizzi agrees. "It's still kind of weird seeing all these species I've never met before. Marlowe's crew seemed nice, though."

That's an approval from Dizzi and Torim, then. "Nek?" I ask.

He folds his arms with a huff. "It makes me uneasy. I have not had much interaction with Gardi, outside the brief conversation we shared on maps and trade. They seemed more agreeable than Ragna, but if they kept their ice magic so close to their chest, they surely are capable of concealing other things." He shakes his head. "I am undecided. As I wasn't there to witness the altercation you described, I will defer to you and Mirzayael's decision on the matter."

Just Mirzayael then. I can sense her conflicted thoughts on the issue already.

"This crusade of yours to prove a single heart can be changed seems a waste of energy and time," she remarks.

"Then consider it a hobby," I say. "It won't impact the time I spend on my responsibilities to the city."

She drums her fingers on one of her legs. "I'll conditionally accept," she says. "The condition being, you offer them a choice: they can be dropped off at Mount Haze with Ragna, or they can remain here in custody with us."

A fair choice. One I'm sure everyone in this room would assume is an easy choice. Why wouldn't Gardi want to go free?

But I have a hunch about them. "I accept these conditions. Thank you," I add. "I have to at least try."

Mirzayael waves her hand dismissively, as if clearing a bad odor out of the room. "Enough talk on the Jorrians. The sooner we never have to mention their country again, the better. I will continue to weigh what is to be done with Salvia, but in the meantime, we have plenty of other concerns to address."

The mood of the room seems to lighten.

"Like the festival?" Dizzi suggests.

"And organizing trade with the city," Nek adds.

Torim frowns. "Will these two events be concurrent?"

"No," I say. "At least, not as they're currently planned. The festival is scheduled for three days from now, while we'll be passing over Deltin tomorrow, and we will arrive at Mount Haze in six days."

"That's going to be busy," Dizzi remarks. "Should we put the festival off?"

"Or move it to coincide with the arrival at Haze," I suggest. "Perhaps it would be good to present a celebratory atmosphere when traders arrive."

"No," Mirzayael says. "We will have it as scheduled."

I look up at her in surprise, given her firm tone. Not that I particularly had strong feelings on when the festival occurred, one way or another, but it's clear Mirzayael does.

"We need a break," she says in answer to my look. Her tone softens. "All of us. Soon our lives will be entwined with these other cities. We're not used to this—to so many people, and so much change. The festival should be just for Fyrethians. A celebration of what *we* have accomplished. One last day to relax among what is familiar and comforting before we are thrust into a much larger world."

I smile softly, and reach over to squeeze her hand. "No, you're perfectly right. A day just for us *is* what we all need. We'll have it as planned."

Mirzayael's hand twitches, but doesn't move. "Good. It's decided then." In our minds, though, her fingers entwine with mine.

The remainder of the meeting turns toward logistics and agriculture, and soon after that it ends. I stretch my arms and wings above my head as I stand. It's only morning and it already feels like I've run a marathon.

Trade tomorrow. The festival after that. Visitors two days later. And dealing with Gardi somewhere in the mix.

Not to mention keeping an eye on Salvia, checking back in on the watchtower's spell circles, and figuring out a way to get more species into my Map Interface without death or murder.

The last one, though, I think I might have an idea on.

I rake my talons through my wings as Mirzayael also stretches herself out, briefly stretching up to an imposing height of almost ten feet. I find a loose feather and comb it out of my wings. Rolling the bright red and orange plumage between my fingers, I offer it to the Dungeon Core as a snack.

Oh yes, it very much would like a snack! The feather blinks from my fingers as the Core sucks it up like a piece of spaghetti. Hm. Soft and squishy, but not much flavor.

I check the Map's catalog next; Harpy has not appeared in the list of tracked species.

Echo, I prompt. *Why did Mirzayael's leg work to populate Arachnoid in the Dungeon Core's Map catalog, but this feather wasn't enough for Harpy to be listed?*

[The minimum mass threshold has not been met,] Echo says.

How much would be enough? I ask.

[For the desired species, a minimum of 1.2 kilograms would be required.]

That's a lot of feathers. But we have a lot of harpies. Not to mention, I'm pretty sure I left a handful of feathers back in the hall, last night, when I ran into that wall.

What mass do we need for dracid? I ask.

[2.4 kilograms.]

I wonder if that's because dracid weigh more than the light-weight harpies.

But I've got an idea for the dracid, too.

"Uh oh," Mirzayael says, looking over at me.

My stomach lurches. "What is it now?"

"You." She smiles slyly. "You felt excited about something. Something weird."

I relax with a laugh. "It is weird. But I think you'll like the results. Dracid shed their skin, don't they?"

Mirzayael raises an eyebrow. "They do. Young dracid especially."

"What is generally done with the shed skin?"

She shrugs. "It's often disposed of. Probably some ends up with the waste, while more might be mixed in with the fertilizer."

"How much do you think we could gather up?" I ask.

Mirzayael wrinkles her nose in distaste. "These results better be as enticing as your excitement promises."

CHAPTER TWENTY

FEATHERS AND SKIN

The Dungeon Core makes retching sounds when it eats all the shed dracid skin.

Oh come on, I think. *You didn't complain with Mirzayael's leg.*

That was entirely different! It was hard and crunchy and was almost like a less delicious rock. This is dry and flakey and gross.

Mirzayael chuckles as she listens in. "Then it will really get a kick out of the feathers."

An enormous pile of multicolored harpy feathers is stacked in a haphazard pile on the floor of the red room, next to an empty space where the much less colorful pile of dracid skin had been just a few moments before. Nek had given me a disturbed look when I told him what we needed help gathering, and Dizzi had about fallen off her chair laughing. She'd been more than happy to go around asking for harpy feathers, at least.

Go on, I nudge. *You had one of these already. You liked it!*

The Dungeon Core dubiously takes a look at the harpy feathers, then pulls all of them into its Inventory at once, like a kid trying to swallow a vegetable whole so they don't have to taste it. It shudders.

There! It is done with the awful treats. It does not think these were treats at all. They were more like medicine.

You don't know what medicine is, I tell it.

It knows about it from me; medicine is the opposite of tasty.

"You'll have to give it that," Mirzayael says, amused. "Did it work?"

I check the catalog in the Map Interface and grin. "In fact, it did."

- Arachnoid

- Dwarf

- Dracid

- Felis

- Harpy

- Human

"That's all the species in the Fortress accounted for," I say. I check my Role Range stat next: 3.425 km.

"That boosted my range to three and a half kilometers," I tell Mirzayael. "The city itself has a radius of about a kilometer, so that means I can fly about two and a half kilometers beyond the city walls."

"Is that enough to reach the ground?" she asks.

"Almost," I say. "The Fortress's buoyancy leveled off around four kilometers above sea level. We could maybe tweak some settings and try to lower it a bit, but if I just barely reached the ground that wouldn't give me a lot of wiggle room: I'd pretty much need to stay directly beneath it."

Mirzayael frowns. "As you said, you've catalogued all the species in the Fortress. And reconnecting the defensive spell circles to the throne helps a small amount, but not much. What else can we do to extend your range?"

"There are more species out there than just the ones who live in our Fortress," I say thoughtfully. Marlowe's crew had a few elves, which looked much like those I'm familiar with from Earth fiction. On the fishing boats, I'd caught sight of some sort of aquatic species called nereids, which were slightly shorter and covered in scales and fins, though they seemed to not have any trouble being out of the water. And there were also the lamia, with a human torso but a snake's tail in place of their legs. So at least three more species for me to track, which means there's bound to be more I haven't even encountered yet.

Echo, can you give me a list of all intelligent species on Lusio? I ask. It hadn't occurred to me to ask before as I'd just assumed all the people we'd run into represented the full variety of species on the planet. The Fyrethians hadn't mentioned others—but they'd also been stuck underground for several hundred years. In retrospect, the question seems obvious.

And happily, Echo obliges.

"Cambion, Dhampyr, Elf, Goblin, Halfling, Lamia, Nereid, Orc," I repeat aloud. "Oh my. That's more than I was expecting."

"Ah. I've heard of some of those," Mirzayael admits. "They appear in a few of our older stories. I wonder if they fled before Fyreneth fell, or if their numbers dwindled thereafter?"

It's an interesting question, though not directly relevant to our needs. "I hope it will be as easy to acquire biological matter from these species as it was with harpies and dracid." For the species with hair, at least, I think that should work for Echo's needs. (Though, it would be *quite* a lot of hair.) But nereids, at least, didn't appear to have any. I hope they shed. I desperately would love to avoid needing to come up with body parts, like we did with Mirzayael's leg.

Mirzayael laughs suddenly.

"What is it?" I ask.

She displays one of her rare open-lipped grins, showing off her thin, sharp teeth. "I was imagining Nek's face when we ask him to add all this to the trade register. Elf hair. Shed skin of a lamia."

I cough out a surprised laugh, too. Those are certainly unnerving things to include on our list of desired goods. More delightful nods to my role of The Dark Lord, however unintentional it might be.

I mean... it *is* merely a coincidence, isn't it? Whatever assigned my Role couldn't have known I'd form a Pact with the Dungeon Core, or needed biological matter to fill out its catalog. Though just about every Dark Lord-like sign I've noticed has been tied to the Core, in some way or another.

I shake my head. Confirmation bias. I'm seeing patterns because I expect them to be there.

"But there is one more way I can increase my Role Range," I say. "Admittedly one I've been neglecting, though it's not as though I've had time to dedicate to it. Leveling up should increase my abilities, which in turn should increase my Range."

"Oh?" Mirzayael raises an intrigued eyebrow. "What would that entail?"

"Leveling up my spells, largely," I say. "Which requires consistent practice with them. I have Spark, Blaze, Fireball, Jet, Psionic Link, and Psionic Touch at my disposal."

Mirzayael settles back with clear interest. Training is something in her wheelhouse. "Walk me through them."

I sit on the edge of the desk and lean back on my hands. "Spark I've largely not had use for since we were able to turn the lights on in the palace," I say. "I don't really use Psionic Touch at all either. I've no use for speaking into anyone's mind who is already close enough to touch. Blaze and Fireball are mostly offensive, which I haven't needed since the Jorrian battle."

"You use Jet consistently," Mirzayael says.

I nod. "That one I've got up to Level Seven simply from how often I've used it these past few weeks."

"What do these levels mean?" she wonders. "Is there any tangible benefit?"

"For most of them it means they cost less mana, so I can use more spells for longer," I tell her. "With Jet, specifically, I've found it easier to control; it takes less conscious effort to think about. Though I suppose that could also simply be from practice."

"Interesting," Mirzayael muses. "These levels sound like arbitrary markers for the natural progression of one's magic. Using a spell over and over again of course makes you more efficient at casting it. And as you said, the more you practice something, the less difficult it becomes. This is true for all magic I know, not just yours."

"It is interesting," I admit. "I've asked Echo about it before, and she said something similar; though other people aren't aware of their levels and stats, they still have them. From what I can gather, it's prescribing them quantitative approximations of qualitative traits. And the System seems to help... *accelerate* the development of these metrics."

That produces a frown from Mirzayael. "A guiding hand helping you to become powerful more quickly?"

"It does sound a bit ominous," I agree. "Though it's not just me, remember. Ollie is in the System, too. And if there's us two, I strongly suspect there are more. The real question is: Why us?"

"Your reincarnation?" she suggests.

"It could be," I agree. "But then that shifts the question to: Why would reincarnation grant us such access?"

Mirzayael shakes her head, and I don't have an answer, either. This was one of the first questions I'd asked Echo when I'd appeared on this world, and I'd received a firm <ACCESS DENIED.> Access from whom, I continue to wonder?

"At any rate," I say, returning to the present conversation, "the last spell I have access to is Psionic Link, which I exercise with you and Ollie every day, so that one I've been working on, at least. Oh, and Psionic Sense, of course. I've used it a few times with Ollie, but not often enough to level it up."

"Can you use it with anyone?" Mirzayael asks.

"Anyone I'm Linked to," I say.

She stares at me for a moment.

"I haven't used it with you!" I hurriedly add. "And only with Ollie when I ask him first. That would be a terrible invasion of privacy!"

"Of course," Mirzayael says. There are more complex thoughts behind her response, but I pointedly don't go looking to find out what they are.

"Well, it seems you could be practicing more spells throughout the day," Mirzayael says, getting the conversation back on track. "Your Spark, for instance—even if it's of no use to you, it also seems to be a trivial mana drain, and if you constantly have one going, that should help you with these Level Ups, correct?"

"It would," I agree. "Though small mana use seems to contribute less to the level progression."

"Pity," Mirzayael says. "So your level progression is limited by your mana pool."

"Well," I say hesitantly. "Not exactly. Spells are just one way to level up."

Mirzayael perks up. "Oh? Why didn't you say something? What are the others?"

I hesitate, because I can already predict where this will be going. "Combat," I admit. "Dealing damage and taking damage both contribute."

Mirzayael grins. This smile feels significantly less good-natured.

"You mentioned this System also gives you healing abilities," she says.

"Yes," I reluctantly admit.

"Then it's settled," she says. "You will participate in sparring and combat training going forward."

I grimace. "I'd really rather not. I think I'd be better served operating in scientific capacities—"

"Fyre," she interrupts, giving me a hard look. "You lead this city by my side. You will be a target to our foes. Your sanity hinges on remaining within these walls, unless or until you become more powerful. What if someone attempted to assassinate you? Or even merely kidnap? What if Ollie isn't there to help?"

My mouth goes dry at the suggestion. Even though we'd been in battle before, it had never really hit me until just now that I *will* become a target for some people, no matter how kind I try to be, no matter how many allies we make. No matter what, there will always be those looking for an opportunity to take advantage of; there will always be edge cases.

And she's right. Alone, I am not particularly strong. Outside of the Dungeon Core's area of influence, I am limited to just my fire and psionic spells. And if I am pulled outside of the Role Requirement's range, I stand to be driven mad and would have little in the way of fighting back.

And what would happen to Ollie, then? I need to stay out of danger for his safety as much as my own. In fact, if I became strong enough to not need protecting, would that help subvert Ollie's Role Requirement entirely?

"You can't afford not to be strong," Mirzayael says firmly.

"You're right," I admit. "There's always just so many more important things to be doing. How will I find time to learn combat skills on top of everything else?" I glance at my arm, and sadly pinch my skin. Like all harpies, my physiology has traded muscles for agility.

Mirzayael laughs. "Weight training was not what I had in mind. You're a mage. You should learn to fight like one."

"Leveling up my spells?" I ask. This seems to have gone full circle.

"No—learning how to *fight* with spells," Mirzayael says. "Evaluating which to use at what time. How to strategically ration your mana. How to position yourself to use them to their fullest effect." She pauses. "Although a bit of basic self-defense couldn't hurt either."

She makes a good point; most harpies used ranged attacks in the Jorrian battle. Wind spells and arrows seem to make up the majority. I have doubts about my ability to learn a bow and arrow, and without wind arcana to guide it, I'm sure I'd make for a very poor archer. But I have my fire spells, and those can be long range, at least.

"You want me to join your guard drills?" I ask.

"No, no. That wouldn't suit your strengths. And everyone witnessing your lack of combat abilities would not help with public image." She taps at the chitin on one of her legs. "I will train you in private. We can co-opt one of the unused halls in an underground tier of the palace. That should give us plenty of room to work with."

I hold in a groan. "When in the world do we have time to work this into our schedule?"

"Well, we're merely talking now, aren't we?" Mirzayael teases. "We can repurpose some of these check-in meetings. Practice sparring while we share our daily reports."

I cannot begin to express how much I dislike this idea.

But it seems to be perking Mirzayael up, at least. "We can add in a session before bed as well. And if we wanted to wake up early—"

"One at a time," I beg. "At least ease me into it."

She chuckles. "Alright, alright. We'll ramp up to more frequent sessions. Come! This should be fun."

"Now?" I ask, the resignation already setting in. "But we are scheduled to descend to the Delta for trade talks tomorrow morning. That's less than fifteen hours away."

"Exactly." Mirzayael snatches up her spear and excitedly pushes herself to her feet. "Fifteen whole hours. Come! We have no obligations scheduled between now and supper."

Grimacing, I use some slate and chalk to write out a note on where we've gone for any of the advisors who might come by looking for us. Mirzayael is waiting for me at the door, her face lifted in uncharacteristically good spirits. She practically trots down the hall as we make for a remote, empty hall.

Think she'll go easy on me? I glumly ask the Dungeon Core. I can abruptly relate to its reluctance to carry out its duties and eat the dried skin and feathers we'd given it earlier.

The Dungeon Core doesn't know what I'm talking about.

No, I think with a mental sigh. *You're right. I don't think she knows the meaning of taking things easy.*

CHAPTER TWENTY-ONE

SPARRING SESSION

Mirzayael picks a large hall with a second-floor balcony. Marbled stone pillars stretch from floor to distant ceiling, and weathered artwork is pressed into the walls. The floor itself is an intricate and spiraling mosaic, and the ceiling looks like it might even be gilded. To think there are so many forgotten rooms like this all throughout the Fortress. It's stunning.

"Create a boulder here, and here," Mirzayael says, pointing to spots on the decorative floor. "And add some stalactites as well. You should practice using variable terrain to your advantage."

I turn to her in horror. "But that would destroy the art!"

Mirzayael shrugs, unmoved. "No one's using it."

"But the history! Wait, I've had a thought." I frown, staring intently at the ground.

Core, I need your help in a very specific way, I think. *Can you remove this section of the floor, but keep it intact? Take the whole block into your Inventory at once.*

The Dungeon Core would have been offended, if it were capable of feeling such things. Of course it can take a big bite! It could take an even bigger bite. It could bite out the whole floor, if I wanted it to!

Er, no that's not necessary, I hastily say. *Just make sure the piece remains whole in your Inventory. Meaning, don't digest it.*

The Core sighs a little sadly. It tastes better when it gets to break them all apart and savor the little pieces. But it won't say no to eating some rocks!

I mentally highlight the sections of the floor Mirzayael had indicated, then pick several random points on the ceiling as well. In a blink of an eye, the swathes of tile vanish.

"There," I say, satisfied. "Now what did you want to put here?"

Mirzayael suggests some randomly sized boulders and stalactites to summon in their place; enough to provide some obstacles. The Dungeon Core cheerfully summons these as well, though it additionally throws in an offhand remark that it would love some *new* stone to chew on, at some point. Recycling the same stuff in and out of the Inventory gets so stale.

"Good," Mirzayael says, surveying the room. "This should suffice. Are you ready?"

"Um, not particularly," I say, eyeing Mirzayael's spear. At least she's in casual clothes today and not in armor, but I still feel hopelessly outmatched. "I don't have a weapon."

"Your spells are your weapons," Mirzayael says. "You don't have the muscle for a sword, or the reach for a spear. Not to mention, you don't know how to wield either, and it would take too much time and effort to learn. Work with what you do have. A significant advantage of magic is that you can't be disarmed."

At least not until I'm out of mana. I Check over my stats.

[Name: Fyre]

[Species: Harpy]
[Subspecies: Phoenix]
[Class: Psion]
[Level: 25]
[HP: 100/100]
[Mana: 500/500]
[Bonus Mana: 227,927,469]
[Role: The Dark Lord]

Of course, the bonus mana is for the Core (and the Fortress,) and not for my personal use. Even as I watch it, the numbers are rapidly flipping down. Rationally, I know it will take months for the store to deplete at its current rate, but it's still disturbing to watch it plummet by the hundreds of points every second. I try to pretend it's not there.

I Check Mirzayael next.

[Name: Mirzayael]
[Species: Arachnoid]
[Class: Silk Warrior]
[Level: 31]
[HP: 235/235]
[Mana: 120/120]

It's interesting that she's higher level than me, but has much less mana. Of course, she has more than double my HP, but it feels like that has more to do with our difference in size than anything. I'm sure she's much quicker, stronger, and tougher than me as well. The displayed stats aren't the only ones we have, just the default values which populate my interface; curious, I ask Echo for any related to speed, strength, and toughness as well.

New stats appear on Mirzayael's list:

[Agility: 55]
[Strength: 40]

[Endurance: 62]

I compare this to my own:

[Agility: 52]

[Strength: 23]

[Endurance: 19]

Well I suppose I should have expected that.

At least my agility rivals hers. That's something. But this effectively confirms the strategy Mirzayael had previously outlined for me: stay back and use magic.

Mirzayael cocks an eyebrow. "Done analyzing?"

I flush, faintly embarrassed to have been found out. "I don't particularly like my chances."

Mirzayael chuckles. "Only because you're ignoring the Dungeon Core's capabilities. If we really were to fight, each at full power, you could end it in an instant."

She's right about that. And I had before with the Jorrians.

"But for this sparring match, no Dungeon Core," Mirzayael reminds me. "The entire point of this is to train for a scenario where you won't have it at your disposal. That said, I give you permission to target me with any of your spells at full strength."

I'm about to object to that, knowing how deadly some of my fire attacks can be—though the times I had used those, I'd also borrowed mana from the Dungeon Core. Perhaps even my basic abilities are not as impressive as they might appear when I'm truly not reliant on others.

"Okay," I say, balling my fists as jitters run through me. "How does this work?"

Mirzayael spins her spear around with a flourish to rest it casually over her shoulder. "I try to subdue you. You try to avoid being subdued."

"Sounds simple enough," I say. I note that my win condition is not, in turn, subduing Mirzayael. Perhaps my pride should be injured, but I rather agree with her assessment.

"Ready?" she asks, still standing casually.

My body tenses in anticipation. "Ready."

She pauses a beat. "Go!"

[Jet activated.]

I blast myself backward as Mirzayael whips her spear around her neck and slashes through the air where I had just been standing. My heart jumps to my throat in alarm until I realize she'd swung at me with the blunt end. I don't have any space to be bothered by the fact that she's going easy on me—I'm just relieved.

The room is wide and tall, and even with the obstacles I added, there's plenty of room for me to fly around and put some distance between us. Mirzayael is a close-combat fighter. Theoretically, I should be able to stay up here and lob Fireballs down on her head.

At least until my mana expires. Then what?

Mirzayael casually strides my way, and I circle the opposite, hoping to keep some of the boulders between us. I need to develop a strategy to end this, not just evade. Perhaps I could use a Blaze to act as a flashbang, then—

Mirzayael launches her spear at me. I jerk to the side in surprise. I hadn't expected her to throw away her only weapon.

She jerks a hand back, and a thread of spider silk catches in the light. The line goes taut, and her spear is yanked back toward her. Mirzayael catches it, then aims again.

So much for her being a close-combat fighter. She must have at-tached the silk when she circled behind one of the boulders and I'd briefly lost sight of her. I notice she's also cocooned the spear tip with a layer of silk as well. It's unlikely to cut me, but it's certain to still hurt.

Mirzayael throws again, and once more I dart to the side. Before she's had a chance to pull the line back in, I summon a Fireball and return fire.

She also easily sidesteps it, and fire splashes harmlessly against the floor beside her.

"Good instincts," she says. "Attack when the enemy is least prepared to guard. But that attack's too slow."

I'm not sure if anything else I have is much faster. Spark is useless here. I'm already using Jet. Blaze is about all I have left, unless I start getting creative and figure out a new application of my abilities.

"Are you going to hover up there all day?" she calls.

Given my Jet spell depletes my reserves at about 15 mana per minute, that's not exactly an option. I summon a second ball of fire.

"Again?" she asks. "I told you it's too—"

I throw it down at her.

Once more, Mirzayael steps to the side. Then, right as it's about to pass her, I yank the Blaze spell to the side and redirect it into her torso.

While Blaze might not have the condensed power of a Fireball, it wins out in versatility, as I can precisely control its size and movement.

Mirzayael stumbles back in surprise. The fire splashes around her and quickly fizzles out. She whips a hand down her shirt to ensure nothing caught fire, and I'm briefly concerned I burned her. Then she laughs.

"Good! That was tricky. But now I'll be watching for it. What else have you got?"

What else indeed? I was rather proud of that Blaze subterfuge, but she's right that it would only work once.

"Nothing?" Mirzayael calls. "Then I guess I'll have to come to you."

The arachnoid becomes a blur of movement. She runs up the side of one of the boulders and leaps for the second-floor balcony, catching it and hauling herself over. I backpedal toward the opposite wall in alarm as she begins to run around the landing that encircled the room. The second floor is not completely continuous; the balcony ends over a gap above the main doors we'd come through. This poses little issue for Mirzayael. Still moving at breakneck speed, she runs up the wall and over the gap, racing along it for quite a ways before dropping back to the landing's floor.

Right. Spiders.

Mirzayael jumps to the nearest stalactite, her many legs digging into the stone and preventing her from falling. Once more she throws her spear at me. This time when it passes by, I aim my Jets at its line; the silk melts and snaps, and the spear clatters to the floor beneath us. That only makes Mirzayael grin wider.

I don't like how much she seems to be enjoying this.

She leaps to a different stalactite, and I circle away, summoning another Blaze. As she catches sight of it, she abandons her perch, jumping back to the opposite landing, then leaping to one of the boulders, and finally to the floor. She snatches up her spear, and I launch the Blaze while her back is turned. She spins around before it reaches her, and I make the fire give chase as she switches direction. Just as I'm about to land a hit, she slashes through it with her spear, dissipating the spell.

Once more Mirzayael is already on the move, rushing beneath my feet. What now? I warily drift back as she passes below and keeps running. What is she—

I lurch, my Jets stuttering, as my wing catches on something. I quickly recover and try to tug my wing away, but it's stuck. For a moment I'm baffled—I'm not near any of the walls or pillars. There's nothing there to get stuck on. Then I try to twist away, and the spider silk catches the light.

Oh. *Oh.* That's what she was doing with all those acrobatics.

I use a Jet to burn through the line, but by then Mirzayael is nearly on top of me. She leaps from the balcony and I jerk back—running into a second line. I twist around to burn that one away, too, and Mirzayael lands on the nearby stalactite. (I'm starting to think these obstacles were more for her benefit than mine.) She stabs her spear at something over my head and yanks it back, and I feel another line pulled against me.

I desperately point one of my Jets toward her, but she deflects it with her spear, catching my wrist on the spider silk as well.

Unable to gimbal my Jets properly, I feel gravity take hold. The silk keeps me painfully suspended in the air. Mirzayael extends another thread between her hands, and I can tell this is where she intends to end it.

[Blaze activated.]

Fire bursts around me, and I funnel even more mana into the spell as it expands around me, hot and bright. Mirzayael flinches back, and the lines I'm caught on evaporate beneath the flames, freeing me.

One factor I had forgotten to take into account was the current positioning of my Jets. The moment the lines are gone, I blast toward the ground. I flail my limbs in a wild attempt to reposition them, but I have less than a second to recover—

I slam into Mirzayael's chest as she catches me, pulling me in close moments before we hit the ground. Her legs compress like springs, but momentum still turns the landing into a roll. The room tumbles around me, my wings tangled with one of her legs. In a panic, I realize I still have my Jets going, and I quickly snuff them out. Then we come to a stop, my head spinning as I find myself on the floor, splayed spread-eagle in the most literal of senses.

Mirzayael is crouched over the top of me, one hand braced against the ground, the other behind my head—the only thing that kept it from having struck the stone floor. She carefully pulls her hand away and braces it against the ground, too. Her front legs are folded beneath her at an awkward angle; only her arms and back legs are keeping her from falling on top of me—and likely crushing me. Both of us are breathing hard.

"Are you alright?" she asks.

"Yes," I say between breaths. My heart is still hammering in my ears. I didn't even take Bludgeoning damage from the fall. I'm not sure the same can be said about Mirzayael.

Then I remember my Jets, and anxiety wells up in me once more.

"Are *you* alright?" I ask, worriedly reaching for her nearest leg. I don't see any scorch marks, but I'm certain I hit her.

"It was only a glancing blow," she says.

Even so I run my hand down the limb, searching for damage. Its surface is cool, smooth, and hard, like a stone from a riverbed. I'm not even sure if a burn would leave damage I could notice, but I feel compelled to check anyway. Nearby is her amputated leg, and its sight fills me with guilt. I've already apologized for the injury I caused when I first arrived in this world, but words don't seem enough.

Mirzayael clears her throat, and I glance back up at her face. I'm not sure we've ever been this close before. I'd never noticed the freckles that dust her cheeks until this moment. Perhaps that's because they're only a shade darker than her already dark complexion—or maybe I was never looking close enough. The smaller eyes that frame her two main ones blink at me.

"I assure you, I am unharmed," she repeats. Mirzayael glances at my hand, still resting on her leg.

"Ah! Right." I snatch my hand away, flushing with embarrassment. "Sorry."

She nods at my words without making eye contact. "One of my legs is hooked around your wing. Can you lift it up? I don't want to injure you."

"Of course." Though it's easier said than done, given I'm lying on them.

Even so, after a minute of awkward shuffling and squirming, we're carefully able to untangle our limbs. Mirzayael pushes herself off of me, then offers a hand, which I gratefully take, and pulls me to my feet.

The burn in my cheeks and neck has yet to pass; I decide to blame my elevated heart rate on the sparring match.

"Well that was quite intense," I remark after a moment of silence.

Mirzayael breathes out a laugh. Then she straightens up, and is back to her typical Captain of the Guard self. "I told you not to hold back."

I look up at her quizzically. "I wasn't."

"*Really?*" she asks in my mind. "*Did you use your psionics?*"

Ah. "I'm not sure I feel comfortable using that combatively."

"I did give you permission," Mirzayael reminds me.

"I know," I sigh. "Something to consider for next time."

Mirzayael raises an eyebrow. "Next time? Oh, we're not done here."

I wince. I was sort of hoping we were. "I'm not sure I have the mana to do something like that again."

"No spells," Mirzayael promises. "You should learn some basic self-defense. Here, hold out your hand. We'll start with an arm bar."

Warring against my weariness, I comply, and Mirzayael walks me through the move. She's very gentle, even when applying slight pressure so I can understand what it's supposed to feel like. Then she has me practice the move on her. I take her hand and clumsily twist her wrist around. She smiles softly at my attempt, then corrects me by shifting my grip around her hand. Like the hard surface of her leg, her fingers feel cool around mine.

I suppose it can be said that training sessions aren't *all* bad.

CHAPTER TWENTY-TWO

WATCHTOWER THREE

Trading with Deltin goes better than I could have hoped.

Thanks to Captain Marlowe's advanced notice, the town is only reasonably nervous to see a giant dragon and a small platoon of harpies descend on their beach from a giant city in the sky. I keep an eye on things through Ollie, and Dizzi once more works her charm on the locals until they're willing to get close enough to see what we have to offer.

And what we have to offer is… not a lot. We're still restricted to what Ollie can carry on his back and what the harpies can carry in their arms. But Dizzi and I are working on that problem. Hopefully we'll have something serviceable before we reach Mount Haze.

We have more woven linens to offer, but as we'd previously deduced, it's the spells that become the real selling point. Dizzi made a couple the last few days, though I worry that this will become a bottleneck for future trade. She's really the only one currently capable of creating such intricate spell circle designs; at least she's been recruiting some of the watchtower researchers to help. I could easily see spell research and production becoming full-time positions for them.

All told, between Dizzi's spells and our other cargo, it's enough to trade for several crates of fish (which unsurprisingly are pretty cheap for a coastal city) and, more excitingly, a fair supply of fruit and vegetables.

These are all new to me. The fruit is called blueseed, which looks something like a black pomegranate with a blue interior. We receive two kinds of vegetables: a bean plant filled with slightly oversized peas, and something called ray peppers, which look and smell much like habaneros. I'm especially excited about these. The vegetables we currently have can be divided into two categories: root vegetables, like potatoes and carrots, and leafy greens—by and large moss, though it's prepared and eaten in a similar way to salad.

Not to mention, mushrooms. We have so, so many mushrooms.

I can't wait to see what our cooks will do with a bit of spice, and they seem equally ecstatic to start experimenting with them. Especially given tomorrow's planned festival and feast.

It takes a couple trips for Ollie to ferry all the items back up to the Fortress, though he doesn't seem to mind. After he's dropped things off, he descends back to the ground empty-handed—an opportunity which he uses to try to shake Meritis off his back. The two find this hysterically funny.

At least we can feel confident in the harness now.

For this mission, Salvia stays behind. It's part of their ongoing punishment for attempting to murder the Jorrians. They accept their orders without complaint or any sort of expression, which worries me. I can't tell if they were humbled by how easily they had been subdued, or if they've simply accepted the discipline and are weathering it until they can return to their normal duties, or if they're still harboring a festering anger that will once more build up until it can no longer be contained.

I honestly still don't know how to address this. They're hurting, and with good reason. Where else is there for them to direct their frustration save the imprisoned Jorrians? I am looking forward to getting the prisoners out of our city. Mount Haze is only another four days away. I hope we can make it that long without another incident.

By late afternoon, we've drifted across Deltin and a good distance beyond. The townsfolk bid us a happy farewell, having warmed up to us over the course of the day (no doubt due at least in part to Ollie frolicking in the shallow waters of the beach like a terrifyingly overgrown puppy). Everyone is in high spirits as we unload, count, and divvy up the day's spoils.

That evening, I go looking for Dizzi, and am unsurprised to find her in the lab. It's almost more her room than mine, now.

"Hey," I say, leaning against a workbench. Dizzi looks up from a chunk of rock she's etching. "How're you doing?"

She grins, waggling the stone at me. "I think I made a breakthrough on our transport problem."

That doesn't exactly answer my question, but I feel safe interpreting it as Dizzi's version of "doing very well."

I hold out my hand, and she flicks the rock toward me. It floats like it's in microgravity, and I pluck it from the air. The cloudstone is smaller than my palm, and flat like a skipping stone. The spell circles she's carved in the surface are connected with more lines and circles, making a bigger spell circle. The etching is as fine as hair.

"This is impressive," I remark. "I don't think anyone else in the Fortress can etch half as precisely as you. You might get stuck drawing spell circles all day if we can't train up some helpers."

"I'd rather do that than play envoy." She pushes her chair back, stretching her hands above her head and kicking her talons up on the workbench. She sighs dramatically, hanging her head over the back of the chair. "People are exhausting!"

I chuckle. "You seem to speak with them easily enough."

"Just because I *can* doesn't mean I want to," she says. "I mean, it's one thing if they know something I just have to learn more about—then I could talk for hours! But this trade stuff is a bore. And yeah, yeah, I know it's important and all that."

"I think we can get you off negotiator duty soon," I assure her. "Ollie's harness did well today under significant duress. We should be able to start sending non-harpies down soon. And once we test this transport and scale it up, we'll have even more options."

She perks back up, eagerly leaning forward in her seat as she tucks her feet beneath her. "Great! Want to see where it's at now?"

I float the stone back toward her, watching the way it lazily rolls through the air with amusement. I wonder if astronauts find this as delightful as I do. "Be my guest."

Dizzi grabs the cloudstone with one hand, activating its spell circle, and picks up a miniature basket with the other. There's a second flat volume in the bottom of the basket, which she slots the cloudstone into. She lets go of the basket, and it floats there between her hands.

"Ta da!"

I grin at her excitement. "That's step one."

She scoffs in mock affront. "Please, Fyre, you don't think I've already figured out step five?"

She grabs a handful of pebbles from the workbench and drops a few of them into the basket. It initially dips with each weight that's added, then levels off. I see she's incorporated some of my negative feedback-loop equations. Using one finger, she pushes it back up to shoulder level, and when she removes her finger, it stays suspended where she left it.

She gestures dramatically toward the floating basket, and I reward her with a teasing golf-clap. She holds up a finger to stop me, then reaches into the basket and removes the pebbles, one by one. Each time she takes one out, the basket bobs upward a little before dampening out. It doesn't rise to the ceiling, however.

"Okay, now you can clap," she says with a grin.

"Well done, Dizzi." I reach out to pluck the floating basket from the air. I feel a faint resistance, like it doesn't want to be moved, but once I've built up a velocity, it continues the motion frictionlessly.

"A neutrally buoyant transport, independent from the amount of cargo it carries," I say. "That really is quite the feat." Something that wouldn't have been possible on Earth. I'm continuously delighted by all the new possibilities this world and magic system has to offer.

"For now, Ollie or some harpies will have to tow it up and down from the Fortress," Dizzi says. "But all we have to do is add some wings and control surfaces, and it'll basically be its own airship!"

"I can synthesize a larger stone for the full-scale model," I say. "I can make it a cloudstone, but I can't put the wind arcana in it."

Dizzi waves off my concern. "I've got enough mana to top it off."

"And how long will it last before it needs to be recharged again?" I ask.

She leans back in her chair, thinking. "A couple hours probably? Plenty of time to get between the Fortress and the surface."

I resist the urge to pinch my nose. "And what if it gets delayed on the ground."

"Er..."

"Is there a way to tell how much time is left before the cloudstone's mana is depleted?"

"Well..."

"Dizzi, what happens if it's mid-flight when it runs out?"

"Okay!" she squawks, fluttering her wings in agitation. "I'll make a tracker for its mana stores, or something. And we can get a couple of harpies to help fill it up so it will last longer."

"Thank you." She's definitely brilliant. Once she learns to see past the invention and anticipate the application, then she'll be a true menace.

I hope Mount Haze has some books we could trade for. Oh, how I've missed books!

Mirzayael wanders in as I'm working with Dizzi on the dimensions for the full-size transport. I won't be able to synthesize it here, as the lab isn't big enough, but we can still finalize the design. I suppose we'll also need to construct a hangar of sorts, once we have a fleet of them. Or a dock—probably something we should create regardless, given the airships we'll likely be engaging with.

"Everything well?" Mirzayael asks, watching us work.

"There's a lot to do before we reach the city," I reply, poring over the calculations. "But I think we'll be ready when we get there."

"Good," Mirzayael says. "Then we have other ways in which we can prepare." Mentally, she adds, *There is time for more self-defense training before supper.*

I grimace.

Dizzi saves me from more pain and embarrassment by looking up in thought. "Oh! That reminds me. I wanted to talk to you two about the watchtower spells."

Mirzayael looks at her. "What about?"

"Well..."

It's hard not to notice how Dizzi's typical enthusiasm has all but evaporated.

"Maybe we should discuss it in one of the towers," she says. "Tower three, specifically."

I have a bad feeling about this.

Mirzayael also seems to understand the seriousness of Dizzi's tone. "Of course. Show us what it is."

Dizzi and I leave through a balcony, while Mirzayael takes a path on the ground. It will take her a few more minutes to get there, so Dizzi and I take our time, coasting and casually looping around the city. I'm getting the feeling Dizzi doesn't want to draw attention to this tower in particular, and all three of us making a beeline for it could certainly stir suspicion in those observant enough.

Since the orientation of the Fortress is not consistent enough to use descriptors like north or south, we've started to name the watchtowers. The first tower, harboring the barrier spell, we've started to refer to as Shield Tower, whereas the tower damaged in the Fortress's ascension has become Broken Tower. (Not the most creative names, I admit, but intuitive, at least.) The third tower Dizzi's team investigated is currently nameless, as she'd quickly moved them onto the fourth tower when she deemed the spell too complicated to decipher.

Of course, she'd told Mirzayael and I that she suspected the spell in Watchtower Three was a weapon; she just didn't know what it did.

I suspect we're about to find out.

Mirzayael joins us in the large room on the top floor where the room-sized spell circle is inscribed. All the rubble and dust has been cleared off its face, though cracks still run through the design, rendering it unusable.

Dizzi paces around the room a bit, then lets out a breath, turning to us. "So, I was right. This one is definitely a weapon." She uses the talons on her feet to point out a few nearby runes. "Fire." She gestures to some other ones. "Concentration modifier." She points out a few more. "Direction modifier. Of course, it's a lot more complex than that, but the crux of it is a giant beam of fire capable of taking out a small army in one go. Kinda terrifying."

That's one way to put it. I can taste bile in my mouth just imagining the scene she described.

"Good," Mirzayael says. "We should repair it and connect it back to the throne's circuit."

I look at her, horrified. "No, we shouldn't! Such an awful weapon—no one should have such power."

"Even if it saves our people?" Mirzayael counters. "I'm not suggesting we look for a fight, but it would be unwise to not have such a weapon prepared, if it were ever needed."

"This is dangerous," I say. "Not just the weapon—but *having* such a weapon. People might view us as a threat just for it being in our back pocket." It makes me think of Fyreneth's story. How, supposedly, the gods determined she was a threat that could not be ignored, and she was destroyed for it. A chill runs down my back.

"Then we will keep its existence secret," Mirzayael says, annoyance tinging her tone. Dizzi looks distinctly uncomfortable, and ineffectively attempts to melt into the wall. "Wasn't that what we had originally agreed upon? We would investigate these spells so long as their nature is kept covert between those who can be trusted."

It *was* what I agreed to. But simply being covert doesn't feel like enough. What if a Fyrethian stumbles upon it? With the company we'll soon be having, what if a non-Fyrethian stumbled upon it? Not to mention there's the researchers, who already know of its existence, at least to some degree. Including Salvia. Do I trust them not to use such a weapon against someone they might see as an enemy?

We will need to keep this tower under lock and key.

Or I could destroy it.

I'm not sure if she caught a hint of that thought, but Mirzayael's expression darkens. "You can't avoid conflict by ignoring it as a possibility. Not everyone we meet will be as congenial as the individuals we've traded with over the last week. We need to be prepared to defend ourselves."

"I know," I say, looking down at the spell circle. But I'm not sure I can bring myself to repair it. I would have a hand in the creation of this weapon. If it's used to kill, would I be able to divorce myself from the death it causes?

"Just… give me time to think about it," I say, unable to meet Mirzayael's eyes.

"How much time?" she asks.

I don't have an answer.

"Fyre, this could go far toward increasing your Role Range," she says, switching tactics. "Even if it's not used, simply having it repaired could label our city as 'better defended.' Isn't that enough reason to try?"

I blow out a breath. "I don't want to do this. I see the reasoning in your argument, but it still gives me a bad feeling."

"What would convince you, then?" she demands. "Or is reason a tool you use only when convenient to your wants?"

Her words stab into my heart. I look up at her in surprise, and her frown falters for just a moment. Is she right? Am I being hypocritical? It's not as though I haven't taken lives. I did what I had to do when we fought the Jorrians. Is this any different? We're not even using the weapon—just arming it.

Somehow, even this doesn't reassure me.

"Alright," I say quietly. "I'll repair the circle."

Dizzi nervously creeps back into the conversation to point out places on the floor that need to be fixed a certain way. I follow her instructions, and the Dungeon Core makes the spell circle good as new.

"There," I say. "It's done."

Mirzayael's shoulders dip. "Good. Thank you." She pauses. "Did that change the Role Range at all?"

I don't check the stat. "No."

"Ah." There's a tense silence. "Well, it was worth a try. Dizzi, was there anything else you wanted to talk about?"

"Uh, no," she says quickly. "That was it. I'll head back to the lab, then, alright?"

She barely waits for either of us to reply before she dives out the window.

Mirzayael sighs. "I'm sorry if I was too harsh."

I attempt to offer her a reassuring smile, but I'm sure it doesn't reach my eyes. "It's okay. I understand where you're coming from."

"I see. Thank you."

We head down the spiral staircase together, an uncomfortable tension still hanging between us.

It is, in no part, helped by my guilt that I'm keeping carefully tucked away as I mentally look through the Dungeon Core's senses, examining the fixed spell circle and the broken circuit beneath the stone that I have not yet connected back to the throne.

CHAPTER TWENTY-THREE
DRESS UP

As soon as I wake, it feels as though the festival has begun.

It's planned to be an evening ordeal, involving a feast, dance, games for the children, and of course Dizzi's fireworks display, but already the anticipatory atmosphere seems to have infected the air.

Arachnoids have strung up silk streamers all over the palace, dyed bright colors of red, orange, and yellow with help from the textile team. The halls smell thick with the steam of a rich and salty stew. Kids are running throughout, laughing and playing with cloudstone balls, which are becoming the toy of choice.

"My kids have mentioned a game using those rocks," Nek says that morning at the daily check-in. "They're developing a sport of some kind." He smiles fondly. "We never had this much time for leisure when I was a kit."

"Hopefully we'll secure more time for the adults to partake in leisure as well," I remark, thinking of the upcoming trade talks at the end of the week. "If we're lucky, we'll acquire some supplies and tools that should take some pressure off everyone."

"The textile group is already finding time to work on side projects between the necessary linen orders," Torim agrees. "Once the needs within the Fortress have been taken care of, perhaps they could focus on creating more clothing and blankets for export."

"Or they could simply enjoy the downtime," I reply, amused. Fyrethians are a hard-working people, mostly out of necessity, I suspect. I wonder if there will be a cultural shift in the younger generation, growing up in a much different climate from their parents.

"We'll have plenty of that at the festival," Mirzayael says, folding her arms.

There's still a faint tension between us from last night's argument. I hate that it's bled into today, which should be a day of relaxation and companionship. Dizzi nervously glances between us, but doesn't say anything.

"Speaking of today," Nek says, "I have the current itinerary."

"Yes, please share," I say, relieved for his intervention.

Nek consults a slate he's carrying. "We'll gather in the main hall at two hands before sunset. They will likely expect some words from one or both of you."

Mirzayael and I exchange an uncertain look. Neither of us are particularly good public speakers.

"We'll have something prepared," she says.

Nek nods. "After that the kitchen crew will begin serving the feast. There will be ten rounds, I'm told, one every half hour; the cooks have all taken shifts so none of them are working for more than an hour." Nek scratches his ear. "I'm not exactly sure how they have it all worked out, but they seem to have a plan.

"Throughout the evening there are various groups that each have volunteered to entertain in some way. The first group is a family of dracid who have a dance they'd like to perform. The last event is Dizzi's explosion display."

"Fireworks display!" I correct, desperately hoping that was merely a miscommunication on Nek's part and not a misunderstanding on mine.

"I mean, they're basically explosions," Dizzi says.

She's not wrong, but the language still concerns me.

"I have a full list of planned events and activities if you want to review them," Nek offers.

"No," I say, "I'm sure they'll all be lovely."

Mirzayael also dismisses Nek's offer. "I trust any Fyrethian with whatever activity they wish to share."

He nods. "Of course. Then the main thing that's left is the preparation of the main hall..."

Most of this involves decorations, but Nek needs my help for some slight adjustments. The main hall is about the size of a large, indoor sports gymnasium, so it can fit all of our city's inhabitants inside at once, but it's a tight fit. Typically, we don't all eat at the same time—and some take the food back to their houses instead of sharing the communal space—so we'll need to make some adaptations for the ensuing feast.

While the meal circles here are mostly designated by rings of fur and blankets that act as pillows, back in Fyreneth's Keep, the meal circles had been shallow depressions set into the floor. Consulting with Nek on what size and variety of circles should be made, I use the Dungeon Core to recreate the indentations, spacing them out to create wide walking paths through the room designed to simplify trips to the kitchen.

Conversely, I also raise a couple shallow platforms above floor level to provide performers a dedicated stage to make them easier to see. And with some convincing on Nek's part, I also raise a portion of the floor at the head of the room, where Mirzayael, the councilors, and I will be seated. I'd previously removed the wall behind us so Ollie could join us for meals, but I take this opportunity to enlarge the pavilion and add more seating space for non-dragon loungers. The space will provide us a clear view of the firework show at the end of the night.

By the time I finish helping with all the adjustments to the main hall and head back to the throne room, I find a new party is awaiting me. A group of felis and arachnoids I recognize from the textile group have arrived, and are speaking with a distinctly-uncomfortable looking Mirzayael.

I join the group after they catch sight of me and excitedly beckon me over. Mirzayael notices with a grimace. "*It's too late for you to escape, now.*"

"*Escape?*" I repeat with curious amusement.

"Lord Fyreneth!" one of the arachnoids exclaims. He has an off-white shell, hair long but drawn up in a bun. Echo identifies him as Yequirael, which is fantastic, as I'd definitely forgotten his name despite having met him a few occasions before. "I'm glad we found you. We were just going over the options with Lord Mirzayael."

"Just Fyre, please," I say. "And options for what?"

The arachnoid holds up a bolt of shimmering cloth. My breath catches in my throat.

It's the most amazing fabric I've ever seen. The texture ripples like water as it passes through the tailor's hands, and a faint iridescent scattering of rainbows glimmer in its folds. A variety of fabrics are being presented to Mirzayael and I; some black, some red, some white or blue. Some have designs embroidered into the cloth, while others are plain—though I would be hard pressed to call any of the textiles plain, given their clear artistry.

"These are amazing," I say, running my hand over the fabric. It's as smooth as silk—which it probably is. Spider silk of some sort, though this is nothing like the durable and tacky lines I've witnessed Mirzayael use in combat.

Yequirael beams. "I'm pleased to hear it. We can tailor them to your fit with a few measurements, but we wanted to see which style you would prefer, first."

"Style?" I ask, thrown.

I've never really had much of a style. At work, it was all suits and collared shirts. The most colorful I got involved silly sock designs. Wearing more interesting clothes was a nice thought *in theory,* but that also involved an eye for fashion I never had. Sticking with the expected attire was the easiest and least unnerving option available.

I helplessly look at Mirzayael. She snorts. "If you think I've any instinct for these matters, you are mistaken."

I chuckle nervously. We really are the two worst individuals to ask about this.

Some of the colors are so bold and beautiful. But are they something I would ever dare wear? Would I look like a fraud?

"I'm not sure," I admit, looking over the dizzying number of options. "Perhaps, is there a color that is representative of our kingdom?"

"Royal colors?" Mirzayael drums her fingers against one of her legs in thought. "I'm unsure. If there were any in Fyreneth's day, I think they've been lost to time."

Not surprising, given the Keep's limited resources for indulging in things such as decorations and dyes. "I'd prefer to leave the decision in your hands," I tell Yequirael. "I suspect you all have a better eye for this than myself."

"Agreed," Mirzayael quickly joins, and I can feel her relief at being able to defer the choice to someone else.

Yequirael exchanges a thoughtful look with his team. "Colors representative of Fyrethians? I think we can come up with something."

Oh, good. Maybe one day I will feel comfortable picking out bold colors and styles of my own, but I am not quite at that point today.

The tailors take us to our individual chambers to take measurements and start stitching our clothes together. I'd been to a tailor once as a human to get my suit properly fitted. Much like now, it had involved a lot of standing still, raising arms, and allowing the tailor to take measurements. However, at the end of that meeting I had left without my jacket, and they had gotten back to me a week later with all the alterations. This experience is somewhat different.

Even as a felis takes measurements, Yequirael is draping cloth over me, pinching edges together, and seamlessly adhering the fabric to itself using what is certainly some type of magic. I try to focus on this instead of my extreme self-consciousness as they begin to fashion the clothes around me in real-time.

Like all harpy clothes, the fabric on the back is split into three pieces, one hanging between the wings, and two hanging on either side, so they can then be tied and secured beneath. A lot of harpy clothes are kind of long and tasselly as a result. Arachnoid clothes are similar, with cloth draping over and secured beneath their abdomen, slits cut in the fabric where the legs are located. Dracid, dwarves, and felis have attire most similar to that I'm familiar with on Earth, though even those have slight alterations to accommodate the felis and dracid's tails. It's probably because I'm still not entirely familiar with harpy attire that it takes me so long to realize what sort of clothes they are making.

It's a dress.

My stomach performs an acrobatic flip.

Mirzayael's mind stirs. "*Is something wrong?*" she asks me.

"*No,*" I reply. I'm not sure how to feel, actually. "*I just wasn't expecting it to be a dress.*"

I can feel Mirzayael nodding along to my words. "*They are not very practical. What if we were attacked while wearing such ceremonial garb? I could trip on the hem.*"

I smile at her priorities. "*I have nothing against dresses,*" I tell her. My chest flutters with sudden nerves. "*I just... I've never worn one before.*"

"*Oh.*" Mirzayael sounds surprised. "*If you have nothing against them, then why haven't you?*"

The butterflies stir up a storm. "*On my world,*" I say haltingly, "*or at least, where I lived, dresses were clothes mostly meant for women. It wasn't common for a man to wear such clothing, and if they did, they were likely to receive harsh disapproval.*"

Mirzayael emanates faint confusion. "*But you are a... Oh.*"

There's something comforting in the knowledge that she had forgotten about my other life, and only sees me for who I am now. But the conversation itself has stirred a flurry of conflicting emotions within me.

"*Are you uncomfortable with this?*" Mirzayael asks. "*We could ask them to make different attire.*"

"*No,*" I say quickly. "*No, this is fine. I suppose I am just a bit nervous.*"

"*What about?*" she wonders.

I'm not sure if I know myself. "*Perhaps, I'm worried it will feel wrong. Or I will look silly.*"

"*Well, if it feels wrong, you can always change,*" Mirzayael says. "*Though I highly doubt your second concern is valid.*"

I smile to myself. Leave it to Mirzayael to berate you for your own self-doubt. My nerves aren't fully calmed, but speaking to her about it has helped. "*Thank you. I'll count on you to inform me if the look is indeed silly.*"

Warm amusement radiates from her mind. Antithetically, it makes my chest hurt.

"*Mirzayael,*" I continue after a moment. "*I want to apologize for last night. I shouldn't have gone back on my promise about the weapon. It's not my decision to make. Having such power frightens me. But it's not my power; this power belongs to Fyrethians, and I shouldn't have fought with you over it. I'm sorry.*"

"*I know,*" Mirzayael says, her tone softer than I've ever heard it before. "*I understand your hesitation. You are a gentle soul, Fyre. So let me be the one to make the hard decisions when you cannot.*"

I'm not sure if I can do that. I don't think letting her make the final call would make me feel absolved of responsibility for the consequences. But I'm touched that she would want to take that burden from me.

Mentally, I move back into the Dungeon Core's interface and navigate to Watchtower Three. Hesitating there for a moment, I repair the broken spell circuit and connect the dormant spell to the network.

The guilt I'd been feeling over the spell circle immediately begins to ebb away.

"*I'll always have your back,*" I tell her, returning to my body. "*Whatever you need, whatever this city needs, I'll be there at your side to support you.*"

Affection radiates from her mind, wrapping around me like a warm blanket. "*Thank you.*"

After a time, Yequirael determines his work is done. He doesn't offer me a mirror, as the tailors want to reveal the two of us at the same time. We're both ushered into the throne room, where a great mirror stretches along one of the walls. The tailors excitedly back us up to each other in what I feel is a fairly ridiculous manner, a sentiment Mirzayael equally shares.

"Okay," Yequirael says. "You both can look."

We turn toward the mirror.

I'm not sure if the spike of awe that jolts through my mind originated from me or Mirzayael, but it oscillates between both of us for quite some time after that.

I'm in a sleeveless black gown that shimmers with an opalescent sheen in the throne room's light. It appears to be made of dozens of sashes, two of which cross dramatically over my shoulders and down to the opposite hip, while more sweep about my legs in a forest of overlapping tassels. The dark hue stands out starkly against my bright plumage, so when I move a leg, a flash of brighter colors briefly blaze from within. The occasional trim and details that adorn the dress come in shades of crimson, gold, and copper.

Mirzayael, meanwhile, is dressed the opposite. The primary shades of her robes are made of the same colors as the highlights in my dress, and the layers overlap in such a way that she looks like she might be wearing living flames themselves. The trim on her attire is the same iridescent black as my dress, matching the hue of her shell.

Mirzayael abruptly laughs, startling me out of my awe. She reaches down to run one of my black tassels through her hand. "They have given you my legs."

When she lets go of the fabric and it collides with the rest, setting them all swaying, I realize she's right—the design *is* reminiscent of arachnoid legs. I look back at Mirzayael's robes more critically, then find myself grinning as well.

"And you have my wings," I say, running a hand over the side of her abdomen where the colors sweep back ornately in the likeness of feathers.

Mirzayael turns to get a better look in the mirror, and she laughs again. "So I do."

They've flipped our color palettes—with a dash of extra drama. It should look silly, but my heart feels like it is about to burst with awe and appreciation.

"You're beautiful," I say before I can think the words through.

Mirzayael's surprise is as obvious in her mind as it is on her face. Both shift quickly to embarrassment. My own embarrassment hits me at the same moment, but I don't regret what I said. I meant it.

"No one has ever said that to me before," she says stiffly. Her mind is a mess of too many emotions for me to decipher.

"Me neither," I admit. "At least, not until I came here."

That seems to shake her out of her shock. "What? Who told you you're beautiful here?"

"Captain Marlowe," I say. "Just a few days ago."

Her expression darkens. "Did he now."

I can't help but laugh over the sudden and obvious jealousy. "I think he was just trying to flatter Dizzi and I."

"Hmm."

"Now, now." I take her hand, and she turns away from the mirror to look at me directly. "Don't let a person who is not even here sour the day. We've a festival to enjoy."

"Yes," she says, her bristled mind melting back into fondness. "We do."

Chapter Twenty-Four

THE FESTIVAL

The hall is a cacophony of happy voices and laughter. Children run around the meal circles with silk ribbons and toss colorfully dyed cloudstone through the air. The councilors are still arriving, meeting Mirzayael and I at the meal circle at the head of the room, while Ollie sprawls on his open-air balcony behind us. Meritis prances around in front of him, showing off his newly dyed feathers in shades of green and blue.

"DO YOU THINK THEY COULD DYE ME GREEN AND BLUE, TOO?" Ollie wonders, delighted by his friend's new colors. *"OR MAYBE RED. OR I COULD BE A DIFFERENT COLOR EACH DAY!"*

"I'm not sure we have enough dye for that," I reply. "Perhaps we could look into some different colors of clothing you could wear instead."

"CLOTHING?" he asks skeptically. *"AS LONG AS IT DOESN'T ITCH. LIKE THE HARNESS DOES SOMETIMES. IT FEELS LIKE A SCRATCHY TAG."*

"I'll see if Sora can find something less abrasive for you," I say.

"THANKS! OH, AND FYRE?"

"Yes?"

"*DO YOU THINK YOU COULD DO A MIND LINK WITH MERITIS, TOO?*"

My mind skips tracks. "What?" I ask, bewildered.

"*IT WOULD BE SUPER COOL IF I COULD TALK TO HIM,*" Ollie says. "*AND BEING ABLE TO TALK INTO EACH OTHER'S MINDS WOULD BE AWESOME! LIKE WE'RE SPIES.*"

I'm rattled. I'd never considered adding someone else into the network—it's permanent and invasive. The ones I formed with the Dungeon Core, Ollie, and Mirzayael were out of necessity in dangerous situations.

But could I—should I—do it for Ollie? He can't even talk to his friend unless I'm there to give him a voice. I don't want to doom him to a life of solitude.

"I... I'll think about it," I tell him, torn.

He drops the conversation just as quickly, however, when Meritis starts talking to him, and Ollie swivels his head back to listen. I fondly watch the two boys as I try to sort through my troubled thoughts. I'm not sure this is something I can come to a decision on overnight. Resolving to talk it over with Mirzayael later, I turn my attention back to the rest of the hall.

I try to remember the last time I saw the entire city gathered like this. Perhaps the only time we did was when the lost colony joined us, and we had a celebratory feast much like this one. The thought summons a brief note of anxiety in me. That feast had been immediately followed by the Jorrian confrontation; I hope that's not an omen for how tonight will end.

We wait until it seems like most people have arrived and settled into the various meal circles. When Mirzayael stands, a hush rapidly falls over the hall.

"Thank you," she says, her voice echoing through the room. "It is my honor to serve as one of your leaders today, as it was my honor to serve as the Keep's Captain of the Guard for decades past. I never expected to claim such a position as this. I never expected many of the things that occurred over the last few months."

She pauses to glance down at me with a faint smile when a murmur of agreement passes through the crowd. I give her an encouraging thumbs up, and she snorts. She turns back to the hall. "We will face new challenges in the coming days, and in the coming years. We will encounter people and situations entirely foreign to us. Some will be for good, and some for ill. We are truly venturing into the unknown.

"But through all that, I have faith in our strength. Our continued existence proves our tenacity, our will to persevere. We will meet all these new challenges head on, and we will overcome them!"

Mirzayael pauses again as a cheer rises. She really seems to be hitting her stride now. She had been so worried about this talk, but it's apparent her fears were unfounded. This seems to be coming naturally to her.

"But those are the challenges of tomorrow," she continues. "Tonight is for our past. Tonight is a celebration of what we have accomplished, and the adversity we have overcome. For those we have lost, and those who we still honor by persisting. This is not a night to celebrate me or Fyre. And though this Fortress is great, it is not a celebration of its majesty. This is a night for you, our people." Mirzayael looks down at me, offering a hand. I take it, and she pulls me to my feet. "For every one of us past, and every one of us here today, this is for Fyrethians!"

Another louder cheer answers her words, and a few chants of "Fyreneth!" resolve among the cheers.

"And now," I call, when it's settled enough for my voice to make it over the din, "let the festival begin!"

Mirzayael lets out a breath as we sit back down.

"You did great," I assure her, answering the question that lingers on her mind, though she's too proud to ask. "It was perfectly brief, and exactly what they needed."

She nods curtly. "Good. I don't think I would have been able to say more, regardless."

"I suppose it's good practice for future feasts," I remark.

She looks at me sharply. "Practice? What other speeches will we need to make?"

I shrug. "We'll be meeting with ambassadors and traders in the coming days. And that's likely to just be the beginning. We'll need to speak with other kingdoms, attend more dinners like tonight, treat with—"

"Alright, alright, I understand." Mirzayael grimaces, rubbing at her head. "As I said in the speech, such nightmares are future concerns. Please at least let me pretend for tonight that this is the biggest speech I will ever be required to make."

I laugh. "I can indulge the delusion for one night, I suppose."

Then the food arrives. The first serving is light; a palette cleanser, I think. It's moss with a hint of something almost citrusy, served with clear cold water from our recently functioning rain collection system.

Ollie is not given distinct servings, but rather a few Fyrethians begin to carry out gallons of broth to fill the oversized stone bowl I'd created for him. We don't have enough fresh produce for him, but he wouldn't want to eat it anyway. It seems his dragon anatomy leaves him desiring a more protein heavy meal, so the cooks separately prepared a stew made from boiled bones and shells of stingers, fish, and the remains of everything we still had from the arctic. Meritis teases him for the pungent smell, but Ollie seems perfectly happy to chug the soup down.

A family of dracids perform a dance with ribbons of water, and later a partition of Mirzayael's guard execute a synchronized form that is symbolic of some battle past. Dozens of different performers take to the stage as more rounds of the feast are served. There's a light, fishy broth, similar to what Ollie was served (though with significantly less bones,) and there are smoked seafood bites. The vegetables and fruits we'd traded for show up in several of the dishes, prepared a variety of ways: some as chopped pieces garnishing a dish, others blended into a puree drizzled over the top. I notice more soup and stew dishes are served between courses that have whole chunks of meat or fruit; likely meant to fill us up and stretch the solid food as far as possible. It's extremely effective, as by the time the last serving is brought out, a frozen fruit treat similar to a snow cone, I'm so stuffed I can barely bring myself to try it.

The evening passes in a blur of delicious food and delightful performances, which leave me feeling increasingly warm and content as the night progresses. Or perhaps that's the alcohol that was brought out sometime around the third course. Every time I reach for my cup, it seems to have been refilled when I wasn't looking.

When Mirzayael nudges me, I realize I've come to lean heavily against her side. I struggle to push myself upright.

"Are you doing alright?" she asks me.

"Yes." My head is swimming a little, but in a fuzzy, pleasant way. "I think I'm drunk."

Mirzayael chuckles. "I've noticed. I believe that's enough libations for you."

"I didn't have that many," I object, focusing on my cup. It's small, like a sake glass. "I've drunk much more in the past."

"As a human?" she asks.

"Mhm." I lean back against her once more, because it's more comfortable than trying to remain upright, and everything feels a bit heavy.

"From what I can tell, humans seem to be larger than most harpies," she remarks.

"Oh! Yes. Of course." I nod along with her insight. I didn't take the difference of mass into account. "Harpies are lighter. The alcohol would be more concentrated. And maybe there's a difference in metabolism... I bet I could calculate the ratio."

"I'm sure you could," Mirzayael agrees. She sounds amused. "Do you feel comfortable getting up?"

Probably, but I'm very content right where I am. "What for?"

"The fireworks," Mirzayael says, gesturing. Others in the hall have moved toward the open wall, or are filing out to view the display from different balconies. "Dizzi just left to get everything set up."

I do recall her leaving, now that she mentions it. "Of course," I say, gathering my legs beneath me. "I can't miss that. She requested notes for improved performance."

I stand up, swaying faintly, but my wings help with the balance. I'm rather proud I didn't need Mirzayael to steady me. I'm not *that* far gone. Hopefully.

Even so, Mirzayael offers me her elbow, and I link my arm in hers as she guides us out onto the platform next to Ollie.

"*YOUR BRAIN FEELS WARM,*" Ollie tells me.

Oops. "Sorry." I try to rein in my thoughts; sharing my inebriation with Ollie or, god forbid, the Dungeon Core, is the last thing I want. "Better?"

"*I GUESS SO,*" Ollie says with a massive shrug.

"Better," Mirzayael assures me.

We sit down between Ollie's forepaws. The fireworks haven't started yet, but Mirzayael's face is turned to the night sky. Light from inside the hall reflects faintly off the metallic texture of her clothes. For a moment, she doesn't seem real. Like I'm looking at this beautifully carved statue rather than a person. I distantly marvel at the surrealness of the moment. How I came to be here, at her side.

She blinks, and the illusion fades.

Embarrassed, I look away, hoping she hadn't heard any of those thoughts. Instead, I follow her look; it's a moonless night, and stars seem to fill the sky like powdered sugar sprinkled across the heavens. It's so many more stars than I'm accustomed to. I suppose it is for Mirzayael as well.

"I don't think I'll ever get used to it," she says quietly. "It's the most beautiful thing I've ever seen, next to sunsets and sunrises."

"I'm not used to the moons," I say.

She feels surprised. "They do not have moons on your world?"

"*ONLY ONE*," Ollie replies. "*AND IT DIDN'T HAVE A NAME. IT WAS JUST CALLED, 'THE MOON.' WHICH IS DUMB. IT SHOULD HAVE A NAME!*"

"It had many names, just not in English," I tell him. "Like Luna."

"*OH! I'VE HEARD OF THAT ONE*," he says.

"I don't know what ours are called," Mirzayael admits. "They were never relevant." She sounds a little sad.

"I bet the other Fyrethians know," I say. "The Lost Colony. They often went outside. They probably remember the names."

"You're right." The sadness shifts to a burst of hope and appreciation. In my mind, I think I can see her shifting emotions much like fireworks. I'm not sure if that's the inebriation. "They probably were able to preserve many such things. It is good to know not all of our history is lost."

I jump with the first *boom*, and many Fyrethians do as well. A second later, a splash of red bursts into the sky before us, like the unfolding petals of a flower. It's quickly followed by a second, smaller pop. The difference between the speed of light and speed of sound. I faintly wonder what other laws like that exist here; is there a speed of magic?

Mirzayael snorts. "Why are you thinking about such things now? Can you never turn that scientist brain of yours off?"

"Sorry," I giggle. "Maybe." I try to focus on the fireworks after that. It's unlike any fireworks I'd seen on Earth.

These are each clearly infused with spells which help shape the resulting explosion. Some swirl into a vortex, while others remain hovering in place. Dizzi layers them so some fireworks burst to life just as others are flickering out, resulting in colorfully overlapping patterns that gradually morph shape over time. There's some that look like stars or flowers; others are scenes, like a mountain range. A theme of fire and feathers is present, of course, to honor Fyreneth. And at the end, there's one that burst into a surprisingly accurate replica of the Fortress itself. Dizzi clearly had fun working on this project.

By the time the last embers flicker out, I'm feeling a bit more clear-headed. As I stir, I realize my arm is still linked in Mirzayael's. I gently slide it out.

"Feeling better?" she asks.

"Yes," I say. "Sorry if I did or said anything foolish."

"If that was you being foolish, you are an extremely mild drunk," she teases.

She's not wrong.

Ollie started to doze in the midst of the fireworks display, and as everyone begins to file back inside, I leave him to rest. It's getting a bit late for the kid. The celebration continues indoors, however, with more dance and drink.

"I think I'll pass on that," I say. "I've had quite enough excitement for one evening."

"Before you head to bed, I've something I'd like to show you," Mirzayael says.

I raise an eyebrow. Mirzayael's done something without my knowledge? That's surprising. She's not really the type to be indirect or sly, and I never caught a hint of anything in her thoughts. "What is it?"

"I'll show you," she repeats, tipping her head toward one of the doors leading out of the main hall. "Come with me?"

"Of course."

She guides me out of the hall and through one of the many well-worn paths of the palace. Even without the Dungeon Core, I feel I could navigate this place with my eyes closed. I realize where we're headed before we arrive.

"The bathhouse?" I look up at her curiously. We turn a corner, and sure enough the entryway to the many-roomed complex of public pools stands before us. We'd just finished draining the drinking water from them into the underground storage tanks a few days prior.

"Yes," Mirzayael says. She pushes open the door. "I seem to recall it was on your shortlist of services you wished to restore to the Fortress when you had time."

Hot air billows out to meet us as we step through the door. The nearest pool is full, a turquoise blue from the tiles that line the basin, and the air feels humid and warm.

"How?" I ask, turning to her in delight.

"I spoke with Torim and Dizzi about restoring the baths," Mirzayael says. "They were only able to collect enough water to fill one of the smaller pools. And Dizzi was able to install new spell circles for thermal heating, since we can no longer rely on the springs. This one is the trial basin, but Dizzi insists it should work perfectly well, and the others will similarly be restored soon."

Mirzayael pulls the door closed behind us to keep the warm air in as I crouch by the edge, dipping my hand into the water. It's pleasantly warm. God, how long has it been since I've had a real bath?

"You can try it out," Mirzayael says. "I've seen to it that no one should disrupt us."

"What about you?" I ask. "You can't expect me to bathe while you sit around and watch."

A flustered embarrassment radiates from her mind, and I can't help but laugh.

"I have only ever had sponge baths," she says. "Submerging in so much water seems like... a lot."

"Then we can take it slow." She probably doesn't know how to swim either—in fact, probably none of the Fyrethians do. I'll have to make sure the pools are kept shallow enough, especially with children around. Perhaps I could install an emergency water-evacuation spell...

I stop my line of thought. A problem for another day.

"Come here," I say, beckoning her over. I sit down at the edge of the pool, hoisting the bottom of my dress up to keep any of the tassels from getting wet. Then I slip my feet in, and sigh as the warmth spreads up my legs.

Mirzayael hesitantly sits beside me. I help pull the hem of her robes away from the water's edge as well.

"Just your two front legs," I suggest. Carefully, she complies, dipping them into the pool. "There. How's it feel?"

"Soothing," she admits. "I can see why you were interested in restoring the bathhouse."

I grin. "Just wait until you get all the way in. It'll be life changing."

"I believe you," she murmurs.

We sit that way for a time, shoulder to shoulder, enjoying the warmth and quiet. Well, my shoulder is about at her elbow, really, since her abdomen causes her to naturally sit higher. But her sturdy presence is reassuring all the same.

Strangely, however, I notice a gradual and faint anxiety growing within Mirzayael. I don't think she's intending to broadcast the thought, so I don't comment on it. She fidgets, one of her fingers picking at a tile at the pool's edge.

"Fyre, I enjoy this," she says abruptly. "I enjoy... being at your side."

"I do, too," I say softly.

Her anxiety hasn't lessened. "I mean, not just physically, but working with you. Serving as a ruler with you. I enjoy the time we spend together."

My stomach flutters, and I look up at her. She is staring fiercely into the water. If possible, her anxiety has only increased. "I enjoy these as well," I tell her.

She nods. "I think, perhaps, it might be to our benefit, and for the benefit of the Fortress, to formalize our partnership." Her voice is level, but mentally she's crawling into a deep, dark hole to die of mortification. "If that is something you would desire."

Her words squeeze my heart, and I don't hold back the affection I feel for her as I take her hand that's still nervously picking at the tile and pull it away. She finally looks down at me. I'm not sure if arachnoid physiology allows for blushing, but I'm sure she would be, if it were possible.

"Mirzayael, are you proposing to me?" I ask.

Her mind lurches in an odd manner as I ask this.

"Ah," she says, her thoughts a maelstrom of embarrassment, fondness, and surprise. "Well. I was intending to ask if you would like to court me. Not that, I mean…"

"Oh!" It's my turn to drown in mortification, and a blush *does* rapidly burn its way up my neck and cheeks. "Oh my goodness. I didn't mean—I suppose I had just assumed, given the political position we were already in—Oh no. I'm so sorry. Please pretend I never said that!"

Mirzayael huffs out a laugh, and the nervousness slowly fades behind the affection. "Then I suppose I should not be concerned over the direction of your response…?"

"Yes," I blurt. "I mean, no, you shouldn't be concerned. Courting—courting sounds lovely." Then I bury my face in the crook of her arm, and consider sinking into the water.

Mirzayael's body shakes with a silent chuckle, and I feel her fingers hesitantly brush through the feathers on the back of my head.

"Lovely," she quietly agrees.

Chapter Twenty-Five

GUESTS

The festive atmosphere is sustained over the next several days, and by the time Mount Haze is in sight, the city seems more excited than nervous to meet with traders.

We've caught sight of distant airships on the horizon for the last couple days, but now the sky is practically teeming with them.

The mountain itself, which appears to be a dormant volcano, climbs about two thirds the way toward our Fortress from sea level. The city fills the caldera and spills over its sides, much like cooled lava, coloring the upper quarter of the mountain with tiered houses and farms. The airships all drift beneath us. I suppose they typically have no reason to fly higher than the mountaintop. But today, a train of ships is rising to meet us.

Having learned from Captain Marlowe's visit, I've adapted the wall around the front half of the city to accommodate airships. There are now pilings for them to anchor to, and stone boardwalks that stretch out into the sky for easier docking. Along with Mirzayael, the counselors, and a dozen guards and messengers, I eagerly await the ships' arrivals. As they slow and slot between the boardwalks, I watch to make sure the alterations were done properly, and mentally take notes for how I can tweak things to make things smoother next time. Six ships pull in to dock, but it's the nearest one with a bright red balloon that I recognize.

"Captain Marlowe," I greet as the man strides off his ship with a wide grin. "I see you've been busy."

"Of course," he says, coming forward to clasp my and Mirzayael's hands in a firm grip. "Couldn't let an opportunity like this slip through my fingers, could I? I hope I'm not too late, however. You two look smart. Haven't been trading without me?"

Mirzayael and I decided we should make a strong impression with the traders. If we appear poor, they might think we would accept less lucrative offers, while if we appear more prosperous, they are more likely to want to impress. We hadn't planned our first meeting with Captain Marlowe, so there's nothing we can do about his first impressions, but this encounter we have more control over.

We're both wearing less ornate versions of the gowns we had worn at the feast. The colors are the same, but the style is more practical; for Mirzayael, the shimmering cloth is looped about her arms, but cinched tight around her chest and abdomen, where she's wearing a light version of her armor. The effect is quite stunning; she looks both warrior and queen.

I myself am wearing a black vest of the same material, with billowing loose pants that almost appear like a skirt when I'm standing still, and a brightly colored sash tied at my waist. While I enjoyed all the tassels on the dress, it simply isn't practical if I want to fly anywhere. This outfit at least doesn't risk getting tangled in my wings or singed by my flames.

"Not at all," I say to the captain. "These outfits are of our own making. But I'll be sure to pass on your compliments to Yequirael. Now, what can you tell us about our guests?"

Captain Marlowe's eyes glint with a hungry and eager look as he catches my drift. His voice drops, not quiet enough to seem suspicious, but enough that I doubt anyone from the other disembarking ships can hear. From a distance, it would appear a friendly and casual conversation.

"The black ship belongs to Calaman, head of the local banking guild," he says. "She's interested in metals. She likes a good wine." He inclines his head slightly to his right. "The ship with the white and blue balloon is carrying Lord Merit; they're the head of a noble house that dabbles in artificing. The lamia, Korzo, is a prominent figure in the airship construction industry—he might be rich now, but he worked his way up from the scrap heap, so he likes a hands-on approach. The smallest ship at the end is a group of scholars who won't have much to offer in terms of trade, but could be a valuable source of information. And the green ship has a couple pursers representing the agriculture guild; they'll be interested in your textiles, if you can impress them with more similar to what you two are wearing. Got all that?"

I'm not sure I do, but I have Echo to help remind me of everyone's names, at least. "I appreciate the insight, and hope you'll continue to facilitate the coming discussions as well."

Captain Marlowe winks. "Wouldn't have it any other way."

The airship crews set about securing their vessels as the important figures of each disembark and meet us on the wall. Many of them are species Echo had mentioned, but I haven't met before today; at least the same can be said for Mirzayael and the other Fyrethians, so I'm not the only one who's trying not to stare.

"My friends," Marlowe says, sweeping an introductory hand toward all the guests. Then he makes a curious gesture; I don't understand what it's for until he continues to gesture as he speaks.

Echo pipes in with, [Foreign language detected. Activate translation?]

I blink. It's some form of sign language. I wonder if one of our nobles is deaf? *Yes please*, I say to Echo, and the motions abruptly take on new meaning within my mind.

"I'm pleased to introduce you all to Lord Mirzayael and Lord Fyre," Marlowe continues. I stare at him in fascination, wondering how my mind can make sense of a language I've previously never encountered. Magic is the answer, obviously, but it still captivates me.

Marlowe repeats a round of introductions, as if he'd not just told me who each group was, and everyone steps forward to clasp hands as they're mentioned. As the lamia, Korzo, greets me, I notice his gaze linger on Marlowe's signs. He must be who the sign language is for, then. But as two more lamia from the scholar and agriculture group also are introduced, I notice a similar pattern. In fact, as I examine them, I realize I can't see any ears on their otherwise human-esque heads. I'm unsurprised I hadn't noticed right away, as my gaze had initially been drawn to the lower half of their body, which is that of a snake's tail in place of legs. Just like the Greek figure of legend. Curious.

Are lamia deaf? I ask Echo.

[Lamia have reduced hearing as compared to most sentient species on Lusio,] Echo replies. [Due to their lack of vocal chords, Common Signs are their primary language.]

Fascinating! *Can I learn it too?* I ask her. *Is there a way you can teach me the movements, similar to how you're translating them?*

[Negative,] Echo says. [Translation may only occur to the user's language, not from.]

Unfortunate, but I suppose I shouldn't be surprised. Echo seems to be acting as a filter in my mind, interpreting what I see and hear into something I can understand, but that doesn't mean she can give me the muscle memory to speak a language I don't already know. Ah well, it was worth a try.

"Welcome," I say once the introductions are complete. Captain Marlowe, I notice, interprets my speech into sign language. "And thank you for agreeing to meet with us. I'd like to give you a tour of the city first, and then we can break for lunch and discuss business from there, if it suits you."

"If it suits us?" one of the scholars, an elf, repeats. "We'd be delighted! It isn't every day a city floats over your home."

"Though anything indoors would be appreciated," one of the agriculture pursers adds. She has grey skin and pointed fangs, is wearing a cowl that casts her face in shadows, and has a strange narrow band fixed over her eyes. Echo calls her a dhampyr, informing me that they have trouble seeing in bright light and their skin is particularly sensitive to the sun. To be honest, they very much look like a vampire. Another species with features similar to Earth mythology! I have so many questions I wish to ask. But I suppose that can wait until we're all more familiar with each other.

"Of course, we'd be happy to accommodate," I say. "Let's get off this wall and make our way to the palace."

As we walk, Dizzi immediately inserts herself into the scholar group—yes, I am vaguely envious—and strikes up a conversation about rune research and theory. I'm sure she's interested to get her hands on any symbols that might have been lost to time for Fyrethians. Lord Merit, the noble whose house is involved with artificing, also drifts over to listen. Nek engages the agriculture group, who we're likely to do the most trade with, while Captain Marlowe continues to chat up me and anyone else who makes eye contact. He really is rather good at breaking the ice.

Mirzayael, for her part, remains largely silent except to answer any questions directly asked of her, which goes a long way toward retaining her imposing atmosphere. Our guests quickly recognize this and field any questions they have toward me, with glances toward Mirzayael that indicate they suspect she's the one actually in charge.

The assumption amuses me, but it also works out in our favor. Mirzayael, who is also entertained by the developing dynamic, will mentally reply to me any time she wants to add something, and I'll voice it as if it's my own thought.

"*They view you as an accessory to me,*" Mirzayael remarks, feeling a mix of flattered for herself and offended on my behalf.

"*It's because you're acting so mysterious,*" I tell her, still nodding along to Lord Calaman, who is explaining the local economic structure.

"*I'm not acting.*"

"*You're right, you're just naturally mysterious,*" I tease. "*But this presents us with an interesting opportunity. They probably believe I have your ear, and they might try to curry favor with me as a means to negotiating advantageous deals with you. We could use this to try to gain insight into what they really want from working with us.*"

Mirzayael glances down at me with a side-eye and faint smile. "*That's rather devious of you. Though for it to work, you'll need to play dumb, and I'm unsure you're capable of that.*"

"*I could!*" I insist, though honestly I think Mirzayael may be right. I'm already itching to join in on the artificing conversation. "*Who knows? It could be fun.*"

She chuckles. "*Don't let me stop you. But I give it two hours before they realize you're more clever than you're letting on.*"

We keep to the shade of buildings as we take the main road up to the palace entrance, and the handful of dhampyrs who have accompanied us gratefully drop their cowls and remove their eye pieces when we step inside. I don't lead them on a complete tour, of course—these are still strangers in our home, and it can't hurt to be cautious—but I take them to all the most impressive rooms available to the public. We stop by the great hall, where we'll be returning for lunch, and visit Yequirael and the textile group, who are operating out of an adapted ballroom. Our guests, and especially the scholars, marvel over the intricate tile work that decorates most rooms, and everyone seems delighted by the bathhouse, even though it's still only half-filled.

By early afternoon everyone is ready to break for a meal, and the group seems sufficiently loosened up and talkative. Nek sets about getting everyone situated in various meal circles as I step away to speak with the kitchen crew and make a few dietary requests.

The main kitchen is an impressively large room, though it's clear it wasn't originally intended to serve the main hall, but rather the smaller dining rooms immediately adjacent. Even so, I've shifted some doors around to cut a direct path between the kitchen and main hall, so servers only have to pass down one hallway and cut through one dining room to get there.

It's as I'm heading through this corridor that something snags my attention. I'm not sure if it was a flicker of motion or a faint rustle of sound, but it makes me stop. I'd just passed by an open doorframe, which leads into one of the palace's many unused rooms. I cock my head and hear nothing. Even so, I'm drawn back.

I pause in the doorway, blinking against the dark of the chamber. As my eyes adjust, my heart skips a beat as I'm alarmed to find there *is* someone there.

I can't make out any details, but since their attire is white, they show up readily in the room's shadows. They're standing at the opposite wall, about ten meters away. A shiver runs down my spine at the eeriness of it all. What are they doing, standing there alone in the dark? They still haven't moved. Are they attempting to hide?

With mounting unease, I decide to act first.

[Blaze activated.]

Fire bursts into my hand, light flaring through the room and chasing away all the shadows. The stranger whips around in surprise as my spell activates, and an unnatural breeze brushes past me.

"Fyreneth?" she asks, her voice full of fascination.

The name summons a lump in my throat. "You are mistaken," I say, frowning at the young woman. We hadn't told any of our guests that we were Fyrethians. I narrow my eyes. "What do you know of her?"

The woman is dressed in white and black—I think I recognize her as one of the scholars—and is wearing a pair of round, black-tinted glasses.

Her look of surprise melts into an easy smile. "My apologies. You bear an uncanny resemblance." She gestures to the wall behind her.

She's standing at the base of a life-sized statue of Fyreneth. Her features have been weathered away, but her name is still carved into the pedestal at its base.

The young woman appears relaxed, but this exchange has me on edge. "Why were you standing here in the dark?" I ask.

"Was I?" She laughs. "Then my apologies again. I was unaware, though I can see how suspicious that might look." She taps her glasses. "The wind helps me see many things, but light is not one of them."

The breeze I felt before stirs faintly around me, barely grazing my skin. I recognize it from all the times I've seen harpies do much the same: an air affinity.

Oh. She's blind. My unease fades into mild embarrassment. "No, I'm sorry. That was rather rude of me. You're with the scholars, correct?"

"That I am. Oh! But where are my manners?" She crosses the room, offering a hand. "I'm Lisari."

I clasp it. "Pleasure to—"

Something prickles at my mind the moment our hands make contact. It's a distant... *pull*. I can't describe it. The Dungeon Core notices, too.

What's this? It's making it *hungry*.

I let go of Lisari's hand, and the moment passes. The Dungeon Core looks around, confused. I've been knocked off balance, too.

"...meet you," I say faintly.

I Check her.

Echo pauses half a second before she replies. [Lisari: Level 21 Human Alchemist.]

"Well, I suppose I should head back to the others," Lisari says, oblivious to the odd sensation I just experienced. She steps around me. "Sorry for wandering off in the first place. It's just such a fascinating city. I can't wait to come back and explore it more thoroughly. I hope this will be the beginning of a rewarding relationship for the both of us."

She hums a pleasant tune as she strolls back down the passage toward the main hall, and I'm left staring at her back, baffled. Had I only imagined it? No—the Dungeon Core had noticed something, too. It wasn't in my head. But Echo hadn't reported anything strange. I'll need to keep an eye on her.

It isn't until she steps back into the main hall that I realize she never answered my question about Fyreneth.

Chapter Twenty-Six

TIME TO MAKE SOME MONEY

By the end of the day, everyone is exhausted, but in good spirits. We create some accommodations for a few of the ships to spend the night, though all but Captain Marlowe and the agriculture team depart. We all meet in the red room after dinner for a debrief.

"Lisari?" Dizzi repeats when I ask her if she'd spoken to the scholar. "Yeah, I chatted with her a bit. Pretty cool application of wind arcana. Must be way more advanced than what I use for her to be able to sense her surroundings with any level of detail. But I'd never thought to apply it that way!"

I'd discreetly informed Mirzayael of the encounter I'd had with the woman as soon as she'd left my line of sight. Mirzayael had kept an eye on her in my absence, but Lisari hadn't done or said anything strange after that. I'm beginning to doubt my own instincts on the matter.

"Did she ask about Fyrethians? Or Fyreneth?" I press.

Dizzi seems surprised. "What? No. Does she know?"

"She found a statue of Fyreneth and seemed familiar with her," I say. Familiar enough to mistake me for her. Or had that just been a coincidence, as I appeared right when she was examining the statue? I shake my head. "Perhaps you can do some gentle prodding tomorrow if she returns. In fact, we all should attempt to discern what these people know about us."

"The murals aren't particularly subtle," Nek says, leaning against a wall, arms folded. "I heard a few comments on the artistry, but none on the content."

"We could ask for history books," Torim suggests. "I realize currently we are trading for more practical supplies, but I'm sure at least the scholars would be willing to help."

"As long as we can do so subtly," Mirzayael says. "If they do harbor feelings similar to the Jorrians, we don't want to expose our history without cause."

My mind drifts to the two Jorrians downstairs. I wonder if they might be able to help with this, actually. Ragna would invite me to shove my request up facets of my anatomy. Luckily, she will be out of our hair by the time we leave Mount Haze. Gardi, however...

"I'll put some feelers out," Dizzi says. "It shouldn't be too hard to slip in, since Lord Merit and the scholars will be returning with some texts tomorrow. I asked if they could bring maps of any locations with ambient magic, so we could evaluate them as potential landing sites." Her feathers ruffle in excitement. "I can't wait to see what they've got!"

"Speaking of," Torim says, "we should prepare for what offers we can anticipate. I was mostly engaged with Lord Calaman, the banker." He looks to Nek.

"The agriculture guild appears open to working with us," Nek says. "They seemed interested in the textile group, but more so with our fertilization techniques. They spoke with Agate earlier, and he told them about the different additives his team uses to alter the acidity of the soil. They seemed interested in procuring some."

That wasn't a trade item I had been expecting. I had produced phosphorus for Agate to add to the soil to help lower the pH, as apparently the soil we currently have to work with is very basic due to all the limestone it had steeped in over the centuries. It makes sense that the agriculture team would be interested in additives that would help their produce.

But is soil in a volcanic city also basic? (Alkaline, if I remember my college chemistry.) Or was it acidic? If it's already acidic, then adding more phosphorus would only be damaging. Not to mention, I'd never considered refining these materials in large enough quantities to trade. I suppose I could, I'd just have to think about how we would store and transfer it all.

"Have them bring a sample of their soil as soon as they're able," I tell Nek. "I'll see what I can do."

We talk through a few more trade options that had arisen throughout the casual day of mingling, until Torim eventually brings it back to the banker once more. "There's one aspect we haven't yet discussed—a few of the others alluded to payment rather than trade. I spoke with Lord Calaman about this. There is local currency as well as regional currency. The local currency is a form of parchment with different denotations of worth marked on the leaves. The regional currency is traded in flat squares, most commonly made from bronze, copper, silver, and gold."

"You mean like, the metal?" Dizzi asks, seemingly confused.

"Yes," Torim says. "It appears the ore is considered highly valuable in this region. Though they don't trade with just the raw material; they're shaped a certain way and imprinted with designs."

"Huh."

I frown, mulling this over. "If we can, we should avoid accepting any of the local currency; it would be worthless once we move to other cities. I'm uncertain about the regional variant. While it could be useful for future trade, we still have immediate needs to attend to, and a ton of flour would be much more valuable to us at this moment than an equivalent weight in gold."

But the other Fyrethians appear more thoughtful.

"They would also accept these metals from us in exchange for goods?" Mirzayael asks.

"Yes," Torim says. "If they're shaped correctly."

Nek hums thoughtfully. He shifts his hand up and down, as if mentally weighing something. "How much would they trade for a kilogram of copper?"

Torim consults his notes. "A single coin seems to be a few grams. So... a kilogram of copper would be roughly five hundred copper coins. They mentioned a blueseed fruit costs one coin. So that would be quite a large crate of fruit."

The Fyrethians appear stunned.

"You're saying we could trade one large copper pot for enough fruit to feed everyone in the Fortress?" Mirzayael asks, baffled.

It finally sinks in what they're all talking about. The Fyrethians spent centuries living in caves, mining whatever materials they could from their surroundings. Most dwarves have a stone affinity, which helped them to form tools from the surrounding earth. While silver and gold is still fairly rare (though not absent) in Fyrethian society, copper makes up most of the cookware that we use in the city. Everything from bowls to cauldrons, and spoons to cups. And while these materials are useful to Fyrethians, they are so common they're mostly considered worthless.

Meanwhile, we served our guests lunch on plates *literally* made of money.

Dizzi whistles. "That's wild!"

"I suppose it explains how polite everyone has been," I say faintly.

"Of course, we will need to shape our metal into the shapes of their coins," Torim says.

"Is that something you could do?" Mirzayael asks me. "If we procured a few coins for you to use as examples."

"What?" the question startles me. "You want me to mint our own coins?"

"I mean, we have tons of copper to work with," Dizzi says, entirely unaware of my mounting discomfort. "That shouldn't be hard to reshape. But you can change the material of things too, right? Can you convert some of that stone in the Dungeon Core's Inventory to silver and gold?"

"I could," I say, hesitating. "Changing the elemental nature of matter costs mana. It would eat into the Fortress's reserves and reduce our flight time. But... doesn't this seem *wrong*?" I pleadingly meet everyone's gaze.

They all return blank looks.

"Why?" Mirzayael asks. "This is something they want, and we can provide it. It seems an ideal trade opportunity."

"Of course, but..." I have no idea how to articulate my instinctive aversion to printing our own money. I'd never really given it much thought before this moment. But printing your own money is clearly unethical, because... "It... it would be bad for the economy, wouldn't it? It could devalue the metal's worth."

The Fyrethians appear unfazed.

"One city's worth of copper could disrupt an entire economy?" Dizzi asks. She's not being critical, just curious.

"Probably not," I admit. We're only a few thousand in number, after all. The single city we're passing over likely has three or four times as many people as we do. And when you take the rest of the continent into account, our impact does seem pretty small.

But it's still *wrong* isn't it?

Isn't it?

But I'm struggling to see the harm. Our intention is not to become wealthy or powerful, but to feed our people. To secure our city and improve our quality of life. That makes it justifiable, doesn't it?

I need to reflect on this matter. No—I need to reflect on my own feelings on this matter.

"Alright," I say, rubbing a temple. "See if you can secure a few of the regional coins tomorrow, and I'll... I'll at least look into it."

Conversations wrap up not long after that, and as the night is growing late, the room disperses.

"Are you heading to bed as well?" Mirzayael asks.

"Soon," I tell her, scanning the day's notes. God, I can't wait until we have a disposable amount of paper at our fingertips. "Just a few more things I want to wrap up."

"Alright." She lingers in the doorway. "Though I have faith in my guards, I still am not entirely trustful of the outsiders who are staying with us. I would feel better if you did not sleep alone and unguarded."

I look up at her, raising an amused eyebrow. "Stationing guards outside our rooms seems a bit overkill. Then we really would feel like royalty, wouldn't we?"

Mirzayael doesn't appear to share my amusement. "That woman you mentioned before leaves me uneasy. Perhaps it was nothing, as you said, but on the off chance there is some deeper conspiracy afoot, I am willing to spend the night in your chambers to ensure your safety."

"And who will ensure your safety?" I tease, shaking my head. "Lisari left with the other scholars. I'm not concerned about any of our guests who stayed."

"If that is your wish," Mirzayael says. "Goodnight, Fyre."

"Goodnight, Mir." I smile fondly as she leaves the room.

I finish up my work and begin to descend through the layers of the palace. I'm halfway to the Jorrian cells when it abruptly hits me: Was she asking to spend the night with me?

I smack my forehead and drag my hand down my face. *Fyre, you fool,* I think. She wasn't even being particularly subtle about it—I'm just that boneheaded. I consider mentally reaching out to her, but I'm not sure what to say. Not to mention, I still have one last task to complete before I turn in. With a sigh, I continue my descent to the Jorrians.

There's a guard posted at each of their doors. I pass over Ragna's cell and ask to step inside Gardi's. The guard unlocks the door to let me in.

Gardi glances up in surprise when I enter. They're lying on the folded blanket I'd given them. Not under it, though; as I'd heard from many other felis, this palace feels unusually warm to them now that it's heated and we're out of the arctic. I might fiddle with the atmospheric spell settings to lower the temperature a bit, if that's what most Fyrethians would prefer. (Yet another task on my unending to-do list.)

"Hello, Gardi," I say as they sit up. "Have you been eating well?"

They give me a curious look. Not the same suspicious look they originally regarded me with, but perhaps a level of puzzlement. Beneath that, though, is an undercurrent of weariness. It's etched deep into the lines of their face.

"Yes," they say as I sit down across from them. "Yesterday I was given soup and greens—at least I think it was yesterday. I cannot keep track of time in this place."

Leftovers from the festival. Good, I wasn't sure if the guards would follow through on my request to send some of the excess to our prisoners. Somehow, we managed to produce more food for the feast than was eaten, so now we're in a scramble to reuse as much as we can before any of it goes to waste.

"Yes, that was yesterday," I tell them. "And right now, it's night. I'll try to get something installed in this passage to better simulate the natural light outside."

"Why?" they ask. Again, not suspicious, just wearily baffled.

"Because it would improve your quality of life," I say. I dig a package out of my bag and hold it out. After a moment, they gingerly accept.

"Have you decided what you want to do?" I ask them as they pick at the twine. "We are currently at Mount Haze, and we'll be dropping Ragna off in the city in the next few days. We could drop you off here, too."

They slowly shake their head as they unfold the wrappings. "She would not wish for me to accompany her. It would be best for me to give her that space." They peel open the package to reveal a brush and a small box. They tip their head. "What's this?"

"The brush I think is obvious," I say. I've noticed how meticulous some felis can be about grooming. "And that is a puzzle box. I figured you could use something to occupy your time. I'd rather offer you a book, but we don't have any yet."

Gardi stares at them for a moment, then up at me. "What do you want?"

"This isn't bribery," I tell them. "I understand how terrible the isolation must be. Without Ragna to talk to... Well, this seemed the only thing I could really offer."

Gardi sighs through their nose, and leans back against the wall. "I don't understand why you are offering such kindness. It's difficult for me to trust you. I still don't quite understand why you trust *me*."

I suspect there's nothing I can say that would change their mind at this point. But perhaps I can show them.

I hold out my hands, palm up. "Here. Let me show you why I feel the way I do."

They eye me suspiciously. "What do you mean?"

"I have a psionic spell that allows me to speak mind-to-mind," I explain. "It only works if we're in physical contact. If you won't believe my words, perhaps you will believe my conviction."

Gardi doesn't move. "You want me to submit to a mind spell? How do I know it's not mind control?"

I give them a disappointed look. "If I wanted to violate your autonomy, do you think I would be asking?" When Gardi still looks unsure, I soften my expression, offering an encouraging smile. "Trust me on this one thing, and I will not ask you to trust me on anything else."

Gardi stares at my hands for a long stretch of silence. I stay still, allowing them to think it through. I feel much like a child attempting to coax a frightened cat out from under the porch with a scrap of food.

"Okay."

They swallow, hesitantly reaching out a hand. I quickly segregate my Psionic Links so Gardi won't catch any of my mind neighbors' thoughts by accident. The felis's fur brushes against my palm as they carefully rest their hand on my fingers with the lightest touch.

[Psionic Touch activated.]

Gardi stiffens, their hair puffing up, as their mind timidly makes contact with my own. I don't say anything, careful not to overwhelm them, but simply open my mind and emanate a sense of warmth and openness, letting them venture forward at their own pace.

It takes some time, but they eventually do. I can feel their fear and uncertainty. Their guilt. Their regret. Thoughts of their family swim through their mind, dripping with heartache; they believe there is no going back. The thoughts are sharp and painful, and tears prickle at my eyes as I feel their emotions as if they were my own.

Gardi wanders through my mind, touching on an occasional feeling or memory. I don't give them access to everything; I retain knowledge of my interdimensional nature. But they find the feelings I still have for my daughter, who I'll never see again, and they find the warmth I feel for the people I've come to know here. They linger at my compassion and resolve, like warming themself before a fire.

Eventually, they pull away. They look down, scratching at their cheek before discretely brushing at one of their eyes. "I'm your prisoner," they finally say, voice hoarse. "You should see me as your enemy."

"Maybe we don't have to be enemies," I say. "And maybe you don't have to be a prisoner."

They look up with a weary frown. "What are you suggesting?"

"A second chance," I say. "You believe you won't be welcomed home. And you have no interest in leaving with Ragna. We could drop you in some far away city, if that's what you prefer—or you could stay with us."

Gardi looks at me like I've just grown horns and a goatee. "You want to free me? You want me to become a Fyrethian?"

"Perhaps in time," I admit. "But your actions against us can't be entirely dismissed. You would need to work for your freedom. Give back to the community. Earn your place among our people."

Gardi continues to stare for several seconds longer, then lets out a mirthless laugh, resting their forehead in their hands as they shake their head. "You are asking me to defect."

"I am asking you to keep an open mind," I say. "Perhaps we are not as evil as you believe."

"I don't believe you are evil, Lord Fyre," Gardi says with a sigh. "The gods have punished those undeserving of retribution before."

I tip my head, faintly surprised by this. I also wonder what other people they might be referring to. "If you don't think we're evil, then why are you set so firmly against us?"

"They're the *gods*." They look up at me. "For Jorria to view me as a traitor is one thing. For the Heavens to view me as a traitor is something much more."

"Is that how most of Jorria sees our subjugation?" I ask them. "Pitiable, but necessary to avoid the gods' wrath themselves?"

Gardi picks up the puzzle box, turning it over in their hands to avoid looking at me. "It's complicated. Varied. Outside of the clergy, most didn't even believe you were more than myth before we marched on your kingdom."

This is an interesting nugget to chew on. The two Jorrian representatives we'd interacted with, Biorne and Alis, had both been in the clergy. Were they *not* representative of the majority of the population? Or is that merely wishful thinking?

I suppose it doesn't matter anymore. "Is it similar with the rest of the world?" I ask, finally getting to the crux of why I came to speak to them. "Do they believe we are a myth?"

Gardi shakes their head. "I don't know. I've never left Jorria. *Had* never left. It wasn't something I ever talked with foreigners about. Though..." They pause for a long moment. "...Though if I were to guess, I'd suspect they've long forgotten. It was already fading from importance within our kingdom, and no one would have more reason to care than us."

This is potentially good news. If the rest of the world doesn't even remember Fyreneth, we have an opportunity to reinvent ourselves without the stigma of being marked by the gods. Indeed, everyone we've interacted with so far seem to know nothing of our history or treat us with any suspicion.

That doesn't mean we shouldn't continue to be careful, however. Things could still be written in history books; those with enough curiosity and determination would likely learn of our origins. The question is, what would they do with that information?

"Thank you for your insight," I say. "And consider my offer. You don't have to decide tonight. Though if you change your mind and would like to be dropped off in Mount Haze with Ragna—"

"No," they say firmly.

But they hadn't firmly said no to considering my offer.

"Just think about it," I repeat. "Whether or not you believe the gods will target us again, you're here now. You'll suffer the same fate as us. The question is, would you like to do something productive with your time while you're here?"

I push myself to my feet. "Rest well, Gardi. Please reach out through the guards if you need anything."

Gardi doesn't say anything else as I leave, and not for the first time, I wonder what I am doing. Mirzayael had asked the same: Why spend so much time and effort on one individual? I'm not sure myself. Maybe I just want to believe they've been misled, and their bigotry stems from an indoctrination of lies rather than true hate.

Or is there any difference if the outcome is the same? I don't know.

Maybe I just want to believe in second chances.

Chapter Twenty-Seven

GOOD RIDDANCE

Over the next few days, we gradually drift across and then away from Mount Haze. It's still within sight, but tonight the last of the airships will depart, and then we'll be alone floating over the wilderness. It seems our max stay for any one city is four days. We could spend more mana to fight the winds and hover over a city for longer, but we don't deem it practical right now. We need to make sure we have an idea of where we want to land and enough mana to get there before we burn too much of our reserves. Unfortunately, Mount Haze was not helpful on this account; hopefully we'll start to gather such information soon. It's been less than a month since we originally set sail, but I'm starting to worry a little.

The next major city, Hetopolis, is a week away, and we're told it doesn't have an airship port; the only airships that might be in the area would be transport from visiting cities. Luckily, we have one of Dizzi's cloudstone transport vessels made, and several more in the works. We can spend the next week testing them out before we arrive.

Not to mention, I might be able to head down to the surface myself this time.

Nek goes over several of the items we've traded for, spread across a table in the red room.

"Elf hair," he says, pointing to several long braids. "Dhamypr hair, and goblin hair. Shed skin from lamia, and shed scales from nereids. Wood grown from a dryad. There aren't any cambions or orcs in Mount Haze, so they couldn't help us there. There are a few halflings, but they didn't have enough hair between them, and weren't too keen on the idea of shaving anyway."

"Well done, Nek," I say, looking over our rather macabre spoils. "I can't imagine these were easy to ask for."

His ears droop. "You have no idea."

"Will it be enough?" Mirzayael asks. "There isn't as much goblin hair."

"The amount of matter the Dungeon Core needs to ingest for the species to be registered is dependent on the species' mass," I explain. "Some sort of ratio, it seems. So we don't need as much goblin hair as we would for, say, an orc."

Mirzayael ticks off her fingers. "We're still missing three species, then."

I nod. "Of the fifteen sentient species on this planet Echo has informed me of, I'd say we're off to a very good start."

"Well," Mirzayael says, "let's see what this much will get you."

"What's your current Role Range?" Dizzi cuts in as I'm reaching out for the first lock of hair.

I pause to Check it.

[Role Range: 3.51 km]

That's a smidge higher than it was last time. Is this a result of my connecting the weapons system to the throne? Or perhaps training with Mirzayael. (Thankfully, she'd put that on pause while we've been in the middle of trade negotiations, but I'm certain she'll restart the practice with great fervor once we leave the city and have more time on our hands. She's also alluded to Salvia or Dizzi joining in, so I could get some pointers from another harpy. I'm even less excited about that.)

I relay the stat to Dizzi, who jots it down on a slate.

"Okay," she says. "Ready. But do them one at a time so we can get data on each!"

"Good idea." I unnecessarily nudge the Dungeon Core, who has been hovering over my shoulder excitedly once it caught wind of what we were planning.

New things to eat! It hopes they taste good. It's sure it won't be as good as rocks, but sometimes new things can be interesting. Like the sea shells! Those were fun to eat.

Yes, I encourage it. *Just like candy.*

Recalling how it gagged down the harpy feathers and dracid skin, I carefully segregate the parallels between that and the current sampling of goods. It's all keratin, I think, and if it didn't like the ones before, it's probably not going to like this.

But to my surprise, the Core slurps down the elf braids like pieces of spaghetti. Hmmm! This is very odd. It needs to try more to decide if it likes it.

"Three point nine nine," I quickly read off before the Core eats the goblin hair next.

[Role Range: 4.43 km]

Then the dhampyr: 5.07 km

Then the lamia skin—

EW! The Dungeon Core shudders in my mind. Oh, no, it remembers this. It did not like this before. So gross!

Mirzayael snorts. *"But it ate the hair completely without issue?"*

"I'm pretty sure it's all in its head," I reply. *"Remember the spring water? As if it doesn't love sulfur when it's in rock form."*

"Five point eight two," I say, trying to tune out the Core's complaints. It starts retching for extra emphasis. I swear, this rock is more dramatic than any person I've ever known.

Come on, I tell it. *Only two more to go. Then...* I wrack my brain for any incentive I can offer it. It's a lot harder when we're not surrounded by stone it can chew on. *...I'll have Ollie go get some more shells for you.*

That perks the Core right back up. Yes, it would love more of the tiny crumbly rocks that shatter between its teeth in the most delightful way! It downs the nereid scales and dryad wood after that. The wood it's unsure about, but it surprisingly deems the scales acceptable. Honestly, who knows with the Core? Its preferences seem pretty inconsistent. Like a kid who will tell you something tastes bad based on what they *think* it will taste like rather than what it actually does.

"I missed the last one," I tell Dizzi. "But after those last two, I'm now up to seven point one three."

Dizzi scribbles a couple more notes. "Yeah, that makes sense. It's not a linear relationship. The more the Core eats, the more benefit it gives your range. Wow!" She looks up from her calculations with a grin. "We basically doubled it. That's great! I think the last three species will get you over ten kilometers."

That would be nice, but I'm already quite pleased with my current numbers. Not only can I now reach the ground, I'll have significant wiggle room to wander around on its surface.

"What are we at, about four kilometer's altitude? That means..." I get Echo to do some quick Pythagorean math for me. "I can range about five and a half kilometers from the Fortress while on the ground. That's over ten kilometers in diameter. That's fantastic!"

"The question is, how to increase it further," Dizzi muses. "After you get some biological matter from orcs, cambions, and halflings, we'll have hit the end of this source of range increase."

"More intense sparring sessions should help," Mirzayael suggests.

Dizzi looks up at us in delight. "You guys are sparring? Oh, I gotta watch that."

"What about the last two watchtower spell circles?" I ask Dizzi, coincidentally changing the subject.

"Those ones are interesting," she says. "Turns out they're not like the other two. What I'm calling Eye Tower has a spell that is less related to offense and defense and more... surveillance, we think. But we haven't been able to suss out the last spell tower yet. It's more complicated, and we don't know a lot of the runes that are used."

That dampens the mood. I dislike a surveillance system almost as much as a weapon system, but I can see the utility in both. If nothing else, I'll connect them to the throne just for the small boost in the Role Range I'll receive.

On the plus side, though, the feelers we've been putting out with regards to the public's perception of Fyrethians have been promising. We obtained a couple of history books from the scholar group, and most of those don't even mention Fyreneth's Fortress—or the Jorrians, for that matter. The only book where we found any mention of Fyreneth was a book about the Ruins, a collection of city remains that leak ambient magic into the world—like the Drifting Isles, which we had originally been mistaken for. While the Jorrians had insisted the Ruins were ancient cities destroyed by the gods, it seems this is not the prevailing theory elsewhere in the world. Fyreneth's city was mentioned briefly as potentially being another Ruin, though no ambient mana has ever been detected there, as its supposed location was too inhospitable for extended investigations.

I'm inclined to doubt her city is in fact one of these remains; we aren't a source of magic for one. If we were, our lives would be exceptionally easier. Additionally, the timeline doesn't seem to add up. Archeologists estimate the Ruins are nearly two thousand years old, while Fyreneth's city was founded—and fell—within the last one thousand years.

It seems we really have been given a fresh start, as long as we can avoid the fanatics in Jorria.

And, of course, the gods.

As the sun lowers toward the horizon, there is only one airship that has not yet departed. We gather at the docks to bid Captain Marlowe and his crew farewell.

"You've made me a rich man," he happily remarks, grinning as he clasps each of our hands in turn. "Hope to see you all around these parts again. Sure would love to continue doing business with you. I've sent some wyverns ahead to Hetopolis with some introductions, so they'll know you're coming."

"I appreciate it," I say. "We wouldn't have been able to do all this without you."

"Nay, you didn't need me," Marlowe says. He pauses before adding," But you wouldn't have done half as well!"

Mirzayael feels mildly offended, but I chuckle along with his boisterous laughter. He's probably right.

In the end, we were able to trade textiles, spell circles, ore (much to the Dungeon Core's remorse), and soil additives. In exchange we came out with some scrolls, loose papers, and an incredible amount of fruits and vegetables, including seeds to expand our own produce selection. Dizzi was delighted to gain a few new artificing books as well, which she's sharing with the spell circle research team, and I have gathered a sample of the regional currency, which I will probably start to duplicate on the way to Hetopolis, despite my discomfort.

Most importantly, though, is one item we were able to export.

A small group of Marlowe's crew escorts Ragna to their ship. She's no longer shackled, but from the way the crew walk tightly around her, it's clear she's not free to do as she pleases, either.

I feel uneasy about releasing her, even though it was my idea. I worry what she might tell others about us, and that they might believe her. After learning how the rest of the world seems to have forgotten Fyreneth, or at least indifferently relegated her to myth, I know I should feel better about letting the Jorrian go. Not to mention, Jorria itself has had plenty of time to warn the gods about us—if that's even something they can do—and they've not confronted us yet. So rationally, I know there is no danger in releasing her. But her obvious disdain, when she glares once more back at me before being walked onto Marlowe's ship, fills me with sorrow.

Perhaps it's not anxiety I'm feeling after all; it might be regret more than anything. I might be winning Gardi over, but we couldn't do the same for her. Which is the outlier?

"I have a parting gift for you," Captain Marlowe says, pulling me from my introspection. He holds out a small stack of letters.

"What's this?" I tease, accepting the bundle. "You want to be pen pals?"

"Each letter is spelled to deliver itself to my ship." He gestures for me to turn them over. On the other side are small, simple spell circles. "Write the letter and activate the spell, if you ever need to reach me."

"Thank you," I say, a little touched. "I'm sure we will be in contact again. You've been a great help. I'm not sure how we'll be able to make it up to you."

"Actually, I *do* have one last request for you all," Captain Marlowe says, grinning shamelessly. "I didn't make any promises, but I said I would ask."

Mirzayael scoffs. "And giving us a parting 'gift' right before asking for a request is completely incidental, I assume?"

"Amazing coincidence," he agrees, eyes crinkled in amusement. "There's a couple people who would like to stay." Mirzayael's eyebrows shoot up, and he makes a placating hand gesture. "At least just until the next city! They could take an airship back home after that. But it isn't every day a castle flies over your home, and you've stoked quite a few people's interest. I'm sure there's more they'd like to learn from you all, and I'd hazard a guess that there's more you could learn from them."

This certainly wasn't a request I was anticipating, though in retrospect, it is something we should have prepared for. Even if he hadn't made this suggestion to us today, our kingdom is sure to receive visitors in the future.

"How many?" I ask.

"Nine individuals," Captain Marlowe says. "A couple are scholars, one is from the airship guild, and the rest, frankly, are just intrigued. Two being my niece and nephew," he adds with a wink, "so I expect for them to receive special privileges."

I can tell he's joking with this last comment, but Mirzayael doesn't feel amused.

"*Spending the night is one thing,*" she says to me privately. "*But staying with us for a whole week? Perhaps more? This makes me uneasy.*"

"*I understand,*" I say. "*But it might not be a bad idea. He's right that it wouldn't hurt us to have people with us who are familiar with the area and customs when we reach Hetopolis. It would help us be more prepared. Besides, we'll need to start making accommodations for outsiders at some point.*"

"*Do we?*" Mirzayael asks, resignation setting in.

"Fine," she says aloud. "You can tell them they may stay. Just to Hetopolis, however. We will reevaluate their hospitableness from there."

"Fair enough," Marlowe says with a wide grin. "Glad to hear it. I'll go let them know, then. Lord Mirzayael. Lord Fyre." He tips his hat. "It's been a pleasure."

The captain saunters back to his ship as Mirzayael tells a few of her scouts to deliver a message to prepare a few rooms. She picks populated locations outside the palace, I notice. Not too close, but still in areas where people can keep an eye on our guests.

For Mirzayael, I consider this significant progress.

Our guests disembark with excited smiles and large travel bags—they clearly came prepared. I'm a little relieved to see that the scholar Lisari is not among them. Marlowe's relatives are a young felis woman and a young human man—at least now I don't have to wonder how these multi-species siblings came to be. They seem ecstatic to meet us, and even Mirzayael isn't impervious to their infectious enthusiasm.

As Marlowe's airship pulls away, and we turn to lead our visitors into the city, I can't help but feel this marks some kind of turning point. I have a feeling the empty streets and houses in the lower tiers of the city won't remain so for much longer.

Chapter Twenty-Eight

Mutual Dissatisfaction

"*I hope you know what you're doing,*" Mirzayael thinks.

"*Me too,*" I agree.

Her mind dances with amusement. "*That's not as encouraging a response as I was hoping for.*"

We're standing outside the prison cells. Ragna's door is open, her cell empty; just knowing she's gone makes me feel a bit less stressed.

Now, for prisoner number two.

"Are you ready to resume your duties?" Mirzayael asks Salvia.

The harpy stands straight and rigid, their eyes filled with fierce determination. "Yes, my lord."

"You will prevent the prisoner from endangering any Fyrethians," Mirzayael says.

"Of course."

"And you will prevent any Fyrethian from endangering the prisoner," she continues.

The briefest impression of doubt flickers over their face. "I understand. My lords, if I may..."

Mirzayael gestures for them to continue. "Go ahead."

Their gaze dips. "I wish to apologize for my previous actions. I should not have subverted your directive. That was... wrong of me."

"I don't blame you, Salvia," I say with a sigh. They look up with faint skepticism. "You were hurting. I'm sure you still are. You want justice for your father—there's nothing wrong with that.

"But justice has been served," I continue. "The ones who attacked your father were slain by Mirzayael and Ollie. The Jorrian behind this wall isn't responsible for what happened. They weren't in charge. They took no Fyrethian lives. The conflict is over. And just as you deserve a second chance, so do they."

Salvia blinks. "My lords?"

I pat Salvia on the shoulder. "Can we count on you to uphold your duties to protect anyone from befalling harm while Gardi is under your watch?"

They stand up straighter. "Of course."

"Good." I nod. "Unlock the door."

Salvia complies, swinging the door open and stepping aside. I duck into the room after them.

Gardi is in the corner, watching me. I'm sure they overheard the previous conversation, but that was the intention. The puzzle box I'd given them is nearby; it already appears solved.

"Want to stretch your legs?" I ask.

Gardi regards me skeptically. "What?"

"Stand up," I say, beckoning them on. "I'll not have you drown in your despair and slowly waste away in here. Let's go."

Cautiously, they push themself to their feet. I step back out of the cell and wait for them.

It takes nearly a minute for them to finally follow. They pause in the door and eye the open cell dubiously. Their gaze alights on Salvia, who glares at them before glancing away. Hesitantly, they step out.

"Salvia will be your guard," I tell them. "They will ensure no harm befalls you, and also ensure you don't try to hurt anyone else or attempt to flee. You'll stay close to them. Understood?"

Gardi appears extremely dubious of this proposal, but nods. "It doesn't seem there would be anywhere to run, anyway."

"That is correct," Mirzayael says shortly. Gardi looks at her, and the worry in their face deepens. The only interactions they've had with Mirzayael have been brief and blunt. Not to mention, she's much more physically imposing than me.

And emotionally imposing.

And verbally.

"Alright," I say, turning for the stairs. "Let's go."

We head down the hall and up a few floors, making our way to Yequirael's workroom. The arachnoid happily greets us, as I'd informed him of our arrival earlier that morning, and sets about taking Gardi's measurements and sorting through some pre-made clothes we have on hand.

Mirzayael, Salvia, me, and the dwarf healer Opal are possibly the only people in the Fortress who would recognize Gardi on sight. They've had other guards, of course, but few of them bothered to look at the prisoners (most made it a point not to) and Gardi had originally been brought in extremely battered and bloodied; the cleaned up felis I'm looking at today, without any Jorrian sigils or attire, would be indistinguishable from any other felis Fyrethian or visitor.

Except, perhaps, this one appears far more tired and nervous. And maybe a little emaciated; I should look into ensuring their rations are enough.

Yequirael has no problem finding something that fits, however, and by the time they've been dressed in clean, umber trousers and a burnt-orange tunic, they look like a completely different person.

"That should do it," Yequirael says, standing back to admire his work. "Compliments your tawny fur very well, I think. Anything else you all need?"

Gardi seems too disoriented to speak, so I jump in.

"No, I think this will do just fine. Excellent work, as always, Yequirael. Thank you!"

"Not a problem, dear." He smiles, checking Gardi over one last time. "Feel free to send any of the other visitors my way, too!"

I promise I will, and we step back out into the palace halls. Gardi's tongue finally seems to come unstuck from their mouth.

"Why are you doing this?" they ask.

That was exactly what Mirzayael had wanted to know when I pitched the idea to her. The motivation is in fact multifaceted.

First, we need to trial Salvia's admittance back into the guard. As much as Mirzayael is sympathetic to their motivations, she was extremely angry that one of her own had disobeyed her and subverted her authority. She had half a mind to permanently remove Salvia from duty, but that was only the anger talking; we both recognize the potential in the harpy, and if they are able to prove their trustworthiness going forward, I suspect they'll one day become Captain themself. Better to foster loyalty in the passionate than to punish and alienate them.

And of course, what better way to test their devotion to their position than to assign them to the very source of their original expulsion? If they prove themselves with Gardi, they can be trusted with just about anything.

Another motivation to the outing is to give Gardi the opportunity to experience our city. If we want to test the possibility of rehabilitation, they need to meet other Fyrethians and learn about who we really are. The visitors who are staying with us for the following week provide the perfect opportunity to do so; no one will be surprised by an unfamiliar face. It gives Gardi the opportunity to interact with Fyrethians without bias or suspicion.

Not to mention, of course, this will test if we can trust Gardi out of their cell.

"You can't expect to spend the rest of your life in that room," I reply to them. "Consider this a trial run. If it doesn't work out, well, we can always drop you off at the next city. Now come on. It's time for breakfast."

We meet up with the other visitors in the main hall. Mirzayael has assigned two guards to their group as well, but with a much more relaxed arrangement than the one between Gardi and Salvia. They've been instructed to look out for any signs of mischief, but otherwise act as guides for the visitors. I suspect Mirzayael picked Zakaiya and Rei because the two are young and friendly. (I also wonder if it might have to do with the fact that they are cultivating a proto-soul with their partner, Jasper, and Mirzayael wanted to give them a break from training so they could conserve their mana.)

Our guests excitedly greet us as we sit down for breakfast. We pick a meal circle that's larger than the leader one we typically sit at, so all fifteen of us can sit together.

Marlow's niece, Pip, and her brother, Alec, are especially excited to speak to me and Mirzayael.

"Uncle Marlowe told us so much about you!" Pip says, her black tail flipping back and forth like a cat ready to pounce on a toy. "What's it like living in a floating city? Where did you guys come from? What do you do with all the refuse?"

I'm sure Dizzi would love to answer that one.

"We're in the midst of a move," Mirzayael replies. "We won't be floating forever. Just as soon as we find an ideal landing location, we will settle there."

"That's so cool," Alec says. The young man shares the same dark eyes and warm brown skin tone as his sister's, but is a human rather than a felis. "What an amazing idea! Why pack up and walk when you can take your whole city with you? So, why *did* you decide to move? How are you able to levitate a whole city?"

"Our city was founded on a significant amount of cloudstone," I say. "It was just a matter of harnessing what was already there."

Luckily, they seem too excited that we're giving them any answers to be bothered by the ones we don't.

Korzo, the lamia who works in the airship industry, pays close attention to our conversation as well.

Echo, I think when Dizzi joins us with a bowl of traded fruit and excitedly jumps in at the next question. *How is Korzo able to hear our conversation? I thought lamia were deaf. Is he lip reading?* I've heard that can be difficult and taxing.

[Lamia have reduced hearing but are not deaf,] Echo says. [However, many lamia carry interpretation stones with them to ease communication. These can translate sounds into vibrations that map to different words.]

Even as she's explaining, I subtly look Korzo over until I realize his gloves are faintly glowing from the enchantments engraved on their backs. His fingers twitch faintly as he watches Dizzi, and I wonder if that's the device Echo was talking about. I'm extremely intrigued by the idea.

But he surprises me again when he jumps into the conversation with sign language. An emerald stone hanging from his neck starts speaking a moment later, repeating aloud the same words he's signing. I Check that as well.

[Translation stone,] Echo says. [Designed to translate from one language to another. In this case, it is translating Coastal Signs into Dunmorish.]

And now I'm even more intrigued. I make a mental note to talk to him about that later.

Gardi doesn't say anything over the course of the meal, but they're more than happy to accept whatever food is offered to them. After trading with Mount Haze, our meals have seen a notable increase in diversity. The cooks seem to be having a field day experimenting with all the new flavor combinations. Some, admittedly, are more successful than others, and I pass on the blueseed-and-moss juice when it comes by. But we also made off with a supply of dark beans which, when roasted and ground, create an impressively similar flavor to coffee. I'm not sure if these are caffeinated, but I'm more than happy to add the hot drink back into my morning routine.

Mirzayael finds it utterly disgusting. ("I might as well save time by eating dirt.") More for me, I suppose.

The meal passes pleasantly, and it's the first time since our festival's feast that I actually feel full. We offer the group a tour of the city after that; a couple of them already completed a circuit when they visited us earlier this week, but they're more than happy to experience it again, and we show them to a few new places they hadn't seen last time.

The Mount Haze residents assume Gardi is one of ours, while Fyrethians seem to assume they're a visitor. This works out fairly well, as they're mostly left alone to blend into the background of our ensemble. Salvia keeps close to their side, of course. I also keep a side-eye on the two, and I can feel Mirzayael doing the same, but by the end of the day, there have been no incidents. Everyone is happy—well, except for Salvia and Gardi—and we discuss plans tomorrow for the visitors to shadow different Fyrethians, depending on their interests, before we turn in. Salvia takes Gardi back to their cell, and then a guard is sent to relieve Salvia so they can have the night off before we all start again tomorrow.

The next few days pass in much the same way. We meet up with the visitors for lunch and dinner, and they wander around the city during the day, working with Agate in the fields, or studying how Yequirael has incorporated metal filings into his silk to create lightweight armor, or sharing recipes with the cooks in the royal kitchen.

In the evenings, after our visitors have turned in, Mirzayael drags me down into the unused halls for more sparring practice. And by sparring practice, I mean her wiping the floor with me. She insists I'm getting better, but I suspect she's mostly trying to flatter.

"I do not flatter," she says, catching the thought as she pulls me to my feet. "What would be the purpose of lying to you about your combat ability? That would only set you up for failure in the field."

"Well, there is always the fact that we're courting," I point out, settling back into the defensive stance she'd shown me. "I've heard flattery can earn you points."

Though, despite our conversation the previous week, we haven't had much time or opportunity to explore our new relationship. Nothing particularly feels different from how it did before. I still feel affection for her, of course, and I often feel similar fondness directed back at me, but we've been too busy with everything else we've been juggling to do anything as a couple—or talk about it, even.

Mirzayael pauses. "I've not had practice in this area, admittedly."

"Really?" I ask, a little surprised. "No one?"

"Just one," she amends, raising her fists. "Long ago." She's crouching so we're closer to eye level. She steps forward, throwing a punch, fast but obvious. I practice the move she showed me, stepping out of the way and grabbing her wrist. I struggle for a moment with the pressure point. She makes this look so easy!

"Is it someone I'd know?" I ask.

Mirzayael, twists her wrist and repositions my hands with her free one, showing me where I'm supposed to push. "Possibly. A dracid named Tautus."

I wrack my brain. "The water purifier who works for Torim? That grumpy old man?"

Mirzayael smiles out of the corner of her mouth. "He was not old when we courted." She pauses. "Though he was still grumpy."

I chuckle. "I can imagine your personalities didn't feed into each other very well."

"No," she agrees, stepping back to reset and let me try again. "It was a brief and unhappy relationship."

"And that was it?" I wonder. "Until me?"

She nods, then punches once more. I step aside, deflect, and twist. This time, she bends away when I press on the back of her wrist. Aha! That's better.

"I didn't let people get close," she admits. "I... closed myself off to many. Nek was a friend from childhood. He's the only one who I managed to stay friends with after my parents' disappearance. Though the effort was largely one-sided, I'm ashamed to admit."

I smile softly. "I don't think he blames you for that." We go through a couple more moves Mirzayael wants me to practice. "So if you didn't pursue relationships after that, did you ever consider making a child on your own?"

"No," she says without hesitation. "I was dedicated to my position, and my low mana reserves means it would have taken years to cultivate one on my own. And... I didn't want to bring a child into our community. The world was too harsh, and I wouldn't have been able to provide them the warmth they deserved. Had I known they would have the opportunity to move back into Fyreneth's Fortress..."

I wait, but she doesn't continue. Maybe she's still not sure what her answer would be.

That's okay. It's not my intention to pressure her.

I pause to stretch and groan, shaking out my aching muscles.

"We can stop for the night," Mirzayael says. "It does no good to overwork yourself."

"The same is true mentally, you know." I continue to stretch out my arms and legs. "I see how many hours you spend working on the Fortress's logistics. I don't know how you manage to squeeze guard drills in with everything else you do."

"It's work that needs to be done," she objects. But she considers my words. "Though perhaps you're right that we both could use a break. It would be to the benefit of no one if we both burned out."

I straighten up, brushing dust off of my clothes. I always feel filthy after these sessions. I would love to go for a bath right now if I weren't so exhausted.

A bath.

"Ah! I have an idea."

Mirzayael looks at me questioningly.

"Perhaps we can find an excuse to mix the work with leisure," I tell her. "A new activity for our guests. But also, an opportunity for us to relax. And perhaps spend some quality time together."

"What would you propose?" she asks.

"Dizzi said the spell circles are functional, and Torim confirmed the pools have all now been filled." I grin. "Tomorrow, we open the bathhouse to the public. I think it's high time we have a pool day."

Chapter Twenty-Nine

Every Book Needs a Pool Day

At the very least, the guests and I are excited about the bath house. Mirzayael, Gardi, and Salvia are significantly less delighted.

"I've ensured all the water levels are low enough to be safe for all species," I tell her that morning. "No one is in any danger."

"I'm not worried about drowning," she says. "I'm worried about the Jorrian."

I raise an eyebrow. "What exactly do you think they'll do in a swimming pool?"

"They have ice abilities," she says. "They could freeze us all in the water."

I'm pretty sure they could already do that without being in the water, but I decide it won't help my case to point this out. "And then what?" I ask.

"Then... they could attempt to escape."

"Where to?" I ask.

"Or they could use the opportunity to try to hurt us," she says, pivoting.

"Then I'll use my fire to thaw the ice and stop them." I take Mirzayael's hands to stop her from worrying them. "Come on, Mir. You know that as long as anyone is within the Dungeon Core's area of influence, they don't really pose a threat to us."

She sighs. "I just don't know how I'm expected to relax with a Jorrian there."

"Let Salvia worry about that," I say.

As we make our way to the bath house, we pick up some silk towels and robes from Yequirael. They're not towels like I'm used to, fluffy and thick: these are wide and thin, much more like tablecloths. I guess Fyrethians haven't yet discovered whatever technique is needed to make the thick, fluffy type of towel I'm used to from Earth. I wonder if anywhere else in the world has it figured out. That's certainly not something I would be able to help with.

We don't have bathing suits, so it's clear we'll all be swimming in the nude. No one seems surprised or bothered by this, so I try to conceal my own discomfort. I'm used to naked bodies from locker rooms, but I've never been in a co-ed type situation before. For a world with normalized gender and sex equality, where one can be in a relationship with any person (or persons) they like, this shouldn't be surprising. I guess it's time for me to catch up.

Even so, I self-consciously slip into a robe after I undress in the first chamber, and I continue wearing it as we head deeper into the bath house.

"Gorgeous!" Pip exclaims, turning in a circle as she takes in the mosaics that cover the walls and floor in the steamy room. At least she's covered in cat-like hair, so there's not much for me to see. I keep my eyes raised over the heads of all those in attendance.

"Can we use any of them?" Alec asks. The bathhouse is a network of rooms connected with open doorways, some larger or smaller, some featuring a collection of private baths, or giant communal pools.

"Go ahead," I tell him, still watching the ceiling. Alec is your standard mostly-bald human, which leaves little up to imagination. "The room with the orange tiles has hotter pools, and the ones with blue tiles are for cooling off. Otherwise, please help yourself."

The group of visitors happily chatter with one another as they spread out and explore.

"*Are you alright?*" Mirzayael privately wonders. "*You feel bothered.*"

"*It's nothing,*" I insist.

Mirzayael feels deeply skeptical.

"*It's a 'me' problem,*" I add. "*I'll be fine once we're in the water. Come on!*"

Gardi and Salvia stick close to us; I'm not really sure which one of them is even following the other at this point. But it's probably for the best to keep them close anyway. The four of us pick out a steaming pool that's about a meter deep—shallow enough that Mirzayael should be able to submerge up to her chest while seated. While the others hesitate at the edge, I quickly disrobe and step into the pool. Any lingering embarrassment is immediately washed away as the warmth embraces me. I let out a long, content sigh, sinking into the water until it's up to my neck.

Mirzayael chuckles. "You sound like you've needed this for a while."

"I certainly have."

I glance back in time to see her stepping down into the water. She doesn't seem as hesitant this time, likely because it's much shallower, and the way all her legs work in tandem to lower herself down is surprisingly graceful. I'm briefly struck by the intensity and sheen of her black carapace—she's usually covered in practical garb or armor, and seeing so much of her midnight-dark shell now is mesmerizing. I quickly tear my eyes away and sink further into the water, blowing bubbles from my nose as heat rises up my face.

"Oh, so that's what this is about," Mirzayael says, settling into the pool next to me with a teasing smirk. She must have caught wind of my thoughts after all. "It's not the first time I've seen you naked, you know."

"What? When!" I drift back to give her more room as she settles all her legs about her. Gardi tentatively steps into the opposite end of the small pool, and Salvia dutifully follows them.

"When we first met," she says, her eyes dancing with amusement. "When you showed up in the caves before me, you weren't wearing any clothes."

I laugh, partially from embarrassment. "I'd forgotten about that." I try flexing my wings, and find the sensation of them pushing through the water very odd. They'll help me float, I recall from when I had first gotten the Dungeon Core to absorb the spring water in Ollie's cave, but I'm not sure how they will help or hinder me if I try to swim.

"It was surprising, given how cold the caverns were," Mirzayael continues. "But you know, you don't have to feel so self-conscious about it."

"I know," I say. "It's a bit of a holdover from my culture. I'll grow used to it."

"Oh." Mirzayael is faintly surprised. "It's nudity in general that bothers you?"

"Yes." I frown. "If you weren't assuming the same, then what did you mean?"

Her smirk fades to a kinder smile, and beneath the water she runs a hand through the feathers of my wing. "I thought it was less cultural and more personal. That you were ashamed of your body in some way. I know it is still new to you. But I wanted to assure you that you have nothing to doubt." She bashfully switches to thoughts. "*You're beautiful.*"

The words seize my heart and sting my eyes. I didn't realize how much hearing that would affect me. Captain Marlowe had said the same the week prior, but that felt different—an attempt at flattery. This, though, this is genuine, and coming from Mirzayael, it means all the more.

"It is still new to me, in many ways." I find her hand that's playing with my feathers, and lace my fingers through hers. "But in a good way. I'm not ashamed of this body. It feels more *me* than the body I had in my lifetime before. But to hear the words from you, it means..." I don't need to explain what I'm feeling. She can feel it.

Mirzayael gently pulls me in. Beneath the water, our bodies clumsily bump into one another, and I chuckle, laying a hand on her abdomen to steady myself. Her free hand goes back to playing with the feathers in my wing. It's soothing, like having a hand run through your hair. I lean my head on her shoulder, close my eyes, and rest that way for a time. Warmth and peace roll through me.

Eventually, some of my muscles start to cramp, so I stir, turning around so my back is to her stomach. I stretch my wings to either side, then experiment using them to tread water as I let my feet float up. Mirzayael's hands are clasped loosely around my stomach, my head on her chest. She gently rests her chin on top of me.

Finally. It took this long to feel as if we're able to exist as a couple, rather than coworkers. I'm not sure where the relationship will lead from here, but in this moment, I'm more than content.

The next moment I realize Gardi and Salvia are staring at us. That's saying something, considering Gardi typically attempts to avoid all eye contact, while Salvia doesn't take their eyes off the Jorrian for more than a few seconds at a time.

"If we're bothering you, you're more than welcome to move to a different pool," I tell them, amused. "You're not required to stay with us."

They both hurriedly glance away, and Mirzayael's chest rumbles with a quiet laugh.

"Apologies, my lords," Salvia says. "I didn't mean to bother you."

"You didn't," I assure them. I glance up at Mirzayael. "Perhaps we should practice showing more affection in public. So everyone can get used to the idea."

Mirzayael shrugs. "Everyone already assumes we are courting."

"They do?" I ask, surprised. I hadn't told anyone about the conversation Mirzayael and I had, and her talking about it with someone is even less likely.

"You can thank Dizzi and Nek for that," she says. "They've been spreading rumors for weeks now."

I laugh. That does make sense.

Gardi has returned to watching us, though this time I can tell they're trying to work themself up to say something. They haven't said two words to me in the last several days that Salvia has been accompanying them around the palace with the other visitors. I'm curious to see what it is that they're willing to speak about now.

They finally seem to summon the courage. "You arrived here naked?"

Mirzayael and I burst into laughs.

"I did," I admit. Salvia is paying attention now, too; they weren't there when I first arrived, so they wouldn't have known. Of course, everyone in the kingdom knows I came from the outside, but only a select few know about my reincarnation and prior life. Given the belief that phoenix harpies can reincarnate, and my similarities to Fyreneth, we decided that was one rumor we didn't want to throw fuel on.

Instead of pressing me on why I wasn't wearing any clothes, however, Gardi has a different question. "Then you're not a Fyrethian?"

"Not originally," I admit. "But being born here isn't what makes someone Fyrethian." I shift my gaze to Salvia. "The lost colony was separated from us for hundreds of years, and they're still Fyrethian. It's not about birth, it's about..."

"A vision," Mirzayael says.

"Values," Salvia says.

"A home," I agree with them. "They took me in with open arms. Well." I side eye Mirzayael teasingly. "Most of them did."

She blows air out her nose in protest, but she's smiling.

Gardi falls silent again after that, but they also let themself relax, resting against the side of the pool. Even Salvia seems to be a bit more at ease.

After a while we switch rooms, finding the others in the large community pool. I can't remember the last time I felt this carefree. We'll certainly have obstacles to face when we reach the next city, but it's nice, at the very least, to have this time to decompress.

The last few days of our trip pass without event. One of the scholars floats the idea of staying longer, as he's enjoying working with Dizzi on artificing theory, and Mirzayael actually seems open to it. She seems more open to a lot of things these days.

As Captain Marlowe predicted, the next city, Hetopolis, doesn't have any airships, so we put Dizzi's floating cargo carriers to the test. We're still too far out for me to land, but in the next two days we'll be within range so I can visit with public officials.

Before I have a chance to go visit them, however, they're more than happy to visit us.

Word of the Fortress is spreading. There's a handful of individuals from nearby villages who came to see us. I wonder if Captain Marlowe sent letters to more than just Hetopolis. Well, we always knew our presence wouldn't be subtle. I guess we'll have to start getting used to the fame. Better than notoriety.

On the third day, Hetopolis has grown from a distant smudge on a field of green, to a sprawling metropolis. Out on the docks, I'm preparing to accompany Ollie down to the city. The previous day we used Dizzi's transportation shuttles to bring more visitors up to the Fortress, and now they'll be returning down with us once more.

Mirzayael is fussing over me.

"I'll be fine," I promise her. "I've double checked all the measurements. And Ollie will be there to protect me if anything happens. You know, we could always adapt Ollie's harness to fit your physiology."

"No," she hurriedly objects. "That's not necessary. Besides, one of us should remain in the Fortress at any given time."

She's probably right about that.

As we're packing supplies (and coins) onto the transports, a familiar voice catches my attention. I'm not sure where I recognize it from until I find its owner.

"...Now *please* do behave yourself. I can't abide you causing any trouble in this magnificent city. Have you met her yet? Not to worry, I can introduce you!"

It's Lisari, the scholar from Mount Haze. She's talking to another woman, this one a felis with calico markings. I frown. How did she get here? Was she one of our guests? I don't recall seeing her arrive. And why wouldn't she have greeted me when she did?

I make my way over to Lisari and the stranger. I Check the second woman for clues, but don't receive much.

[—]

[Blair: Level 20 Felis Paladin]

I frown. That was odd. It was like Echo glitched for a moment.

"Oh!" Lisari turns my way with a smile when she notices my approach. "Lord Fyre! It's great to see you again. I'd like to introduce you to my friend, Blair."

The felis regards me sternly and doesn't offer a hand to shake; I don't either. Something about the two is setting me on edge.

"Welcome to our city," I say to Blair. My gaze shifts back over to Lisari. "How did you get from Mount Haze to Hetopolis before us?"

"Oh, I took an airship," Lisari says, smiling broadly. "Had to go pick up my friend first. I just couldn't wait to show her what you all have accomplished. She was so excited to see it for herself!" She claps Blair across her shoulders, and the felis doesn't react. She gives Blair a friendly shake. "She was so excited to see it for herself!"

"Indeed," Blair belatedly agrees, without any hint of excitement.

"I don't recall you two coming aboard," I say.

Lisari waves her hand about as if the question is frivolous. "Oh, I didn't want to bother you. But if you are offering another tour today, I'm sure Blair would just *love* to accompany you."

"No," I say slowly. "We're about to head down. When did you say you arrived?"

"Oh, with the last group," Lisari says.

I Check both of them again, just to be sure, but Echo doesn't have anything more to say.

"*Mirzayael,*" I reach out to her. "*Something's wrong.*"

"*What is it?*" she asks, immediately alert.

"*Can you check the visitor logs?*" I ask. "*We have some unexpected passengers.*"

"*Stowaways?*" she asks. Out of the corner of my vision, I can already see her talking to one of her guards.

"*I'm not sure,*" I admit.

"Well, we'll get out of your hair," Lisari says after my extended silence. "I'm sure you've much to take care of. It's been a delight to speak with you again."

I look at the Dungeon Core Map Interface as she talks.

I blink.

I zoom in further, double checking the dots on the map. I glance around my surroundings, then back at the map.

There aren't any markers where Lisari and Blair are standing.

But human and felis are in the Map's database. The only reason they wouldn't populate, is if...

"What are you?" I ask as Lisari starts to pull away. My fingers tingle as I prepare to summon a flame. Is it an illusion? Shapeshifting? Something else?

"Pardon?" Lisari says, tipping her head.

"What are you really?" I repeat, lowering my voice. Mirzayael is headed back our way.

Lisari laughs, and the sound sends a shiver down my spine. "Oh, she's good."

She turns to Blair with a grin. Somehow I can tell this is a *real* smile, not something rehearsed. Even her tone of voice has shifted from something practiced to something more threatening and sharp.

"Didn't I tell you this would be fun?"

Chapter Thirty

PLAYING WITH FYRE

My stomach is cold with dread. I don't know who these people are, but they're clearly not supposed to be here—and I wasn't supposed to notice anything was wrong. What do they want? Are they Jorrian? I need to get them away from everyone else. If something happens, I can't let anyone get hurt.

"*What's going on?*" Mirzayael asks, picking up on my fear. "*What is it?*"

At the same time, Ollie bursts into my mind. "*FYRE! ECHO SAYS YOU'RE IN DANGER.*"

A chill runs through me. "*Ollie, stay where you are. These people aren't what they seem.*"

Lisari laughs, draping her arm around Blair. "Now, now. Let's not be hasty. I brought you here to meet her, not smite her."

Smite? The chill crystalizes into ice.

Blair glares at her. "Enough of your games. She was not fooled. The time for passive observance has expired."

"Oh, don't be like that," Lisari says. "Surely you see there's no harm in chatting? It's not like she's going anywhere. How did you figure it out, by the way?"

I unstick my tongue from the top of my mouth. "I could see…" I stop myself before I say anything else. They don't need to know about the Dungeon Core or Echo, and my explanation wouldn't mean anything to them anyway.

Or would it? I Check them again, and again it seems like Echo hesitates for a fraction of a second before responding. My alarm is mounting. Are they affecting the System in some way? How is that possible?

"Our stats?" Lisari suggests when I don't finish my sentence. "That's odd, I thought we had them locked."

And for a moment, for just the briefest second, her numbers change. It happens so fast, I almost think I imagined it, and though I couldn't take in all of them at once, I did manage to glimpse one change: her level briefly flickering to 100.

A pit sinks in my stomach. Between Lisari's amused indifference and Blair's cool scrutiny, from all the clues they've already let slip, what they are seems as obvious as it is unbelievable.

"You're… gods."

It would be a ridiculous conclusion in any other circumstance. But at this moment, my instincts are screaming at me that I'm in danger, and faced with the presence of these two, the idea suddenly doesn't feel so far-fetched.

Lisari grins, snapping her fingers as she points at me. "Got it in one."

And then their stats change—permanently, this time. Their HP and Mana skyrocket. Their levels flicker and are replaced with 100.

Their classes change—and Roles appear. The only thing that stays static is their names.

[Name: Blair]

[Title: God]

[Class: Temporal Paladin]

[Level: 100]

[HP: 15,000/15,000]

[Mana: 9,000]

[Role: High Partitioner]

Unlike Blair, however, Lisari's name also changes:

[Name: Shirasil]

[Title: God]

[Class: Anarchic Alchemist]

[Level: 100]

[HP: 10,000/10,000]

[Mana: 11,000]

[Role: The Inquisitor]

My stomach falls through the ground as I take in their real stats. I feel frozen in place.

"*Mirzayael, stay back,*" I hurriedly tell her. "*Stop!*"

"*What?*" she asks. "*Why? Fyre, tell me what's going on!*"

"*FYRE, WHERE IS IT? WHERE'S THE DANGER? I CAN'T FIND IT!*" Ollie's voice is starting to sound panicked, and my heart squeezes.

I'm hyper aware of all the people around us. Everyone is so vulnerable and exposed. I need to get the gods away from them. From Mirzayael and Ollie.

"Please," I say, keeping my voice steady. "Can we move somewhere more secluded? No one else has to know."

Lisari pats Blair's arm. "See? We can still be civil. It's just a chat!"

Blair holds my gaze for a long moment. There's a calculating look in her eyes. It's not hard to guess which one of them is triggering Ollie's Role Requirement. But if this goes on any longer, he's going to suffer.

"I have someone dependent on me," I try again. "If I'm endangered, it causes them pain. Please, I don't have time to explain, but—"

[Your Role has been identified,] Echo abruptly says.

Blair glances around the dock. Her gaze lands on Ollie a moment later. "The dragon. I see."

She shrugs Lisari's arm off her shoulder and shakes her head with a sigh. "Fine. We may speak somewhere more covert."

"*OH!*" Ollie says. "*IT STOPPED. THAT WAS WEIRD!*"

Mirzayael reaches us, spear drawn. "What's going on?" she demands.

"Don't," I tell her, holding out a placating hand. "Put the weapon away. None of us need to escalate anything."

Blair's gaze flickers over Mirzayael and almost as quickly glances away, as if her presence is inconsequential.

"This is getting a bit crowded." Lisari reaches out, and even as I'm taking an instinctive step back, her fingers brush against my shoulder.

The sky vanishes, replaced by stone walls. Disorientation washes over me as I stumble away from Lisari. She and Blair are standing exactly where they had been before, as if we haven't moved, but rather the world shifted around us.

"*Fyre!*" Mirzayael's voice cries in my head, panicked. "*Where are you? What did they do? Are you alright?*"

"*I'm in the throne room,*" I reply, heart nearly beating out of my chest. Mirzayael didn't come with us. It's only me, Blair, and Lisari. At least they didn't bring Mirzayael along; if something happens to me, the city still has Mirzayael. I try to hold onto that nugget of comfort.

"*I'm coming,*" Mirzayael promises.

"*No!*" I object. "*Stay away. Don't let anyone near.*" Even as I tell her this, I'm speaking with the Dungeon Core, asking it to seal the room's doors and windows. It joyfully complies, and rock slams down in every opening.

Blair glances at the nearest door that's now become a wall of granite. "If you think this will contain us, you have sorely misjudged the situation."

"It's not to keep you in," I say. "It's to keep others out."

Lisari laughs, spinning away from the two of us. "I told you she was smart, didn't I?"

"*Fyre, what are you doing?*" Mirzayael demands. "*Talk to me!*"

"*I don't know what—*" I can feel my composure crumbling. "*I'm sorry. I need a moment to think.*" Panic and fear threaten to well up inside me, but I fight them back down. These are gods. Actual gods. What do they want? Are they here for the Fyrethians? Will they attempt to destroy everyone I care about?

Could I even stop them? I'd have to try.

There's too much to parse, too much I need my complete focus for, to be distracted by secondary conversations. "*I'm going to throttle my connection with you and Ollie so I can focus,*" I tell Mirzayael, desperately attempting to maintain my calm. "*Please don't let anyone attempt to reach me.*"

"*Fyre, don't—*"

"*I'm sorry.*" Guilt squeezes my heart as I tune her out. I don't have much time to dwell on it, however, when I realize Lisari is heading over to the throne. A growing pressure is pressing at me the closer she gets. The Dungeon Core can feel it, too. Actually, I'm the one feeling it through the Dungeon Core. It doesn't hurt, but it's... unsettling. It's making the Dungeon Core agitated.

"Stop," I say, taking a step her way. Blair moves between me and Lisari. But she does stop.

"You can feel it?" Lisari asks. "Interesting. I didn't think a Pact would be enough."

Blair speaks over her shoulder. "We should take it and be done."

"No!" I object. Fire licks at my fingers with the beginnings of a Blaze, but I snuff the flames out. The last thing I need to do is antagonize them. "It's keeping this city afloat. Without its control, we'd fall. Everyone would die."

A hint of surprise flickers over Blair's stony face. "You're able to harness its power for such things?"

"Yes," I hurriedly reply. Anything to keep her focused on me. Anything to keep her talking. The more time I can buy, the more time I'll have to think of a solution. Come on, Fyre, think. Think! "All the spell circuits in this city operate through magically conductive ore. By regulating the amount of mana that is stored in the cloudstone, we can control its lift. We also use it to monitor all the control surfaces in order to manage our heading, pitch, yaw..."

"You can monitor so much information at once?" Lisari asks, sounding genuinely curious.

"No." I try to keep myself steady. Calm. Focused. "I set up self-correcting feedback loops in the spell circuits."

Lisari barks out a laugh. "This is wonderful! How did you have the time to design such a complex spell network?"

Despite her laughs and smiles, I still feel as tense as a compressed spring. Blair continues to watch me with that appraising look—not a glare, exactly, but like she's trying to decide something about me. I hope I meet whatever standards she's judging me by.

"I didn't," I reply to Lisari. "The vast majority was already built into the kingdom. I just plugged some new hardware into the computer."

"Computer?" Blair asks.

"Oh, um. It's like a complex system of logic gates."

Blair turns to Lisari, and despite her shaded glasses, they seem to share a look. I try not to react. *What? What did I say? What part of that was significant?*

"You worked with these computers in your world?" Blair asks.

My world. How much do they know? "I did," I say carefully.

"See?" Lisari is addressing Blair. "That's at least *one* good reason not to partition her."

I don't know what that means, and I'd love to not find out.

"But your world doesn't have magic," Blair continues.

How does she know all of this? "No, it didn't. I've leaned on the knowledge of others since... arriving here."

"Dizzi, right?" Lisari says. "I like that girl. Sharp as a needle. She'll do big things one day, mark my words. Why, I've half a mind, too..." Blair shoots a look at her, and Lisari holds her hands up with a laugh. "Calm down! It was just a joke. I've already got plenty on my hands as it is. I tell you, these Travelers can be more trouble than they're worth."

"Is that why you haven't already recruited this one?" Blair asks.

"What, Fyre?" Lisari asks. She waves a dismissive hand, turning away from us to curiously circle the throne at a more respectful distance. "She's too measured. Not really my type. You might like her, though, if you stopped posturing like some kind of Lorata-wannabe."

Blair bristles, and I'm overcome with an abrupt sense of impending doom. But the tension gradually leaks from Blair's stance, and when she returns to considering me, it's with less hostility and more curiosity.

I take a steadying breath as an overwhelming array of emotions continue to wreak havoc in my head. I can't function like this. I need to focus. Mentally gathering all my feelings like an armful of flowers, I wrap them up, box them away, and push them toward the peripheral of my conscience. The panic dulls slightly. There. That's better.

Mind still racing, but now with a more controlled clarity, I attempt to assess the situation. These *are* gods. But they don't seem to view Lorata with high regards, and she was the one who ostensibly attacked Fyreneth all those years ago. An enemy of my enemy?

Too soon to tell. I try to pull everything else I know together.

They know about me and Ollie. They know about Earth. They took me, but not Mirzayael.

A small piece of the picture abruptly slides into focus.

"You're not here for the Fyrethians," I realize. "You're here for me." They didn't come after me because I was a leader, they came after me because I'm from Earth. But—no, that can't be all of it. They're ignoring Ollie.

For now, at least.

"Another excellent deduction," Lisari says. "You're on a roll. Make it three in a row, and I'll give you a prize."

"Ah, no thanks," I decline before I can think better of it.

Blair snorts, a faint smile pulling at her lips. That's the first positive reaction I've gotten from her so far.

Luckily, my response summons another laugh from Lisari and not her ire. "Rude! But wise. See, Blair, this is what I'm talking about. I don't need that kind of energy in my life."

Lisari really *does* seem to be treating this all like a game, or at least some form of entertainment. Blair worries me, but she also strikes me as more direct. Yet, they both appear to not be entirely aligned with the head of the pantheon, and I'm not sure if that should worry or reassure me.

If nothing else, it presents an opportunity to peer behind the curtain.

"How many more are there?" I ask, taking a chance. I don't expect Blair to reply, but Lisari appears to have loose lips. "People like Ollie and I. Are they alright?"

"We're in the process of cataloging them all," Blair says, surprising me, and also managing to not answer either of my questions.

Lisari, of course, is more than happy to fill me in. "One hundred and seventy-two others," she says. "Well, one hundred and seventy-three, technically. Do you know someone named Kanin?"

"Who?" I ask, baffled.

Blair shoots her a glare. "Shirasil, enough."

"What!" Lisari throws her hands in the air. "It's a fair question. And it's not my fault you hate fun."

"This is important," Blair says, glowering.

"Fyre." Lisari points to me. "Are important and fun mutually exclusive?"

"Um. No?" I say, perplexed by the current exchange.

Lisari turns to Blair. "Hah! See? And *she's* smarter than you."

I'm not thrilled to realize I'm being positioned between the two gods, and decide to maneuver the conversation back to safer ground.

"You said you came here to talk to me." I glance between the two in an attempt to gauge reactions. "Was there something you wanted to address specifically?"

Lisari sighs. "Getting back to work, are we?"

Mentally, I feel a distant sort of tinnitus—it's Ollie or Mirzayael trying to reach me, I think. I try to ignore it for now.

"There wasn't anything specific I wanted to speak with you about," Blair admits, watching me. "Rather, I wanted to see *how* you would speak to us."

That's cryptic. "And how have I spoken to you?"

"Well enough. At least, in current circumstances." Blair turns away from me, also heading over to the throne. I tense as she approaches it, getting closer than Lisari had. The tension builds again as she reaches out for the Dungeon Core, embedded in the top of the throne.

"What are you doing?" I ask, my voice tight. I try to not make it sound like a demand, but some of my nervousness slips through. The Dungeon Core is also getting jittery. What's this? What is this feeling? Is it something it can eat? It wants to eat it. Can it try?

You can't eat living things, I tell it, but I falter even as I think the words. The Dungeon Core doesn't qualify as living, but it is still a thinking... *entity.* Are gods alive? Can something that is immortal be considered living?

No, you can't try to eat it, I add to the Dungeon Core. At least, not yet.

Blair hovers her hand before the jewel, as if warming her fingers before a fire. Then she lowers her hand and turns back to me. "I want to see you use it."

I don't move. I don't know how, but this feels like a trap. "I already did. When I closed the doors."

"You control it remotely?" she asks.

"I can communicate with it remotely, yes." So they haven't noticed me talking with the Core. That's something.

"This is a result of your Pact?" she asks.

I hesitate, wondering how much I should reveal. Every sliver of information I hold that they don't have has the potential to become leverage. Yet, lying or holding something important back might be just as dangerous.

[Your magic has been identified,] Echo abruptly speaks.

"She has psionic spells," Lisari says. "That must be how."

I resist the urge to scowl at her. And I'd started to think she was on my side. "That's correct." At least they don't seem to know about my connection with Mirzayael and Ollie, yet.

"Interesting," Blair says. She points to the jewel. "Still, I want to see you wield it—while you're wearing it."

It's not a request. But I'm not sure I can. "Will touching it work?" I ask her. "I don't think I can wear it right now. If I remove it from the throne, it might interrupt the spell circuit it's interfaced with, and since the Fortress is dependent on the spells to stay aloft..."

Blair doesn't appear pleased by this, but thankfully she doesn't press the matter. She steps away from the throne, gesturing me forward. "Physical contact should be sufficient."

I cautiously approach, wracking my brain for why she's asking me to do this. She wants to see me wield the Dungeon Core. Even though, according to legend, the Core is what drew the gods' ire in the first place. Not to mention, the gods' presence seems to be unsettling the Core in some way. Making it jumpy... and hungry. So if it poses some threat (why else would they have wanted it buried?) then what motive do they have for wanting to see me wield it, and within such close proximity to them?

To measure my control.

That has to be it. They are judging not just the Core's danger, but what level of threat it might pose in my hands. Then I'll have to show them it's benign. I'll show them that I have complete control over it.

Even if I'm not sure either of those things are true.

Okay, Core, I think, reaching the throne. I nervously keep an eye on the gods as I rest my hand on the arm. *You're going to need to listen to me, alright? Listen to me completely.*

Okay. Why wouldn't it? It hears me all the time. I think so much, it astounds the Core! Why, the Core can go for years without having a single thought—

I mean, you're going to need to do exactly what I say, I tell it. I reach up and touch the Core's jewel, embedded in the throne. *We're just going to do a small demonstration.*

The Dungeon Core gives me the mental equivalent of a shrug. Okay. But then can it eat the tasty thing in those people? It *knows* they would be delicious.

No, I tell it, try to keep my expression level. What is it talking about? I can't see or sense whatever it is the Core has latched onto. *Absolutely not. Now, we're just going to move a bit of earth around.*

Oh, well, alright, it supposes it could do that, too.

I have it summon a random cube of stone from its Inventory, which falls to the seat of the throne. At the same moment, the room shakes. I jump, glancing around.

Blair raises an eyebrow. "Was that—"

The room shakes again, and a scattering of pebbles falls away from the sealed balcony. Outside, I can hear muted voices. The tinnitus has gotten worse. Cautiously, I crack open my mental connections.

Mirzayael and Ollie burst into my mind.

"*—S OKAY, I CAN HIT IT ONE MORE TIME*," Ollie is saying.

"*Aim here*," Mirzayael replies.

My chest feels tight, and blood rushes in my ears.

"They're trying to break in," I tell Blair and Lisari. "They're worried about me. Please, don't hurt them."

Lisari turns to Blair with a disappointed sigh. "See what all your posturing has done! You've scared her."

As if I didn't find Lisari just as terrifying.

"We can leave," Blair says. "I've seen enough for now." She fixes me with a look. "I would recommend you don't disclose our nature to the residents of this city."

"I think that would be wise." I agree. Are they really leaving? Just like that? My hand trails off the throne, and I find it's trembling.

"Oh well," Lisari sighs. "I suppose the fun had to come to an end at some point. But don't worry," she tells me with a grin. "I'll be sure to visit again soon."

That feels more like a threat than a reassurance.

Blair is still holding my gaze when the two of them abruptly vanish. Like they were merely an image, and someone's just turned off the projector.

I stand there for a moment, too mixed up inside to process how I'm feeling. Then another impact shakes the room, and I quickly have the Dungeon Core dissolve all the barricades I'd previously formed.

Ollie and Mirzayael spill in from the balcony.

"*FYRE!*" Ollie cries. "*ARE YOU OKAY? WHO WERE THOSE PEOPLE? MIRZAYAEL WAS REALLY SCARED!*"

I let out a shaky breath, control over my emotions wavering. All at once, my strength seems to leave me. I sway, then wearily lower myself to the ground at the throne's side.

"Fyre!" Mirzayael sprints across the room. She moves so fast, I distantly realize she's been holding back during our sparring sessions. She skids to a stop at my side, going down to her knees. Her legs cage me in like a defensive barricade of spears. "Are you alright? What happened?"

Her fear is overwhelming, spilling over into me. Or perhaps I'm finally acknowledging my own. She grabs one of my hands, and I lean into her as she pulls me into a hug.

"I'm okay," I assure them both. "They're gone now."

"Who were they?" Mirzayael demands. Now that she's confirmed I'm safe, her fear is crystalizing into a fierce protectiveness.

I want to feel safe in her arms, but now that the adrenaline of the last several minutes is wearing off, dread is settling heavy in my gut.

"They were gods."

CHAPTER THIRTY-ONE

SIMMER

As soon as I think the words to Mirzayael, I recall the last thing Blair had said to me. She didn't want me telling the Fyrethians of their visit. But Mir is different. She's a leader—she's my partner—and she deserves to know as much as I do.

Mirzayael stiffens. "What—"

"*Don't say it aloud,*" I quickly think. At least I had only shared the thought with her, and not Ollie. Not that he'd be able to spread the rumor anyway, but I don't want to alarm anyone I don't have to.

"*They said they were leaving, but I don't know for sure,*" I quickly explain. "*I can't see them on the Map Interface—that's how I first knew something was wrong. But they could still be here listening. They didn't want anyone to know what they were.*"

Mirzayael lets out a breath, letting me go to give me a searching look. "*Are you sure?*"

"*Yes,*" I say, and I find I'm trembling again. They hadn't even done anything, and I felt so helpless.

And I hadn't even believed in them before now. Not *really*.

I'm such a fool. I'd told the Fortress I would protect them against the gods. I challenged the Jorrian prisoners, asking why their pantheon hadn't yet intervened on their behalf. All that brave talk because some part of me still dismissed it as superstition.

I pride myself on being rational and open-minded. But in this matter, I was shamefully ethnocentric.

"*I'm sorry,*" I tell Mirzayael, guilt swirling through me. "*I should have believed you. I didn't realize I was still harboring such biases. I didn't know. No. I did know. You all told me. But—*"

"Calm down," Mirzayael says aloud. Now that I'm safe, her fear for me has leaked away, exposing a faint yet simmering anger. I cast my gaze to the floor in shame. "They're gone, right?"

"I think so," I say.

"Then we'll discuss their visit later," she says.

Not the response I was expecting. "Alright. What—"

"Why did you shut us out?" Mirzayael demands with a hiss, her anger boiling over. "How can we help you if you keep us away?"

I flinch as her distress lashes against my mind, shocking me like a slap to the face.

"*I WAS REALLY WORRIED,*" Ollie adds. "*BUT NOT AS WORRIED AS MIRZAYAEL!*" He's too big for the throne room, his shoulder blades hitting the ceiling even when he's flat on his belly, but he tries to shimmy further inside anyway. He makes it far enough to reach me, and he lays his head down at Mirzayael's side.

I reach out and pet his nose. "I'm sorry. I was trying to compartmentalize. My mind was scattered. I needed to focus."

"Making excuses is not an apology," Mirzayael snaps.

I cringe. "You're right. I was trying to keep you two from being involved—I thought that would keep you safe. That wasn't fair." I shake my head, running my hand over Ollie's pebbly hide. Its texture is soothing. I try to force some of the wound-up tension out of my limbs, but that just makes them start to tremble.

"Ollie, that especially wasn't fair to you," I say. "Your Role is dependent on my safety. I can't keep you safe by keeping you away. I'm sorry I did that. I'm sorry I scared you."

"*IT'S OKAY*," he says, but I can still feel the worry and sadness in his voice.

"No, it's not," I say. The poor kid only has me and Mirzayael to talk to, anyway. Cutting him off from being able to communicate with me—even if only for a few minutes—was cruel. "I'll do better. I promise. I love you."

He rumbles out a sigh, closing his eyes and turning his head so I can reach a better spot to scratch on his muzzle. "*I LOVE YOU, TOO.*"

I have to wait until my throat is no longer tight before I try to speak again. The anger is still swirling through Mirzayael's mind, and knowing it's aimed at me makes my heart ache. I turn to her next. "I'm sorry. We're a team, on the throne and off. Shutting you out doesn't help anything. You need to know what's going on just as much as I do."

For a moment, she holds my look with a sharp gaze. Then she sighs, her form crumpling, and she casts her gaze down as her anger simmers into frustration and shame.

"I'm not mad at *you*, Fyre." She grimaces. "I'm mad at myself. When you needed me most, there was nothing I could do. I'm sorry for snapping at you. That was an overreaction. I just. I feared..."

Flickers of her thoughts float close enough for me to glimpse: when I went silent, she was afraid something terrible had happened to me. She was terrified I'd died.

My throat tightens up all over again, and I take her hand, squeezing her strong, calloused fingers in my own. "I won't shut you out again."

She nods along to my reassurance, but still looks miserable. "And I'll try to give you space, if you need it. I don't want to distract you when something else needs your full attention. I'll—I'll work on trusting you more."

She already does trust me, I can feel, but I understand what she really meant; it's hard for her to trust that I can take care of myself. It's hard for her to step down when she wants to join the fight.

It's hard for her to imagine what losing me would be like, when I'm the only one she's opened her heart to since she locked it away decades ago.

She doesn't linger on the thought. Already I can feel her settling back into a tactician mindset, wondering about the gods, what they wanted—if there was anything she could have done to protect me.

"I still don't understand why they would only take you," she thinks to me privately. *"If they've been watching, they must understand we are both rulers of the Fortress."*

"This wasn't about Fyreneth's legacy," I tell her. *"Well, not entirely. It involves the Dungeon Core. But they didn't only wish to speak with me because I'm connected to it—they cornered me because they know I'm from another world."*

Mirzayael blinks. *"Why would they care about that?"*

"I'm not sure," I admit. Though I'm starting to form some theories. I sigh, leaning against the side of the throne. Its cold stone presses against my back. *"I'm still trying to sort through everything. I'm not sure I understand it all yet."*

Mirzayael's shoulders slump as well. She's itching to ask a hundred questions of her own, but she holds back. "Come. You should get some rest. We will discuss what transpired when you're ready." She pulls a silk spider messenger construct out of her satchel. "I'll inform the guards the situation is resolved."

I quickly sit up. "Oh—the trade talks!" I had forgotten about our planned descent into the city amongst the chaos. "I should get back—"

"You can go tomorrow," Mirzayael says firmly. "We still have three more days over Hetopolis. "I'll tell Torim and Nek to take your place."

I'm not sure if rest is what I want, but when I glance up at the Dungeon Core, I realize the idea of leaving it miles away makes me uneasy. Not that my presence would do anything to stop the gods if they wanted to take it.

I've never felt so powerless.

"You won't be going on my behalf?" I ask her.

"No," she says simply. "The others can handle it. Ollie?"

He opens his eyes. "*YEAH?*"

"You don't have to accompany them down today if you don't want to," she says. "You can stay here instead."

Since I'll be staying, he'll probably want to keep near me. I'm sure Mirzayael realizes the same.

But he surprises us. "*CAN MERITIS RIDE WITH ME IN-STEAD?*" he asks. "*I WANT TO SEE THE CITY, AND SO DOES HE, AND HE DIDN'T GET TO GO DOWN WHEN WE WERE IN THE LAST CITY.*"

That's because in the last city, they came to us.

My parental instincts briefly summon an objection to my lips. I don't want to let him go by himself. I'm worried about him.

But he won't be by himself. He'll have Dizzi, Meritis, Nek, Torim, and all the others to take care of him. I can still contact him—and even look through his eyes—if I need to. If this is him interested in exploring a bit of independence, I shouldn't punish him for it.

"Alright," I say, trying not to grimace. "As long as Meritis's parents agree."

"*YAY!*" Ollie lifts his head with a happy rumble. "*OKAY I'LL GO ASK. WELL, MERITIS WILL ASK. I WISH I COULD TALK TO HIM. ARE YOU READY TO DO THE MIND LINK WITH US, YET?*"

"I've got a different idea in mind," I tell him, thinking back to our previous guests. "But I do think I'll find a way for you guys to speak soon. Just a bit longer, alright?"

"*ALRIGHT!*" Ollie begins wiggling backward, and I have the Dungeon Core remove some stone around the balcony's entrance to help. Mirzayael sends off her messenger spider as Ollie slides back out of the throne room.

"How did you get up there?" I suddenly realize. She and Ollie had come in the same way.

"I rode on the saddle," she says shortly.

I blanche, aghast. "But it's not designed for you."

"It was very difficult to stay on," she agrees. "The experience was terrifying. I will never do it again." She stands up, pulling me to my feet, and the two of us wearily leave the throne room.

"I'm sorry I scared you," I repeat.

"I know," she says softly. "But I'm glad you're alright."

She leads us back to her chamber instead of mine. I don't object. Inside, she settles into her nest-like bed, and I wordlessly climb in with her, curling up against her chest. She pulls a blanket over the two of us and wraps her arms around me.

Her limbs envelope me in a warm fortification, as if she's trying to shield me from the world.

I wish it made me feel safe.

I doze restlessly, disrupted by vague and anxious thoughts that don't quite resolve into dreams. Eventually I rouse, too agitated to nap any longer. Mirzayael gets up with me, and we head to the dining hall. It's not really near any meal time, but the cooks graciously throw something together for us, and we sit down to eat. Over the course of a seemingly silent meal, I tell her everything.

Mirzayael is just as baffled as me. "*And you're **sure** they were gods?*" she asks when I'm done.

I recall the stats I'd seen on their displays. "*Pretty sure. Echo described both of them as having the title "God," and they were both level 100. Lisari's class was Anarchic Alchemist and Blair's class was Temporal Paladin.*" Interestingly, they both also had a Role, like Ollie and I. They're the first other people I've seen with a Role stat.

They both also clearly had access to the System, since they were able to see my and Ollie's Roles and deduce information about my spells. Was that the connection? Only people who could see and interact with the System had Roles? But why? What are they for?

"*It's strange,*" Mirzayael muses. "*I am no expert in the gods, but I don't recognize either of those names. And the fact that they made reference to Lorata in some sort of disparaging way... I don't understand it.*"

"*Lisari's name displayed differently in her Stats,*" I recall, trying to think back. "*Blair called her by that name, too. Shirasil, I think.*"

"*Oh.*" Mirzayael takes another bite of our smoked fish, frowning. "*That name **does** sound familiar. They're a god of chaos, I think. And knowledge.*"

"*Chaos and knowledge?*" That was an odd combination. But given a class like 'anarchic alchemist,' it does sort of fit. And their Role had been the Inquisitor. I have no idea what that might mean. They did seem curious, if nothing else.

"Do you know anything else about them?" I ask.

Mirzayael shrugs. *"They sometimes appear as a man or woman, though I believe man is more common. They're blind. They wield power over wind and shadows."*

"Oh." I had begun to believe that Lisari's blindness was an act. To what end, I have no idea, but I suppose I had just assumed that a deity wouldn't have disabilities. *"Can't she fix her sight, if she's a god?"*

Mirzayael shrugs again. *"Perhaps she doesn't want to. I don't know much more about her than what I've already said. She's often trouble, I think."*

"Trouble for mortals, or gods?" I wonder. *"If she has some disagreement with Lorata, could that be a good thing for us?"*

Mirzayael shakes her head. *"I don't know. But I don't trust the motive of any god. They wouldn't be here if they didn't want something."*

"Like the Dungeon Core," I muse. I also have to shake my head. *"I can't sort through it all. Blair suggested taking the Dungeon Core from us, but stopped when I told her how that would doom our city. That seems to be the opposite of what happened with Lorata in the legends—burying the city seemed to be the point. Yet, they still wanted something with it. Or with me. Or the both of us, since we're connected. And that feeling when they got too close..."*

I don't know what to make of it. *"If they're testing my control over the Dungeon Core, to what end? And why did they want knowledge of their presence to be concealed? If this is being done against Lorata's will, or without her knowledge, why?"*

"I have no answers," Mirzayael says.

Me neither. But perhaps there will be a way to get more. *"We should gather texts on the pantheon while we're still over Hetopolis. Perhaps that will help prepare us for their next visit."*

Mirzayael's face darkens. *"We can prepare in more ways than one."*

"I don't think it would be a good idea to antagonize them," I tell her. She already knows that, of course, but her pride won't let her suggest it. *"But we might stand to learn something from them if we play along."*

*"We will **not** align ourselves with the gods,"* Mirzayael snaps.

"Even if some might be working against Lorata?" I ask.

"No," she says firmly. *"I don't care who is aligned with whom. It is against everything we stand for."*

"Maybe," I say. But I'm not convinced the pantheon is as monolithic as Mirzayael sees them. Not from the clues Lisari was dropping.

Was that intentional? Blair kept implying Lisari was saying too much. Loose lips, or trying to send a message?

I guess I won't know until they return. And hopefully when they do, they'll continue to just want to talk.

Chapter Thirty-Two

COMMUNICATION 101

I don't end up visiting Hetopolis. The idea of leaving the Dungeon Core unguarded makes me uneasy, no matter how irrational the thought may be. Instead, I spend the next three days showing more visitors around, working more trade deals, and making money. *Literally* making money. I feel guilty every time I do it, but we need the supplies, and the merchants are more than happy to accept our gold and silver.

True to my word, I also commission a custom piece of artificing for Ollie. I hope the alterations to the base design I requested will work as intended. I'm expecting it to arrive today, in one of the last shipments before we leave the city behind.

The gods don't return in that time. I should be relieved, but it just makes me more anxious. Are they actually here, but watching in disguise? I wish they would return already so I could stop worrying about when it was going to happen.

I unhappily poke at my blueseed salad, attempting to summon an appetite.

"Something is bothering you," Gardi says.

I look up in surprise. While they've started answering others in monosyllabic responses, it's rare for them to start a conversation themself. Salvia, sitting on their other side, eyes them suspiciously. Our visitors have all left or are preparing to leave, so lunch is just the three of us, and unusually quiet.

"I've had a lot on my mind lately," I admit. "I keep waiting for things to slow down so I can catch my breath, but each day only seems to be getting more busy and complex. I suspect things won't actually settle until we find somewhere to make our permanent home."

"Why not put down here?" Gardi asks, continuing to surprise me. "You formed good relations with the people on this coast already."

"That is a fair point, but there's no reason to rush into a decision," I say. "We've a few months of flight left before we run out of mana. Not to mention, I think the Fyrethians would prefer a cooler climate to a tropical one. And it would be vastly preferable if we could land somewhere with access to mana ore."

While the mana we have is keeping the city floating, it's also keeping the city powered. All our water collection and atmospheric spells, all the lights in the palace, all the cauldrons in the kitchen, run off the magic that had been absorbed by the Dungeon Core when it consumed all the nearby mana ore before we left Jorria.

The bonus mana that's now in the Core's interface is a limited resource. The Dungeon Core could recreate the mana ore it had previously consumed, of course, but that version would be empty, and it would take a very long time for the ore to re-accumulate ambient magic from its surroundings. In an ideal scenario, we'd find a new mana ore vein somewhere and land there. Once it's wired into the Fortress, we'd be able to regulate how much mana we could sustainably drain from different parts of the ore, while allowing the rest to recharge.

Gardi snorts. "Good luck with that. Mana ore is a coveted resource. Unless you've got a way to find an undiscovered vein, it's unlikely any mines will be willing to sell theirs to you."

I frown. I suppose I should have expected that. Stone that can capture magic from the air and store it for anyone to use is probably a highly valuable resource, now that I'm thinking about it. Which means we can probably even sell the drained mana ore the Core has in its Inventory for a pretty penny. But that doesn't help us with trying to find a sustainable way to power the Fortress.

"Fair point," I reply. "I suppose we'll have to keep our options open, then. And what about you?" I ask. "Today's your last chance if you want to be released in Hetopolis."

I can practically see them retreat back into their shell. They look down at their half-eaten meal. "It's too close to Mount Haze." *'And Ragna'* goes unsaid. "Perhaps the next city."

I decide to change the subject before they can cloister themself up once more. "By the way, I've been meaning to ask you. Have you heard of a god named Blair? Some kind of... temporal paladin."

Gardi pauses, then gives me a curious look. I guess that did a good job of surprising them out of their self-isolation. "I didn't think any of you would be interested in learning about the gods."

I attempt a casual shrug. "It never hurts to be informed. One of our visitors mentioned her, and since I know basically nothing about the gods, I thought I would ask."

This isn't entirely true. I've spent some time interrogating Echo about Blair and Lisari since their visit. At first, neither name got me anything from her: [The database does not have accessible information on the subject.] But when I asked about Shirasil instead, Echo had provided a little more.

[Shirasil: a prominent god in the pantheon. Sometimes referred to as the Inquisitor, they are often associated with invention, exploration, and the pursuit of knowledge. However, scholars typically choose Lorata over Shirasil as the patron god of choice, given Lorata's association with foresight is often seen as a more reliable guiding force than Shirasil's idiosyncratic ingenuity.]

Two days ago, I was also able to get my hands on a scroll about the pantheon, and I've been poring over it ever since. Again, no Lisari was mentioned, but there was a Shirasil, and the accompanying illustration seemed to match Lisari close enough. The scroll mentioned Shirasil was often depicted as a human, with eyes filled with black smoke, and alchemic tools hanging at his hip. I'm not sure what Lisari's eyes looked like, hidden behind her dark glasses, but she also presented herself as a human alchemist. It's enough parallels for me to believe they're the same person.

But once more, there was no mention of Blair. I couldn't even find a god similar to her domain: High Partitioner. Then again, I wasn't entirely sure what that meant.

"The name Blair is not familiar to me," Gardi says after a moment.

I'm disappointed, but not surprised; like Lisari, she could be using a pseudonym. "Thanks anyway. Though I would be interested in picking your brain about some other gods at some point."

They give me a skeptical look. "I'm sure you can learn more from a book than from me."

"True," I agree, "but talking to people about it and getting their perspectives can often be more enlightening."

Gardi goes back to eating their meal. Salvia continues to watch both of us, intent but quiet. I never know what's going on in that head of theirs.

We finish up and start to make our way back down the city toward the dock, where our last supply-run should soon be arriving. As we walk, Gardi speaks up again. I hope it becomes a trend.

"Which gods did you want to know about?"

Lorata is probably an important one to get a Jorrian's opinion on, but that's also a rather touchy subject—for both individuals present. I decide to focus on the one god I do know a little about.

"What can you tell me about Shirasil?" I ask. "I know he is some sort of scientist god, but that's about it."

From my research, I've learned there are forty-one gods all told, though only a handful are prominently featured in stories, while the rest appear less powerful, or at least, less well known and worshipped.

Drawing parallels to Greek mythology, Lorata, god of light and head of the pantheon, would be their Zeus. Shirasil would be on the level of Olympian Gods, like one of Zeus's children (though as far as I can tell, none of the gods on this world are related, and all seem to be childless). And I suspect Blair—or whoever she really is—might be on a lower tier, though that is merely speculation based on how the two interacted with one another.

"Shirasil is often associated with alchemy," Gardi says. "The fusion of artificing and potionry. He is said to be curious, meddlesome, and... volatile."

Curious and meddlesome matches what I experienced. "Volatile?"

"There are conflicting stories about the god," Gardi admits. "Some paint him as patient and helpful while other stories show him being angry and destructive. In some tales, he is Lorata's closest ally, and in others, he resents her for a past slight. It's difficult to tell if this is because some of the stories are incorrect, or if they are all true and Shirasil's mood changes like the wind."

It's becoming more and more clear that Shirasil has some history with Lorata. That probably doesn't bode well for us if she finds out—no matter if he's her friend or foe.

"She's also associated with wind," Salvia abruptly adds.

Right—Gardi isn't the only one here with some knowledge on the gods. I imagine the lost colony would have had more opportunities to interact with the outside world than those trapped underground; it makes sense they might know more than the average Fyrethian.

"But Rinviu is the true wind god," Gardi quickly counters.

Salvia sniffs. "I never said Shirasil was the *true* wind god. Merely that she can sometimes be associated with it. Shadows, too."

For a moment I marvel at the two sharing a conversation. Or, more of an argument, really. But I'll take it.

"Sorry," I interrupt when it's clear Gardi is about to disagree with Salvia again. "I hope this isn't insensitive. But Gardi used 'he' for Shirasil, and Salvia you just used 'she.' I've also received some mixed information on this in my research. Is Shirasil a man or a woman?"

They shrug. "Either," Gardi says at the same time Salvia says, "Both."

This doesn't entirely clear up the matter for me, but at least I got the two to agree on something. Kind of.

"So to sum up," I say, "she's associated with alchemy, wind, shadows, and meddling?" I get affirmative nods from the two. "That doesn't sound very... cohesive."

Gardi chuckles. "It's not. But that's why he's the god of chaos."

"No," Salvia interjects. "It's not chaos. It's change."

Gardi scowls. "But all of his stories are ones of destruction."

"Change can be destructive," Salvia counters. "Which fits with the association of alchemy. And wind! You said so yourself earlier—her mood changes like the wind."

"That's coincidental," Gardi grumbles, clearly annoyed their words are being used against them. "And change can *also* be chaotic. But given his association with shadows..."

I back out of the conversation and let the two go at it. I have no idea who's right, but it's good for them to be finding more constructive ways to express their friction with each other.

When we get to the dock, they're still bickering, though the conversation has now moved onto Rinviu, the god of wind, and whether or not their domain overrides Shirasil's.

I meet up with Nek as Gardi and Salvia fall behind me, too engaged in their heated debate to pay attention to much else. Nek stares at them.

"I think it's an improvement," I say with a chuckle. "At least they're not trying to kill each other."

"If words could kill, it would be a bloodbath." Nek peels his eyes away from them. "We've just finished unloading the last transport. There's one package that was marked for you personally."

I brighten. "Excellent! I've been waiting for this. Where can I find it?"

Nek shows me over to the cargo as I mentally reach out to Ollie. *"Are you busy? I've got something for you at the dock."*

Ollie perks up in my head. *"FOR ME? WHAT IS IT?"*

"A present." I grin when his mind starts bubbling with excitement. *"I'M COMING, I'M COMING!"*

Sure enough, the dragon arcs around from the opposite side of the Fortress, beating a hasty flight in our direction.

I laugh. *"Slow down! The present isn't going anywhere. Unless you knock it off the wall with all that wind of yours."*

His wings immediately snap into a glide, which he maintains the rest of the way to the wall. When he touches down on his landing pad, only a faint breeze accompanies him.

"WHAT IS IT?" he asks, craning his head over to us. He can't quite reach, but he's learned to stay on his platform and off the dock, both so

he can move without worrying about squishing someone, and so the dock workers can continue their jobs without having to worry about being squished.

Nek hands the package to me. It's the size of my hand.

"Smaller than I expected," I admit. Nek is clearly curious, so I beckon for him to join us. As I head over to Ollie's perch, I unravel the twine and unwrap the burlap, and when I pull the last layer aside, I reveal a glittering blue jewel. It's as big as my fist and shaped like a rhombus. Holding it up for Ollie to see, it feels pitifully small in comparison.

"*OOOOOH!*" Ollie says, his eyes going wide. "*TREASURE! AND IT'S FOR ME?*" He raises a claw like he wants to grab it, but knows he's not supposed to and would probably hurt me, so instead settles for pawing at the air.

"It is. Now, hold on."

I finish unwrapping the jewel and find it's already attached to a small metal chain—the variety designed for a human's neck, not a dragon's.

"I might need your wife's help to come up with a better way to secure this to him," I tell Nek. "But I guess this will do for now. Ollie, hold out your hand."

He eagerly raises a claw, bumping lightly into me in his excitement. I grab his massive finger to hold it steady, then slip the necklace over it like a ring.

"You might need to close your hand around it," I tell him. "The jewel has to be touching you for it to work." At least, I hope it will work.

Ollie curls his claws into a fist, and the stone vanishes beneath his grasp. "*WHAT WILL WORK?*" he asks me.

At the same time, a very quiet and muffled, "What will work?" comes from his paw.

Nek gasps. "Is that a translation stone?"

"*WHOAAAAA!*" Ollie says, and a tiny "whoaaaa" comes from the stone. He turns his paw over to look at the stone. "*IT SAYS WHAT I'M THINKING!*"

"It says what I'm thinking!"

The voice is quiet, sounds a bit robotic, and is definitely not that of a child, but it's more than I could have hoped for. I grin as relief and joy overtake me.

"*BOO!*"

"Boo."

"*ECHO!*"

"Ech—"

"*NO, NOT YOU, ECHO, I WAS TALKING TO THE SAP-PHIRE.*"

"No, not you, Echo, I was talking to the sapphire."

Ollie breaks down into a fit of giggles, which the jewel replicates in a robotic and very creepy manner. Well, it's *almost* everything I could have hoped for.

"It is a translator stone," I reply to Nek. "I spoke with one of our lamia visitors about the devices they use to communicate with those who can't sign, and thought it might help bridge the communication gap for Ollie, too."

"Amazing," Nek says, looking up at Ollie in awe. "Ollie... can you hear me?"

"*I CAN ALWAYS HEAR YOU,*" Ollie replies.

When the translator repeats this, Nek tears up. "Of course. Well, I'm happy I can finally hear you."

He's going to make me tear up, too. After all this time, finally, *finally*, he'll be able to talk to people and make friends. He'll be able to regain a sliver of the childhood he deserves.

I pat Ollie's hand to regain his attention. "You asked if I could form a psionic link with Meritis so you two could communicate. I'm not ready to add anyone else to our mental network, but I thought this might be a good alternative."

"*I LOVE IT!*" Ollie cries, and the translator repeats. "*I CAN'T WAIT TO SHOW MERITIS! EVEN IF IT'S VERY TINY AND QUIET.*"

"Dizzi might be able to help with that," I muse. She didn't have any of the runic knowledge to make something like this before, but we've obtained several magic theory books over the last few weeks, and Dizzi is soaking up every piece of literature placed in front of her like a sponge.

"In the meantime, be careful with it," I tell him. "Until we can find a better way to secure it to you, if you drop it, that's it."

"*I WON'T DROP IT,*" he promises, excitedly bouncing up and down. The wall rumbles with each hop. "*CAN I GO SHOW HIM NOW?*"

"Sure," I say with a laugh. I can't imagine the look on Meritis's face when he hears Ollie speak for the first time. "Go have fun."

"*YAY!*" Ollie spins away, and Nek and I have to duck to avoid getting hit by his tail. Ollie opens his wings and crouches, ready to launch, then just as abruptly whirls back to face us, like he'd forgotten something.

He excitedly nuzzles me, which feels a lot like getting punched in the chest by Mirzayael during a sparring match. I stumble, throwing my arms around his nose to keep from being knocked to the ground.

"*THANK YOU!*" Ollie cries ("Thank you"). "*THANK YOU, THANK YOU, THANK YOU! I LOVE YOU, FYRE!*"

"I love you, too, Ollie."

Then he spins around and jumps into the air, letting out a gleeful roar.

CHAPTER THIRTY-THREE

SHOPPING SPREE

By the time we reach the next city, people have started coming to us. Airships move much more quickly than our city does, and word is clearly spreading. I'm not sure if we really have anything of value to offer in trade, but I think people are more excited to visit a castle in the clouds than anything. I hadn't expected "tourism" to become our main industry.

They also soon discover we have a talking dragon, and Ollie quickly becomes a source of fascination. Ollie, of course, basks in the attention, and is more than happy to accept (and even request) gifts to add to his growing collection. I'm going to need to keep an eye on the effect it might have on his ego. The last thing we need is a spoiled eight-year-old the size of a house.

Thank goodness he's out of his tantrum years.

"*COME ON, FYRE!*" Ollie encourages me. "*DON'T BE SCARED!*"

A much tinier voice from his translator echoes, "Come on Fyre, don't be scared!"

"You don't have to mentally talk to me when I'm right here," I remind him.

"*OH YEAH*," he says, still replying mentally. "*I FORGOT.*"

Sora did in fact create a leather band for Ollie to wear, which keeps the translation stone pressed against his neck. This also helps make the voice sound more like it's coming from his head than his hand. The jewel looks absurdly tiny on him, but he parades it around with pride, happy to point it out to anyone new he meets. Dizzi examined the stone but was hesitant to alter any of the spells in an attempt to increase the volume lest she break something. Now that we're at a city again, the plan is to find another language artificer who might be able to help.

"And I'm not scared," I tell him. "Just nervous."

Ollie giggles. "*THAT'S THE SAME THING.*"

"*Don't worry,*" Mirzayael assures me, picking up on our conversation. "*I'll stay in the throne room the entire time you're away.*"

I wish that was at all reassuring. But Mirzayael insisted I couldn't stay cloistered up in the palace forever, and she's right about that. We can't hang everything on what the gods may or may not do.

"Fyre!" Dizzi flutters over to us as Ollie and I continue to wait for the cargo shuttles to finish being loaded. "I'm glad you'll be joining us today. I can't wait to explore this city. There's been so many things I wish I could have shown you in the last couple!"

"You make it sound like it's a shopping trip rather than a business excursion," I lightly tease.

She shrugs. "Same thing, right?"

She's starting to sound like Ollie.

"I'm a bit concerned about taking Ollie into the city," I admit. "He must take up their entire streets."

Dizzi waves off the concern. "Don't worry, I've already talked to them about accommodations. We'll be meeting outside the city this time. The last two cities had giant squares that Ollie could sit in without much trouble. And he only destroyed one cart!"

"He what?" I ask, alarmed.

Ollie ducks his head. "*IT WAS AN ACCIDENT.*"

"And we paid them back, so don't worry about it!" Dizzi quickly says. "But actually, I *do* have something I've been trying that might make it easier for Ollie to maneuver in the city while we're on the ground. Want to see?"

I have no idea what she could mean by this, but I am curious. "Show me."

She leads me over to one of the cargo shuttles, where helpers are finishing loading the last crate of supplies. It's filled with blankets, ore, spell scrolls, crops, soil additives, and of course, a few chests of manufactured coins. (Yes, I still feel bad about that. Once we have enough sustainable trade, I fully intend to stop producing currency.)

"Check this out," Dizzi says. She pulls a paper out of her pocket and unfolds it, revealing a complex spell circle. I can read some of the runes related to size and material, but it isn't until I have Echo Check it that I realize what it's for.

Dizzi sets it on top of the last crate that's loaded, and taps the circle, which illuminates beneath her finger. At first, nothing appears to have happened. But after a few seconds, the space between the crate and its nearby cargo appears to have become bigger—because the crate itself has become smaller. It continues to shrink, very slowly, but it's shrinking nevertheless.

"It'll take about five minutes for it to complete," Dizzi says. "And then it will be about the size of a blueseed fruit. Can you imagine how much more we could pack on these shuttles if I made a circle for everything here?!"

The spell circle itself is still glowing, I note: so it can't be used simultaneously for multiple pieces of cargo. We'll need to replicate the spell dozens—or hundreds—of times. But it does pose exciting potential for our deliveries going forward.

"How long will it last?" I ask.

"A couple hours," she says.

"Amazing." I crouch down next to the cargo, watching the crate dwindle at the pace of a snail. "I'm surprised everyone doesn't use such methods for cargo delivery."

"Well, I'm still working out some kinks," Dizzi admits. "It's smaller, but it's not lighter, for instance. Which is okay for us, since we've got the cloudstone to carry it around on, but it wouldn't help if you wanted to put it in a bag—the fabric would probably tear before you'd be able to lift it. Also, I haven't figured out how to make them become big again. I just have to wait for the spell to expire."

I give her a look. "So they're going to be like this when we need to trade them?"

"Uhhh." Dizzi smiles guiltily. "I said I was working out some kinks! We can just trade the other stuff first. It should be back to normal by lunch!"

"It's an interesting spell," I tell her. "But I think it would be best to hold off on trying something like that on Ollie until you've worked out all the kinks."

"You're no fun at all." But she gives me a wink and a smile before heading back to finish overseeing the last steps of securing the cargo.

"DO YOU WANT TO RIDE ON MY BACK, TODAY?" Ollie asks me as we prepare to launch.

"Meritis won't be accompanying you?" I ask.

Ollie shakes his head, which doesn't entirely work for a dragon with a long, snake-like neck, but I get the idea. *"HE'S HELPING*

HIS PARENTS WITH SOMETHING. PLUS, HE LIKES TO FLY ALONGSIDE ME ANYWAY."

"Then I'd be happy to," I say.

Ollie gives a pleased rumble.

I climb up his neck, wary of using my Jets lest they accidentally burn him, and carefully strap my legs and waist into the seat. I could fly alongside him, of course, but Ollie seems to enjoy taking others for rides—and then terrifying them with loop-de-loops and barrel rolls. At least the harness has been well-tested at this point.

"Ready?" Dizzi calls to me from the cargo shuttles. A dozen harpies are assisting to tow the three shuttles up and down, but other non-flying Fyrethians are also onboard.

I wave back to her. "Let's go!"

Ollie launches into the sky.

Riding on his back is entirely different from flying on my own. I'm not in control for one, and Ollie is *much* faster. I squeeze the handholds on the harness and lean down against his neck, the wind pulling tears from my eyes. Ollie is laughing in my head, and as he abruptly folds his wings to drop into a free fall, my stomach lurches into my throat, and I find myself laughing from the thrill—and terror—as well.

I can see why Mirzayael has sworn off flying for good.

At Dizzi's direction, we alight in a large field at the edge of town. That was a good call on her part. Not only is Ollie unable to break anything out here, we can also avoid inadvertently terrorizing the citizens.

Already a good number of officials and merchants are out waiting for us. As I disembark, I look up at Fyreneth's Fortress, closer to the horizon than overhead, but breathtakingly massive nonetheless. No wonder everyone seems so awed by our city.

After an hour or so of hammering out logistics, we divide up into a few different groups: one will stay here and handle any of the merchants who come to trade with us (and any of the townsfolk who want to meet Ollie) while the rest of us will take various items into the city to meet with businesses who have expressed interest in working with us. I'm reluctant to leave Ollie, but of course he's done this many times by now, and seems to know the drill better than me.

The next few hours are a flurry of talk and trade. I'm very glad to have other people with us who have become experienced with such negotiations, because it's hard for me to stay focused on the conversations at hand.

The city is amazing! I can't stop staring at all the ways magic has been infused into even the most mundane aspects of their society. One square is shaded by a floating canvas that gradually changes colors, simulating a sky that shifts from starry nights, to rolling thunderstorms, to brilliant sunsets. Constructs like Mirzayael's silk spiders skitter along a miniature raised walking path that runs along the street's gutters. Giant armadillo-like creatures pull carts, and something that looks part way between a bird and a dinosaur is frequently used as a mount to carry people quickly through the streets.

And that's just in the marketplaces. I can't wait to visit some of the shops and see what other more specialized magic tools and resources might still be waiting for us to discover. Maybe we'll find something here that can help us find the mana ore veins we need to power our city once we land.

After a quick break for lunch with Ollie and the rest, we wind down the last of our mass-item sales and trades and begin to scour the marketplace for the niche items on our list that various Fyrethians have requested.

I use this opportunity to head off with Dizzi in search of an artificer to help with Ollie's translator. He won't be able to communicate with those we left him with while we're gone, but he's plenty used to that, and we should be back within a couple hours, anyway.

Translators are a bit of a specialty item here, as it turns out, so the hunt is a bit more involved than we'd hoped. Eventually, we're pointed toward a shop called *Arcane Accommodations*.

But just as we're about to step inside, something prickles the back of my neck. I pause, turning back to scan the marketplace. It doesn't take long to find someone who is looking back.

Blair.

A chill runs through me. Why here? Why now?

"Fyre?" Dizzi asks, lingering in the doorway.

"You go on ahead," I tell her, not taking my eyes away from the god. "There's something I want to go take a look at. I'll catch up in a moment."

Too distracted by the promise of new spellwork, Dizzi doesn't question it and ducks inside. A pit of dread settles in my stomach as I cross the street to Blair. Arms crossed, she's leaning against a wall near the edge of a square, tucked into a sliver of shade.

"Hello, Fyre," she says passively as I join her. "Pleasure to see you."

I wish I could say the same. "Blair. Here to test me again?"

"No, actually," she says. "I was in the area for a different reason, but I thought I might stop by before leaving."

That's not the answer I was expecting. Caught slightly off guard, I ask, "Why?"

"Just to see how things are progressing." She nods her head back toward the edge of town. "That was a good idea with Ollie's transla-tor."

"Thanks." I stand there awkwardly, unsure how to even react to all of this. In the square, kids are playing in a fountain, laughing and shrieking as they chase magically swirling loops of water. It feels surreal to be speaking with a god while the city continues to move around us, entirely unaware.

I quickly scan the rest of the crowd. "Is Shirasil not with you today?"

Her eyebrow faintly twitches. "I see you've been doing some research." Last time when she had spoken with me, her tone had been cool and calculating. Curiously, she sounds more indifferent today.

"It wasn't that difficult to figure out, since you said his name." I pause. "Her name?"

Blair chuckles lightly. "Either will do."

This is not the kind of interaction with her I had been dreading over the past week and a half. She's acting so casual now. I decide to push my luck. "I couldn't find *your* name in my research, however. Or your domain. Are you obscuring elements of your stats?"

Her already faint smile fades. "Yes."

I wait, but she doesn't say anything else. Well, I guess that explains that. Kind of anticlimactic, really. "Can you also *change* your stats?" I ask.

She tips her head. "How do you mean?"

"Our Roles," I say. "Can they be changed? Mine is restrictive, but it's Ollie's I'm worried about. Can you help him?"

I'd tried asking Echo about changing Roles before, but all I'd gotten was a bunch of <ACCESS DENIED>s. If the gods don't have access, I can't imagine who would.

Blair is silent for a moment. I half expect her not to answer. Finally, she shakes her head. "No, I'm afraid not. Altering an individual's Role is not within my power. The fact that you all even have them..." She pauses, as if reconsidering her words. "We are still looking into the matter. For now, the best we can do is partition them."

I'm starting to suspect this is not going to be the answer I'm looking for. "What do you mean by partition?"

Instead of meeting my gaze, Blair watches the children playing in the fountain. "Some Travelers have Role Requirements that they haven't or couldn't adhere to. We have locked those individuals in a temporal state to prevent their Sanity Stat from further degrading."

She says this as if it should sound reassuring, but there's something ominous behind her words. I take a guess at what that might be. "Are those the only Travelers who have been partitioned?"

Blair is silent for a long moment before her intense gaze slowly moves back to me. I have to steel myself to not look away.

"No," she finally says. "Those deemed a threat have also been taken into custody."

It's easy to read between the lines: these "partitions" are obviously some kind of imprisonment. But they're gods—what would they deem to be a threat?

"That's why you wanted to test my control over the Dungeon Core," I cautiously guess. Does that mean I passed?

"Partially, yes," she admits. "So far, I don't believe it necessary to confine you."

"I appreciate it," I say.

Blair again returns to people watching. "I would not be so fast to thank me. Should you give me any reason to believe that Core of yours poses a threat, I will reconsider my position."

Briefly, I think of the Fortress's weapon systems, and I go cold.

"Do we have anything to worry about?" I ask. "Not me and Ollie—but the other Fyrethians? I've only been told stories, but given what I know about Fyreneth and Lorata..."

"You would be wise to worry," Blair admits, which is not the answer I wanted to hear. "But not because they are Fyrethian. There are as many diverging opinions in the pantheon as there are gods. Neither Lisari nor I wish ill to befall your city, but others will disagree. Most gods would likely seize your Dungeon Core the moment they lay eyes on it—regardless of the consequences to your kingdom. My advice: keep its existence quiet. Use classic arcana and cloudstone as the explanation for your city's flight. Find somewhere to land quickly."

Easier said than done. Her advice feels more like a warning of impending doom. I'm not sure what to do with this. If two gods have already found us, it's only a matter of time before more come.

But then she speaks up again.

"I can't hide you and the boy from the pantheon," she says. "I will not report your existence, and I will do what I can to steer others away, but that is as much as I can interfere. I will also not report the Dungeon Core. But should it prove to be as dangerous as I believe it has the potential to be—should you demonstrate a loss of control over the remnant—I will not hesitate to partition you both. Do you understand?"

"I understand."

Her words are a threat, I have no doubt about that. But they're also a show of mercy.

On the one hand, it's a relief to know the gods don't care about the Fyrethians themselves; it's the Dungeon Core that they seem to be concerned with. On the other, we sort of need it to not drop out of the sky. If we're able to land first, then a god seizing the Dungeon Core would be bad—it would shut down the city and cripple our infrastructure—but it would not be a death sentence like it is now. Clearly, getting out of the sky needs to move up in the priority list.

"Thank you for your help," I say. "It sounds like you are taking a risk on our behalf. I was not expecting to encounter kindness from the gods. I will take your words to heart."

Blair grimaces in response. "As I said, we are not a monolith. Some do pose a threat to your kingdom. But the prevailing mindset within the Heavens is shifting. So long as the safety of this world is first ensured, I believe Travelers can be left..."

She pauses, glancing to the side as if something caught her eye. I look as well, but there's only a storefront in that direction, and as far as I can tell, there's nothing noteworthy about it. When I look back, I realize she's not looking at something in the square—she's looking at something in the System.

Blair abruptly clenches her teeth in a snarl, and—as if I couldn't be even more shocked by the current encounter—she lets loose a stream of alarming and colorful swears.

At the same moment, Ollie cries out in fear.

Chapter Thirty-Four

FRIEND OR FOE?

I'm blasting out of the city with my Jets before I even have a moment to consider my options. Dizzi is still in the shop. I probably scorched Blair with my flames, which certainly wasn't a wise move. But all I can think about is Ollie, whose alarm is spiking through me, indistinguishable from my own.

"What is it?" Mirzayael asks. *"Is Ollie alright?"*

"I don't know," I admit. I'm high enough above the city I can see Ollie and the clearing we'd landed in. *"Ollie. Ollie, what's happening!"*

"HE STUCK ME!" he cries. *"HE TRIED TO STICK ME!"*

"What?" I ask, desperate. It takes me less than thirty seconds to rocket out of the city. *"Who? What happened?"*

As I get close, I can make out a lot of raised voices—and Ollie's growl. It's a low rumble that resonates in my chest. I've never heard him make that noise before. I also notice his alarm has shifted to anger.

I land hard, cutting the Jets before I'd fully slowed down, and stumble across the grass. Both Fyrethians and locals are yelling, though it's so chaotic I can't tell what they're yelling about, or if it's even at each other.

Ollie swings his head toward me as I run up to him. "*FYRE! WHAT DO I DO?*"

"About what?" I ask, quickly looking him over. He's laying down where we'd left him, and I'm relieved to not see any blood. When I Check him, he's missing one point of HP. "I still don't know what's going on!"

"*ABOUT HIM!*" Ollie says, nodding his head toward the ground.

It takes me that long to realize there's a person pinned beneath Ollie's claws.

The man appears to be an elf. He has brown skin and short black hair, but that's about all I can make out beneath his continued frantic struggle—and Ollie's massive paw. Ollie's claws have dug into the ground around the man, one on each side of his head, and two more beneath his arms, effectively ensuring he won't be able to squirm free.

"Let me go!" the man cries. "Please! Someone help!"

As I'm staring at this, baffled, Salvia hurries to my side.

"We confiscated his weapon," they say, gesturing to an unsheathed sword they're carefully holding to their side.

"What happened?" I ask for about the tenth time.

"He tried to stab Ollie," Salvia says, looking back at the elf, who's given up the fight and is now laying there, hyperventilating. The giant dragon paw pressing down on him is probably making it hard to breathe, but I'm too mad to feel very concerned for his safety.

"Tried being the operative word," Salvia continues. "Ollie pretty quickly took care of that."

"*THAT'S WHAT I ALREADY SAID,*" Ollie grumbles. "*HE TRIED TO STICK ME.*"

"Well done, Ollie," I tell him, willing my heartrate back to normal. "And ease up a bit, will you? I've got questions I want answered before you squish him."

"HE'LL WIGGLE FREE," Ollie protests. But he shifts his weight anyway and lifts his paw. Sure enough, the man starts fighting, trying to slip one of his arms out. Ollie quickly presses down once more, and the man lets out an audible "oof" as the air is knocked from his lungs.

I quickly relay the situation to Mirzayael as I stomp over to the stranger, my own anger rising.

"Who are you?" I demand as I Check him. "Why did you attack Ollie?"

[Check,] Echo says, his stats populating my vision.

[Name: Sandro]

[Species: Elf]

[Class: Spellsword]

[Level: 28]

[HP: 112/120]

[Mana: 127/150]

[Role: Dragon Slayer]

My breath catches in my throat. He's like us. He's from Earth. But that Role fills me with dread.

"Ollie, Check him," I say as I crouch down at Sandro's side.

"DRAGON SLAYER?" Ollie exclaims. *"THAT'S MEAN!"*

And it also explains why he attacked Ollie.

Echo can I see someone else's Sanity Stat? I ask her, examining the man as he stares up at me, wide-eyed.

[Permissions granted,] she says. A new stat appears above the man's head. [Sanity: 85%]

Damn. I had suspected as much. I keep an eye on the stat, but so far it remains static. I'm still very upset on Ollie's behalf, but I try to soothe some of my anger away. This isn't his fault. At least, not entirely.

"Hello, Sandro," I say, and his eyes widen as he looks up at me. "I don't appreciate you attacking my kid."

"What?" he gasps. "How do you…"

"Did you Check Ollie first?" I ask him. "Did you know what he was and try to hurt him anyway? I find it hard to believe you ran into a fight with a dragon without attempting to scope out his level first."

"Check? Level?" Sandro repeats. His frantic gaze appears to dart randomly around the clearing before settling back on me. "You—you can see it too!"

Oh boy. This is not going to be an easy conversation, is it?

The chaos is starting to settle down now, with the Fyrethians and townsfolk giving me and Ollie a wide berth.

I turn to Salvia. "Do you have something to secure him?"

"Yes, Lord Fyre," they say, passing Sandro's sword off to another guard as they produce a loop of spider silk from their bag.

I gesture them forward as I step back. "Ollie, you can let him go. We'll take it from here."

Ollie lets out another low growl, and Sandro goes very still. "*ARE YOU SURE? HE'S NOT GOING TO TRY TO HURT ME AGAIN?*"

"Salvia will tie him up so he doesn't," I promise. "You did a great job, Ollie. I'm proud of you."

His growl turns into a pleased rumble—a purr, maybe, for an enormously oversized cat.

Ollie lifts his claws away, and again Sandro tries to make a dash for it. He yelps, flipping onto his back as his cloak flaps out behind him, and he awkwardly crab-walks backward.

"No, wait!" he cries, grabbing at his neck. "Stop!"

I stare at Sandro, baffled, but it isn't until Salvia pounces on his legs and pins him in place that I'm able to parse what I'm seeing. He makes a strangled noise as his cloak continues to flap wildly at his back. But there's no wind.

The cloak is moving on its own.

The *cloak* is trying to get away, and it's dragging Sandro along with it.

Sandro gasps in a breath when the cloak stops strangling its owner to whip around toward Salvia instead. I jump forward, grabbing the cloak before it manages to wrap around their head. The cloth thrashes in my grasp, surprisingly strong. Strong enough that I'm beginning to think I made a mistake.

"No!" Sandro cries. "Please stop!" But he's not fighting us, and Salvia takes advantage of the moment to quickly bind his feet. I try to pull away from the cloak, which is terrifyingly attempting to encircle my torso like an anaconda.

Salvia binds his hands in seconds, then jumps on the cloak with me, yanking us apart. The cloak goes for Salvia next, but by then several other Fyrethians have rushed to our aid and are able to wrestle the magical cloth to the ground.

We all lay there panting for a moment.

"*WOW!*" Ollie suddenly says. "*THE CAPE IS ALIVE. THAT'S SO COOL! JUST LIKE DOCTOR STRANGE.*"

I Check the cloak, still quivering beneath the four guards it's pinned beneath.

[Check,] Echo says. [The Shuddering Shroud. This powerful and ancient artifact is dedicated to the protection of its wearer, enhancing their agility and evasiveness. It is even capable of acting independently from its wearer in order to ensure their safety.]

I suppose dragging its wearer across the ground by their neck is *one* way to save them.

It takes some work, but five guards working in tandem are able to wad up and secure the cloak. It looks a bit ridiculous, crumpled into a ball and bound against Sandro's back, but at least it's no longer trying to strangle anyone.

Sandro glances up at me, eyes wide with terror. "Please don't kill us!"

"I'm not going to kill you," I say, grunting as I push myself back to my feet. "Not unless you try to attack Ollie again."

"Ollie?" he repeats, looking around wildly.

Is he even using his System access at all? "Can you disable that cloak?" I ask instead, focusing on the more pressing issue.

"Uh, no," Sandro admits, shaking—*actually shaking*—beneath my glare. "I think it's stuck on me. It won't let me take it off. It's terrified of being removed—well, it's terrified of most things, really."

Not just a magical cloak, but a consciousness? That sounds strangely like the Dungeon Core, if you substituted fear for hunger. This raises more questions, but Ollie's safety comes first.

"Can you add it to your Inventory?" I ask him.

He blinks. "My what?"

A gust of wind washes over us as Dizzi lands nearby. "Fyre! What happened? I turned away for like one minute and you disappeared." Then she notices Sandro, bound and surrounded by five guards. "Uh, it looks like I missed some things."

"Do you have Ollie's translator?" I ask her.

"Yeah, sure." She digs it out of her bag. "It's not updated yet, though. I left before we were able to discuss much of anything."

"That's alright. This will do for now." I take the blue stone and head back over to Ollie. He lifts his chin so I can put the translator back into the leather band on his neck.

"How's that?" I ask.

"Blah blah blah blah—oh! It's working," his translator says.

Sandro gapes. "It—it can talk!"

I sigh. He really *did* run into a fight with a dragon without Checking its level.

"*He* can speak through the translator, yes," I say. "And his name is Ollie. You *do* know how to Check things, don't you?" Even Ollie had figured that out before meeting me, and he's eight years old.

Sandro's gaze darts between me, Ollie, and Salvia as if any one of us might eat him at any moment. Well, that is a possibility with Ollie, but his continued fearful reactions strike me as far more extreme than they should be. "Of course I can do that. But what has that got to do with anything?"

"Our Roles," I emphasize, managing not to sigh again. "We're the only three that have them. Or hadn't you noticed?"

"I noticed!" he objects. He nervously glances at Ollie again. "Oh. Well, his Role is the same as his species. I might have missed that."

"No, my Role is The Dragon but my Species is FROST dragon!" Ollie's translator says. He opens his mouth, and the back of his throat begins to glow white in demonstration.

"Ollie," I warn.

He snaps his mouth shut, and a puff of cold air and flecks of ice roll over us. Ollie giggles. "That felt like snorting milk out my nose."

"He's eight years old," I feel obligated to explain to Sandro. "And his role is 'The Dragon,' which is... complicated." I Check his Sanity stat again, but it hasn't changed. "But I think you better explain your Role first."

Sandro is still staring at Ollie. His expression and tone have bounced around a lot over the last few minutes, ranging everywhere from surprise to abject terror. We're back to some level of surprise again now, except this time it's tinged with something else.

"He's a kid?" Sandro says quietly. He looks helplessly back up at me. "I—shit. I didn't know. I'm sorry. I—"

Ollie hisses. "He said a bad word!"

"We try to keep our language PG around Ollie," I tell Sandro.

"Uh." Sandro is staring at Ollie, whose hissing does sound quite menacing if you don't know it's his mocking version of 'oooOOOoooh!' "Okay. I'm, uh, sorry about that."

"Apology accepted," Ollie says. "I guess!"

Finally, I let myself relax. Sandro doesn't seem to have any ill intent, despite his initial attack. I suspect he was operating under the influence of his Role. Which doesn't mean he poses no threat, but it does mean he can be reasoned with.

At least, until his Sanity stat gets too low.

It's that Shuddering Shroud that I'm more concerned with at this moment. Per its description, and Sandro's previous objections, it appears to be acting independently of his will. That makes it a bit of a wild card.

I turn back to Salvia and Dizzi, who were watching this play out with various levels of confusion and interest.

"I think I've had enough excitement for one day. I'm going to head back up with Ollie." I nod my head back toward Sandro. "Bring him back with us. There are still many questions I need answers for."

"Yes, Lord Fyre." Salvia bows and departs, heading off to help pack up the traded goods.

Dizzi watches Sandro curiously. "He's from your world?"

"Yes," I say, lowering my voice. "Though perhaps that is a detail we should keep to ourselves."

She tips her head. "I thought you were trying to convince everyone you're not from around here so they don't conflate you with Fyreneth."

"True," I admit, recalling Blair's warning. "But things have changed. It's fine to acknowledge I'm not originally Fyrethian—I doubt I could hide it, really—but where I am from, specifically... I'll explain later."

Dizzi looks curious but she doesn't argue. "If you say so. Well, guess I'll start to get this show packed up. What a way to end the day..."

I watch her head off to start organizing how the transports should be loaded up. I still haven't told her about our visit from the gods—only Mirzayael knows. I've been worried about saying too much aloud, in case the gods were nearby and listening, but after speaking with Blair today, perhaps I'm being too cautious. I decide we'll have to have a talk with all the council members later to catch them up.

I look back at Sandro, the Dragon Slayer.

For now, I've got a bigger headache to worry about.

Chapter Thirty-Five

CATALYSIS

Ollie and I head up to meet Mirzayael and soothe her worries as Dizzi and the rest continue loading the shuttles. They'll be bringing Sandro with them when they're done. Unsurprisingly, the town claims no responsibility for his actions, and are more than happy to let us take him off their hands.

Mirzayael is already waiting for us when Ollie lands.

"Everyone's alright?" she asks, quickly checking Ollie over. When she finds no injuries, she turns to me.

"We're okay," I assure her for the seventh time in as many minutes. "Though it looks like we might be needing to put Ragna's cell to use once more."

I gave her the short version of events while Ollie and I flew back up to meet her. She expressed concern about bringing Sandro back with us, but I'm more worried about letting him go and then not knowing where he is or what he's doing. Mirzayael suggested a more permanent solution that I quickly shot down.

"*His Role is not his fault,*" I privately tell her. "*I can't kill someone over something they're being compelled to do.*"

"*If you don't, Ollie's life will be at risk,*" she points out.

"I will not let anything happen to Ollie." My response is a little more fierce than I intended. *"But as long as there's a chance of finding a way to help them both, I have to try."*

"I don't even know if there are any dragons left in the world, Fyre," she says. *"And if there are only a few, would you be willing to endanger them for this stranger?"*

I don't have an answer for that.

"There's more," I say aloud with a sigh. But first I turn to Ollie. "You can go play with Meritis if you like. Mir and I need to talk about some boring adult stuff."

The dragon manages to roll his eyes. *"I'M NOT DUMB! I KNOW YOU GUYS ARE GOING TO TALK ABOUT SOMETHING IM-PORTANT."* He waits a moment. *"BUT I **AM** GOING TO GO FIND MERITIS, BECAUSE IT PROBABLY WILL BE BORING."*

I chuckle, patting his nose. "Have fun."

We wait until Ollie has jumped off the wall and circled up toward the palace. Mirzayael turns to me expectantly.

"Blair found me in the marketplace." As I relay the conversation I'd had with the god, I lean against the dock's parapet and look down over the land far, far beneath us. It's a breathtaking sight, one Mirzayael does everything in her power to avoid.

"I don't trust her," Mirzayael says once I've finished. "Why would she help us? There's no motive."

"Besides doing the right thing," I point out. "Maybe she just doesn't want to see a couple thousand people die for no reason."

Mirzayael scoffs. "It didn't stop them before."

"What if it's true that there is some discord in the Heavens?" I ask. "What purpose would she have to lie about that? If they all wanted us dead, at this point, we would be."

Mirzayael shakes her head, letting out an annoyed sigh. "Perhaps some of them might disagree on some things. Perhaps those two *don't* want us dead. But that doesn't mean they have no ulterior motive for helping us. They'll ask for something in return, mark my words. And when they do, it won't be an ask."

I hope she's wrong. But deep down, I suspect she isn't.

"Either way, I think Blair's warning is authentic," I say. "The longer we remain aloft, the more we run the risk of drawing the attention of a god who is not interested in our wellbeing. We should try to find somewhere to settle soon."

Mirzayael scowls. "Easier said than done. Did you have any luck finding information about mana ore mines?"

I grimace. "Not yet." In fact, it's with growing concern that I'm realizing Gardi's comment might be correct: finding somewhere to land that will provide an ambient source of mana for the Fortress may be more difficult than I first thought.

As we wait for our ground crew to return, Mirzayael orders a couple guards to go prepare Ragna's cell. It's another ten minutes before I can make out the dots of harpies and our shuttles in the sky.

"Oh," I say, my mind returning to Sandro. "There's something else about the man I forgot to mention before. I think it's unrelated to his Role. But he was wearing this magical cloak when we caught him. I'm not sure if we'll be able to take it off; it appears to be sentient, and tried to fight us when we bound him. Our cells should hold Sandro just fine, but the cloak will cause us some trouble if it manages to escape."

"A magical cloak?" Mirzayael repeats. "Strange. I've heard of garments imbued with proactive spells, but nothing that moves on its own. Are you sure he wasn't controlling it? Perhaps with some form of Attunement?"

"I'll double check when he gets here, but I'm pretty sure it wasn't him." I watch as the flying dots start to resolve into recognizable shapes. "I guess we'll find out soon enough."

"This should be fun."

I jump, head whipping to my right. Lisari is casually standing there, grinning.

Well, I can *feel* it's Lisari.

The figure beside me has the same black and white clothes, potion bottles at their hip, dark hair, pale skin—but that's where the similarities with the scholar end. The Lisari before me now appears taller, male, and though his hair is black, it's because it's made of faintly wafting smoke. Similar black fog drifts from his eyes. His very presence seems to exude power.

And danger.

I had felt it with Blair and Lisari before, but now I can also see it: *this* is a god.

I swallow down the pit forming in my throat. "Shirasil?"

Mirzayael's head snaps in my direction. "What? Is he here? Where?"

I gawk at Mirzayael, then turn back to the man standing right next to me, feeling as though I'm losing my mind.

"She can't see me," Shirasil says, resting an elbow on the parapet and his chin on his fist. "Don't bother."

Then I catch sight of Blair, on the other side of Mirzayael. Like Shirasil, she now appears in a far more celestial form, with a subtle glow beneath her skin, and clothes that seem to drift around her body like she's underwater. I'm sure she hadn't been there a moment before. A chill runs through me.

"Shirasil is to my right and Blair is to your left," I mentally tell Mirzayael, attempting to quell my panic. She looks wildly around. *"They must be hiding themselves from you somehow."*

"Why are you here?" I ask Shirasil, since he's the closest. Though he's also the most likely to answer my questions, I wish it was Blair I was speaking to. Somehow, despite Blair's aloofness and Shirasil's persistent cheerfulness, she feels the less dangerous of the two.

"Careful, now," he teasingly warns. "Talking to yourself? That can't be a good look. What will your people think?"

He rests his hand, palm up, on the wall between us. "Psionic Touch would save you the trouble."

I stare at the hand, abruptly reminded of the helplessness I'd felt the first time the gods had cornered me. I try to stuff down the instinctive panic, focusing on keeping my head clear. I lean faintly away from Shirasil until I brush up against Mirzayael's side. She leans back, providing a solid, comforting wall, and wraps an arm around me.

"Tell me precisely where," she mentally replies. *"I'll strike at those places."*

"And then what?" I ask. *"Run? No—no. I don't think they're here for us."* I glance at Blair out of the corner of my eye. She's not looking my way, but at something below the fortress.

"Is this another test?" I ask aloud, despite Shirasil's offer. I try to follow Blair's gaze, but there's nothing of note except our approaching shipment of supplies.

"No, no, of course not!" Shirasil says.

But Blair says, "Yes." She's still not looking at me. "The most important test of all."

"I'd call it more of an experiment," Shirasil says, grinning madly as he also turns away. "Hypothesis: the remnants will react capriciously but the Travelers will maintain authority."

"Predicting that results will be unpredictable is not a real hypothesis," I say before thinking better of it.

But Shirasil just laughs. "I suppose we'll find out." Then he casually places his hand on my arm.

I stiffen. His touch is cold, and I brace for whatever he's planning next. But he doesn't do anything else. He doesn't squeeze my arm or try to hurt me. Does he want me to use my Psionic Touch?

I glance toward Blair. She's on the other side of Mirzayael, at an angle where she wouldn't be able to make out what Shirasil was doing. Is that intentional? Does he not want her to know?

"Not much time left now," Shirasil remarks, leaning forward. The comment could have ostensibly been for Blair, but I'm fairly certain he's trying to tell me something.

I take in a nervous breath.

[Psionic Touch activated.]

"*Smart girl,*" Shirasil says in my mind, and I shudder. The voice is somewhere between Shirasil and Lisari's—or perhaps both speaking at once.

"*What do you—*"

"*If the impending encounter goes poorly, Blair will take you, the boy, and the Dungeon Core, resulting in the destruction of this city and all its inhabitants,*" he says. My heartbeat quickens. "*Take hold of the Dungeon Core now... if you can.*"

I tense, then privately reach out to Mirzayael. "*Say nothing,*" I tell her, trying to remain calm. "*Don't react.*" I quietly open her link into the Psionic Touch.

"*Why?*" I ask Shirasil, reaching out to the Dungeon Core. "*What's about to happen?*" The Dungeon Core stirs at my attention, happily greeting me, but I'm at a loss of what to do. Take hold of it? Its mind is not some tangible thing I can wrestle into submission.

"That depends on you," Shirasil says. Mirzayael stills, but doesn't make a sound. *"Perhaps nothing will happen. Or perhaps we're about to have a significant problem on our hands, and things will get very exciting. Either way, the boy won't have any say in how this encounter resolves."*

"The boy?" I echo. *"Ollie?"* No. Ollie's back in the palace, and the gods are looking out away from the city. Waiting for someone to approach.

Like our traders.

"Sandro," I realize. What about him? The way his Role could impact Ollie? Or... *"The cape. It had a mind of its own. It's like the Dungeon Core, isn't it?"*

Shirasil grins.

"But why is it up to me?" I ask, still desperately trying to imagine myself wrangling the Dungeon Core under control—an entity whose consciousness has expanded to be larger than the city itself. *"If something happens between the Dungeon Core and his cape—can't he stop it?"* A cape seems far easier to control.

Shirasil's laughter rings through my head. *"You've spoken with him. He has the mental fortitude of a wet rag."*

"And you think my mental fortitude will be enough?"

"I'm not here to flatter you," Shirasil says, his amusement dancing through his words even as my anxiety winds tighter. *"We'll soon find out. But I think there's a chance. You demonstrated your ability to think on your feet and stay cool under pressure the last time we met. And even now you had the wherewithal to slip someone else into our conversation to eavesdrop. Hello, by the way."*

Mirzayael's grip on my shoulder tightens.

"*Why are you doing this?*" she demands, now that her presence has been exposed. "*Why are you hiding this conversation from your fellow?*"

Shirasil chuckles. "*You told her about Blair, too? Of course you did. It's quite simple: I don't want you to fail.*"

"*And Blair does?*" I ask, skeptical. She had just been telling me how she would be willing to cover for me and Ollie... as long as I maintained control of the Dungeon Core.

"*No,*" Shirasil says. "*Neither of us want you to fail. But Blair won't stop you from doing so. She believes organic encounters produce organic results. If she knew I was helping, she'd be extremely cross with me.*" He sounds far too amused while he is saying this.

"*How are you helping?*" I ask, exasperated. "*I still don't know what to do!*"

"*Its power flows through you,*" Shirasil says. "*Don't forget that you hold the reins. Its area may be wide, but its influence is small... for now, anyway. Don't constrain your mind to what you see: imagination has no bounds.*"

I don't understand all of what he's telling me, but the comment about holding the reins—he's right about that. I control the mana that allows the Dungeon Core to exert its influence over the city. I'd once pictured it as a pipe of running water, where I could increase or decrease the rate of flow.

"*Time's up,*" Shirasil says, removing his hand from my arm. He eagerly leans forward. "Here we go."

The shuttles are so close, I can make out everyone's faces. I check the Dungeon Core's Map: they're just outside its area of influence, still invisible to the Dungeon Core's eyes, but that will change in a matter of seconds.

"*Mirzayael,*" I quickly say, but she's already read my mind.

"I'll secure Sandro," she promises. *"You focus on the Core."*

And then they're within the Core's range. Its attention latches onto the cape like magnets snapping together. It startles me with its suddenness, even knowing something like this was coming. A rumbling hunger overtakes the Dungeon Core, and it grows jittery and excited. It wants to eat this. It wants to eat this more than it's wanted to eat anything!

At the same time, raised voices drift across the air. "No!" I can hear Sandro shout. "No, don't!"

I'm having a similar mental conversation with the Core. I grab the faucet to the Dungeon Core's flow of mana, and I hold it tight. *No,* I tell it. *You can't eat it.*

Mirzayael gives my shoulder one last squeeze, then sprints from our place at the wall, drawing a line of silk as she rushes for the docks. I grab the edge of the parapet, white-knuckled as I clutch the stone, and feel the Core push back against me.

But it wants this thing. It wants it so bad! And it would be so easy to eat, it wouldn't even take that much mana. Or maybe it would savor it, tearing it apart piece by piece—

No, I say firmly. *I won't be giving you mana for that, and that's final.*

The Dungeon Core sours. Why won't I let it have this one thing? It's not asking for much. And it needs it! It *craves* this thing, this food that feels so distantly familiar.

It can still sense my resolve, however, and it grumbles with growing agitation.

Fine. If I won't let it have any more mana, then it will just have to take some.

It takes a fraction of a second for me to realize what it means. I'm still letting mana flow through our connection. I have to if we want to keep the city aloft and operational. But not every function it's powering is necessary. If it diverted all the mana I'm giving it for powering the lights in the palace, for instance—

I shut it down. I shut every single non-essential spell down, throttling the Dungeon Core's mana flow simultaneously. My ears painfully pop and cold wind blows over us as the atmospheric spell powers off. In the castle, every fire, every light, every stove and water pump stops functioning. All I leave running are the spells that are keeping the city floating and stabilized.

The Dungeon Core throws a fit. It thrashes at my mind. It complains and demands and cries. It's acting like a toddler, lashing out at my conscience with ineffective blows. I've only ever seen it remotely act like this before when I immersed it in the thermal spring water it hated so much—and this is much worse.

But I've overcome it before, and I'll do so again now.

I steel myself. I imagine my mind as solid and unyielding, and the Core's attempts to throw itself at me suddenly become a whisper. Shirasil was right; though its influence affects a large area, I still hold far more power over it than it does over me. I can't let its abilities skew my perception of reality. I'm in control.

Ollie surfaces in my mind. "*WHAT'S IT DOING? IT'S BEING SO NOISY!*"

"*Sorry. It tried to eat something it couldn't have,*" I tell him.

"*OOOOOH.*" Ollie sounds very understanding. "*SORRY, CORE. SOMETIMES YOU CAN'T HAVE CANDY, AND IT'S NOT FAIR. WANT ME TO GET YOU SOME MORE SEA SHELLS?*"

Finally understanding the futility of its struggle, the fight goes out of the Dungeon Core, and it puddles to the floor of my mind, pathetically sad. It supposes some sea shells would be nice.

"*OKAY!*" Ollie happily says. "*ME AND MERITIS CAN GO GET SOME NOW! IT'LL BE FUN. BE BACK SOON!*"

The Core encourages him to come back quickly. And maybe grab some of those pink shells, they're the Core's favorite.

I slump, loosening my grip on the wall. *"Thank you, Ollie. That was a big help."*

Ollie, who seems unaware of how close we were to catastrophe, happily accepts the praise before his attention switches back over to Meritis, who is speaking to him.

I also return to the Dungeon Core. *Will you behave now? That's the only way you'll be getting back access to all that mana.*

The Dungeon Core gives a heavy, defeated sigh but agrees to not eat the tasty thing. Can it have more mana now?

One good thing about the Dungeon Core is that it doesn't seem to have any concept of lying, or the ability to do it itself. If it says it won't try to eat something, then it means it—even if it might change its mind about it later. For now, though, I think I can trust it to behave.

I begin funneling mana back through the Core and turning the city's spells back on. My ears feel stuffy as the air pressure and temperature start to slowly rise back toward their previous levels.

The shuttles pull into the dock, and Mirzayael is on Sandro in an instant.

I look over at Shirasil. Per usual, he's smiling.

"And you said that wasn't a real hypothesis," he teases.

I grimace. "It was more like a prediction, anyway." Shirasil chuckles, and I turn to Blair next. "Did I pass, then?"

She gives me a considering look, then nods respectfully. "You did well."

Maybe that would fill me with more reassurance if I hadn't known she'd been inches away from dooming the entire city.

Chapter Thirty-Six

DRAGON SLAYER

To my disappointment, the gods don't leave after we haul Sandro off the transport. They also don't reveal themselves to anyone else, instead preferring, I suppose, to continue providing me with a personal haunting. I privately let Mirzayael know but otherwise ignore them, too busy keeping an eye on the Dungeon Core—and Sandro's cape.

"Good job, Salvia," Mirzayael says to them as Sandro is turned over to us. "You may return to your duties with Gardi."

The young guard scowls. That means letting the Jorrian out of their cell so the two of them can join in with the activities of our city's visitors, which is an extremely fair punishment, in my opinion. But they don't object. "Yes, my lord."

Mirzayael looks Sandro up and down. "So this is the one." She glares, leaning over him in a manner that looks intentionally intimidating.

Sandro appears thoroughly intimidated.

"Look," he says, nervously glancing between the two of us. "I don't want any trouble. I was just trying to satisfy my Role. But I don't want to hurt a kid—I didn't know what he was. I'm really sorry."

"I know," I say. "That's why I brought you back with us. You're not the only one with an unfortunate Role, but I'm hoping we can work together on figuring out how to resolve them." I make eye contact with Blair and Shirasil (well, with Blair anyway) as I say this. "There are other questions I want answers to as well. But let's find somewhere more private to chat."

It's a long walk back up to the palace, and Sandro turns his head every which way, looking at the city in awe as we march him through the streets. In the end we settle on one of Ollie's outdoor pavilions, so he can also be part of the conversation when he returns from his Dungeon Core errand. This platform is just outside the throne room, so no one else is around. The balcony gives us a stunning view of the land and clouds beneath us, shadows stretched far to the east as the sun lowers in the sky.

I lost track of Blair and Shirasil when we were heading through the city and palace, but now that we've reached the private pavilion, they reappear once more. I'd dared hope they decided to leave us for a time.

"...rather rude, don't you think?" Shirasil is saying to Blair. "I mean, *I* provided the tip."

I try to ignore them as Mirzayael and I figure out what to do with Sandro. The stuffed-up bundle on his back that's covered in about a hundred loops of spider silk trembles.

"Can I trust you to be untied?" I ask Sandro. We settle him on a stone bench designed for those of us who are not dragon-sized. It has another bench on either side, situating us like a U around a small central table. It's designed for casual chats between friends, but I've never had the time or opportunity to use it.

Sandro nods eagerly. "I won't do anything—I promise. I don't even have a weapon if I wanted to. That one harpy took it."

"Your class is a spellsword," I note. "What kind of spells do you have?"

"Oh," he says, as if he'd forgotten. "Right. Uh, they're all sword related. Making the blade hot, or poisoned, or move faster—stuff like that."

"And your cape?" I ask.

Annoyingly, Blair and Shirasil are continuing to speak with each other in the background.

"This time, at least," Blair says. "But what if it encounters a stronger remnant?"

"Do you know of any?" Shirasil asks.

Blair hesitates.

I'm not sure if they have forgotten about me, or are intentionally doing this to remind me of their presence. Shirasil might just be doing it to annoy me.

Sandro winces. "The Shuddering Shroud. It's, um, a bit different. It has a mind of its own. It won't attack you unless it feels threatened." He pauses. "But it sort of always feels threatened."

"How reassuring," Mirzayael says dryly. She turns to me. "Your call."

"We can untie his hands," I decide. "He didn't pose much of a threat with his sword, anyway."

Sandro grimaces.

"But we're leaving your cloak secured for now," I add. "Alright?"

Sandro looks downright miserable. "Sure."

Mirzayael cuts his bonds, and Sandro mumbles an awkward thanks, rubbing his wrists, then tucks his legs up onto the bench as well, as if he's trying to make himself appear as small as possible.

Given he's an elf, it's a bit odd to watch him acting so awkward and nervous—though perhaps that's Tolkien biases playing into my expectations. I ask Echo to Check his age: 25. An adult, then, but it's hard for me to not think of him as a kid. Twenty-five was half a lifetime ago.

"So, um, you guys are all from Earth, too?" Sandro asks, nervously glancing around at us. "I thought it was just me. Do you know if there are more?"

"Sandro," I interrupt, suspecting he was about to continue nervously asking questions until we cut in. "I've a few questions I need to ask you before anything else."

"Oh! Sure, sure." He hurriedly bobs his head.

"That depends on if and when we find this Kanin fellow," Shirasil is saying, despite my efforts to tune them out.

Blair shakes her head. "That's tangential. They will remain a problem no matter the reason for their summoning."

"You can't tell me you're not curious," he says. "You especially."

"My duty is to the realm before all else."

"*Fyre*," Mirzayael mentally prompts.

I drag my attention back to her and Sandro. "*Sorry. They're distracting. What was I saying?*"

"*Questions for Sandro.*"

"*Right. Thank you.*"

"Your Role, Dragon Slayer," I say, focusing on Sandro. "What are its requirements?"

"The Dragon Slayer has to slay a dragon," he recites with a shrug. "It's pretty straight forward. Unfortunately. Do you know how many dragons I've found before today? None."

"Sandro, focus," I say. "How does Echo define the term 'slay'?" Maybe there's a loophole here that can be exploited. I've already asked her myself—and was provided the obvious answer—but I have to make sure there aren't any differences between our interfaces.

"Um." He pauses, tipping his head with a wince. "She says slay means to kill in a violent way."

My budding hope withers once more. But this is only a part of the picture, I remind myself. "Your sanity stat is at eighty-five percent," I note, Checking it again. It's the same as it was when I first met him. "Has that changed at all since you arrived here?"

"Yeah," he admits. "It started at one hundred percent, but it's been slowly ticking down. I didn't notice it at first, but now there's this… buzzing in the back of my mind. It's kind of annoying." His brows pinch together in sudden worry. "Is that bad? Will I be okay?"

"Don't worry. You'll be fine," I lie.

If it started at one hundred percent, and it's decreased fifteen percent in the last few months, it sounds like he loses a point every four days or so. Theoretically, that's almost a year before he hits zero. But does he have that long? When my sanity stat was plummeting, I lost all sense of self far before that point. And if his Role Requirement is starting to bug him now, then it might be more than he can ignore before long. I estimate we have two, maybe three months before it becomes a serious problem.

And even if I find some other dragon for him to kill in that time, what then? Will the number reset to one hundred percent, just to start ticking down once more?

This is even worse than the Requirements Ollie and I are bound by.

And what a cruel Role this is. Why would this System want to force someone into violent conflict? I don't understand it.

But perhaps there is someone who is willing to enlighten us.

"You're not holding out on me, are you?" Shirasil asks. "I thought introducing you to Fyre, here, was more than a show of good faith."

"It's a start," Blair says. "But if you want to sway Yua Tin, you're speaking to the wrong person. I'm no longer her—"

"Would you care to join the conversation?" I ask, raising my voice. Trying to speak with Sandro and Mirzayael while the gods continue to talk over us in the background is absolutely maddening. "I assume there is some reason you have remained."

Sandro nervously glances around. "Who... who are you talking to?"

Blair regards me coolly, and I realize my frustration may have resulted in me addressing them a bit too casually. "With all due respect," I weakly add.

"You should not have been privy to that conversation," Blair says. She looks at Shirasil.

"Wait, was *I* supposed to conceal us?" he asks with transparently fake surprise. "Oh, no! Sincerest apologies."

Blair lifts her eyes to the sky in a moment of exasperation before collecting herself and turning to me. "The reason I have remained is because I still have some time left in the mortal realm before I need to depart. I am here for Sandro, not you. I've been shadowing him to gauge the danger of his cloak. After today, I think it is safe to say it poses very little threat."

"Oh," I say awkwardly.

"But thank you for the invitation!" Shirasil says, "What do you say, Blair? The more the merrier."

"Shirasil, do not—"

Sandro gasps, and Mirzayael jumps, her head whipping toward the gods. Well. I guess everyone can see them now.

Blair pinches the bridge of her nose.

"Erm," I say. "Sandro, Mirzayael. This is Blair and Shirasil. They're gods." That part probably wasn't necessary, given their appearances.

Mirzayael's grip on her spear tightens, but to my relief, she doesn't do anything rash. Yet.

Sandro, meanwhile, starts shaking. "Oh no. Oh, no, no, no. Please don't kill us! Please!"

Mirzayael gives him a disgusted look. "Pull yourself together! This is embarrassing."

It does seem like an extreme reaction, but he's been shaking worse than a chihuahua since I first saw him.

"It's not entirely his fault," Shirasil says, strolling over to us, hands clasped behind his back. "It's the remnant's influence, most likely. Their personalities can be strong, but... one dimensional. Though he does seem particularly bad at shutting this one out. It's not even that powerful."

Similar to how the Dungeon Core only cares about eating? I recall what Sandro said about his cloak a few minutes before. "You're saying his cloak is... anxious?"

Shirasil shrugs. "That seems to be a fair assessment."

I'm still digesting this as I feel Mirzayael's shifting mood. There's a smoldering anger inside her that is never quite extinguished. Sometimes it's only a few embers, buried far in the back of her mind. But right now, it's growing, flames licking up her subconscious.

I put a hand on her arm. Her muscles are so taut, it feels like steel wires lay beneath her skin. "*Steady.*" I try to soothe her.

"These... remnants," I say, turning to Blair and Shirasil. "Why do they want to harm each other?"

Shirasil brightens. "Excellent question!"

"That we will not be answering," Blair cuts in.

Not that I *want* the gods to come back, but I'm going to need to pin Shirasil down by himself one of these days to pry out some answers.

"Fine," I say. That question was out of academic interest anyway; what I really need to figure out is a way for Ollie to not become a target of Sandro's. "Perhaps you can help us with something else. Blair already mentioned that you can't change or alter our Roles. But can you at least help us manage them?" I gesture to Sandro. "His Role is forcing him to commit violence. And it might put Ollie in harm's way. Is there anything, *anything* about these Roles you can tell us that might help?"

Blair's frown softens into a sympathetic look. "You all did not receive Roles through the proper process. We are still trying to understand how and why each of you received the Roles you did. It's possible they were applied randomly."

"Some of them don't even make sense," Shirasil adds, gesturing to me. "What even is a Dark Lord?"

"Oh." I look at the two of them in surprise. The gods didn't know about this. "It's the name for a storytelling trope from my world. It refers to a villainous leader."

Both gods appear surprised to learn this. Then Shirasil starts laughing. "You? Villainous?" He laughs even harder.

Mirzayael gives me a pointed look. She doesn't speak into my mind, but I can hear the "I told you" anyway.

I frown, chewing on a nail in thought. "Then the System is creating Roles based on knowledge from our world. Yet, my Role seems to have been influenced by Fyrethian history. Fyreneth, from an outside perspective, would have fit the 'Dark Lord' trope. She was a leader of a country that was deemed 'evil.' Or at least, Forsaken. And I ended up being given a Role that fit the hole she left."

"The System is drawing on concepts from Travelers, but merging them with relevant context where they appear in our world," Blair muses. "I assume the boy's Role also means something to you?"

"Ollie? Yes," I say. "The Dragon is another motif. It refers to a powerful entity who works for the Dark Lord. Which *can* be a dragon, but doesn't have to be."

"Oh," Mirzayael says. "I was wondering why it was 'the dragon' and not simply 'dragon.'"

But why did we receive *these* Roles specifically? If they're random, as Blair suggested, but based on some initial conditions around where we manifested in the world... In programming speak, we'd call this a seed. Perhaps this System really is some sort of magical computer.

"See?" Shirasil says, spinning to Blair in delight. "I told you speaking to them would be a good idea. Now we know why some of the Roles appear nonsensical."

I look between the gods skeptically. "Are you saying no one had even asked any of us about the significance of our Roles before now?"

Blair actually looks uncomfortable.

And oddly, Shirasil seems to lose some of his amusement with the situation. "Why, yes, Blair, why *haven't* we been speaking with the Travelers?"

"It was not my order to partition them," she says.

"Oh, of course. Following orders absolves one of all responsibility," Shirasil says, a hint of bitterness entering his tone. This shift in his character sets me on edge.

"Could you not speak with those who have been taken into the custody of the gods?" I ask carefully. Blair had mentioned this "partition" before, but only briefly.

Shirasil gives a mirthless laugh. "They're not really in a talkative mood."

I look back to Blair for elaboration, hesitant to push this clearly dangerous subject too far. We're also getting off track from my original ask. None of this helps with Sandro or Ollie's Roles.

"Then about Sandro's Role," I say, trying to shift back into safer territory. "To kill a dragon. Is he going to have to continuously perform this Role? Or will it be complete after he does it once?"

Both of the gods are silent for a moment. Sandro is hunched in on himself as if trying to appear as small as possible.

"It will reset," Blair says, sounding disappointed. "He will need to achieve this feat at least once per year."

"But that's..." I don't even know how to finish the sentence. Horrific? Cruel? Unfair?

"This is the danger of harnessing a hurricane," Shirasil murmurs.

"Partitioning seems a mercy in this case," Blair says to him.

Oddly, he doesn't reply. He seems lost in thought.

"And this partitioning would prevent his Role from affecting him?" I hesitantly ask.

Shirasil appears to snap out of his thoughts. He scoffs, turning to Blair. "Is that what you told her?"

She stands a little straighter, looking indignant. "It's the truth."

"The truth," Shirasil says, turning to me, "is that every Traveler who has been snapped up has been frozen, slowing any passage of time they experience a thousand-fold. This renders them *mostly* unaware of their surroundings, and *delays* a lapsed Role Requirement from enforcing a decrease in their sanity stat."

"*Mostly* unaware?" I repeat, horrified.

Blair remains quiet.

"Over a few decades, they will experience a few days of consciousness," Shirasil says. "And their Sanity Stat will still decrease—excruciatingly slowly. But that won't stop it. They'll exist in that null space until a solution can be reached. And study on Roles has been ongoing for about... what, Blair, two thousand years?"

I physically recoil. "These people will be imprisoned for eternity, slowly and inevitably going mad? That's horrific."

"Depending on what Role the individual is being compelled to fulfill, it can be a mercy," Blair objects.

"Can be," Shirasil shoots back. "And tell me: How many have been suspended out of mercy?"

Blair shakes her head. "I do not have time to argue this with you now."

"Of course." His voice drips with sarcasm. "Don't let me keep you from more important matters." He turns away from Blair and walks toward us. Mirzayael goes taut once more.

"Find a bestiarian," he tells me, still walking toward us with no sign of slowing. "Your kid isn't the only dragon in the world."

I take an alarmed step back right as it seems he's about to walk into me, and he abruptly evaporates, collapsing into a cloud of smoke that dissipates into the air as it washes over me.

Blair shakes her head. "He means well. But he's lost sight of our purpose." Then she also walks over to us. Unlike Shirasil, she stops, looking at both Mirzayael and I.

[Permissions Updated,] Echo abruptly says.

"It *is* a mercy," she insists, voice low. Her gaze briefly flickers to Sandro. "If you can find no solution, don't forget there always remains another option."

And then she, too, simply vanishes.

We both stand there for a moment, stunned.

Behind us, Sandro whimpers. "Are they gone? Oh, thank god."

Mirzayael's lips peel back in a sneer. "No. *Fuck* the gods."

CHAPTER THIRTY-SEVEN
SURVEILLANCE

Sandro is... a handful.

The Shroud, at least, pretty much leaves everyone alone; it's too busy tripping Sandro up by wrapping itself around his body at every possible threat. Threats include, but are not limited to: loud sounds, bright colors, Ollie, flocks of birds, Mirzayael, shadows, and people walking into the room. Though I can't entirely fault the Shroud for being so nervous with the Dungeon Core's presence persistently looming over it, wondering if today is the day I'll let it eat the tasty-looking cloak.

Sandro himself, meanwhile, is almost more clingy than his cape. He keeps close to whomever he's with, bumping up against or even nervously grabbing the arm of whomever is closest. He's a never-ending stream of questions, which normally I wouldn't have a problem with, but in his case it's less curiosity and more along the lines of "Who is that? Are they dangerous? Is this place safe? Where are you going?"

Mirzayael keeps Salvia on Gardi, which Salvia actually appears relieved about, once Sandro's anxious attachment style makes itself apparent. Zakaiya and Rei are the two unlucky guards who get assigned to the boy. While Sandro is emotionally draining, the job at least lets them continue to conserve their mana for their gestating soul.

Before our Fortress leaves Hetopolis, I take advantage of Shirasil's parting advice to look for a bestiarian. This city isn't big enough to have anyone so specialized, but I purchase a couple of bestiary books and scrolls that include at least a passage or two on dragons. In about two weeks we'll be crossing over a major capital city, and there I'm sure I'll find someone who might be able to help. Sandro's Sanity stat should only decrease from eighty-five percent to about eighty percent in that time. Hopefully, it won't be an issue.

More pressing, however, is Blair's threat of other gods finding us and discovering The Dungeon Core. I've considered rearranging the throne room to move the Core somewhere more secure, but I'm not sure that would make a difference to a god.

Mirzayael and I talk through these concerns while we separately go about our daily tasks. Dizzi is giving me an overview of all the watchtower findings, while Mirzayael is doing drills with her guards.

"Perhaps if the gods do find us and sense something, they will attribute it to Sandro's Shroud and target him instead," Mirzayael suggests.

I don't disguise how aghast I am with this idea.

"It's better than them taking the Core and killing all of us," she objects.

"I know." But that doesn't mean I want Sandro to be stuck in that semi-conscious, semi-frozen state the gods alluded to. At least... not unless we can find no other alternative.

"We'll just have to focus on finding somewhere to land," I reply. *"Any word on viable settlement locations yet?"*

"We gathered as many ambient mana and geological surveys as we could find," Mirzayael says. *"Chert is working on it now. The mana*

maps are less useful, due to these Ruins that appear to be scattered over the world. Their high mana-concentration obscures the more subtle mana-ore locations. But he seems to think with the geological maps he'll be able to find something, in time."

I wish time was something we had.

Once more, I glance at the new option in the corner of my vision. Blair unlocked some portion of the System I previously didn't have access to. It's not much, but it's something:

[Contact List.]

[Current Contacts: Blair.]

It's not a mystery why she gave me this capability. I recall the last thing she told me before she left. "It *is* a mercy. If you can find no solution, there always remains another option." It's clear what choice she's waiting for me to make.

"Fyre?" Dizzi prompts. "You with me?"

"Sorry, yes," I say, turning to her. "How's the progress?"

"We're ready to hook this one up," she says, gesturing to the ground. We're in Eye Tower, which contains the mass-surveillance type spell. The defensive spell in Shield Tower, and the weapon spell in Watchtower Three, are already connected into the circuit. Broken Tower's circle is almost entirely gone, destroyed (and eaten by the Dungeon Core) beyond repair. Dizzi is still puzzling out the fifth and final watchtower with the other researchers, which appears to be the most complicated circle yet.

Chalk markings cover the spell carved into the floor, filling in damaged portions of the circle and detailing how I should alter the stone to repair the floor.

"What can you tell me about it?" I ask.

"This one creates a field," Dizzi says. "I know I said I thought this one was some kind of surveillance type spell, and it is, but it's less about tracking people within the city, and more about setting up alarms for people crossing the barrier in or out of the city."

"Interesting," I say. "What sort of things could trigger the alarm?"

"It's a bit tricky to pin down without activating the spell," Dizzi admits. "But it seems pretty flexible. Like, it could alert someone in the throne room every time, say, a harpy passed into its range. Which I wouldn't recommend, because then you'd have the spell triggering constantly. I think you can set it to alert for individual people, too, but they would have to pass through the field at least once for it to log them."

"Interesting." I step up beside her and take her hand, activating Psionic Touch.

Dizzi laughs giddily in my head. *This is so cool. I feel like a spy.*

After the gods' latest visit, Mirzayael and I decided to loop Dizzi, Nek, and Torim into what was going on with Shirasil and Blair. They can't act as our advisors if they don't know what's going on. I performed a group Psionic Touch with them at the time so we could discuss things freely without the gods eavesdropping on us. The revelation had made Nek and Torim extremely concerned—with good reason—but Dizzi only seemed disappointed she'd missed it. I warned her to be cautious around Lisari, if she showed up disguised as a human again, but I suspect Dizzi will be anything but.

"Do you think this spell can work on the gods?" I ask her.

"I don't know," she admits. *"We might have to turn it on first, and have at least one of them come back. Then once they're in the system, we'll be able to see if we can set it to alert on any future visits—and if we'll be able to set it broadly to alert to any god, or if it will only pick up on the individual."*

I think back to the stats I'd witnessed with Blair and Shirasil. *"In my System interface, both of them still had species, like anyone else; felis and human. But they also had a Title, that I haven't seen on anyone else, and that was what designated them as a God. Perhaps we could set this alarm system up to activate if anyone with a God Title enters."*

Dizzi shrugs. *"You could try. Will this spell even know about this System of yours? I guess we won't know until we flip it on."*

"Then let's do so."

[Psionic Touch ended.]

I let go of Dizzi's hand to crouch down and touch the floor instead. I call the Dungeon Core's attention over and point out the chalk marks and tell it what it needs to do. It's happy to comply, and sets about fixing all the runes and snapping all the breaks in the circle shut. Dizzi walks around, inspecting it all, then gives me the all-good.

I step back and Check the repaired circle.

[Check: Greater Detection Spell. Mana requirement: 1 mana per second.]

"Wow," I say aloud. "That's a much better magic consumption rate than the others. One mana per second."

"Probably because the defensive and offensive shields are temporary," Dizzi muses. "They also need to be able to expend and absorb a lot of energy on a very high scale. Meanwhile, this spell is far more passive. And that's, what..." She pauses, her finger flicking through the air in a mental calculation. "Still almost a hundred-thousand mana a day to keep it active around the clock."

I have Echo do some math for me as well. "Over thirty-million mana to keep it going for a year."

"Ouch," Dizzi says.

"Indeed. We really need to find some mana ore to settle on."

I double-check how much magic the Dungeon Core and I still have.

[Bonus Mana: 199,838,512]

That's down from about two-hundred and forty million that we first launched with. Theoretically, this will keep us aloft for another four months, but we almost certainly need to land before then. If I started this spell today, it would only shorten our flight time by two weeks. That's more than worth the risk, in my eyes.

"Ready to see it in action?" I ask Dizzi.

Her face lights up with glee. We haven't activated any of the other spells due to their high mana cost. "Would I ever!"

I grin, confirming the spell circle is connected back into the throne room. Then I tweak the Bonus Mana flow rate dripping into the Core, adding just one more mana per second, and I activate the spell circle.

The floor illuminates, casting a red glow around the rest of the room. Dizzi would have to go back to the Throne Room to access the spell, but since I'm mentally linked into the Dungeon Core, itself embedded in the throne, I can start looking through it remotely. I offer my hand to Dizzi once more, and when she takes it, I activate another Psionic Link, so she can experience the new spell's capabilities with me.

"This is so weird," Dizzi says, grinning.

"*Keep any remarks in our head,*" I remind her. Not that the gods probably couldn't figure out how these spells worked on their own, but I'm learning not to tempt fate.

"*It seems to be in effect,*" I note. The spell itself is populating metrics on the city's inhabitants. It doesn't tell me the location of each individual, like the Dungeon Core's Map interface, but it does provide a list of populations which can be ordered by qualities such as species, affinities, and age. "*I didn't feel anything when the spell turned on. I never would have known.*"

"*Age,*" Dizzi immediately says. "*That's what you can use to filter for the gods. They're all, like, what... thousands of years old?*"

"*Great idea,*" I say. "*What's the oldest age a mortal species on this planet could be?*"

"*Uhhhh... Hm.*" Dizzi tips her head. "*Good question. For Fyrethians, dwarfs are the longest living species. They can go up to two hundred, but that's pretty rare. I'm not totally sure about some of these new species we've met.*"

I ask Echo the same question.

[On Lusio, the longest-living mortal and sapient species is the dryad, capable of living up to two hundred and fifty years,] she says.

"*Oh my gosh,*" Dizzi cries. "*I heard that! Woah! I mean I knew you had a voice in your head, but I had no idea it was so literal. Hey. Echo! Echo! Can you hear me?*"

Echo does not reply.

"*Awww,*" she thinks, radiating disappointment for roughly two seconds before it snaps back to excitement. "*Well, it was worth a shot!*"

"*Two hundred and fifty, then,*" I say. "*Let's do three hundred, just to be safe.*" I don't want the klaxons going off on an elderly dryad visitor.

The spell accepts the age parameter I set, and that seems to be it. I guess we'll find out if it works the next time Blair or Shirasil pay us another visit.

I once more release my Psionic Link spell. "Okay," I say. "That should do it."

"Sweet," Dizzi says. "Did that do anything for your Role Range?"

Good question. It's funny how the others seem more worried about my range than me these days. I guess I don't see much point in being able to head miles from the city when we're already miles in the sky, and everything I care about is right here. Still, the freedom to leave if I need to is useful. If any gods do ever come for the Dungeon Core and me, would my Role Requirement activate if I'm whisked away to the

Heavens? Are the Heavens even on this plane of existence? If they're not, how would distance from the Fortress be determined?

I suppose none of that really matters; as long as my Role Requirement activating puts Ollie in danger, I need to make sure it never happens.

[Check,] Echo says. [Role Range: 24.57 km]

"Holy shit," I say.

"What?" Dizzi asks, alarmed. "Are you okay? Is it Ollie?"

"No, no," I quickly say. "It's just the Role Range."

"Oh." She looks relieved. "You never swear, so I thought it was something big."

"My range is almost twenty-five kilometers," I tell her. "It must be because the detection spell is currently in effect."

Dizzi stares at me. "Holy shit."

Chapter Thirty-Eight

DRACUS

When I have a chance to dig into the scrolls I purchased to research dragons, they're less illuminating than I wanted them to be. One of them is about the value of dragon bones and scales, and the arcana applications of such ingredients. It also makes it abundantly clear how rare such items are, due to the rarity of dragons themselves. That itself doesn't bode well.

The bestiaries contain stories, mostly. Some read like history, while others sound more like myth. It's clear that dragons *did* exist at some point in this world, but the danger they presented made them targets of beast hunters, and eventually the bounties on their heads became so high that the animals were hunted to extinction. Again: this isn't boding well for Sandro's Role.

"Good morning," I greet everyone as I sit down for breakfast. Gardi (and Salvia) are sitting with Sandro (and his guards) along with a handful of other visitors we've acquired along the way. Some of them are participating in knowledge exchanges with our own experts—Agate for farming, Yequirael for weaving, Dizzi for artificing—while others are paying their way simply for the novelty of it all. The Fyrethians have grown a lot more used to visitors by now. I'm sure it's a welcome change of pace from the experiences they had with the Jorrians.

"Good morning, Lord Fyre," Rei greets me. The young felis has black and white fur. "Is there anything we can help you with?"

"What, I can't share breakfast with you all without needing something?" I tease. She's right, though; I typically sit in the meal circle at the head of the room with Mirzayael and the other leaders. Today, however, they've already eaten and set about their daily work. I'm a bit late due to the dragon scrolls I was poring over.

"Okay, I do have some things I wanted to talk about," I admit with a guilty smile. "Actually, I was hoping to chat with Gardi and Sandro."

Gardi looks surprised. Sandro looks concerned. His cloak quivers.

"It's about dragons," I say. "Gardi, were you aware of any other dragons like Ollie in the arctic?"

"I don't think any dragon is like Ollie," they admit, glancing toward the head of the room. Ollie isn't currently on his pavilion, so we're met with the sight of blue sky and distant clouds instead.

"As far as I know, dragons aren't supposed to talk," Gardi continues, peeling their gaze away. "But, no. As far as I know, the last ice dragon was killed long before I was born."

Unfortunate. But I had sort of expected that. "Have you heard anywhere else in the world they might exist?" I extend the question to some of our guests sitting in the circle, passing a questioning gaze over them as well.

Gardi shakes their head.

However, it's Salvia who speaks up next, surprising me. "Ollie can do magic, right?" they ask. "He has affinities."

"He does," I admit, wondering what that has to do with anything. But I'm curious to indulge. "Ice and wind."

"Animals aren't supposed to have magic," they say. "Sometimes it can happen if a creature has lived long enough. It's said they absorb magic from the world. Over a lifetime, that can add up."

"Creatures can also gain affinities through concentrated exposure to magic," one of our visitors adds. She's a lamia with light brown skin, wavy dark hair, and a blue and yellow pattern over the snake half of her body. She wears a green jewel around her neck, which glows as it repeats her signed words aloud.

"It's common for creatures that live near Ruins to gain magical affinities," she continues.

Salvia nods along. "Well, dragons need a wind affinity to fly, right? So probably you'd be looking for something very old, which means it would be very secluded. Or," they add, gesturing to the lamia woman, "near a source of wind arcana."

"The Drifting Isles is a source of wind arcana," another visitor, this one a dhampyr, suggests. "We mistook your city for the Isles at first."

A narrative I've heard several times now. If there are dragons left in the world, could they have retreated to an ancient, remote land hidden in the clouds? I have to believe there are dragons out there *somewhere* for Sandro's Role to not be a death sentence. Blair had said his role would reset even after he slayed a dragon, so it's designed for more than just one.

Though I still loathe the idea of hunting an endangered species for the benefit of one person. There has to be something I'm missing. There must be a nonviolent solution to this. But can I solve it in time?

Gardi scowls, a rumbling sound building in their chest. "Ruins are dangerous. The gods destroyed them for a reason."

"What?" the dhampyr says with a laugh. "No, they didn't. It was a natural disaster."

"In all the Ruins at once?" the lamia counters. "No. Something happened. But I suspect it was arcane in nature. Perhaps a weapon."

"Or disease," a felis suggests. "We know the world's population was significantly reduced at that time. Perhaps without people to run the cities, their technology fell into disrepair, leading to the mana leakage we see at those sites today."

Gardi does not appear to be pleased by any of these suggestions. "Gods make the most sense. All of these civilizations, destroyed at once? What else has such power save the Heavens?"

"If the gods wanted those cities destroyed, there wouldn't be any trace of them left," the lamia points out.

Gardi hesitates. "They could have left the remains as a warning to others."

"A warning about what?" she counters. "If their remains are intended to dissuade us from doing something similar, what are they warning us not to do?"

Gardi frowns, looking down at their breakfast. "I... I am not certain."

Salvia seems to find this conversation highly entertaining, grinning smugly when Gardi happens to glance in their direction, which just sends the felis into an even deeper scowl.

I take a bite of the meal, attempting to hide my own smile. This is good for Gardi, even if they might not want to admit it.

"So dragons require a wind affinity to fly," I say, bringing the conversation back on track. "Does that mean some dragons can exist, or did, without the ability to fly, assuming they never obtained a wind affinity?"

The lamia woman shrugs. "Possibly. There are many dragon-like creatures that still remain in the world without a wind affinity. Drakes. Wyverns."

I perk up at that. "Is there a clear-cut definition for what defines a creature as a dragon versus dragon-like?"

Everyone looks around at each other uncertainly.

"I don't know," the dhampyr finally says. "Beast classification is not my area of expertise."

The same seems to be true for everyone else as well. But this brings me back to the words Shirasil had said to me before departing: *Find a bestiarian. Your kid isn't the only dragon in the world.*

This must be significant. What if there are creatures that may not be a dragon in name, or even appearance, but will qualify for Sandro's Role Requirement?

"Sandro," I say, and the boy startles. Goodness, I need to work with him on separating himself from his cloak's feelings, somehow. "I'd like to speak with you in private once we're done with the meal, if that's alright?"

He nods, a little too quickly, and starts shoveling food into his mouth.

"Er." I raise a hesitant hand in protest. "You don't have to rush."

He swallows down an overfilled mouthful of fruit that I'm not even sure he'd finished chewing. It moves down his throat in a visible lump. That has to be painful. "I'd rather get it over with."

"It's nothing bad," I promise.

Somehow, that makes him look even more frightened.

I wonder if this world has some form of anxiety medication.

Despite my assurance that he can take his time, he finishes the meal in another couple of minutes, everyone watching him in bafflement. I excuse us, promising the others (mostly his guards) that I'll bring him back shortly.

Sandro is tall and gangly, at least a head taller than me, but the way he hunches makes him seem small.

"Are you doing alright?" I ask him as we casually meander toward the open wall. I figure some fresh air might do him good.

"Sure," he says, his eyes darting around, as if at any moment someone is going to pop out and grab him.

"I know things have been hard since you arrived here," I tell him. "We've all been through certain... trials. But I want to help you. You don't have to go through this by yourself."

The cape hugs his shoulders like a kid wrapping themself in their blanket. "Why do you want to help me? I attacked Ollie."

"You didn't know he was a person." We step out into the sun, and my skin tingles pleasantly under its warmth. "And I have a feeling that without the Role Requirement, you'd have no interest in fighting dragons anyway."

"I don't!" he cries. "Please, you have to believe me—"

"I do!" I interrupt, unable to hold back a small laugh. "I already do. That's why I want to help. Ollie and I also both have Roles, you know. We're all just trying to figure out how to manage them."

He looks at me in surprise. "You do?"

I manage not to shake my head in disbelief. "You should consider engaging Echo more often." I hold out a hand. "I have an ability that lets us speak mind-to-mind. It will give us more privacy. Is that okay with you?"

The horrified look he gives my offered hand indicates that no, it's not okay with him. He takes a breath, holds out his hand, hesitantly draws it back, then quickly snaps his hand out to clasp mine, as if forcing himself to touch me before he could change his mind.

I smile encouragingly. "Thank you. You're doing great."

First, I take a moment to ensure our conversation is kept private from Mirzayael, Ollie, and the Core. Not that any of them would mind, I'm sure, but I suspect Sandro would panic if someone else popped into the middle of our talk. Once the communication lines have been segregated, I activate the spell.

[Psionic Touch activated.]

Fear hits me like a truck. I flinch, nearly letting go, as anxiety washes over me in waves. I have the abrupt urge to run, to hide, to look over my shoulder—

I mentally stabilize myself and push the feelings back. They're not mine, they're Sandro's. And they're not originally Sandro's either; I can feel the Shroud cowering in the back of his head, emitting wave after wave of intrusive thoughts. They hammer into Sandro, and he bends beneath their incessant weight. In response, I try to emanate calm thoughts. The two emotions intersect, and like oscillating waves of opposite phases, they cancel each other out.

Sandro blinks. He straightens a little, looking around us in awe. "How did you do that?"

"Emotional self-regulation," I say. "It always came pretty naturally to me, but you can learn it, too."

"Wow." Sandro closes his eyes for a moment. "Thank you."

"*You're welcome,*" I think, and he jumps again. This one is a bit understandable. "*Try responding to me through the Link.*"

"*Like this?*" he wonders.

I pat his hand. "*Perfect. At some point I'd like to work with you on separating your mind from that cloak of yours, but that's not why I wanted to speak with you today. I'd like to get more information on your Role without anyone else listening in.*"

He tips his head, looking at me curiously. "*You mean the gods?*"

Without the Shroud affecting him, he's a lot more observant than I was expecting. "*Exactly. The two you saw before **might** be on our side, but I don't think they can entirely be trusted, and other gods even less so.*"

He nods. "*What about my Role do you want to know?*"

"You said you have to slay a dragon," I say. *"I want you to ask Echo to precisely define what she means by dragon."* I've already asked Echo this myself, but I have to be sure that the answer isn't any different with respect to his Role.

He raises an eyebrow. *"Uh, sure. One second."* He pauses for a moment. *"Okay. She said, 'A Dragon is a member of the dracus family.' So I asked her what a dracus family was, and she gave me a whole list of things. Do you want me to repeat it? It's kind of long."*

He already beat me to my next question. *"A long list is great! It sounds like we have options, then. Go ahead."*

It turns out, the long list is, in fact, long. Echo lists at least ten different types of elemental dragons, which is a bit redundant, but then goes on to list other names, some of which I have heard of, and some of which I haven't.

Wyverns, wyrms, drakes, amphipteres, hydras, and sea serpents all make the list—as do dracids, which surprises me. I suppose I should have guessed as much from the name, but I figured the association was more due to appearances rather than any actual genetic relation. Perhaps dracids are to dragons as humans are to chimpanzees. Once again, a field of science entirely outside of my wheelhouse. But the important thing is, we have options.

"This is great," I say. *"If the others were correct, then many of the species on this list may already be extinct, or at least too rare to find. But there's several on here that I think we can work with."*

"I'd love to not fight a hydra," Sandro thinks, some of his own authentic worry creeping in.

"I'd prefer that as well," I say. *"But this is a starting point. I've heard of wyverns and drakes before, so they must not be as rare as the others. Perhaps some of these creatures could be hunted for meat and supplies."*

If it could be used to benefit others, it would make me feel a lot better about needing to kill one.

I can feel Sandro's relief, but there's still a degree of reluctance. *"Even if we find one, I don't know if I can beat it. When I tried to attack Ollie, it wasn't even close."*

"Does Echo say you need to defeat it by yourself?" I ask.

He pauses another moment. Then he grins. *"No,"* he says. *"I don't."*

"Then we'll be there to help you," I promise. *"I'm sure Mirzayael would love to train you up a bit with that sword, too. All we have to do now is figure out where these creatures live."*

And which are the closest to our location. I still haven't forgotten about the need to find a place to land the Fortress. As much as I want to help Sandro, I can't let his quest to find a dragon delay our increasingly urgent need to find a place to land.

Echo, can you tell me where each of these creatures can often be found? I ask her, recreating the list of names Sandro read off as well as I can remember. I leave dracid off for obvious reasons.

[Affirmative,] Echo says. A moment later, a list appears in my vision.

A lot of the ones with "dragon" in their name have "Unknown" listed beside them. I assume that means they either are extinct, or there at least haven't been any recent sightings. But five other species populate with lists of locations.

My gaze lingers on one of the locations provided for wyverns, and an abrupt, drastic idea occurs to me. Maybe we can hit two birds with one stone; find a place to land *and* satisfy Sandro's Role at the same time. Just imagining Mirzayael's expression when I pitch this idea to her makes me grin.

"Thank you," Sandro says aloud, drawing my attention back to him. "You were right earlier. I *have* been all alone. And scared—though I suppose I can thank the Shroud for that. But I appreciate having someone who understands." He pauses, and I can feel his swell of emotions as he becomes choked up. He quashes the feeling a moment later. "I'll do whatever I can to make it up to you."

"I promise that's not necessary," I tell him, letting go of his hand and letting the Psionic Touch end. "We're all in this together."

Sandro visibly wilts as soon as I let go. He winces, glancing around nervously, but his gaze returns to me. "Okay. I trust you. Should, um. Should I go find Mirzayael now? To help with training?"

I pat his arm. "Maybe we should work on that emotional regulation, first."

Chapter Thirty-Nine

BETTER LIVING THROUGH PHARMACEUTICALS

No one within the Fortress knows of any spells to help with anxiety, though they do seem to believe something like that exists within the field of Life arcana. We have a couple of healers in the city, but our most competent and knowledgeable one is retired.

I hope she won't mind being pulled back into the workforce for this one task.

"Anxiety?" Beryl asks, hobbling about her room to prepare me and Sandro some tea, despite my protests that it really wasn't necessary. She's living in a communal housing network just outside the palace; most of the houses out here are connected, or have been made connected since the Fyrethians moved in. I'm glad she has others around.

"Aye, I could make a potion for that," she says. Sandro's hunched shoulders slump in relief. "It's only temporary, though. Should last about two hours, but one brew is enough for six potions."

Then the entire brew would only give Sandro twelve hours of relief. And it's not reasonable to ask Beryl to make this every day—assuming we even have all the ingredients to make it indefinitely.

"You might need to ration them," I tell him. "We could try to find something else in the long term, but this will have to do for now."

Beryl tosses some mushrooms into a pot, and I'm unsure if that's for the potion or our tea. "Mind magic would be better," she muses. "Healing magic will do in a pinch, but it's not as strong for this sort of application."

"Another thing to look into when we get to the next city," I think aloud.

Beryl scoffs. "Why get someone else? You need to practice."

I pause. "Me? I don't..."

I trail off while Beryl gives me a pointed look.

Okay. So I do have two spells that let me speak mind-to-mind. Which is obviously mind magic. I just hadn't spared much thought about trying to learn any other types of mind-related magic. The entire field feels ripe for abuse. And given my Role...

"I'm not sure how I would learn other mind spells," I say cautiously. "Or if I even want to."

Beryl sets two mugs before us, then goes back to her cabinet, pulling out more ingredients for her potion. The cauldron of water over the fireplace has started to boil. I can make out an inert heating spell circle carved into the hearth beneath the crackling fire and kindling, but it's clear Beryl has opted to use the more traditional approach.

"Sometimes you have to do things you don't want to do," Beryl says.

I wrap my hands around the mug, letting the warmth radiate through me. "Yes. That's what it means to be a leader."

"Hmph." Beryl tosses some herbs into the cauldron. "That's what it means to be alive."

I smile wryly. She got me there. But I'm still a bit nervous to explore mind magic too deeply. I fear venturing in that direction might open

Pandora's box. What if I use an ability that violates someone's autonomy?

What if I become reliant on it?

Then again, perhaps it's something I've been neglecting for far too long. When I break my Role Requirement, my Sanity stat begins to decrease. But it's a stat like anything else. If Health can be reinforced, if my Mana can be trained up—is there any reason why I wouldn't be able to stabilize my Sanity and slow its degradation as well?

I eye Sandro warily, who in turn manages to shrink into his seat even further, the Shroud hunched around his shoulders.

"Do you have any advice?" I ask Beryl. Theoretically, I know from experience that spells can be learned simply through applying already-known spells in new ways. But mind magic sounds more dangerous to experiment with than fire, even. "I'd rather not make anything worse."

Beryl snorts, her back still to both of us as she works. "Mind magic is all about will. You want to hurt him?"

"No!" I quickly object.

"Then you won't."

I suppose that's a bit reassuring, though Sandro certainly doesn't appear to be. I think back to how I'd been able to help him the previous day, with simply willing the Shroud's influence back. I wonder if that's something I can repeat—and something I could turn into an intentional ability.

"What do you think?" I ask him. "We can wait until Beryl is done with the potion. Or we can try something else in the meantime."

Sandro's gaze darts between the cauldron, me, and (inexplicably) our tea. His jaw works for a moment before he speaks, still looking down at his drink.

"Could you do the thing you did yesterday?" he asks. "That... that helped."

"Of course," I say, holding out my hand. He pauses for a moment before taking it.

[Psionic Touch activated.]

This time, I've braced for the Shroud's mental onslaught, and though it still causes me to suck in a startled breath, I'm able to resist the impulse to pull away. I don't know what Shirasil was talking about; the Shroud doesn't seem weak to me.

Then again, we probably have vastly different definitions of 'weak.'

I start to press back against the Cloak's presence, then stop.

Sandro's hand trembles in my grasp. "What are you doing?"

"*Thinking*," I mentally reply, reminding him to do the same. "*You need to be able to resist its influence without my help, or the moment I let go, you'll be back to square one.*"

"*But how?*" he asks, desperate.

The Shroud can sense that I'm here. It's alarmed at my presence—there shouldn't be another mind in our mind!—and its fearful ripples lash out in my direction in an attempt to kick me out. It's not the worst instinct, really. If I were a malicious entity, it would be protecting Sandro. But it doesn't seem to be able to tell the difference between friend and foe. Not that Sandro is particularly trying to convince it otherwise; if anything, he's trying to keep his distance.

Mentally, I move closer to him. I'm able to feel his emotions and thoughts more strongly, and I'm sure he can sense the same from me. I try to imagine myself as a stable force. A laminar island in the turbulence of his mind. Something steady to latch onto.

Which is precisely what he does. I'm not pushing away the Shroud's anxious attempts to repel me, but I'm also not letting it overwhelm me. As Sandro moves closer to me, I provide a small reprieve from intrusive thoughts.

"*Thank you,*" he thinks, huddling against my presence. "*Can you stop it completely? Like you did before?*"

"*I could,*" I admit. "*But maybe you should try to do that yourself, first.*"

Physically, he frowns. "*I don't know how.*"

"*Why don't you give it a try, anyway?*" I suggest. "*Right now, its fear is feeding your reluctance to push back; you're afraid to try. But you're going to need to stand up to it if you want to do this on your own.*"

His mind shudders. "*It's just so strong. How can I beat a creature like that?*"

"*Maybe you don't have to,*" I think. "*Instead of fighting it, have you tried talking to it?*"

Sandro blinks, looking up at me. "*Talk to it?*"

"*I think I've heard you trying to speak to it before,*" I say. "*You were trying to stop it from attacking us. But that had been more desperate cries and objections.*"

Sandro feels a bit embarrassed at hearing this.

"*However,*" I continue, "*you might be more persuasive if you tried reasoning, first.*"

"*I suppose,*" he says, sounding dubious. "*It's just so... so **alien**. It doesn't think like a human—or, a person, I guess.*"

"*I know what you mean,*" I assure him. "*I'm connected to the Dungeon Core in a similar way. Sometimes its power can be frightening. And its priorities are very different from mine. But I've found a way to work with it. When you know what it wants, it can be easier to channel its energy into something productive. So what is it that your Shroud wants?*"

"*It wants to be safe,*" he immediately replies. "*That's why it's terrified of everything.*"

That's a good start. *"Do you think you can help direct that?"* I ask. *"Maybe if you tried talking to it, you could tell it what things are and aren't worth worrying about. Maybe you can help nudge its general anxiety into a general alertness, instead."*

I can feel that Sandro is afraid to try talking to it, and not all of that fear is from the Shroud itself. I catch brief flickers of memories as Sandro recalls them: his first moments in this world and the disorientation he'd felt. Coming upon the cloak soon after, and the panic he'd felt when it had wrapped itself around his neck. The new voices in his head he's done everything in his power to try to ignore.

It's interesting that he stumbled upon the Shroud soon after arriving here in much the same way I'd also stumbled upon the Dungeon Core. Both were close to where we woke up. I wonder if there's some significance to this—but it's not something I have time to dwell on now.

"I'm not sure how to direct it," Sandro says. *"Will it even listen?"*

I shrug. *"I suppose you won't know until you try. Here."* Now I do push back against the Shroud's influence, creating a small sphere of calm that encompasses both myself and Sandro. His grasp relaxes in my hand, and the lines of worry carved into his face smooth out.

"I'll maintain this while you try talking to it," I tell him. *"Hopefully this will make it easier."*

"It does," he says, confidence returning to his tone. I just hope he'll be able to do this without me here to hold his hand.

Sandro's attention shifts from me to the Shroud while I continue to focus on maintaining my sphere of calming influence. I don't attempt to eavesdrop while Sandro addresses his cloak—more specifically, I don't want to get in the practice of overhearing thoughts that aren't meant for me. My gaze wanders over to Beryl, who's hard at work with the potion. With my free hand, I take a sip of the cooling tea.

I jump and nearly spill it all down my front when Echo abruptly speaks up.

[New Spell Obtained,] she says. [Emotional Radiance: a spell which creates a spherical area in which the user is able to impress desired emotions upon the occupants. Mana cost: 3 per 10 cubic meters per second.]

Well, Beryl was right about that. All I had to do was try a new application and keep it up for a bit of time; pretty much exactly how I discovered all the other spells I didn't receive by default. On the plus side, this is something I could use to help Sandro. But I don't like that it can be used for blanket emotional manipulation. Not to mention, it's not targeted, it's a spherical field; this could be used against enemies as well as allies, if they all get caught in its range.

I activate Emotional Radiance anyway, keeping the area small enough just to encompass Sandro and I, then deactivate Psionic Touch. Radiance is more mana efficient, and this way Sandro can have his privacy.

I sip at my tea—which doesn't have mushrooms in it, I'm pretty sure—while I wait. Sandro is silent, but his eyes are open. He's squeezing his own mug, still untouched, as he frowns at a spot on the table. Every once in a while, his cloak flutters on its own.

As the silence stretches, I watch Beryl work. The old woman holds her hand over the cauldron, and a light blooms from her palm before descending into the pot. The water hisses and illuminates as it's infused with magic.

"What would you think about staying aloft indefinitely?" I finally ask Beryl. "Settling in the sky, instead of finding somewhere stationary to land?"

Beryl pauses to give me a skeptical look. "Why ask me?"

"Because you were their leader before Mirzayael and me," I say. "I don't want to know if this is the most optimal choice, but if it's one you would have wanted."

"It doesn't matter what I want." Beryl turns back to her brew. "It matters what everyone wants."

She'd said as much before when I'd spoken with her about launching the Fortress in the first place. We had put it to a city-wide vote, and the response had been overwhelming.

But raising the Fortress and leaving Jorria was the obvious solution. If we now choose to remain in the sky rather than land, that's subverting the original promise—and I worry it might make us more of a target than if we were to land.

"What does Mirzayael think?" Beryl asks.

"I haven't asked her yet," I admit. "It's still just an idea. I worry it may be too... dramatic. And dangerous."

Beryl raises an eyebrow at me, waiting for elaboration.

"Staying aloft might draw the gods' attention," I explain. "Not only has Fyreneth's Fortress risen once more, but to forever fly above the ground would be like declaring 'we will never be buried again.' I just worry this might draw their ire."

Beryl grunts as she begins ladling the potion into a handful of flasks. "The gods will do what the gods will do. We can't live our lives catering to their whims."

I worry that's too simplistic. Blair specifically warned me that drawing attention like we are is dangerous. Then again, what I have in mind might just get us to safety faster. If it works, then even if the Dungeon Core *is* removed from the Fortress, the city will no longer be at risk of falling from the sky. That safety—the ability of the city to not be reliant on the Dungeon Core—is the best possible protection I could buy for the Fyrethians.

Sandro finally stirs, blinking and looking around the room.

"How did it go?" I ask him.

"I'm not sure," he admits with a frown. "It doesn't trust me. I don't think it trusts anything. I tried to tell it what things it should and shouldn't worry about, but that didn't seem to help much. After a while I got a bit angry and snapped at it, telling it to stop pushing its feelings on me. And it cowered, like *it* was afraid of *me*." He smiles wearily. "As if it hasn't been terrorizing me all this time."

A work in progress, then. But progress, nonetheless.

"I'm going to stop my spell now," I warn him. "Maybe see if you can push some of its influence back on your own?"

"I'll try," he sighs, clearly disappointed that the reprieve is about to end.

[Emotional Radiance ended.]

Sandro tenses up, and I watch him carefully. Wrinkles return to his forehead, but he doesn't hunch quite as much as he did before.

"I think..." He speaks haltingly. "I think that helped. I think I can push back against it. A little."

"Keep working at it," I encourage him. "I'm sure it will get better in time."

"And in the meantime, use these," Beryl says, setting the flasks down on the table."

"Thank you," Sandro says, looking between the two of us. "Both of you. Really."

His earnest gratitude warms my heart. "That's what we're here for."

Beryl curtly nods. "It wouldn't be Fyreneth's Fortress if we turned away those in need."

Sandro smiles, and abruptly, I realize I feel a hint of affection for him. Like Ollie, he's just another lost soul in need of family and support as he adapts to this new life.

It also probably doesn't help that he's the same age as my daughter.

Mirzayael's mind stirs at the edge of my conscience. "*Why do I feel like you're about to adopt someone else?*"

I cover my mouth as I turn away to grin.

CHAPTER FORTY

MIDNIGHT SNACK

When I wake up, my room is dark. It's the middle of the night. I shift in my bed, the blankets hushing around me, as I wonder what woke me up. Everything is quiet.

I gently reach out to Ollie and Mirzayael's mind—they're both still sleeping. Then I reach out to the Dungeon Core.

It's fretting over something. I quietly ensure my mind isn't broadcasting to Ollie and Mirzayael as I speak to the Dungeon Core, so I won't wake them. *What is it?*

The Core affects the mental equivalent of a surprised jump. It doesn't know. It didn't do anything!

Well, that's not suspicious. *Core, what have you been doing?*

It wilts in my mind, like a kid caught with its hand in the cookie jar. It has to do *something* with the extra mana. It's not the Core's fault! And it wasn't anything it wasn't supposed to, it was just a few nibbles!

I'm briefly alarmed, before I finish parsing through the Core's guilty thoughts. Then I quietly laugh, my voice echoing in the dark.

It's been active while I sleep. Bored, probably. And it noticed something I didn't; I don't throttle the mana I have trickling into its interface when I go to bed each night. The Fortress requires a consistent draw of mana for many of its spells—flight, maintaining the atmosphere, and so on. But there are certain capabilities that are used less during the night; like our lights and kitchens. The Core, apparently, has been using the surplus of mana for its own entertainment.

It's gone around taking samplings of different rocks in the Fortress. Mostly just some pebbles here and there, but also, I'm now learning, the occasional nibbles off of new, foreign materials that are brought into its domain. If any of our visitors have noticed their belt buckles or boots have obtained holes or small worn patches since entering the city, no one has said anything.

And just now, it had been in the middle of digging through Ollie's horde, looking for anything new and interesting to nibble on. It's embarrassed at being caught, because it rather likes Ollie, and it knows it shouldn't eat his things.

We're going to have to set some ground rules about your midnight snacks going forward, I tell it. But my amusement is fading, because while the Core was being a little mischief maker, it's not what woke me up.

The Core is relieved to know it's not in trouble. Now can I turn that loud noise off for it?

I finally notice the hum. It seems to be pulsing from the Dungeon Core. No, not from it—through it.

It's coming from one of the spells wired into the throne.

I sit straight up, mentally skimming through the spell network to figure out where the alert is coming from. It doesn't take me long to find it.

The Greater Detection spell. Someone older than 300 years has passed within its range and triggered it.

Ice washes over my skin. I try to stay calm. It must be one of the gods. Blair or Shirasil? It doesn't fit their previous pattern—they seem to be more interested in observing me, Ollie, or Sandro. The timing of this is alarming. Why would they arrive in the middle of the night?

I bring up the Map interface. The dots that mark the city's inhabitants are still, apart from a handful of pairs stationed around the prison, on the city wall, and patrolling the street. Mirzayael's guards. I'm glad now she assigned them in pairs, as it makes it easy for me to identify them; the Map interface itself doesn't provide any information on individuals aside from their species.

Then, a single dot moves.

It catches my attention because it's in the palace. A lone cambion. We were able to trade for cambion horns in the previous cities—apparently a rare ingredient used in some spells—but I've never met one myself.

Echo, how old can cambions live? I ask her.

[A long life for a cambion ranges between 150 and 200 years.]

I quietly slip out of bed and head to my chamber door.

It sounds like a god to me. Only, Blair and Shirasil hadn't appeared on the Map interface at all. And we definitely had humans and felis catalogued at that point—unless they are only appearing like those species as a disguise. I don't understand. I'm missing something.

I don't activate any of the hallway lights as I traverse the palace, using the Map interface to navigate while I follow the progress of our unexpected visitor. I can't tell where they're headed. For a moment my heart quickens as I think they're heading for the Dungeon Core, pausing outside the door to the throne room, but they move on soon after, and are now traveling in the direction of the kitchens. I frown. What are they looking for?

I consider waking Mirzayael or Ollie. I don't want to send the guards after our intruder—I fear it would only end poorly for them. But would Ollie or Mirzayael end better? Ollie's appearance might provoke them, and I'd rather not have the child involved regardless. Mirzayael's *words* might provoke them.

But this is her kingdom, too.

As gently as I can, I reach out to her and nudge her mind until I feel it stir. *"Remain calm and quiet,"* I tell her. *"There's an intruder in the palace."*

Despite my words, Mirzayael feels anything but calm as she startles awake. *"Who?"* she demands, even as she's still shaking the fog of sleep from her mind. *"Where?"*

"A cambion," I tell her. *"Possibly a god. They triggered the detection spell, so they're at least three hundred years old. I think they're heading toward the food hall."*

Mirzayael's mind is spinning with alarmed disorientation—I can't really blame her, given the way I woke her up—but she's quickly switching over to tactician mode. *"Stay in your room. I will investigate."*

"Too late. I'm headed up the main stairwell." I smile when I feel her exasperation, but it's partially from my nerves.

"I'll cut them off and come from the side steps, then," she replies. *"Keep me updated on their location."*

"I will."

"Good. And Fyre?"

"Yes?"

"Thank you for waking me." A swell of relief and affection accompanies her words.

I feel a little guilty about almost not waking her, but I'm glad I ultimately made the right call. At least, I hope I made the right call.

I'm not nearly as stealthy as Mirzayael, but I'd like to hope that navigating the halls in almost total darkness helps me a bit. The cambion is in the main hall now; they've crossed from one side to the other a few times, stopping in various doorways. The movement is odd. It less seems like they're looking for something, and more like they're exploring. Another interesting detail—the Dungeon Core doesn't particularly seem interested in them the same way it had noticed Blair and Shirasil's presence. What's going on?

Mirzayael and I continue to coordinate as we approach the hall from opposite sides. I'm near the kitchen—not far from where I first encountered Lisari, standing alone in the dark, examining a statue of Fyreneth.

A detail from that moment abruptly returns to me: the surprise clear on Lisari's face when she noticed me. *"Fyreneth?"* she'd said.

Had she known her? I never asked.

I stop for a moment as footsteps echo through the hall. They're close enough to hear, now. I duck into a side room, across from the one I'd just been recalling, and hold my breath. They're coming my way.

I'm briefly filled with doubt. This trespasser clearly didn't want to encounter anyone, given the time they chose to visit. What exactly do I think I can do against someone like Blair or Shirasil? At least neither of those two seem to wish us ill—for now. But someone who doesn't share their restraint? Lorata herself?

I don't know what I could do.

I update Mirzayael on their position as their footsteps grow closer, and a light flickers down the hall. I press myself further into the wall of the side room I'd ducked inside. They won't be able to see me unless they step in, but if they do, they'd spot me in an instant. There's nothing to hide behind. I hold my breath.

The footsteps stop. A flickering orange light spills into my room from the hallway, cutting a stripe of color across the floor.

"I'm almost there," Mirzayael tells me, her voice tight.

"Show yourself," the cambion says, her voice low and smooth.

Shoot. The jig is up. I guess, for better or worse, it's time to learn who our intruder is.

I'm about to take a step forward when the firelight swivels and her shoes scuff the ground in a pivot.

"Hello," Mirzayael says. My stomach twists. "I don't recall letting you into our city."

"I don't suppose you would." The woman sounds indifferent. She took a step toward Mirzayael when she turned around, which puts my doorway behind her. I wait until Mirzayael speaks again, then I shift, as slowly and quietly as I can, in an attempt to catch a glimpse of the cambion.

"Is there a reason you're sneaking around our halls in the middle of the night?" Mirzayael asks.

I Check our intruder the moment I can see her back. She's carrying a flame in her hand, much like one of my Sparks, so she's backlit from my perspective.

[Name: Zetaru]
[Title: Demigod]
[Species: Cambion]
[Class: Celestial Kindler]
[Level: 81]
[HP: 450/450]
[Mana: 5000/5000]
[Allegiance: Yua Tin]

I've never seen a cambion before, but Echo has told me about them. She has long black hair, red skin, two golden horns that curl back around her head, and a thin tail that droops nearly to the floor, its arrow-shaped tip waving lazily back and forth. Her clothes are surprisingly nondescript—but so were Blair and Shirasil's when they first arrived.

Unlike them, however, this one appears to be a demigod. And she doesn't have a Role. Interesting.

I relay as much of this information as quickly as I can to Mirzayael.

"I was following someone," Zetaru replies. She sounds almost bored with this conversation.

Echo, what is a demigod? I ask.

[Demigods: mortals infused with a fraction of a god's power, the most common of which are champions.]

I wait a beat. *And what are champions?*

[Champions: servants who act as their god's proxy in the mortal realm.]

I guess that explains the Allegiance stat. Yua Tin is another god I've read about; they have to do with the stars, I think. But if champions are supposed to be the gods' eyes and ears in the mortal realm, why did Blair and Shirasil show up in person? Where are their champions?

I suppose those questions aren't important at this particular moment.

"Who are you following?" Mirzayael demands, sounding far more threatening than I would in her shoes.

"It is none of your concern," Zetaru says.

"As I am the ruler of this city, I should think it is."

Zetaru is quiet for a moment. "Perhaps so, then. Have you met a young woman named Lisari?"

Champions of one god tracking down another? What is going on here? Blair said the pantheon is not a monolith, but I suspect I am only beginning to catch a glimpse of how tangled this web truly is.

"Yes," Mirzayael says shortly, and I'm glad she didn't lie. I suspect Zetaru knew the answer to that question already.

"What did she speak with you about?"

Now Mirzayael is quiet for a moment. I can feel her weighing her options. I'm about to make a suggestion when she speaks up. "That information depends on what your relationship to her is. Are you her enemy or ally?"

I am both proud of and terrified for Mirzayael. She's not even flinching in the face of someone who could likely crush us both. When I was confronted by the two gods, I was terrified. Yet Mirzayael is treating this demigod no different from anyone else we've made trade deals with over the last month.

But Zetaru doesn't seem offended. In fact, she chuckles. "Whether she is an enemy or ally depends on the information she shared."

"Unfortunate," Mirzayael says. "Then we are at an impasse."

Zetaru still sounds amused, which is increasingly worrying me. "Or you can tell me the information I seek and I leave here peacefully."

What she might do if she isn't provided the information, hangs unspoken and heavy in the air.

I consider casting Emotional Resonance. Perhaps I could deescalate the situation—make Zetaru feel calm and friendly. But the potential for it to backfire if she realizes what I did is far too risky.

Instead, I take a different risk.

Zetaru spins around as I step from the room, eyes narrowing. She truly didn't know I was there, then—it seems even with eighty levels, these demigods are not as preeminent as they project.

"Who are you?" she demands.

I pause. Can she not get Echo to Check? Does she not have access to the System? Does this have something to do with the fact that she doesn't have a Role? It's becoming a pattern; those with Roles can see the System and those without Roles can't. I thought someone connected to the gods might be different. But this means I actually wield some form of advantage over her.

"My name is Fyre," I say. "Mirzayael and I are..." I trail off thoughtfully, trying to find the best descriptor.

"Co-rulers," Mirzayael supplies.

My mouth twitches with a smile. "I think we're a bit more than that."

Embarrassment and self-consciousness floods from Mirzayael's side of our link. "Partners, then."

"We haven't really put a label on it, yet," I explain.

The demigod looks between us, unamused. "I do not care which relationship status you claim."

"My apologies," I say. "You wanted to know about Lisari?"

Zetaru focuses on me. "Speak."

While Shirasil's relation with Lorata appears to be conflicting, I read one account that said he was friends with Yua Tin, who is apparently this champion's god. I'm very aware that the mortal records could be flawed, but I decide to chance it.

"She said she was here to observe," I tell her. "She warned us others might not be."

Zetaru remains expressionless as she considers this. "You are protecting a Traveler with a remnant."

I try not to react to this. She doesn't know I'm a Traveler—she might not even know about the Dungeon Core. Mentally, I access the interface and tell the Core to sink into the throne, obscuring its jewel with the rock.

"We are," Mirzayael admits. "A boy named Sandro."

My heart skips a beat. *"Mirzayael, what are you doing?"*

"Diverting attention from you," she tells me.

"But you'll make him a target!"

Of course, that's the point. "He has a magical cloak," she tells Zetaru.

The demigod turns back to Mirzayael. "Why are you shielding him? You realize it puts your city at risk. And your castle isn't particularly subtle."

"Taking in anyone who needs a home is what this city was built for," Mirzayael replies, surprising me before I can respond. "Anyone who may condemn that is no one worth capitulating to."

Zetaru snorts. "You're brave. But bravery will not protect you."

"Doing what's right is not contingent upon what is safest."

I might be proud of her if she hadn't just thrown Sandro to the wolves in an attempt to mask that the Dungeon Core and I are the primary subject of interest. But I can't entirely blame her, either; everyone's life in this city is dependent upon the Dungeon Core not being taken from us.

It's the only reason I haven't contradicted Mirzayael. As much as using Sandro as a diversion fills me with shame, we achieve nothing and risk everything by revealing my connection to a remnant, too.

Zetaru shakes her head. "Lisari was right," she says, looking between us. "You're in a dangerous spot. If you care about the safety of your city more than the safety of this individual, you should consider handing him over."

"I suspect we could not stop you if you wanted to take him," I remark.

"You'd be correct," she says. "It is not in my lord's nature to force hands, but champions with less compassion and more cruelty will also investigate your home. It's merely a matter of time. You would be wise to pick your allegiances carefully."

Then she turns and heads my way. Mirzayael steps toward her as I step back—but Zetaru turns, instead passing into the room I'd been hiding in. Her fire snuffs out a moment later, and the alarm spell that's been buzzing in the back of my mind abruptly stops. I peer around the doorframe, but the room is empty.

I sigh. "She's gone."

Mirzayael moves quickly to my side. She reaches out, then seems to not know what she intended to do, so I take her hand in mine. "Are you alright?"

She can already feel the state of my mind—the question is more one of impulse.

I find I'm actually not nearly as bothered as when Lisari and Blair first confronted me. I don't know if I'm getting used to all this, or if it's the knowledge that even these champions, dozens of levels higher than myself, don't have some of the resources I do.

Either way, however, her presence here was a clear signal: more will be coming. The time for evaluating our best options is over. We need to act.

"We need to land," I abruptly say, instead of answering Mirzayael's question. "We need to land quickly, and so far I've found no other viable solution. Perhaps if we had more time…"

Mirzayael tips her head. "What are you suggesting?"

"I know a location that could power our city," I admit. "It would also solve Sandro's Role problem. But it's risky. It will put us more firmly on the gods' radar—that is, there would be little chance of hiding our presence in this location."

Now her interest is piqued. "Which country is this land located in?"

"No country," I admit with a smile. "How do you feel about landing on a Ruin?"

CHAPTER FORTY-ONE

ONWARD AND UPWARD

It had started as a search for dragons. Once I figured out that Sandro's Role Requirement counted anything from the dracus family as "dragons," our options widened significantly.

Specifically, one species caught my eye in particular: wyverns.

Wyverns appear to be small winged lizards that people have bred to use for everything between messengers, pets, and even livestock. In fact, Captain Marlowe had been on the hunt for these when he ran into our city instead. Wyverns aren't typically found in the clouds because they feast on beetles and other grubs. However, there is one such source of grubs and wyverns that can be found in the sky.

The Drifting Isles.

According to Echo, the Ruin is a collection of flying chunks of land that wanders the world wherever the winds take it. It's much larger than the Fortress, so we would have no trouble finding a place to land inside its swirling cloudy walls.

And most notably, it's an inexhaustible source of wind arcana.

"That's better than finding mana ore, even," Dizzi says as I pitch my idea to the council. "Which we were already struggling with. But if we can get the city hooked up to the storm arcana source, we'll never have to worry about keeping the kingdom powered again!"

"It will also provide sufficient mana to keep the watchtower spells activated," Mirzayael says. "Our city will be much more secure with such a source of magic."

"And we'll have more land to expand into for agriculture," Nek adds.

Torim is the only one who seems unconvinced. "I've heard rumors of the Drifting Isles," he says. "Especially that it's treacherous. We can't be the first people to consider making this land our home. Why hasn't anyone else settled it before now?"

"Fair question," I admit. "Part of it is due to accessibility. Only harpies or those with an airship can reach it, and since it's constantly moving, it would be difficult to shift any ground-based population to the Ruins. By the time you delivered a few ship-loads of people and supplies to its terrain, it will have already floated beyond the range of the city.

"Not to mention, given its altitude, it is likely cold and has thin air. Similar to why we established the atmospheric spell around our own city, living at such an altitude would be difficult for most people." I pause.

Torim notices. "And what is the other part due to?"

I smile guiltily. "The danger. There are rumors of territorial and arcana-infused beasts that live there."

"So, it's treacherous," he says flatly.

"It is," Mirzayael says. "But it's also an exceptional opportunity. If we can claim the Ruin, we will be one of the most protected, and potentially one of the most powerful, cities in the world."

The comment tugs a bit of Earth history from the recesses of my memories. During the Cold War, a common sentiment was "He who controls space, controls the Earth." I find the parallel slightly chilling given our current circumstances. Once again, I uneasily wonder how much my Role Requirement might be playing into this, or if it's merely an irrational connection I'm drawing due to my own anxieties. We certainly aren't trying to rule the world—though it's undeniable that being able to drop weapons on the heads of your enemies from miles above is an incredible advantage.

I suppose all we can do is hope this won't provoke anyone into viewing us as a threat, and continue to cultivate friendly relationships. I recall Captain Marlowe suggesting such a future for our city; he imagined we could become a kind of traveling Library of Alexandria, where scholars all across the world could come to learn and share their knowledge. I certainly like this image for us more than an orbiting weapons system.

I think Fyreneth would have liked this for her city, too.

"But most importantly," I add, "this will remove the threat that losing the Dungeon Core would pose to us. If it's taken, we'll have to rewire the city's spell circuits to directly use the Ruin's ambient magic—and we'll likely need many operators to control the spell circles manually in place of the Dungeon Core's automatic control—but we at least would not be left dead in the water."

And once we land, we're no longer at risk of falling from the sky if the Dungeon Core is taken from us.

Landing on the Drifting Isles and integrating its magic into our city will, ideally, make the Dungeon Core and I obsolete. The only way to know that for sure will be to see how doing so affects my Role Range. But I'll feel a lot safer with the knowledge that even if the

Dungeon Core and I are taken by the gods, the city will be able to prosper without us.

Not that I intend to let that happen. The Dungeon Core belonged to Fyreneth, and so it now belongs to the Fyrethians. And, as Mirzayael pointed out, once we connect to the Ruin's magic, we might have a way to defend against any gods who do take too much of an interest in us.

Assuming we can make it to the Drifting Isles, first.

"Alright," Torim finally acquiesces. "I can see the advantages. We'll put it to a city vote. However," he adds before we all (mostly Dizzi) can celebrate, "if it does prove too dangerous, I want a backup plan. We can't expend the rest of our city's mana to get somewhere that ends up being filled with murderous beasts."

Completely fair.

"We could do a scouting mission first," Mirzayael suggests. "A small, skilled party to scope out the Isles. And if all seems safe, we can then proceed."

"And I will continue to search for backup landing locations on the surface," I add. "But I don't believe we should wait on that possibility." Not with the presence of the gods looming overhead.

Torim lets out a long breath, and finally nods. "I see the reason in this. I am in favor of the plan."

"So is this happening?" Dizzi asks, looking around the room as her feathers ruffle in excitement. "Are we really about to land our home in the magical epicenter of the flying remains of an ancient civilization that mysteriously disappeared?"

Nek winces. "On second thought..."

"It's decided," Mirzayael says. "It's time to hunt a Ruin."

The vote to make the Fortress a permanently flying city is overwhelmingly in favor, as it had been to launch the city in the first place. I think some of it is motivated by the perception of freedom; even if our flight will be determined by that of the Drifting Isles, the ability to wander the world stands in stark juxtaposition of the lives they've previously known, buried underground. I can't blame them for wanting to retain this mobility; living in the clouds is a childhood dream come true.

In the next city, we start researching the Drifting Isles. It seems that there's no way to actually predict its flight, or at least, no one has been able to do so thus far. I suspect the storm arcana that the Ruin leaks might be part of that, altering its course in unpredictable ways.

There are sightings of it, however, that some scholars compile. Even if we can't tell which direction it might end up turning, we should at least be able to find its most recent sightings and try to intercept its path from there. One advantage of being a floating city ourselves is that we have an exceptionally large field of view.

Even so, we're unable to find answers in the cities we scour. This is specialty knowledge, it seems. Eventually we're pointed to a conclave of wind arcana scholars in East Dunmora, though how we're supposed to get *there*, I'm uncertain. They're nowhere near our flight path. We could risk spending a significant portion of our mana to fly there, but then we'd have to hope we'd still have enough left to direct our flight toward intercepting the Drifting Isles.

Instead, I dig up Captain Marlowe's parting gift. After I finish drafting a letter asking for his help, I tap the spell circle that's stamped into the page, pressing some of my mana into it. The letter shudders, lifting off the desk, and I'm delighted to watch it fold itself into a paper bird and promptly fly away. I worry that it won't make it to its target, but I'm pleasantly surprised to get a response only a few days later. He agrees to forward my bid for help onto the Wind Conclave, and says I should expect to hear back before the week is up. Even so, we anticipate it might take longer simply for the mages to gather whatever information they need to find the Drifting Isles.

In the meantime... We live.

We trade, we fix up our city, entertain guests, share knowledge, work on our gardens. It would be nice, if it weren't for consistent interruptions from the gods.

The first time the Detection spell goes off again, I startle and nearly drop a mug of hot tea in my lap. Just then, Shirasil—or, Lisari, I suppose, since she appears as a young woman—casually walks by, joining a group of visitors in our meal hall. I narrow my eyes, and though she doesn't turn my way, her smile broadens.

She doesn't approach me, and I don't approach her. After a time, the alarm spell deactivates, and the god appears to be gone.

Blair is the next to appear a few days later. Again, she doesn't approach me, but she does appear to be observing. And again, she vanishes when I'm not paying attention, and the detection spell goes inert once more.

The champion Zetaru doesn't return in that time. Just Lisari and Blair, almost never at the same time, always in the background, merely observing. It's like they don't want to interrupt me, but do want to make sure I don't step out of line.

To be frank, it's starting to become extremely annoying. No matter how sympathetic they may claim to be, I don't take kindly to being under surveillance. One day, using a Psionic Touch, I privately speak with Dizzi and have her shift her team's research back to the final watchtower spell, focusing on the mysterious spell circuits that connect it to all of the other towers. So far, we haven't been able to deduce a purpose of the network, but I have a sneaking suspicion on what it might be for.

Sandro is adapting well, even venturing outside his comfort zone to timidly ask Mirzayael if he could join the guard's practice and training sessions. Salvia takes him under their wing, teaching him some basic moves while Gardi watches from a bench on the sidelines. Gardi uses the time to call out helpful pointers—mostly for Salvia, to their extreme annoyance. Sandro seems completely oblivious to their combative dynamic, just relieved to finally learn how to use his sword properly. I'm glad to see them all (mostly) getting along. But the more days that pass, the more worried I become.

If Sandro's Role Requirement becomes too pressing, we may not be able to wait until we reach the Isles. Of course, knowing that wyverns will satisfy his Role, there is always the option to purchase a domestic one from a city we pass over. But that option turns my stomach. I'm not much more thrilled about what he'll have to do once we do reach the Ruin, but I can at least partially justify hunting wild wyvern flocks to myself; at least I know nothing would go to waste.

And then, we get a response from the Wind Conclave.

They seem quite excited by our request and send us atmospheric maps of the world. Lines move over the pages much like meteorologists would create with computer graphics on Earth. Even in the midst of examining what they've sent us, I can't help but be thrilled to find another way in which magic has taken the place of technology on this planet. Every new application I discover fascinates me.

The atmospheric maps help us better predict our own heading, but will also be a large help when we discover the last Drifting Isles sighting, as the wind lines will provide strong predictors for the city's most likely path of travel.

Unfortunately, the most recent sightings present a slight drawback. They were all over the continent of Valenia (which is, relatively speaking, to the north-east of us) while we are over Dunmora. Theoretically this isn't a big problem, because we are directionally ahead of the Drifting Isles, meaning we could drift north, slow our eastern progression, and have the Isles intercept our trajectory.

However, once the Isles pass over the Emerald Sea, pretty much all sightings of it stop. We can attempt to guess where on the west coast of Dunmora it will next emerge, but it will be just that—a guess. And if we don't position ourselves correctly, it will likely pass us by. I begin to eye the city's mana reserves with increasing levels of concern.

A break comes two weeks after first corresponding with the wind arcana conclave; they recently received notice of a tracker spell designed to provide live updates of the Drifting Isle's position—something that would only be achievable if a tracker was installed on the Ruin itself.

The catch is that the conclave can't pass the tracker onto us. Or, won't. It seems the inventor of the tracker is reluctant to hand it out to just anyone. I offer an extremely generous payment, but I'm still turned down. After some back and forth, Captain Marlowe actually heads to speak with them in person. Eventually, he finally writes me back: talks went well, and he'll be delivering the tracker to us personally.

The letter is suspiciously devoid of details on what talks were had or how he obtained the tracker. I do hope he didn't strongarm anyone. Yet, I'm grateful for his assistance. Our clock is ticking down.

Stumbling upon this Drifting Isles tracker is lucky. Almost *too* lucky—the timing too convenient. I have a sneaking suspicion the gods are involved, some way or another.

The next time the Detection spell goes off, I'm in the middle of working with Dizzi to draft instructions for our city's atmospheric spell, which we'll be sending to the Wind Conclave as thanks for their help. I pause, sitting up to look around.

"What is it?" Dizzi asks.

"Nothing," I absently tell her. The gods aren't here in our workshop at least. "I need to go check on something. I'll be back soon."

"Uh, okay! If you say so," she says, but I'm already hurrying out of the room.

The Dungeon Core's Map interface doesn't help me find them, since the gods are invisible to it, but I have a suspicion I won't have to look far. Sure enough, I step out onto a balcony overlooking a lower tier of the palace and find Blair already there, as if she were waiting for me.

I frown. "When you implied you'd be monitoring us, I didn't expect it to be this frequently."

"It is unusual for two Travelers with remnants to be in such close proximity," she replies. "Periodic check-ins are not unwarranted."

"What are you expecting to happen?" I ask. "You think these objects are a threat to one another, but if nothing has happened yet, I don't understand why you think that would change."

"In truth I do not expect it to change," the god says, looking down over the balustrade. "But in the unlikely event it does, the danger is too great to ignore."

In the courtyard below are some of our guests, including Gardi and Sandro, both still shadowed by their guards. At this point I don't believe either are a danger to anyone, but I know continuing to monitor them makes Mirzayael feel better.

"Danger to who?" I ask.

Blair regards me for a moment. "Everyone," she says gravely.

A chill runs down my back. "If these remnants coming in contact is such a threat, is there anything I can do to lessen it?"

"Not likely," she says, turning back to the scene below. A group of young Fyrethians are using the courtyard to play a cloudstone sport. When they catch sight of the guests, they beckon them over, and begin to teach them how to play.

"You proved yourself capable of controlling the remnant with respect to Sandro," Blair continues. "Hopefully that is a restraint you can continue to maintain. However, I can't guarantee that you won't come in contact with a stronger remnant. And if your Core is on the losing side..."

A pit grows in my stomach. All this time I'd only been considering the gods a threat to the Dungeon Core. But if there are more entities like it in the world, and if they're capable of simply waltzing (or flying) into our city, then that's even more reason to land as soon as we can.

"I hope it never comes to that," I say. "But if it does, you're the first I will reach out to."

She looks back at me, faintly impressed. "You're willing to trust a god?"

"I trust your intentions," I say. "I trust that you don't want to see our city destroyed, if it can be helped. I trust that you wish to avert some sort of disaster. That's enough to know that, if it comes to it, you'd be our best chance at avoiding something dire."

She's quiet for a moment. "I can't help you, you know. The best I can do is deflect attention for a little while."

"That's enough," I say. "As soon as we land on the Drifting Isles, the brunt of the danger to us will have passed."

Blair appears surprised. "You intend to land on the Drifting Isles?"

Now I'm surprised, too. "I assumed it was you who facilitated its tracking."

"No." Blair frowns. "I doubt Lisari would have, either. She enjoys meddling, but not doing work for others."

Then who was responsible? Was it truly just good fortune? I suppose stranger things have happened. Of course, I can't count my eggs before they hatch; we don't yet have the tracker in hand.

"Be careful with the Isles," Blair says after a moment. "Settling the Ruins will draw attention. If you're able to keep the Core concealed, you may pass beneath the attention of the Heavens. But there will be other obstacles to contend with."

"I appreciate the warning," I say truthfully. Concealing the Core was precisely what we were intending. But we have other plans for dealing with the champions. "And thank you for buying us time," I add. "It sounds like doing so may come at a risk to yourself. I'm grateful you're giving us a chance." I gesture down to the group running about the square, shouting and laughing as three more balls are thrown into the match and chaos unfolds. "These people deserve a chance. One their predecessors were not given."

Blair's expression softens. "I can see you care about the Fyrethians very much. But you have not known them for very long."

"That's true," I agree. "I don't think anyone would need to. It's hard not to like them. To root for them."

My gaze drifts over to an abstract mural of Fyreneth carved into one of the walls of the square. It's so artistic, it's more flames than harpy.

"Did you ever meet her?" I ask suddenly. "Fyreneth?"

Blair hesitates. "No. I did not learn of her city until after its fall."

A lump forms in my throat, and my grip on the balustrade tightens. She didn't even know it existed? As if Fyreneth's whole kingdom was insignificant. Just wiped from the earth like someone flicking an ant off a table.

"They didn't deserve that," I say, trying to keep my tone in check. "What Lorata did to them was cruel. How can so much death be justified in any circumstance?"

Blair doesn't argue, grimacing instead. "What was done..."

Then she stops mid-sentence, turning her head to the side as if noticing something in the corner of her vision.

"I must leave," she says abruptly, her voice suddenly tight. Nervous, even? "Perhaps you will not believe me when I say this, but you have shifted my perspective on Travelers. I wish you luck with the coming storm, Fyre. You will almost certainly need it."

I open my mouth to ask what she meant—with the Drifting Isles, was she referring to a literal storm? Metaphorical? Both? But she's gone in the blink of an eye, silently vanished as if she were never there at all.

I sigh. More questions than answers, once more. The gods are being infuriatingly evasive—though I suppose I should be grateful they are only that.

Behind me, someone scoffs. "Meddle? I don't meddle. Can you believe she said that?"

When I turn around, I am unsurprised to find Lisari sitting on the edge of the balcony, legs casually dangling over the side as if it weren't a lethal drop. She tips her head back toward me with a smile.

"I like to think of myself as more of a catalyst."

Chapter Forty-Two
THEORIES

"Lisari," I greet with a flat tone. "I'm surprised you want to chat."

"You are?" she asks, feigning surprise. The god hooks her legs over the balustrade and leans back toward the balcony until she's hanging upside down. From this orientation, her grin looks like a grimace. "But I *love* a good information exchange. Whatever gave you that idea?"

I have to hold in an annoyed sigh. "All the skulking around you've been doing lately. I figured if you wanted to talk to me, by now you already would have."

"Skulking!" Lisari pauses. "Oh, actually, I quite like that. Yes, I've been skulking! But I was waiting for you to come to me with any questions you might have."

I raise a skeptical eyebrow. That easily, she's offering to answer questions? I suspect I will only get half answers—or ones that come with strings attached. Despite Lisari acting far more open and friendly than Blair, I trust her far less.

Perhaps because Blair is blunt and direct—much like Mirzayael, in some ways. Meanwhile, Lisari treats serious subjects with more levity than I feel they demand.

But if she's offering, then there's one thing that's been itching at me for a couple days now. "Were you responsible for creating the Drifting Isles tracker, or pointing us its way?"

Lisari slips from her perch, but her hands catch herself before her head can knock into the ground. She turns the move into a handstand, and then cartwheel, righting herself. "No... I wasn't aware mortals had any way to track it. That's interesting."

Huh. So it really was luck, or some twist of fate. And even the gods seem unaware of it—or were, until I just told them.

Lisari hops back up on the balustrade, and despite the fact that she's a god and certainly in no danger, the sight makes my stomach flutter anxiously.

"Why are you offering to help us?" I ask. I can't imagine it's from the goodness of her heart.

She chuckles. "Life's more fun when there's danger in it, don't you think?" She strolls along the wall, swinging her feet out over the drop with each step. "Consequences. I don't think I remember what fear feels like. Not really. Surprise, though—your lot is stoking quite a bit of surprise in me again. It's delightfully refreshing."

"So we're just a bit of entertainment for you?" I ask skeptically. "You'd betray the rest of the pantheon just for that?"

"Not *only* for that," she says with a grin. "You may not believe me, but I do have your best interests at heart. And betrayal?" She laughs. "Don't be so dramatic. I'm just bending the rules, a bit."

As if I'm the dramatic one here. But if she's really as authentic as she claims, then it will be easy to verify—and I'm not about to pass up this opportunity to get as much information out of her as I can.

"Blair didn't know Fyreneth," I say, deciding to start with safer subjects that don't have to do with the System. Maybe her lips will be looser by the time I get there. "But you acted like you recognized her when we first met."

Lisari sticks her arms out to the side as if balancing. "Is that a question?"

I mentally sigh. "I just want to know what she was like. Why it all had to end the way it did."

Lisari hums. "I'm still not detecting any questions."

I shoot her an entirely pointless glare. "What can you tell me about Fyreneth and the fall of her city?"

"Aha!" She jumps back down to the balcony. "That's one. And I would be happy to answer it." She pauses.

"...For a price?" I guess.

She grins. "Well, if you're offering."

There's the catch I'd been waiting for. I eye her warily. "I don't know if I have anything you couldn't already obtain for yourself."

She waves a dismissive hand at my words. "What nonsense! A riddle for you: what I'm looking for is something so common that everyone has it—yet it is the rarest thing of all, as no two are the same."

I frown, puzzling through her words. After a moment, I take a stab at it. "Experience?"

She points at me. "Bullseye! So, what do you say?"

"You want to exchange question for question?" I ask skeptically. I was expecting something more along the lines of a nebulous favor or an owed debt. "What sort of questions?"

"Well, you won't know until I ask them, will you?" She grins. "What's the harm in a few questions?"

I'm inclined to agree, but wary enough to wonder what sort of trick might be involved. How could she twist a question in some way that might be to my detriment?

No way that I can obviously see. I'm not hiding anything she doesn't already know about. Yet it doesn't hurt to be careful.

"Oh, come on," she says while I'm hesitating. "Indulge my curiosity, won't you?"

"So long as it's merely curiosity," I say.

"What else could it be?" she asks. She cocks an eyebrow. "You're not hiding anything, are you?"

"No," I say, belatedly realizing there is one thing I've been keeping from the gods, though she's not specifically the one I'm worried about learning of it. Even so, my desire for answers gets the best of me. "Alright. I'll play along."

Her face lights up. "Wonderful! Then to answer your first question, I met Fyreneth once. She was bold. Ambitious. Perceptive. Quite a bit more like your arachnoid friend than yourself, actually. Her only soft spot was for her people; she believed fiercely in her kingdom and its potential. She would stop at nothing to ensure their prosperity—ironically, the reason for her downfall. Had she paced herself and withheld the source of her power, she may not have drawn Lorata's attention."

"You're talking about the Dungeon Core," I surmise. "Why was it so important that thousands of innocent people needed to pay for it with their lives?"

Lisari waggles her finger at me. "Ah, ah. My turn now."

Will she ask about the watchtower spells we're uncovering? The surveillance circle that lets me know whenever one of them are spying on us? I steel myself for whatever question she might have.

Lisari claps my hands, eagerly leaning forward. "Is it true your world only has humans? As the only dominant intelligent species?"

I blink. "Er, yes. That's true."

"Fascinating!" She lets go as she throws her arms in the air and does a little spin before coming back to face me. "Alright, next question."

I stare at her. Really? That's all she wanted to know? Was she really just curious after all, without any ulterior motive? Somehow, that idea is throwing me more than anything nefarious she could have done.

"Alright," I say, thinking carefully about my wording. I don't want to ask something that could be answered with a simple yes or no. "Why did Lorata want to destroy the Dungeon Core?"

"She didn't," Lisari says. "My turn!"

"Hey," I object. "That's barely an answer."

She takes on a lopsided grin. "No more so than 'That's true.' Come now, you can't think you can get away with two-word responses and expect a lecture in return from me."

"Fair enough," I admit. "Then what else about my world would you like to know?"

"Everything," she admits, a hungry undertone to her words reminding me very much of the Dungeon Core. "But for now I think I will satisfy myself with this: What does your world know of souls and magic?"

I spend a moment to think about it. "That's a complicated question. Our world had countless cultures with countless perspectives on both those subjects. I will say that neither were considered scientific bodies of knowledge; neither were observable. Many people theorized about souls and magic, but they were not a part of our technology or day-to-day life."

Lisari nods along, and doesn't seem particularly surprised by any of this: I wonder if she already had been told as much, but was using this opportunity to confirm what she'd learned. Perhaps there *is* something to what I've learned about Shirasil's disposition. Some sources describe him as the embodiment of chaos, but others describe him as an alchemist: a scientist. Curiosity incarnate. Is Lisari that side of him? A young scientist, eager to dig down to the truth of things?

It's a nice thought, just one that feels strangely at odds with the persona I've previously been presented with. Is one an act, perhaps? And if so, which one?

"I didn't think magic or souls were real until I came here," I continue. "And even now I question the reality of souls, at least as our world understood them. I thought I caught a glimpse, in that dark place between worlds..." I shake my head. "I don't know what I saw."

Lisari seems to listen more intently at this last part. "What place between worlds was this?"

So I *do* have information she doesn't already know. Interesting. "My question first. Why was Fyreneth's kingdom targeted by Lorata, and what did the Dungeon Core have to do with it?"

"That's two questions," she teases. "But I will allow it. You once again make an incorrect assumption. Fyreneth's kingdom was not targeted: The Dungeon Core was. Your jewel is one of many such objects called remnants."

"You and Blair have mentioned that before," I recall. "Blair said they are dangerous entities, especially if they interact. But she didn't say who they were a danger to. I can't imagine the gods would feel threatened by much...?"

Lisari smiles, dark and ironic. "We are not so impervious as the Heavens may have led you to believe. Lorata deemed the Dungeon Core dangerous enough to apprehend. Fyreneth refused to give it up. Lorata's champion fought Fyreneth, and both perished in the fight. With the city buried and her champion dead, Lorata deemed the Dungeon Core lost—which it did seem to be until you unearthed it."

I frown. "Lorata didn't want to secure the Dungeon Core herself?"

"Our all-seeing superior prefers not to leave the Heavens, leaving her champions to act in the mortal realm on her behalf." Lisari grins. "That's two questions, so now I get two!"

She leans forward excitedly. "Tell me everything you can recall about how you arrived here."

That isn't technically a question, but I decide it best to play along. She is giving me answers, after all.

"I died," I say, and I'm surprised to realize how much those words summon a swell of regret within me—but not as surprised as I am to see Lisari's smile fade. She waits for me to continue, abruptly serious. The shift in her attitude unsettles me.

"I died," I repeat, turning to lean on the balustrade and look back down on the square. Not that Lisari has eyes to meet, but it helps to not be looking at her when I talk about this. The young Fyrethians are still playing in the courtyard below, completely unaware of the god's presence above them. Gardi laughs at something, then grabs Salvia by their arm, pulling them into the game as well.

"But though the world faded away, my mind didn't," I say, thinking back. "I found myself without form, in a place without light, or shape, or... I'm not sure. The space itself was difficult to conceptualize. But I soon realized I was not alone. There were many other presences. Souls, I now think, though I hadn't understood it at the time."

"Did you speak to any of them?" Lisari asks.

"I tried to," I say, closing my eyes as I attempt to recall the nebulous experience. "I'm not sure if 'speak' is the right word. I could sense them. Feel their fear and confusion. There was one who was full of so much regret. Not for the life they'd lost, like many of us, but... I'm not sure. It was like they were apologizing *to* us. I tried to reach out and ask what was wrong, but they didn't seem to hear."

I pause in an attempt to recall what came next, but Lisari stops me.

"What else can you remember about this soul?" she asks. "Did you glean a name?"

I shake my head. "It was such a brief interaction. I think, perhaps, they said something like, 'they didn't mean for this to happen.' But it was hard to hold on to with the malice all around us."

Lisari tips her head, brows pinching in a faint frown. "Malice? In the Between? That shouldn't be."

All I can do is shrug helplessly. "I don't know what should or shouldn't have been—all I can tell you is what I experienced."

Lisari nods, still frowning, and scratches at her chin as she begins to pace the balcony. She waves a hand in my direction. "Continue."

Oh, well, so long as I have permission. "It's hard to explain what happened next. There was some sort of struggle, I think. Like the malice itself was alive and fighting with something. Or someone. Then it was surprised—and most of the souls around me seemed to slip away. That made it angry. It seemed to clamp around me like teeth. The sensation was so corrosive. Like my very soul was being... digested..."

My chest tightens at the realization. It had all been so confusing in the moment, but now, with the benefit of hindsight, the experience is abruptly snapping into new clarity.

I turn to Lisari. "Was it the Dungeon Core?"

She shakes her head. "Not specifically. But I expect it was something very much like it."

Not *specifically*? What does that mean? It should be a yes or no question, shouldn't it? I'm about to ask for clarity, but Lisari continues musing, and as long as she's volunteering information, I'm not about to interrupt her.

"This is more than anyone else has been able to recall. Why?" She turns back to me, frowning with unnerving intensity. "Perhaps your Core *is* relevant in some way. A magnetic draw, or..."

My mind races to put everything together she's telling me. What was drawn to what? Me to the Dungeon Core? But why? Something to do with the entity of malice? Similar to the Dungeon Core. Something like...

A remnant. Was that what I was contending with in that place between worlds? Then it wasn't entirely chance that I ended up emerging into this world near the Dungeon Core.

Which also explains why people like Sandro also encountered a remnant.

And if we all have had an increased likelihood of coming in contact with a dangerous remnant, it also explains why the gods are so interested in finding us.

"Oh!" I cry and Lisari jumps.

She actually *jumps.* "What?" she says, lifting her brows in expectant curiosity.

It occurs to me at this moment that we've stopped all pretext of the answer game. We're conversing like any two people would—not like a god and a mortal. And the expression she's given me feels so much like that of a student waiting for an answer—like she really is a young woman in her twenties.

"I think I know how I manifested a body on this world," I say. "Unless that's something you already know and can inform me about."

She gestures for me to explain. "I have theories but would be happy to hear yours."

"The Dungeon Core has an incredible amount of mana it's absorbed from its surroundings," I explain. "It ate a large amount of mana ore, specifically."

"That does sound like something it would do," she says dryly. "But you think the Dungeon Core has something to do with your body's formation? That seems unlikely."

I shake my head. "Not the Dungeon Core *specifically*." My mouth twitches at the word choice. "As you said—something very much like it. It was a remnant that caught us in between worlds, wasn't it?"

"Very likely," Lisari agrees. "In the Between. It's a dimensional source of null arcana."

I light up. "Then that explains it! So if some other remnant had absorbed an incredible amount of mana, and, as I understand it, it takes a large pool of mana to give gestating souls form, then perhaps when our souls spilled out into this reality, we took some of that mana with us."

Lisari is silent for a moment. Then, she howls with laughter, doubling over to brace her hands on her knees.

"You think you were *birthed* into this world?!" She cackles, clutching her stomach as she staggers back to lean against the balustrade.

So much for her acting serious and genuine.

"Well, not precisely," I say, slightly flustered, heat rising in my cheeks. "But by a similar mechanism, if nothing else."

Lisari continues to crack up, and I'm distinctly reminded of Mirzayael reacting similarly when I first asked about the formation of children in this world.

When it's apparent Lisari is nowhere near finished, I raise my voice. "Unless you have a better idea?"

The woman wipes a finger at her eyes, grinning with mad delight. "Oh, no. I think it's a delightfully accurate theory. I can't wait to meet the parents!"

I sigh through my nose, casting my gaze to the heavens. "I don't think that's how it works."

"Oh, indeed it is," Lisari says, still tickled to death, but gaining a contemplative look once more. "The magic of Between would be more than enough to provide the energy required—and if a remnant was the one who donated it... Though it's possible another could be involved."

"What?" I ask, surprised. "Who?"

"I'm unsure myself," Lisari admits. "I've yet to meet them, and have many questions to ask when I do. But that's irrelevant." She waves a dismissive hand. "I enjoy your theory. And your account of the Between and the remnant lurking there provides the last missing puzzle piece for many of the questions I've had. The bodies each of you assumed were likely influenced by environmental factors."

"People's remains," I suggest. "Which is why I resemble Fyreneth."

"Quite possibly so," Lisari agrees. "That would fit with patterns that have emerged from other Travelers."

As Lisari oscillates between humor and consideration, I fear I'm in danger of losing her to cryptic responses once more. But there's so much I still have questions about. So much I need to learn. I quickly try to prioritize my questions.

"How many of these other Travelers have you met?" I ask. "You previously mentioned there were one hundred and seventy-five of us. Have you met them all?"

"No, no, not nearly," Lisari says, turning away to rest her elbows on the balcony's rail in a bored posture. "Only a handful like you. A few dozen more in the Heavens, though it is *slightly* more difficult to hold discrete conversations with those residing under Lorata's watchful eyes."

I pick my next words carefully. "Blair indicated some of them might be wrongly held."

"*All* of them are being wrongly held," Lisari abruptly snaps. "What is there to be gained from captivity? What is to be learned from stagnation? This is an unprecedented opportunity for empirical research that Lorata is choosing to squander out of short-sightedness!" She scratches her hand across the rail in agitation, and her nails carve grooves in the stone. It's a jarring reminder of just who and what I'm speaking with.

Still, I need to know if this is something I can use. "It seems their freedom is something both of us would prefer."

Lisari goes quiet and still. So still, I'm not even sure if she's breathing—as if she's nothing more than a statue. Then, she chuckles, quiet and low. The sound sends goosebumps prickling over my skin.

"You are bold, Fyre," she says. "I like that. But even if, *hypothetically*, the Travelers were to be released, there is nothing to stop them from being captured once more."

"Not even other gods?" I ask.

"Not enough of us."

Then there's more like Lisari and Blair who might want to help—or at the very least, not wish us ill—but not a majority. Still, those are names worth gathering.

But over the course of this conversation, she's let slip some interesting nuggets of information, whether or not that was her intent. While she appears unwilling to stick her own neck out for me, she seems more than happy to offer hints from the shadows. Like the fact that gods have more vulnerabilities and blind spots than I thought. The surveillance spell is proof enough of that.

"*Hypothetically*," I venture, watching Lisari carefully, "there might be ways to protect Travelers that wouldn't require assistance from the gods."

Lisari's mouth twitches in the hint of a smile. "Indeed. There have long been theories of spell networks that could rival the power of the Heavens. However, it would require an exceptional well of magic."

My pulse quickens as I realize exactly what it is she's suggesting. "And if such protection were established..."

Lisari laughs, throwing her hands in the air. "Then, who knows? Perhaps a situation to access the imprisoned Travelers would arise."

Vague. "You wouldn't be able to—"

"I would never conspire against the Heavens." Lisari grins. "Even suggesting as much could be dangerous! Besides, you're setting your cart before the horse. It is my understanding that such a protective spell network doesn't yet exist."

"No," I agree. "Not yet."

"Well," she says, spinning around with a flourish. "I'd love to catch up when that changes."

Even as she begins to walk away, Echo flickers to life in my mind.

[Permissions updated,] she reports.

I raise an eyebrow. "What—"

But when I look back up, Lisari is gone.

CHAPTER FORTY-THREE

GEODESIC

With Captain Marlowe still on his way to deliver the Drifting Isles tracker, we're left to predict the Ruin's path on our own. Based on the data the Wind Conclave sent us, we can roughly determine where the Isles will be located, at least for the next two months, within about a five-hundred-mile radius. After that, the uncertainty begins to increase beyond reasonable estimates. We'll need the tracker to lock onto the Ruin once we get close, but even without it, we can tell we're currently not on an interception course.

The easiest option is to wait until Marlow reaches us and then plot a direct course to the Isles from there. However, the most direct course isn't always the most efficient—and the straightest path isn't always the shortest. Better to make small changes early that will propagate into large-scale differences over a long enough path.

At our current mana expenditure rate, we'll run out in three months. If we knew where the Isles were today, we could plot a direct course, pour all our mana into the effort, and rendezvous with the Drifting Isles in as little as two weeks. But that would leave us with only days of fuel to spare. Too risky.

Instead, we can spend mana over the next month to make a gradual arc to the correct hemisphere and region as the Drifting Isles, leaving us an additional month of mana to spare. That month can be used to pin down the Ruins with the tracker, or, should the worst occur, find an alternate landing location.

One month will pass quickly, and we'll be kept busy with ever more trade and visitors, as news of our city spreads, but I'm equally worried it will take too long. Already one champion has found us; how many more might visit in that time? How many more will simply be willing to observe? Will we be able to keep the Dungeon Core's presence obscured that long? Having Sandro here helps, as much as I hate using another person as a red herring. But if our plans have time to finish executing, we won't remain exposed for much longer.

At least, I hope that to be true. Lisari had implied as much, and I find that I trust her, however unwise that may be.

Once more, my gaze is drawn to my system interface and the new name that appeared in my Contact list: "L." Even though this feature appears to be private, it seems she's still playing it safe. If I access her name, the option to send a message appears in my vision. I haven't taken advantage of this new feature so far, for her or Blair.

As Mirzayael and I walk along the dock, overseeing the last-minute efforts to secure all loose items before we execute the Fortress's trajectory maneuver, I watch Ollie and Meritis perform daring acrobatics in the nearby sky. I bring up the Contact menu and focus on Ollie.

The System responds with a new prompt. [Add Ollie to Contacts?]

Curious, I think, *Yes.*

Ollie's head jerks in surprise and he lets out a rumbly chirp. Meritis appears to ask him something, and he circles around back in our direction.

"FYRE? I JUST GOT A THING THAT SAYS 'FYRE HAS RE-QUESTED TO ADD YOU TO HER CONTACTS.' I CAN PICK ACCEPT OR DECLINE."

"That was me," I reply. *"Sorry I didn't give you a head's up. I wasn't sure it would work."* Interesting to note Ollie has an option to decline my request. Lisari and Blair provided me no such choice. I suppose I shouldn't be surprised.

"SHOULD I PICK YES?" He appears to finally pick me out of the crowd, and banks toward his landing platform. Gusts of wind are sent around the dock as he flaps his wings and lands. One of our lighter-than-air transports, which is in the process of being tied down, is pulled from its workers' hands and starts to float out into open air. A harpy squawks in surprise and dives after it.

"Whatever you like," I reply aloud, now that he's close enough to hear me. I turn to Mirzayael, who's giving me a questioning look. "It seems Ollie can be added to this Contact list as well."

"I don't like it," Mirzayael says, though she's already said as much when I first told her about it. "What if it can be used to track you?"

"I suspect if they wanted to, I wouldn't have much say regardless."

"OKAY, I DID IT," Ollie says through his translator. Dizzi was able to find a way to increase the stone's volume, only now Ollie seems incapable of remembering to use it at lower levels. *"OOH! NOW I HAVE A CONTACT LIST, TOO!"*

Sure enough, Ollie's name appears beneath L in my list. I mentally select his name, and once more I'm provided with an option to message him. A bit redundant, given our mental communication, but I'm not opposed to fallbacks.

"I don't see any option for it to tell me Ollie's whereabouts," I tell Mirzayael, though of course that means little when the gods clearly have access to more features than we do. Still, it's a potentially powerful tool. Especially if this means that by requesting to add contacts, we can unlock this feature for others as well.

I focus on Mirzayael the same way I had with Ollie, but Echo remains silent. I mentally prod to add her as a contact, but the feature doesn't respond. Ah well, it was worth a shot.

"I'm still worried nothing good could come of this," Mirzayael says, planting her hands on her hips as she pauses to watch the rogue transport wrangled back into position and secured to the dock.

"You're just saying that because it came from a god," I remark.

"Yes. I am."

"It's a tool," I say. "And we'll be careful with it." Mentally, I add, "*And it's one we might be able to use against the Heavens. We may be able to build up a network of communication between Travelers, given enough time. A network other gods might not even realize we have access to. It's worth exploring.*"

I can feel Mirzayael finds the idea of using a god's tool against them appealing, but it's still labored with a healthy level of wariness. "*We will need to meet more of these Travelers of yours for such a network to spread.*"

"*We've already met one,*" I point out, thinking of Sandro. At the thought, I attempt to add him to my Contact list as well.

[User must be within line of sight to request Contact,] Echo says.

So the rules appear to be: only System users can be added, and it must be done in-person. A bit limiting, but still powerful.

"I don't think meeting new people is going to be an issue," I respond aloud, looking down over the lands slowly drifting below us. The forests have thinned into planes, and according to our maps, they'll soon give way to a desert.

"Let's just hope they're the right people," Mirzayael grumbles.

On that, we agree.

It's another half an hour before everything is in order. Ollie has finished frolicking in the clouds, and everything in the Fortress that isn't already anchored to the stone has been tied down. Dizzi lands beside us in a flurry of feathers, grinning madly.

"Ready, Oh Great Leaders?" Her feathers flutter in excited anticipation.

Mirzayael gives her a flat look. "You are far too excited for this."

"What?" she cries. "How can you not be? I'm about to pilot a giant floating city halfway around the world! How cool is that?"

Mirzayael turns to look at me. "Fyre..."

"She'll do great!" I insist. "I have complete faith in her." Mentally, I add, "*And I'll be watching over everything through the Dungeon Core. I can seize control at any moment. But we need more people capable of steering the Fortress and familiarizing themselves with its spells than just me.*"

"I promise I won't run us into the ground!" Dizzi enthusiastically declares.

I manage to maintain my encouraging smile without falter. Thanks, Dizzi. Very helpful.

Mirzayael shakes her head, but flicks a hand in a dismissive gesture. "Fine. Go get ready."

Dizzi snaps her hand to her head in a dramatic salute. "Aye, Captain!" Then she launches herself into the air, distant *whoops* of glee following her spiraling flight up to the throne room.

Mirzayael watches her leave with a grimace. "I can't believe you picked *her*, of all people, as your pupil."

I chuckle. "We need that kind of enthusiasm now more than ever." I take her hand and give it a squeeze. Her expression softens, and she squeezes back. "We're going to face serious threats one of these days.

The more hope and unity we can foster in that time, the better we'll weather the storm."

She settles into a more casual stance, lowering her abdomen so we're closer to eye-level with one another. "Hope is something you're good at cultivating in people."

"I'm glad," I say. "It's something I want to do, even if I don't really know how. But I'm happy to hear it's working."

Mirzayael radiates soft affection, and she doesn't attempt to hide it. I share some of my feelings back, and her mouth twitches with a faint smile.

"*I'm not sure I understand what it is you see in me,*" she privately admits. "*There is so much we don't see eye-to-eye on.*"

"*But the places we do are the places that count,*" I say. "*Your passion, your love for this city and its people, your fierce protectiveness. You feel so strong. A rock to lean against.*"

She takes my other hand, a rare undercurrent of shyness swirling through her emotions. "*I think you have it backward. You are **my** rock.*"

She leans forward, and I do as well, and our foreheads bump lightly against each other, noses brushing. The way light reflects in her eyes is like stars in the night sky.

"EWWWWW!" Ollie cries, mentally and vocally. "ARE YOU GO-ING TO KISS? GROSS!" He gags for effect, which amounts to a shuddering roar that startles several people nearby.

Meritis is sitting on Ollie's neck, elbows propped up on his head. "Adults are disgusting," he agrees.

Mirzayael pulls away as I laugh. "There is nothing disgusting about expressing affection."

"That's exactly what an adult would say!" Meritis cries.

Mirzayael narrows her eyes. "Just because you have developed the bad habit of treating Lord Fyre with informality doesn't mean the same extends to me."

Meritis pales. "Sorry, Lord Mirzayael." He slides down the back of Ollie's neck until he's out of sight.

I chuckle. "They're just being kids. Comes with the territory."

"I've never done very well with children," Mirzayael admits, stating the obvious.

"You're doing well with Ollie," I say. "And getting better every day. No one is born knowing how to be a parent. It's something you just sort of fake your way through." And learn from. There's much I can do better this time. I just wish Carolyn had been afforded that chance.

Mirzayael watches Ollie for a moment longer, who has sidled away from the adults to talk with Meritis in conspiratorial tones. She turns abruptly to me. "A parent?"

"Oh," I say quickly. "Not to assume anything for you. I was mostly talking about myself. And I never want to assume anything for Ollie, either. I can never replace his parents. But for as long as I'm able, I want to be his guardian."

There's a thread of irony there, given his Role.

"You see him as your son," Mirzayael says.

My heart clenches as I watch the dragon. "Despite the strangeness of our circumstances? Yes, I do. I care about him very much."

Mirzayael wraps an arm around my side, and I lean into her. "I care about him, too," she says quietly.

She didn't have to say it aloud. I already knew.

The ground lurches beneath my feet, and Ollie yelps as several others let out a surprised gasp. The motion is gone a moment later—like an elevator reaching its floor. But ever so slowly, I note the land beneath us shift in a different direction.

"WE'RE MOVING!" Ollie cries, craning his head over the wall. We were, of course, already moving before, but I decide not to point that out.

"Everything in order?" Mirzayael asks. Nervousness threads through her thoughts, though you'd never know it from her voice.

I dip into the Dungeon Core and begin sifting through information from all the spells in its interface. Dizzi's doing a fine job. I tweak a few decimal points, but from what I can see, the trajectory change is implementing just as we planned it. It will take another hour for the maneuver to complete as we gain speed and shift directions; in that time, I'll try very hard not to look at the plummeting Bonus Mana numbers.

"I CAN'T WAIT TO SEE IT." Ollie mentally taps on the Dungeon Core like it's a pet behind a window. *"DID YOU KNOW? WE'LL BE LANDING SOON! AND THERE WILL BE MORE ROCKS FOR YOU TO EAT."*

The Dungeon Core jitters with excitement. More rocks! When? Now? It would really like to try something new.

"Soon," I tell it, looking out over the horizon. The world feels vast from this vantage point. And perhaps it is—we've barely scraped the surface of all the people and nations there are to meet. But with the Drifting Isles to carry us, we'll have the opportunity to meet all of them.

"Soon."

CHAPTER FORTY-FOUR

FRIENDS NEW AND OLD

A week into our journey, an airship approaches our city. It isn't the first, and it certainly won't be the last, but this one is familiar. Its balloon is bright red.

"Captain Marlowe," I greet as his ship docks and the man strides down the plank with a wide grin. "Glad to see you again. I must say, you had me wondering what to expect with that last cryptic message of yours."

He clasps my hand with a strong, warm grasp. "Cryptic? I promised you a tracker and I've got one!" He grins, a mischievous glint in his eyes. "Well, in a manner of speaking."

"Do I want to know?" I ask as he pays respect to Mirzayael next.

Marlowe rests his hands on his belt, turning to look back to his ship. "Why don't you see for yourself?"

His crew is already done securing the ship and has started to unload a welcome supply of fresh produce to trade. He probably expects to get a good deal from us for the supplies, and he'd be right. But the individual who steps off the ship is clearly the primary motivation for his visit.

Mirzayael briefly tenses beside me, and I also experience a moment of alarm. Red skin, black hair, orange horns, and golden eyes: a cambion. Zetaru is the only one I've actually met to date, as her species seems more rare, or at least more reclusive, than most. But it takes just a second to realize this person is not Yua Tin's Champion. Even if the differences in appearances hadn't clued me in, their nervous yet excited expression is about as far from Zetaru as you could get.

The cambion has a sort of bookish look to them, with round spectacles on their nose and a bouquet of writing implements protruding from their breast-pocket. They shield their eyes as they look up at the city in awe. "Amazing! What style of architecture is that?"

"Lord Mirzayael, Lord Fyre," Captain Marlowe says, drawing the cambion's attention reluctantly away from the city. "This is Attiru. They're a map-maker and apparently have a bit of experience with the Drifting Isles."

They don't particularly look like the dangerous adventurer type, but I know better than to judge a book by its cover. "I heard there was a tracker of some sort?"

They blink at me for a moment, as if caught off guard, then step forward to sweep into a respectful bow before Mirzayael and I.

"Yes, my lord." Their voice is heavily accented, but they seem fluent in Dunmorish nevertheless. They straighten back up. "However, I've yet to determine if that is a resource I'm willing to offer you."

Mirzayael bristles. "If you came all this way to extort us for wealth, you've misjudged the situation."

Attiru frowns, but Captain Marlowe jumps in first. "I assure you that's not the case. Come, we've traveled a long way to get here. Perhaps this conversation can take place after some food and rest?"

That seems wise, at least to diffuse the small friction that's arisen between Mirzayael and Attiru, if nothing else.

But the cambion surprises me. "That's not necessary—I'm well rested from the flight here. And actually, I came to talk. If it was money I was after, I could have sent an invoice. But I wanted to get to know the people I'd be distributing my map to, first. Captain Marlowe has spoken highly of you."

Purely out of good will, I'm sure, and not also to help broker this deal. I catch his eye, and he gives me a good-natured wink.

I can't help but like the man, even if he's in this at least partially out of his own self-interest.

"Would you like a tour?" I offer. "We could speak along the way."

Attiru's eyes light up. "That would be wonderful. This is such a fascinating city! I think I can guess why you're interested in the Drifting Isles."

We begin walking up the gently sloping main street that leads to higher tiers of the city.

"We'd like to settle there," I admit as we walk. "Our city operates on arcana, so being able to draw from a large, natural well would benefit us greatly."

"That's a nice idea," Attiru says, head craning back to peer at every house and street we pass. "But it sounds dangerous. You realize there are wild animals out there?"

"We can handle a few beasts," Mirzayael says shortly.

Attiru looks her up and down. "I'm sure you could."

"It sounds as though you visited it and returned in one piece," I remark.

"By no small miracle!" Attiru laughs. "But I had help from some friends who are far more apt at combat than myself. And I have a feeling you two would do just fine. But can you say the same for the rest of your residents? What happens when a flock of gryphons attacks the city?"

"Irrelevant," Mirzayael says, clearly not enjoying having the security of the Fortress questioned. "We would have to deal with wild animals no matter where we land."

Attiru shrugs. "True enough."

But it's a fair concern, and I'd rather not wait to be attacked. "We were already planning to scout the Ruins before we land," I tell the mapmaker. "We could also use the opportunity to remove the largest threats."

"You make it sound easy," Attiru chuckles, but I can feel that Mirzayael approves of this plan. I get the feeling she's been itching for more action for a while now.

We take Attiru on a leisurely lap around the city, speaking with townsfolk and stopping to admire squares in the process of having plants installed. Attiru doesn't seem daunted at all by being thrown into conversations with strangers in a foreign language, and is even awed and delighted to meet Ollie. (His speech stone certainly helps smooth out new introductions and convince visitors that he is probably unlikely to eat them.)

"If you don't mind my asking," I say as we wind up a staircase of the palace, "why do you want to get to know us? Is there a reason you're being judicious about who you give this information to?"

"Of course." Attiru runs a hand up the stone banister, gaze still plastered to every new mural and statue we pass. "Most of the world's Ruins have been plundered over the years. The Drifting Ruins less so, due to accessibility. If my map becomes widespread, then the resulting destruction—and almost certainly death—will be on my hands."

I can see their perspective. Even if they wouldn't be responsible for what was done with the tool they created, it would be hard not to feel guilty for the harm that resulted from its use.

"You've already shared it with some people," Mirzayael points out.

"The wind mage conclave, yes," Attiru agrees. "I have a good relationship with them, and I trust them to use the knowledge wisely."

"And what does 'wisely' look like to you?" I wonder. Mirzayael had been about to respond in a similar but far more abrasive manner.

We come to the top of the landing, facing a wide, open pavilion designed for Ollie's use. Attiru stares out over the city, their eyes following a harpy as it glides through the air.

"I'm a cartographer by trade, but I have a background in history," they explain. "I like to think we stand to learn a lot from our own past. It would be a shame to see these Ruins picked apart in search of anything valuable—especially now that I've seen them with my own eyes."

Mirzayael is entirely unmoved. "You can't be that worried about the destruction of something that's already been destroyed."

Attiru gives Mirzayael a curious look. "Just because something has fallen into disrepair doesn't mean it can't be refurbished." Their gaze goes past her and up toward the spires of the palace. "Don't you think?"

Unease stirs in my gut. Do they know what this city is? Who we are? I suppose it would be foolish to think Jorria wouldn't spread the word even after we'd left. I had just hoped we'd be in a more secure position before our origin became known.

"Perhaps we should take this conversation somewhere more private," Mirzayael says, (literally) reading my mind.

Attiru agreeably bows their head. "I think that would be wise."

They don't appear to be making a threat, though their reference was clearly intended to let us know that they know who we are. The question is: why tell us, and what do they want?

I inform Marlowe we're heading to the dining hall, and he waves us on, deep in conversation with some cloudwood traders currently staying in our city. The three of us settle into the meal circle at the head of the room as Mirzayael asks a nearby guard to inform the kitchen of our arrival.

She turns back to Attiru once we're alone. "So you know what we are."

Attiru gives a smiling grimace. "That certainly confirms my theory."

Mirzayael narrows her eyes, and I put a placating hand on her leg.

"No one else has seemed to have figured it out," I remark. "How did you put it together?"

"I've seen drawings of the city. Tiered. Five towers, red roof tiles." They look up at the ceiling and the fiery mosaic that decorates the stone. "The harpy motif is also a bit of a giveaway. There was a statue of Fyreneth in one of the halls we passed." They look back at us with a chuckle. "Though I'm not surprised no one else has made the leap. Most people consider her castle a myth."

This is the most information I've managed to gather about the rest of the world's perspective on us to date. I should have sought out a historian before now rather than relying on books—defaulting to texts over people is a persistent flaw of mine.

"We've been keeping our origin a secret," I tell Attiru, despite Mirzayael's dismay. "We weren't sure if the rest of the world would act as Jorria did."

"You met the Jorrians, did you?"

"That's one way to put it."

Attiru gives a derisive chuckle. "They're certainly a zealous lot. They almost make home look enticing. But no, if you're worried about the rest of the world sharing Jorria's view of Fyreneth, then you can rest easy; most don't believe the story, and those who do likely wouldn't care. Everyone's got their own problems to worry about."

I slump against the stone backrest, a weight lifted from my shoulders. We don't have to hide. We're free to be ourselves.

Mirzayael is far less relieved. "One account is not enough to believe. You could be attempting to trick us into revealing ourselves so we become a target."

Attiru splays their hands with a shrug. "Then don't believe me. I don't particularly care. Although I must admit I *am* a bit curious how you lifted an entire city off the ground."

I glance at Mirzayael. "*I think we can trust them.*"

She mentally grumbles. "*You're probably right, as much as I don't like it.*"

A kitchen helper appears just then, and we all get up to assist with passing the dishes down.

Perhaps it's a risk. But if they were interested in betraying us, they wouldn't have let us know their suspicions in the first place.

So, as we eat, I tell them about the Fortress and the spell networks Fyreneth created within it. I tell them about the cloudstone that keeps us floating, and the mana ore that was used to power the city. I don't tell them about the Dungeon Core, but even without it, the bones of how we took off—and why we eventually need to land—are there.

Attiru is an enthusiastic listener, and clearly forgot about their food the moment I started talking. They take a hasty bite when I finish my explanation.

"Amazing," they say. "So the Drifting Isles is the answer you came to for solving the mana problem? Not the easiest solution, but certainly the most creative."

"There are other reasons we'd like to make it our home," I explain, "including its mobility."

Attiru nods thoughtfully, finally digging into their salad. "Why do you want to remain mobile?" They look between the two of us.

"To learn everything I can," I say wistfully. "To meet different people and go to different places and absorb all there is to know. To see the world."

They raise an eyebrow at Mirzayael next.

"Freedom," she says simply. She glances between us, as we're both clearly expecting more. "And to see the world."

Attiru snorts, and I chuckle.

"That's a lot coming from her." I give Mirzayael a playful wink. "Trust me."

"I do," Attiru says. Then they shake their head with a laugh. "Terrible habit of mine, being so trusting. It's gotten me in quite a bit of trouble as of late. But I'd like to help." They smile. "Another dangerous vice."

"Thank you," I say. "We'd greatly appreciate it."

"Do you have this map with you?" Mirzayael asks. I elbow her. "And yes we're very grateful."

Attiru's eyes dance between us with a knowing smile. "Not exactly. I wasn't interested in it being stolen from me if I ran into trouble." They tap their temple. "But I can make you a copy in about an hour."

"That would be amazing," I say. "If there's any way we can repay you, just say the word."

"Well, I wouldn't mind repayment with a payment," they tease. "I *do* still have to feed myself."

"You will be compensated for your labor," Mirzayael assures them.

"What an enticing offer," they remark.

Their subtle needling is really getting under Mirzayael's skin, but she manages to hold back a retort.

"There's just one request I'd like to ask of you before I get to work," Attiru says, sobering.

"Of course," I say. "Anything you want."

"Not *anything*," Mirzayael adds.

Attiru pointedly ignores this. "Once you land, try to preserve the Ruins, would you? You don't seem like the lot to go around destroying historical sites, but as you start getting more and more visitors, some will surely seize the opportunity to do some impromptu excavating."

That hadn't even occurred to me, but now that they pointed it out, that outcome does seem likely.

"We can set something up," I say, glancing questioningly at Mirzayael. "A guard rotation?"

She wrinkles her nose. "Over some old buildings?"

"This city is old buildings," I point out.

She huffs. "Fine. Once we land, we'll likely want to secure the area anyway. In the long term, perhaps an independent team could be assembled to oversee the Ruins specifically."

I brighten. "An archeological team! Oh, I'm sure we'll find plenty willing to help with that."

Attiru chuckles. "Myself included, if you wouldn't mind. I'm glad to see such enthusiasm. I believe I am making the right choice, entrusting you with this compass." Then their face scrunches up in a grimace. "That is, I'd love to be involved in archeological efforts once the area is safe. There are quite a lot of dangerous animals in those clouds."

Mirzayael's faintly bored gaze abruptly clears as her attention snaps back to Attiru. "What did you encounter? Anything you can tell us would be extremely useful."

Attiru blinks at her abrupt engagement. "Of course. I'd rather not have you all go through the same ordeal we did. The first thing you need to watch out for are amphipteres..."

Attiru spends the rest of the afternoon with us and the other councilors, relaying everything they can recall about the Drifting Isles and what lived there. They also give us the location of the tracker spell that they installed—largely so we won't accidentally destroy it and make their compass useless.

"I went through quite a lot to get it up there," they say. "I'd be very appreciative if you didn't make all that effort for naught."

When they sit down to draw out the sister spell circle that will link to the one on the Drifting Isles, Dizzi joins us, bouncing on her heels as she leans over Attiru's shoulder—careful not to jostle them, yet unleashing a stream of questions.

"Some of this *does* require concentration," they tell her at one point. "If you could reduce your interrogation to one question per minute..."

"Sorry!" Dizzi says, giving them a bit of space. "It's just exciting to watch a master work. This technique is fascinating. And there's even a couple runes I don't even recognize!"

Attiru spares a glance up at her. "A couple?"

"Three," she admits, pointing them out while taking care not to touch the page. She may be excitable, but even she seems to respect the work of a spell in progress.

"Those are the most obscure ones I use in this design," they say, sounding fairly impressed. "You're well read. If you ever want to study mapwork spells, come find me."

Dizzi preens at the compliment; that will buoy her for weeks, I'm sure.

By sundown, we have a rough map of the Drifting Isles, a list of what creatures to expect and where, and a magical compass that's pointing us to the Ruins. It's far more than I ever could have hoped for. For the first time since we took flight, I feel prepared for what is to come.

"Thank you for the hospitality," Attiru says as they pack up their things. "It was a pleasure to see this city."

"You're not staying?" I ask. "We wouldn't turn down your expertise navigating the Isles."

Attiru laughs, holding up their hands. "Please don't ask me to stay, or I might say yes. I've had quite enough of that Ruin for one year. Though perhaps I will visit in the next one."

"That would be lovely," I say.

"Yes!" Dizzi adds. "Please come back. And teach me more about that tracker spell... if I haven't reverse-engineered it by then."

"I suspect you will," Attiru says with a chuckle. As they look between us, their expression softens. "Good luck, and be careful. I'd rather not see our world lose this city a second time."

"You won't," Mirzayael says. Her tone is filled with conviction.

And you know? I have faith we'll pull this off, too.

CHAPTER FORTY-FIVE

SCOUTING PARTY

With Attiru's compass, it only takes three weeks to reach the Drifting Isles, but in that time I notice a decline in Sandro's mental health. His Sanity Stat is at 77% now, and it was about when he crossed the 80% threshold that the effects became more noticeable. He's jittery and jumpy—though that's nothing new—and has taken to rubbing a temple when he thinks no one is looking. Even when I use Emotional Radiance to give him a reprieve from the Shuddering Shroud's influence, he's still twitchy and nervous. We need to resolve his Role Requirement sooner rather than later.

So when we finally reach the Ruins, I decide to bring him along on our initial scouting mission.

"Are you sure that's wise?" Mirzayael asks as we wind through the lower streets of the city, making our way to the dock.

An enormous storm engulfs the sky before us. The cloud must stretch for dozens of miles. Occasional lightning flashes from within, and thunder rumbles through the air. When a strong wind cuts through the clouds, impressions of hidden structures fade in and out of view. It's an imposing sight.

"Don't tell me Sandro can't be trusted," I reply. "You're the one who gave his sword back and offered to train him with the guards."

"So I can keep an eye on him," she objects, then grimaces. "Though, you're right—I don't think he means us any harm. It's his mind I'm worried about."

"Which is why he should come," I say. "We need to satisfy his Role Requirement *today*. Before it becomes a problem for the rest of us." Not to mention, Ollie.

We climb the final steps up to the city's wall, which looks out over the dock. Hundreds of other citizens are already here, looking up at the cloud in awe. They should have been able to see it clearly from anywhere in the city at this distance, but I admit there's something magnetic about its presence. The knowledge that there's the remains of an ancient civilization just before us—that we'll soon be diving into—elicits an electric anticipation within me. I'm not sure if I'm more excited or nervous.

"And by satisfying his Role Requirement, you mean killing a drag-on," Mirzayael says.

I grimace. "I'd hoped to find some work-around before now." Though I am by no means a vegetarian, I still hate the idea of killing a creature just to satisfy some arbitrary demand. It seems like such a callous waste.

Maybe there's still something... I shake my head. I can't keep dodging this inevitability.

Mirzayael pats my shoulder. "Not everything is a puzzle to be solved. Sometimes things are just exactly what they appear to be."

"True enough," I sigh. A muted wind brushes against us. It must be strong to reach this far into our atmospheric spell. "Then you understand why we should bring him on this mission."

"Best to clean the wound before it festers," Mirzayael reluctantly agrees. "Though the mission will be dangerous enough as it is; keeping an eye on Sandro is a distraction we don't need."

"Zakaiya and Rei are still assigned to him, aren't they?" I ask. "They could keep watch."

Mirzayael hesitates. "Those two are low on mana reserves currently."

Ah, right. The proto-soul they're tending to. "One of your other guards, then?" I suggest.

"My lords, if I may."

I turn to find Salvia—and by extension, Gardi—have approached us. Salvia dips their head in a respectful bow as Gardi meets my gaze before quickly glancing away. But they incline their head, just the slightest fraction.

"I would like to accompany you," Salvia says. "I could watch Sandro if need be. I am one of our best guards; I won't be a hindrance to you on this mission."

Mirzayael regards them. "You already have a ward. If we reassign you from Gardi, we'll need to find someone else to escort them."

Gardi stirs, like they want to say something.

"What is it?" I prompt.

They sheepishly scratch one of their ears, looking anywhere but at us. "I could come along. If that simplifies things."

Mirzayael and I exchange a surprised glance.

"You won't have to worry about my well-being either," they say. "So I won't slow you down."

"Gardi, of course we care about your well-being," I say, exasperated.

Salvia snorts. "See?"

Gardi shoots them a glare, but there's no anger behind it. Salvia's mouth twitches with the threat of a smile.

"I can also take care of myself," Gardi adds, turning away from Salvia's mocking look. "You've seen my ice abilities. I won't get in anyone's way."

"I believe it," I say. "What little I saw was quite the impressive display. But I have to ask, why do you want to come? It can't just be because Salvia volunteered." ...Could it?

"I'd like to see the Ruins," Gardi admits. "I've only heard stories. Seeing it in person would be like a children's tale come to life."

They'll be seeing it regardless, as our city will be headed there as soon as it's safe to do so. But instead of arguing the point, I raise a questioning eyebrow at Mirzayael.

"*They're Jorrian,*" Mirzayael mentally says.

"*Yes.*"

"*They're still technically a captive,*" she adds.

"*They are.*"

She hesitates. "*That's it. That's all I've got.*"

I grin. "*What, you're not going to add 'I don't trust them?'*"

Mirzayael exhales through her nose. "*Just tell them they can come already. I'm not going to do it.*"

"Alright," I say aloud, holding back a laugh. "You both can come, so long as you understand you'll need to take care of yourselves, as we might not be able to protect you, if things get hairy."

Salvia stands up straight. "Of course! Thank you, Lord Fyre."

Gardi also nods their head, and mumbles something that sounds like it could be somewhere in the vicinity of a thank you.

"Hurry up and prepare," Mirzayael says. "We'll be departing within the hour. If you're not present, we'll leave without you."

I doubt that's true, but it does light a fire under their heels.

"Thank you," Salvia calls back, already hurrying away. "We'll be quick!"

We head over to Ollie next. Dizzi and Sora are in the process of finalizing the makeshift saddle that's strapped to his back. It's one of Dizzi's cloudstone transports, adapted to carry people instead of supplies. Meritis is helpfully flitting around and pulling on whatever lines Ollie thinks are too tight or loose.

"Just finishing our safety checks," Dizzi calls down when she catches sight of us.

"We might need some last-minute adjustments," I say. "Plan on enough restraints for five."

Dizzi sighs, long and dramatic. "Wish you would have told me that last week. Or yesterday. Or an hour ago."

"Is that going to be a problem?" I ask.

"For me?" Dizzi grins. "Nah. Oy! Chert!" She leans over the other side. "Go grab some more of that spider silk, would you?"

Ollie swings his head around to nuzzle me, nearly knocking me off my feet. I give his snout a squeeze, as much as I can get my arms around.

"THIS IS EXCITING," his speech stone says. "I CAN'T WAIT TO EXPLORE AN OLD CITY! JUST LIKE INDIANA JONES. I LOVE THAT MOVIE. EXCEPT FOR THE KISSING PART. AND THE PART WHERE MOM COVERED MY EYES. FYRE, WHAT HAPPENED AT THAT PART?"

"Er," I hesitate. "I'm not sure. It depends on when she did it."

I'm saved from diving down that rabbit hole when Sora calls for his attention, asking him to give the 'saddle' a good shake.

Before long, everything's declared in working order and ready for our flight. Mirzayael straps her spear to the floor of the transport, along with Salvia and Sandro's swords. Neither Gardi nor I have weapons, but we've all at least changed into more practical attire—no loose pieces of cloth to get caught in the wind.

Or a claw.

"Good luck," Nek says, clasping Mirzayael's arms. "Be safe. If you need more soldiers..."

"It's just a scouting mission," Mirzayael says. "Ideally, we'll be gone for less than an hour, and return with a more concrete understanding of the cloud's interior. You'll be the first I call upon when we begin hunting missions."

Nek nods, not pressing the subject. When Sora wanders over and hooks her arm in her husband's, it's not hard to understand why.

"Ready?" I ask our motley crew. Two harpies, an arachnoid, an elf, and a felis prepare to climb on a dragon: it sounds like the set up for a joke.

For a moment, I pause to absorb the strangeness of my life now—or more accurately, how none of it feels strange at all. Like I'd been dreaming for decades and only just woke up. I'm not sure I believe in things like fate or destiny, but deep in my bones it feels like this is where I was meant to be. In this city. As the person I am today. With these people. I can't imagine a world without them.

"Fyre?" Mirzayael prompts.

I refocus my gaze. "Sorry. Lost in thought. Let's get to it, then."

Salvia leaps up to Ollie's saddle with a burst of wind, tossing a line back over to help Gardi and Sandro climb up. Mirzayael can reach the lip if she straightens her legs all the way, so she half pulls-half crawls up to the saddle as well.

Ollie giggles. "THAT TICKLES."

I opt to take the rope as well, not wanting to risk singeing anyone with my flames.

At the top, a series of crisscrossing straps and makeshift seatbelts are waiting for us. Sandro eyes them warily.

"Need help?" I ask, taking the seat next to him as I start to strap myself in. Of course, Salvia and I don't technically need to be strapped in, what with their wings and my Jets, but without knowing the condition of the Drifting Isles, we deemed it wise to keep all of us tied to Ollie to prevent anyone from being separated.

"No," Sandro says, quickly taking a seat. The cloak wraps around his shoulders like a comforting hug. Well, as comforting as a hug could be from a sentient, anxious, and deadly cloak. "Just worried."

"I'm not expecting any trouble on this flight," I tell him. "You're just along in case we find a wyvern nest."

He grimaces. "That's what I'm worried about."

"The wyverns?"

Sandro straps himself in, fending off a corner of the cloak that's unhelpfully trying to wrap around an arm as he clasps his harness. "Yeah. I'll finally have to kill one, won't I?"

I also grimace. "Unless we can figure out an alternative..."

"I didn't even stand a chance against Ollie." He wilts pathetically, then turns toward Ollie's head. "Still sorry about that, Ollie."

Ollie looks back at us with one eye. "IT'S OKAY! IT WAS A MISTAKE. AND YOU DIDN'T EVEN LEAVE A SCRATCH."

That doesn't leave Sandro looking reassured.

"This will be different," I tell him. "Wyverns are the size of a cat, I'm told."

His eyes widen. "Really?"

Gardi snorts. "Did you think we were about to dive into a nest of Ollie-sized dragons?"

"I didn't know they were small!" Sandro objects.

I'm certain I did, in fact, tell him they were small, but I try not to blame the guy with his sanity degrading as it is.

"And whatever you slay, we can bring back to the city and find a use for," I tell him. Making the best of a bad situation, I suppose.

"Right," Sandro says, slumping into his seat once more. His corner of the transport seems to be radiating a tangible aura of gloom. Everyone else exchanges uncomfortable glances.

"Well," Mirzayael says, cutting through Sandro's fog of self-pity. "It seems we're all secured. Ready Ollie?"

"READY!" he cries, wiggling his hips like a cat ready to pounce. It jiggles our saddle back and forth.

"I know you wanted to evaluate the Isles' threat level for yourself," I say to Mirzayael, "but I'm surprised you didn't send someone else on this scouting mission in your stead. Last time you rode on Ollie's back, I distinctly remember you saying 'I will never do that again.'"

"It was an overreaction." She casually leans back against the transport, hooking an elbow over the side. "I can handle a bit of—"

"GO!" Ollie cries, diving off the platform.

Mirzayael gasps, desperately grabbing her straps as our stomachs lurch in a moment of free-fall. Sandro screams. Salvia seems entirely unmoved, and Gardi gives a nervous laugh. Then Ollie's wings snap open and a powerful wind blows around us. And in the next moment, we're flying.

Mirzayael quickly lets go of the straps and smooths the terrified look off her face. I don't think anyone else noticed, but I have to stifle a laugh.

"*Not a word,*" she mentally grumbles.

Nearby, Gardi's claws are digging into the saddle's floor, their eyes glued to their feet. Salvia puts a hand on their shoulder. "It's fine," the felis grumbles.

I feel a pang of regret—I'd forgotten about the panic attack Gardi had the last time they were confronted with heights. They seem to be doing better this time, however, and at least they have Salvia nearby to comfort them. I would, but I'm a bit preoccupied trying to get Sandro to uncurl from the ball he's folded himself into.

"It's alright," I tell him. "We're steady now."

I prod Ollie's mind. *A little more gently next time, if you please.*

"*SORRY!*" he thinks, emitting amusement rather than remorse. He did that on purpose. This kid better not be entering his rebellious phase—I don't even know how I'd handle it.

The rest of the flight to the storm cloud goes much more smoothly. We keep a wary eye out for lightning as we approach, and Salvia activates a storm arcana spell often used by harpies that's supposed to repel electricity. I've not studied it yet myself, but I'll have to hope it's as effective as other harpies claim.

As we get closer, the clouds melt into the air around us, our path forward gradually growing less opaque. Everyone is silent, peering into the dim as if we're collectively holding our breath. Solid shadows emerge from the fog, and Ollie banks around these. It would be easy to get lost in here. I can see why this Ruin is especially hard to find.

Then, like a switch being flipped, blindingly bright light spills over us. I squint, raising a hand to my eyes, but the clouds reflect light back at us from every angle. It's as if we're in the eye of a hurricane. A swirling wall of white creates a breathtakingly large funnel, reflecting sunlight from the open sky all the way down to the lowest layer of the Drifting Isles, far below us. Sunlight scatters through the mist at just the right angle to dust the air with a prismatic sparkle. A flock of birds takes off at our appearance and spirals down the funnel. My gaze follows their descent. Sandro gasps, and my breath catches in my throat.

"OH," Ollie exclaims. "PRETTY!"

Far beneath us is land. Not the planetary surface, but a valley at the bottom of this cloud, floating much like our own city. Above it, however, is more land. Dozens—hundreds—of giant slabs of stone spiral upward, tethered by vines like balloons on a string. Echo confirms it's all cloudstone—much more than makes up the base of our own city.

But the stones themselves look odd, and it takes me a moment to recognize why. They're sections of a city, long overgrown by plants and half crumbling away. It's as if someone shattered ancient Rome and sprinkled what remained across the sky like pieces of a puzzle.

"Amazing," Gardi breathes.

"I've never seen anything like it," Salvia agrees.

Even Sandro has nothing fearful to add.

Mirzayael turns to look at me, and perhaps it's just the light, but her face seems to glow with happiness. "Ready to explore our new home?"

I grin. "You read my mind."

Chapter Forty-Six

TO VANQUISH A DRAGON

I have Ollie land on the nearest floating rock so we can take stock of our surroundings. It's a wide, flat surface, at least a hundred meters across, overgrown with wild grass and speckled with trees. There's also hints of crumbled buildings here; glimpses of white marble protruding from hills, like bones half buried in the ground. Ollie digs his claws into the edge of our platform and peers over the ledge.

"Let's take a moment to observe, first," I say, scanning the land below. "Attiru said there was a flock of griffons where they set up their tracker. Let's avoid that area if possible."

"And an amphiptere somewhere near the base," Mirzayael adds.

"What's an amphiptere?" Sandro asks.

"It's like a dragon without legs," I tell him. "Just two wings. Technically it would also satisfy your Role Requirement, and we will need to deal with it eventually, but it would probably be around Ollie's size, so…"

Sandro gulps and quickly nods. "Let's stick to the wyverns."

"A DRAGON WITHOUT LEGS?" Ollie repeats. "OH MAN, THAT WOULD STINK! HOW WOULD YOU HOLD THINGS?"

"With your mouth?" Gardi suggests.

"EWWWW!" he cries, despite the fact I've seen him put things I would consider extremely foul in there already. "MAYBE I COULD USE MY TAIL."

We're getting off track. "Everyone, keep an eye out for wild animals. Call out whatever you see, no matter how big or small. I don't want to be caught off guard."

Mirzayael nods. "Let's do a few laps down the cloud, as shallow as you're able. I want to descend slowly and carefully. We'll land on another stone a third the way down and reassess from there. Sound good?"

Ollie wiggles in excitement. "I CAN'T WAIT UNTIL I CAN EXPLORE THIS PLACE. I HAD A SECRET HIDEOUT IN THE WOODS BEHIND MY HOUSE. I BET I CAN MAKE ONE HERE, TOO!" He glances back at us. "SORRY, ADULTS AREN'T ALLOWED."

At least I have Psionic Link and Psionic Senses if I need to find him. "Once Mirzayael deems the area safe, you can do as much exploring as you wish. Ready?"

"OKAY," he says, tensing. "HERE WE GO!"

I hurriedly add, "Slowly this time—"

He spreads his wings and jumps. Mirzayael strangles her harness in a death grip, and Sandro's cloak snaps around him in alarm. But a wind catches us before we have the opportunity to drop, and we glide smoothly downward. Ollie turns an eye back on us with a mental giggle.

We slowly leapfrog our way down the Drifting Isles, pausing regularly to watch for animals and document our surroundings. Attiru had provided us with a general map of the Ruins, but it had only gone about two-thirds the way up, along a single route, leaving a majority of the other floating pieces of land a mystery.

"Over there," Salvia says abruptly, pointing to a large stretch of land. "See? In the trees."

I squint until I finally make out an indistinct form among the leaves.

[Gryphon,] Echo reports, confirming my suspicion. [Native to west Dunmora and also found in the Drifting Isles, these predators hunt in packs and are highly territorial.]

"At least we know where to avoid," I say. It sounds like they are going to be a pain to deal with, though.

We encounter other creatures on the way down, though none of these are dangerous, thankfully. A flock of silver birds scatter at Ollie's approach, swirling up to a different level of the Ruins. A herd of jackalopes race across a field, sparking with electricity as they run—a good reminder that wind magic is only one subset of storm arcana. When we alight on another platform, a giant swarm of burnished beetles take flight, rising around us with a melodic hum like gemstones floating into the sky.

Sandro nervously swats at the lazily drifting beetles, and Salvia rolls their eyes at him. "They're just bugs."

"They could be magic bugs!" he objects. "They could have venom! Or be carnivorous! Or electrocute us!"

Gardi plucks an emerald one from a nearby strap. It buzzes futilely in their grasp until they let it go. The bug hurriedly (but still rather lazily) flutters away. "I don't think they're dangerous."

"IT'S SO PRETTY!" Ollie says, head craned up to watch the cloud of glittering bugs ascend to other less-dragon-filled chunks of land.

"And to think this will be our home," Mirzayael says quietly, also watching the display. "After so many lifetimes in the dark."

I can only try to imagine what that must feel like. My heart aches—both in sorrow for what they've endured, and in joy for the future they'll have access to now.

I catch Gardi watching Mirzayael with a conflicted look on their face. They glance at Salvia next. I'd pay a pretty penny to know what they're thinking.

Well, I could always lean over and touch them, but that would ruin the moment.

"What's that?" Sandro cries, panic rising in his voice.

I consider activating a sphere of Emotional Radiance to calm him down, even though it might be a waste of my mana, but when I turn to follow his gaze, I realize there actually is something to be worried about.

A dense flock of creatures is racing up toward us. Birds of prey, I think, each the size of a hawk. But when Echo checks them—

My heart leaps. "This is it!" I cry. "Ollie, stay put. Sandro, get unbuckled and grab your sword. It's a flock of wyverns. Now's your chance!"

I'm already undoing my own harness, and the others are as well. Not that we all need to be involved, but I'm sure everyone is ready to stretch their legs, and if one of us can catch a wyvern for him, we can get this whole ordeal over with.

Sandro shakily pulls himself to his feet, drawing his sword and clutching it like a lifeline. Abruptly, I think it would be wise for all of us to put as much space between Sandro and ourselves as possible. The others also seem to have come to this conclusion, as Gardi has moved to the opposite end of the transport, Salvia has taken flight, and Mirzayael has crawled back along Ollie's neck, narrowing her eyes at the swordsman. I also leap back, activating my Jets as I clear Ollie's side.

Then the wyverns are upon us.

The lizards do really look like miniature dragons, largely green, brown, blue, and white, most some combination of the four. Their haphazard flight reminds me of a cloud of bats, fluttering every which way yet somehow managing not to run into each other. The wyverns snap up the beetles still slowly trying to escape, their wings stirring up gusts of wind that send the helpless bugs spiraling off course. They completely ignore us, as if they're used to the presence of people, or at least don't see us as a threat. And with their extreme speed and agility, hovering, flipping around, and darting through the air in a blur, I can understand why.

"It's okay," Sandro is saying, his voice tight as his eyes dart around the sky. "They won't hurt us. It's just a bunch of bugs and lizards. Don't freak out. We got this. Don't freak out!"

His cloak is quivering, the bottom hem jerking back and forth like a cat's tail. One wyvern loops around Sandro, and he lets out a yelp, swinging his sword through the air. The slash isn't even close, and the wyvern is gone before it likely even knew he was taking a swing at it. The cloak squeezes around his shoulders, restricting his arms.

"That's not helpful!" Sandro cries. "That's the opposite of help-ful!"

Ollie laughs, looking over his shoulder. I'm about to gently ad-monish him for laughing at someone else's struggles, before he says, "LOOK! THEY LIKE ME."

Sure enough, many of the wyverns have landed on Ollie's neck and tail to finish crunching down their snacks. "CAN I KEEP ONE?" he asks. "I COULD NAME IT PEANUTS THE SECOND."

They really do seem harmless. One even lands on the front of Gardi's shirt, its wings hanging onto the cloth as it finishes gobbling down its last bite of beetle and swings its head around for its next target. Gardi leans back, shaking the front of their shirt until it lets go and darts away. I should have asked them to grab it for Sandro, but I probably would have had the same instinct. Besides, I just don't have the heart.

Sandro is in the process of wrangling the cloak off his arms—this partially explains how ineffective his sneak attack on Ollie had been—when a wyvern lands on his head. Sandro shrieks, dropping his sword. He smacks a hand to the top of his head and actually manages to land a hit. The wyvern screeches and flaps its wings, but its claw catches in his hair. Sandro scrambles to wrench the creature away, getting a hold of its neck. He yanks it out, along with a tuft of hair, and then thrusts his arm as far away as he can manage, wide-eyed and panting.

I feel a mix of relief and regret at the sight. He's done it—he's caught a dragon. Now he'll be able to satisfy his Role Requirement... once the poor creature is dead.

Sandro still has the wyvern by its neck, and the animal is thrashing wildly in his grasp. It flaps its wings and bites at his gauntlet with angry hisses, its tail flailing wildly. I grimace. I'm not sure I can watch this next part.

But Sandro doesn't move to pick up his sword. He just continues to stare at the wyvern, eyes wide.

He looks at me. "She says my Role Requirement has been satisfied."

"What?" I check his Sanity stat. Sure enough, it's back to 100%.

Sandro lets go of the wyvern, and it delivers one last angry chirp, its tail whipping against his head as it flies away. Sandro looks stunned.

"How?" I say, hovering a bit higher so I can be over the transport when I cut my Jets. I fall into a crouch, wings flaring to help cushion the impact.

"I don't know," he admits. "I thought I was supposed to kill it."

"Thought?" I narrow my eyes. "Sandro, what is your Role Requirement?"

"To slay a—"

"Word for word," I interrupt. "Exactly what Echo says."

Sandro shrugs. "She says 'The Dragon Slayer must vanquish a dragon.'"

"Vanquish?" I repeat. "It says vanquish?"

"Yes?" Sandro blinks in confusion.

Mirzayael and Salvia cautiously climb back into the saddle, looking very unsure.

I groan, rubbing a temple. I can't believe he's been giving me the wrong wording all this time. I'm briefly irritated, but it's quickly overcome by relief.

Nothing has to die.

"Sandro, vanquish doesn't mean 'kill,'" I say, shaking my head.

Sandro leans back with a frown. "What? No. It says I'm a Dragon *Slayer*. I have to slay one."

"And my role says I'm a Dark Lord," I reply, laughing in relief. "The names don't have to fit. Or perhaps we're sort of being ham-fisted into something that only partially fits. But that's irrelevant. It's what Echo *means* with the description. Vanquish means to defeat. To subdue. To conquer. It doesn't have to include death."

"No way," Sandro says. "But it's always used for things like, to vanquish a foe."

"That still doesn't have to mean kill." How could he have not known this? Then again, I hadn't gone digging into the true meaning of my Role Requirement until it was too late. I suppose I shouldn't be too hard on the kid.

"Ask Echo to define the word," I tell Sandro.

His eyes unfocus for a moment. Then he slaps his hand against his face. "Oh my god."

Now that I'm thinking about it, he hadn't actually asked Echo to define what 'dragon' meant either, until I'd asked him to do so. "You know, you really should try to use Echo more often."

Sandro collapses back into his seat. "Sorry. I've been trying not to. She scares the Shroud."

Ah. That does explain some things.

"Well," I look around at the others. "All's well that ends well, I suppose."

"Then it's resolved?" Mirzayael asks.

"It seems so." I watch Sandro, who's in the process of sheathing his sword. "As long as he captures a wyvern every couple of months, his Role Requirement will no longer be a problem."

Gardi looks between all of us, faintly baffled. "Is this some sort of Fyrethian custom?"

Salvia lands beside them. "No. I'm equally confused."

"It's a curse," Mirzayael says before I can even begin to think about how I'd explain everything. "Discretion is appreciated."

Salvia bows their head. "Of course, my lord."

Gardi still just looks confused.

As the air starts to clear of both beetles and wyverns, Mirzayael gestures for everyone to return to their seats. "Get strapped back in. We've just the last few levels to go, then I am happy to call this scouting mission complete."

As everyone gets secured, Mirzayael mentally nudges me. *"I wish your Role Requirement could be fixed so easily."*

"Perhaps it will," I think. *"Moving the city within the Ruin's ambient storm arcana will likely help. And finishing up the watchtower spell circuit should also be a significant contribution."*

"And if they aren't?" Mirzayael asks as Ollie pushes off to glide down the last of the floating islands. *"What could you do then that would begin to compare to providing the city with infinite power and developing defenses against the gods?"*

Those do sound like significant accomplishments to outshine. *"Then I'll be quite happy to remain close to the city,"* I tell her. *"But let's cross that bridge when we get there."*

As we approach the floor of the Ruins—a green valley with a lake filled from a waterfall draining from layers above—we do indeed run into the amphiptere Attiru warned us about. It hisses, slithering from the clouds. Before I even have time to shout a warning, Ollie whips his head in its direction and lets loose a thunderous roar. The serpent, about half Ollie's size, shrinks part way back into the clouds, uncertain. Ollie launches an Ice Beam at it next, and the amphiptere beats a hasty retreat, its tail briefly whipping through the mist as it flees.

"That was easy," Mirzayael remarks. "Attiru made it sound like a bigger threat."

"Without a dragon on our side, I suspect it would have been." I glance around the valley as Ollie flaps his wings, slowing for the landing. "It might still be trouble for your guards to root out, but now at least we know where to find it."

"A problem for another day," Mirzayael agrees. "Unless there's anything else we should take care of, I think we can start to head back."

"I'M THIRSTY," Ollie says, folding up his wings and stretching like a cat. "AND TIRED."

"A nap will have to wait until we're back in the Fortress." I glance over at the lake and waterfall. "Do you suppose it's potable?"

"For a dragon, maybe," Mirzayael says, sounding dubious. "I doubt it's salt water, but I wouldn't drink it without running it through the dracid's purification system first."

"I'll grab a sample of it, then," I say. "It could affect where we want to settle the city." I gesture for the others as I get unbuckled. "Might as well stretch your legs."

Everyone dismounts, and Ollie bounds over to the lake, the rest of us trailing casually after.

"Where should we put the city?" Mirzayael muses, looking around the valley. It's about five times the size of the Fortress, so there will be plenty of room to expand. The lake is off toward what I decide to call the north side, while the lowest hanging "stepping stones" of the Drifting Isles are roughly to the east. Along the south side is a field of exposed ruins.

"We could set down there," I say, gesturing to the empty west section. "Though it might be better to have easier access to the stepping stones. We could settle between them and the lake, but then we'd be further from the ruins, if we wanted to investigate them."

"We could always just land in the middle," Mirzayael suggests. "Equal access to everything. We'll just need to be mindful of land that we could use for agriculture..."

We continue to chat on our short walk to the lake. To my surprise, Salvia and Gardi are speaking, too. Sandro appears the most relaxed I've ever seen him, and he even smiles faintly as he cranes his head up at our surroundings.

Ollie leans down to take a drink, and just as his chin touches the water, the surface erupts in a geyser.

Chapter Forty-Seven

Hydra

A wave blasts into us, knocking everyone but Ollie from their feet. My fingers drag through the flooded grass as I try to claw my way to a stop. The air resonates with a deep roar—not Ollie's roar. I cough out a mouthful of water and wipe more from my eyes, looking up.

A long, serpentine neck cranes above us. Its face is somewhere part way between a dragon and a snake, with catfish-like whiskers, yellow eyes, teal scales, and a fan of fins crowning its head and sweeping down its neck. Its head is smaller than Ollie's, but it towers above us, and its neck is almost certainly longer.

"Oh god," Sandro cries, staring up at the sea serpent. "We're screwed!"

"Everyone get up," Mirzayael shouts, hauling Sandro to his feet. Gardi and Salvia are nearby, also picking themselves up. "We're not screwed. Weapons out!"

"And back away," I add. "Slowly. Don't take your eyes off it. It's aquatic—let's just get away from the bank."

"But—" Sandro starts.

"Move!" Mirzayael shoves him behind her, her gaze flickering to me, then Salvia and Gardi.

The serpent flicks its tongue at the air, craning its head down toward us. From its length, it could easily pick any of us off.

Ollie steps forward, roaring into its face. The sea serpent flinches back with a hiss, its attention turning to Ollie. My heart skips a beat. By sheer strength I'm sure Ollie would win the fight, but I'm still worried about him getting hurt. What if it's venomous?

I Check the creature.

"But guys," Sandro tries again, his voice lifting an octave in desperation. "I don't think getting away from the water will work! It's a—"

[Check,] Echo says. [Hydra.]

The water to the left of the serpent's head ripples.

"Ollie!" I shout. "Get back!"

A second head explodes from the water, darting toward Ollie as he's still focused on the first.

"*AH!*" Ollie startles as he jerks away. He swats a paw at the second head, batting it away, while the first takes advantage of the distraction and lunges for his neck.

I blast my Jets on, sending up a spray of water and dirt as I rocket toward him. The first head bites down as Ollie tries to twist away, its teeth glancing off his shoulder. I don't have time to feel relieved, as the second is already striking again, the two heads keeping up a relentless assault.

"*ICE BEAM!*" Ollie thinks as he unleashes a blast at the nearest head.

At the same time I launch a Fireball at the other. Ollie's ice clips the neck of one, frosting its fins, while my Fireball catches the second in a hiss of steam. Both heads shriek, and dive back underwater.

"Fall back!" I shout, swooping down toward Ollie. My flight is clumsier with the water weighing my feathers down, but it's the least of my worries. I cut out my flames, falling to Ollie's neck. I grip his spines with hands shaking from adrenaline, watching the two ripples where the heads had disappeared. "I'm here. Get back!"

Which is when the third head strikes.

This one doesn't burst from the water. It moves slow enough I don't even notice it until the tip of its head breaches the surface. Mirzayael must see it, too, because she lets out a warning shout.

The head stays flush with the ground, darting out over the grass. It's the furthest from Ollie and I, but the others are within striking distance.

I can feel Ollie inhale a breath, readying for another Ice Beam, while Sandro draws his sword, and Mirzayael and Salvia ready their spears. The hydra's mouth opens, revealing two giant fangs.

Instead of striking, however, a jet of water blasts from its mouth. It strikes Salvia and Gardi head-on, and knocks Mirzayael and Sandro from their feet. Ollie lets loose his second Ice Beam, and the head snaps away, retreating back into the lake.

"Gardi!" Salvia shouts.

The harpy managed to dig their spear into the ground to anchor themself, but the wave of water swept Gardi into the lake. The felis isn't far—already they're struggling to push themself to their feet in waist-deep water, but a V shaped ripple is rapidly shooting their way.

With a burst of wind, Salvia leaps after Gardi, splashing down at their side.

At the same time, the other two heads reemerge, one going for Ollie and I, the other for Mirzayael and Sandro.

Ollie snaps at the one targeting him, and I summon another Fireball. My heart is in my throat. I want to help the others, but we can barely protect ourselves.

"Mirzayael—" I think, following up Ollie's attack with a blast of flame to keep the serpent at bay.

"I'm fine," she replies shortly. *"Focus on your fight. I'll take care of this one."*

Salvia and Gardi have stopped running for the bank, both turned and ready for the head that's coming for them. It bursts from the water, mouth wide. Salvia slashes their spear, a blast of wind accompanying it. The head is knocked off course. Salvia wraps an arm around Gardi, crouches, and then the water around them is blown back with a sharp gust of wind.

They're clearly not used to carrying so much weight—given the harpy's lightweight bone structure, Gardi must weigh at least twice as much—but it's enough to launch them back toward the bank. They both hit the sodden ground and go skidding back in a spray of mist.

For a moment, I think they're out of harm's way. Then the heads lift from the water, along with two sinewy claws, as the hydra pulls itself up the bank. Running away just became a much less viable option.

Ollie lurches to the side, and I pull my attention back to our fight. I can't afford to be distracted—Ollie needs my help. As soon as we're done with this one, I can worry about the others.

I take a steadying breath and try not to let myself panic. All those training sessions with Mirzayael can't have been for nothing. Focus on my strengths: spells, information.

I quickly skim the rest of the description Echo had given me about the hydra—I hadn't had time to take in what she was saying in the moment, but it's imperative to know if this hydra is like the one in Earth legends.

[Hydra, level 48.] That's higher than Ollie's forty-five. [These reptiles are solitary creatures, though their multiple heads effectively make them pack hunters. Ranging from one to five, a hydra can continue to live so long as one of its heads persists.]

The heads won't regenerate if they're cut off? I ask quickly, pushing a Blaze in the shape of a wall toward the hydra's head.

[Negative,] Echo says to my extreme relief. [No known variety of complex animal can live once its head has been cut off.] She might as well have thrown on an 'obviously' at the end.

"Sandro!" I call. He's hesitantly backed away behind Mirzayael. She whips her spear in a blur before her, forcing the hydra to back off. "You can kill it. It won't grow back!"

"Are you sure?" he calls, not taking his eyes off the serpent.

"Yes!" I throw another Fireball at the hydra. "It's not like Earth hydras. Fight back!"

"*What?*" Mirzayael mentally wonders.

"*Explain later,*" I think.

[Mana depleted,] Echo reports. [Further uses of mana will access Bonus Mana.]

Shit. That's the mana dedicated to keeping the city afloat. Of course, we have a few weeks' worth of mana left, but if I use too much, we won't have any choice but to land here; there won't be enough left for any backup plans.

I grit my teeth, torn.

"*Mirzayael, is this it?*" I quickly ask her. "*Are we committed to this place?*"

Mirzayael has lashed several threads around the hydra's head, and it's thrashing in her grip, threatening to yank her off the ground.

"*Is now the time?*" she grunts.

"*Yes,*" I say. "*Quickly. Is this it?*"

The hydra snaps at Salvia, catching their spear in its mouth. It jerks its head to the side, cracking the weapon in two and jerking it from their hands. Salvia is sent sprawling to the ground.

"*Yes,*" Mirzayael says. She yanks with all her might, wrestling the hydra's head toward the ground. "*This is it. Monsters or not, we will make this place our own.*"

That's just what I needed to hear.

"Ollie, try to pin it," I tell him. "I'll distract."

"*PIN? OH, UH, OKAY!*"

I tap into the bonus mana and summon the largest Blaze I've ever made.

The third hydra's head lunges for Salvia. Gardi steps in front of them, launching a jet of ice straight down its throat.

Mirzayael shouts, "Now!"

Sandro races forward, bringing his sword down on the hydra's neck. It doesn't cut all the way through, but the creature screams.

I circle the wall of flame around our own hydra's head, placing it behind the sea serpent. It hisses, following the fire. I pull back, and the fire races toward it. The head jerks away from it—toward us. Ollie lunges forward, snapping it between its teeth. The serpent shrieks, whipping around. There's enough of its neck left exposed that it could bite Ollie back. He slaps a paw toward its head, blocking its strike, then slams it into the ground.

Ollie lets go with his teeth, planting his other paw further down its neck, keeping the hydra pinned despite its desperate thrashes. He's breathing hard, but swings his head back toward the others.

Sandro retreats as the hydra he and Mirzayael are fighting pulls free of her silk, but its head is hanging awkwardly and bleeding profusely.

Salvia and Gardi's hydra is encased in ice, thrashing desperately. Gardi helps Salvia to their feet.

Time for me to end this quickly, before anyone has a chance to get seriously hurt.

I jump off Ollie's back, activating my Jets to slow my fall, and land near our hydra's head. "Keep it still," I tell Ollie. I point a finger at the creature's head and focus another Blaze at my fingertip.

I focus the flames, compressing them as tight as I can manage while funneling more mana into the attack. Denser... denser...

"Ollie, how are Mirzayael and the others doing?" I ask.

As soon as Ollie turns to look, I let go of the attack. A blindingly bright condensed beam of energy shoots straight through the hydra's skull, and it goes limp.

[New spell obtained!] Echo says. [Lightbeam. A spell which focuses a burning beam of light on an intended target: the power of the spell scales with mana expenditure.]

"*I THINK THEY'RE OKAY,*" Ollie says, oblivious to the execution I just performed. He survived the battle with Jorria; he hunts live animals. He's no stranger to death. Yet it still doesn't feel right to have him watch as I kill the creature he's holding down. "*THE OTHER HEADS ARE STILL FLAILING AROUND, BUT THEY'RE SLOWER NOW.*"

"Then let's help them finish it," I say.

Ollie looks back at the head he's standing on. "*OH! IT STOPPED MOVING. I MUST HAVE KILLED IT.*"

He says it so casually, like he's remarking on the weather. I need to forge a better life for this kid. I can't let him become numb to death.

"HEY!" Ollie's translator calls, comparatively quiet. His thunderous leaps do a far better job of announcing his presence. "LET ME HELP!"

I sigh, Jetting after him.

As Ollie stops by Mirzayael and I fly to catch up, I keep an eye on Salvia and Gardi. The hydra's head is engulfed in so much ice, I'm not sure it can even breathe. Salvia leaps into the air, pausing above the hydra's slowly thrashing head. They blast themself down, ramming into the hydra's neck and sending it crashing to the grass. Gardi fires more ice at it, anchoring its head in place.

Salvia lands beside them. I can't hear the exchanged words, but Gardi appears to say something, touching an arm that Salvia's holding awkwardly against their chest. Salvia shakes their head with a smile.

"Ollie, grab its head," Mirzayael says as I land beside her. "It's too far back for my lines to reach."

"OKAY!" Now that the hydra is injured and moving slower, it's exceptionally easy for Ollie to bite the hydra's head. He sits down with it, resting his chin on the ground. "LIKE THIS?"

Sandro steps forward, a yellow light washing over his sword. He's frowning—not out of fear, but concentration. When he swings the blade down, a fan of magic follows the strike, and his sword passes through the hydra's neck as easily as if it were made of foam.

"Ollie," I start to say, but he's already tipped his head back and crunched into the severed hydra head, and in a few more quick bites, it's down his gullet. Sandro has returned to looking extremely nervous, which is understandable given the carnage that's dripping from Ollie's mouth.

"THAT'S TASTY," he says, licking his muzzle. "LIKE FISH, BUT ENOUGH FOR ME TO ACTUALLY EAT!"

I head over to Gardi and Salvia next. "Everyone all right over here?"

"Salvia's arm is injured," Gardi says.

"It's nothing," Salvia objects. "A guard should be able to handle far worse."

"Even so, make sure you check in with Opal to get that looked at when we get back," I tell them. "It won't help anyone for you to not be operating at your full capabilities when we need you."

They bow their head. "Of course, my lord."

Gardi snorts. "Sure, you'll listen to her but not me."

"Why would I listen to a prisoner?" Salvia's tone is teasing, like they're partaking in some sort of inside joke.

Gardi's eyes dance with mischief. "I can think of a few reasons."

Huh.

"*It's your fault,*" Mirzayael thinks, amused. "*You forced them to spend all their time together for the last few months. What did you think would happen?*"

"*I was just hoping they'd come to not hate each other,*" I admit. "*Technically, mission accomplished.*"

Mirzayael laughs.

As Salvia and Gardi continue to flirt, I step away to examine the frozen hydra. It's stopped moving, but it doesn't hurt to be safe; I put another Lightbeam through its skull.

[Hydra defeated,] Echo says. [EXP threshold met. Level up!]

"Oh!" Ollie lifts his head. "Echo says it's defeated."

"I got a Level-Up," Sandro says, his gaze going distant.

I turn my attention to my own Stats. "Me as well."

I'd actually managed to level up a couple times over the last few months, training with Mirzayael and practicing my spells. Defeating this creature pushes me up another two.

[Name: Fyre]

[Species: Harpy]

[Subspecies: Phoenix]

[Class: Psion]

[Level: 30]

[HP: 100/100]

[Mana: 650/650]

[Bonus Mana: 7,925,173]

[Role: The Dark Lord]

That Bonus Mana is starting to make me nervous. By my count, it will last for another four days of flight—more if we power off non-essentials. We should still have time to move the Fortress inside, but it's cutting things a lot closer than I'd like.

[Threshold met,] Echo continues. [Path of the Mage: +150 mana.]

Goodness. My mana pool has quadrupled since I first arrived on this world. I'll pass Ollie's mana pool soon enough—though I suppose his health being twenty times that of anyone else I've seen (save the gods) probably makes up for it.

"This is very odd to witness," Mirzayael remarks, watching the three of us.

"What are they talking about?" Gardi asks.

I blink my stats away. "It's a... quantitative type of magic. Don't worry about it."

Salvia raises an eyebrow. "I wasn't before you said that."

"Later," Mirzayael says curtly. "For now, we need to get back to the Fortress—before we run into any more surprises."

Salvia straightens. "Yes, my lord."

We check each other over for injuries, then check Ollie's saddle to make sure the transport's harness wasn't damaged in the fight. Everything appears in order, so we climb back aboard, and Ollie is more than happy to fly us home.

Mirzayael, who's seated next to me, holds out a hand, and I take it, resting my head against her shoulder. She traces feathers down the back of my hand.

Gardi and Salvia are also seated next to each other, speaking in private tones. Seeing them like this makes me smile.

And Sandro is seated alone, looking out over the floating rocks and clouds we pass by. His legs are tucked up close, and the Shroud is wrapped tightly around him, but his hands are loosely clasped around his knees, and he seems to be holding his head a bit higher. Perhaps speaking with the Cloak, or just reacting to a thought, his face lights up in a grin. I've never seen a smile like that on him. Maybe defeating that hydra was a much-needed boost to his self-esteem.

Mirzayael mentally chuckles at this last thought. "*It seems he got to slay his first dragon after all.*"

She's right. I let out a sigh, closing my eyes. "*May it be the last.*"

Chapter Forty-Eight
New Horizons

Four days pass a lot faster than you would think when hitting the time limit means your city falls out of the sky.

After our initial exciting foray into the Drifting Isles, the next time we return it's with most of the city's guards. We spend the next two days taking as much of the hydra meat as we can back to preserve it, while rooting out any other major threats. The flock of griffons are a real danger, but they also appear to stick to their territory, so they can be dealt with later. The amphiptere also makes a cautious reappearance, but with Ollie around, it keeps its distance.

Ollie and I spend the time mapping out as much of the ruined city as we can, documenting the different levels and their contents, and recording which animals can be found where—and which territories to avoid. I'd like to leave as much of the ecosystem intact as possible, only killing when it becomes apparent that the predators will be an active and persistent threat. From the hydra alone, we already have more meat than we know what to do with.

Only one day's worth of mana is left as we slowly ease the Fortress into the Isles, which is significantly more troublesome than it at first appeared.

Some of the floating stones, especially toward ground level, are too large to easily move out of the Fortress's way. And since they twist up the funnel like a spiral staircase, finding a suitable gap in the mesh of vines and cloudstone is easier said than done. All this is made double difficult by the storm arcanum-infused cloud, which prevents anyone from seeing through it, no matter how many harpies try to blow it apart.

Even so, we're able to inch the Fortress inside. The city takes up about a quarter of the area on the base level, and we hover there, the lowest stabilizers just meters above the ground, as we position the Fortress over the land where we plan to set it down. In the end we decide on the middle; it puts us equidistant from the stepping stones, some ruins, and the lake, while also leaving a large, open field that could be developed for agriculture.

Landing the city is its own ordeal.

"We're in position," Mirzayael thinks. *"Don't wait too long or Dizzi might have a heart attack. She's flying circles around the other harpies, making sure everyone knows what to look for."*

The plan is for Dizzi and the other harpies to act as my eyes, and to relay any needed adjustments through Mirzayael. In an ideal world I'd also be outside, tweaking things on the fly, but I know the modifications I'm about to make to the city will likely pull me too deep into the Dungeon Core to be aware of my body. In a rare turn of events, I'm actually seated on the throne. I can almost feel the Core's presence in the stone just behind my head.

"You can tell Dizzi I'm about to begin," I reply to Mirzayael, mentally reaching for the Dungeon Core.

Much like Dizzi, the Core is also buzzing with excitement. It knows it's about to have more rocks to explore. The longer we've been aloft, the more the Dungeon Core has been bemoaning its extreme boredom. Whenever it's gotten especially depressed, Ollie has flown down to the surface to bring back a clawful of dirt and rocks for the Core to eat, reminding it that we'll be landing soon. That always cheered the Core right up, but the effect was only temporary, and the days between its complaints have been steadily decreasing.

Is it time? The Core ping pongs around my head. Can it eat all the tasty rocks it wasn't allowed to eat before? It has done so well at not eating the tasty rocks.

Yes, I think with a chuckle. *You've done very well. But we're going to have to go about this methodically; we only have enough mana for one shot. I'll be maneuvering the city down while you devour the cloudstone base from the ground up. We're going to have to time this carefully so we don't drop the city. As soon as we make contact with the ground, I'll give you more mana to expand into the surrounding land. Alright?*

Surrounding land! It can't wait to expand.

After we touch down, I emphasize. Though honestly, I'm not really sure it absorbed any of those instructions; I've yet to see evidence it can hold onto more than one thought at a time. I'll just have to walk it through what I need as I need it.

Alright. Here we go.

First, I put us into a gradual descent. Very gradual. Momentum can build up far too quickly with this much mass.

After a few minutes, Mirzayael speaks up. *"Dizzi says the lowest rudders are about to make contact."*

Core, I think, maneuvering our mental Map. I bring us down to the bottom of the base of the city and point out the lowest hanging stabilizers. *You can eat these first.*

Okay! The Core happily munches up the rock. Rock that I used the Dungeon Core to create in the first place. Usually it complains about eating rock it's already eaten once before, but it's either just desperate to eat anything, or wildly inconsistent with what it does and doesn't like to eat on any given day.

Probably both.

Once those are gone, I continue to lower the city. Mirzayael gives me updates on the space between the surface and the lowest point of the cloudstone base, and I continue to have the Core gradually erode the cloudstone beneath us.

And then we make contact. Mirzayael tells me at the same time I feel it: the Fortress won't lower any further because something is in our way. I start to feed a trickle of mana into the Dungeon Core so it can expand into the ground, allowing us to "see" it. This is where things will start to get tricky.

There is so much cloudstone beneath the city that if we stopped now, the city wall would be a good five stories above ground level. I'm not sure we'll be able to fully get it flush with the ground, but I'm going to try to get it as close as possible.

The Dungeon Core sets to work following my plan, eating away at both the ground its range is expanding into and the bottom of the Fortress. Gradually the Fortress lowers, and through the Dungeon Core I can feel the weight of the Fortress increasingly pressing down on the earth below. It's getting heavier by the minute, picking up speed as its buoyancy decreases and its base sinks further into the earth.

We're going too slow. I'm worried about dropping the city if we erode too much cloudstone too quickly, but now a fresh danger has presented itself; if we don't get the Fortress settled soon, the city might tip onto its side.

Stop eating the cloudstone, I quickly tell the Core. *Eat away the earth beneath it instead. Anywhere the cloudstone touches, take that dirt into your Inventory.*

Yay! New dirt!

The Dungeon Core happily complies, sinking its teeth into the ground.

I pay close attention to every contact point as the Fortress steadily sinks. My mind is spread across the base of the entire kingdom, keeping track of dozens of elements at once. I feel stretched, my mind split so many ways. But I can't stop now; the fate of the entire city depends on it. I strain to stay focused, leaning on the Dungeon Core for strength as it easily splits its attention a hundred ways at once, steadily carving out the ground.

After an eternity, Mirzayael's voice reappears in my mind. "*It's level,*" she reports. "*The base of the city is flush with the ground. You did it.*"

I let go of the Dungeon Core, falling back into the throne with a gasp. *That's it,* I tell the Core, breathing hard as if I'd just run a mile. *You can stop.*

Awww. But what if it doesn't *want* to stop?

I rub my forehead. The world feels like it's tipping. If it weren't for Mirzayael and Dizzi's confirmation that I've settled it properly, I'd think we were leaning to one side.

You can explore the area, I say, giving it more mana to expand into the Drifting Isles. *But no eating just yet.*

It fakes a pout, but it's actually quite happy to go tunneling through the ground. I put some space between our minds as I try to clear my head.

There's a strange sound outside. A faint roar. It's only when I hear someone closer, within the palace, that I realize what I'm hearing.

It's cheers. The entirety of Fyreneth's Fortress is cheering.

It takes that long for the reality of the situation to sink in. We did it. We found our new home.

There's still much to do to make this place our own. There's arcana not just in the ground, but in the air as well, and as we start measuring the magic density in the area, we find that the source is somewhere near the top of the Drifting Isles, and the magic is effectively pouring down, level by level, to the base. We won't be able to directly connect the Fortress into that source of the magic, but there's so much all around us that it's not an issue. Dizzi's team of researchers and artificers gets to work on creating spell networks to collect and direct the ambient storm arcana so we can feed it directly into the Fortress's networks.

I keep, and even expand, the airship dock that we created along the top of the wall. I anticipate we'll have even more visitors than before. Soon we'll need to start making airships of our own.

"At that point, we'll be able to take you to a city of your choice," I tell Gardi. We're outside the city, overseeing all the developments that are taking place. It feels so strange to be outside of the Fortress, looking up at it. For a moment I recall the first time I saw it, briefly illuminated by my flames in those distant, dark caverns.

"I see," Gardi says, exchanging a look with Salvia.

Mirzayael had told Salvia that they no longer needed to escort Gardi around the palace, but they'd continued to spend most of their time together. How strange.

"*Now you're just being cruel,*" Mirzayael mentally teases.

"*Not intentionally,*" I object. "*Think of it as a nudge.*"

"The same offer extends to you, Sandro," I continue, watching workers up on the dock. "If you want to be taken anywhere..."

"Oh, no," Sandro quickly says. "Definitely not. I'd much rather stay here." Then he looks uncertain. "If that's okay? I don't want to assume—"

"Of course it's okay," I chuckle.

Relief spills over his face. "Good. Because I was thinking. They say people use wyverns as pets and messengers, right? Well, what if I started training some of them? It would be fun! And also satisfy my Role Requirement. And then maybe we could trade some of them?" Once more he pales. "Unless that's a terrible idea."

"It's a wonderful idea," I assure him. "In that case, Gardi—"

"My lords, if I may," Salvia blurts out. They're standing stiffly, staring at the air between me and Mirzayael.

"Yes?" Mirzayael prompts.

They continue to look at neither of us. "I would like to vouch for Gardi's character. They may be from Jorria, but it does not define them. They are kind and honest. When fighting the hydra, they saved my life."

"Only after you saved mine—" Gardi starts.

"As such," Salvia says, raising their voice. "I would like to request that Gardi be given the opportunity to reside here and become a citizen of our kingdom if they so desire."

They take in a breath after pushing all their last words out in one.

Mirzayael stares at them for a moment. "Your approval is noted. But I'd like to hear Gardi's opinion on the matter."

"Me?" Gardi's fur poofs up slightly. "I... I don't know what you want me to say."

"What you want, dear," I say gently. "If this is where you'd like to stay, or if you'd like to leave. There are no wrong answers. But we must hear it from you."

Their tail nervously flicks back and forth, and now it's Gardi who's avoiding our gaze.

"Ever since Ragna left, I haven't known what I want," Gardi admits. "Home feels so far away—and not just by distance. I'd never felt so alone, and you went out of your way to make me feel included. I've realized that... a lot of what I was told about Fyrethians isn't true. That's been difficult to work through. But you've been so patient with me. Probably more than I deserve."

I smile softly. "Gardi—"

"Please let me finish." They finally meet my eyes. "I am not yet ready to call this place my home. It is so different from everything I've known. I am still adjusting. But Salvia has helped ease that process. And while I am not sure where I want to live, I know that I will be content as long as I am at their side." Gardi steps forward and takes Salvia's hand. Salvia is blushing fiercely. "You see, we are courting."

"Oh!" I say, trying my best to look surprised.

I clearly don't do a very good job of it.

"You knew?" Salvia says.

"Well," I say, glancing at Mirzayael, "we had some suspicions..."

"Wait, it was supposed to be a secret?" Sandro says.

Gardi dips their head in embarrassment.

"Sorry!" Sandro quickly backtracks. "Was that rude? It's none of my business. Even if it was very obvious."

Salvia shoots Sandro a glare.

"I mean, in a good way!" He shuffles back, his Shroud rippling nervously. "I think I'm going to leave now."

As Sandro follows through, I find myself chuckling. At Sandro, at Salvia and Gardi, at myself. Why do we make relationships more difficult than they need to be?

Salvia is still holding their chin up, even though their face has nearly turned red from mortification. "I understand if we don't have your approval. I am willing to accept whatever punishment you administer, though I will not terminate the relationship."

They're so fierce—so fierce, and so young. I can't stop a small laugh from escaping my lips.

"You are not going to be punished," I assure them. "You are free to date whomever you like."

Salvia looks between me and Mirzayael, halfway between suspicious and surprised. "Even if they're not Fyrethian?"

Now it's Mirzayael who chuckles. "It would be hypocritical of me to condemn a relationship with a foreigner." She looks at me. "Being Fyrethian is not where you're born. It's who you choose to be."

Affection swells within both of us, reflected back at one another.

"*EWWWW!*" Ollie abruptly cuts in. "*YOU GUYS ARE BEING MUSHY AGAIN!*"

I laugh, sequestering our thoughts away from the kid.

Salvia bows low before us, and after a moment of hesitation, Gardi awkwardly dips their head as well.

"Thank you, my lords," Salvia says, straightening up. "I understand our circumstances are unprecedented, but I appreciate your understanding."

"Perhaps not as unprecedented as it feels," Mirzayael says, turning her attention back to the couple. "Our people have been at odds for generations, but in Fyreneth's day, her city was open to everyone. She encouraged people from every species and kingdom to visit and make a home within her walls. Maybe it's time we more proactively seek to revitalize her vision."

I'm overcome with such pride to hear Mirzayael speak those words. She's had such a cold life, filled with hardship and loss. And yet, she was brave enough to open her heart to someone new. She was strong enough to look past Gardi's origins. She's compassionate enough to recreate Fyreneth's vision, despite every instinct she learned warning her otherwise.

In the time that I've been at her side, I've witnessed her bloom in ways I never would have imagined.

Then again, I'm sure I've also changed in ways that have taken place too slowly and subtly for me to notice as well.

"Thank you, my lords," Salvia repeats. They're still holding Gardi's hand. They both stand there awkwardly for a moment.

"You can leave," I permit, trying not to laugh. Ah, to be young. "And to reiterate, Salvia, you are no longer assigned to accompany Gardi. And Gardi, you are no longer to be monitored. You will be considered a guest to the Fortress until you have any desire to change that. Perhaps you can help them find appropriate accommodations, Salvia?"

"Right away, my lords," they say, taking the suggestion as seriously as an order.

I don't have the opportunity to clarify myself before the two are hurrying off. Gardi says something to Salvia, and then the harpy does something I haven't witnessed since their father's death: they laugh.

Mirzayael and I stroll through the valley, blue sky far overhead and soft grass beneath our feet.

"What you said about proactively pursuing Fyreneth's vision," I venture. "I have a selfish question to ask."

"Somehow, I doubt it," Mirzayael remarks.

"It is!" I insist. "In a way." I watch some of the workers picking their way over the hydra's carcass, cleaning and disassembling the bones. I'm not sure what we'll use them for, but I'm certain they'll be put to use.

"I'd like to try to find more people like Sandro," I finally say. "I worry that a lot of them are suffering from their Role Requirements without support. Blair and Lisari indicated there were many more—both captured, and freely wandering the world. I'm not sure what I can do for those who are already in the gods' custody, but our mobility at least makes it easier to search for the ones who haven't yet been captured."

"And how exactly is this selfish?" Mirzayael asks.

"It might put Fyrethians in danger," I say. "Now that we're somewhere stable and have access to a new supply of magic, losing the Dungeon Core doesn't mean we lose the Fortress. But accumulating Travelers will likely make us a target."

Mirzayael snorts. "Fyre, are you planning to leave the Fortress?"

"What?" I cry. "No! Of course not."

"Is Ollie?"

"No..."

"Sandro?"

I think I see her point. "Us being here already makes us a target."

"I doubt the number of Travelers you find will change that," Mirzayael says. "But it's an irrelevant fear, regardless." Her eyes flash with sudden fierceness. "I will not allow the gods to take you away. I will not allow them to hurt anyone under our kingdom's protection."

There is a part of me that is frightened by her conviction. I worry she'll do something rash to back those words. I wonder if Fyreneth had sworn something similar.

But her determination isn't without justification. The final watchtower is nearing completion, and that will be the real test of our ability to withstand the gods.

I try to let go of my fears. There's nothing we can do about it at this moment. For now, it's enough to have Mirzayael's steadfast support.

"Thank you." I look up at her to find she's already looking down at me with a fond smile. "For everything."

"Everything? That's quite a lot," she teases.

I shake my head with a quiet laugh. "Alright, then. Thank you for this life."

Her playful look fades. "That's still quite a lot."

"It is," I agree. "But this life has been more than I ever could have hoped for. I've never been so happy and felt so much at home. Sometimes it feels like more than I deserve."

"Fyre," Mirzayael says quietly. She bends her legs to lower herself to my eye level. It's close enough to see her faint freckles. I love her freckles. She reaches out to cup my cheek. "You deserve the world."

She's got it entirely backward. How can she not see that? I place a hand over hers, but before I can say as much, she gently pulls me in.

As we kiss, the evidence I was assembling to the contrary crumbles away.

EPILOGUE

"That should do it," Dizzi says, straightening up as she claps dust off her hands and then plants them on her hips. She looks critically at the spell circle beneath her. "We've double and triple checked the runes. We've measured each line to within five millimeters. We've learned as much as we can on spell theory from the surface. As far as I can tell, there's nothing more we can do to prepare. I'm ninety-nine percent sure this will work."

"That's very confident," I remark.

"Okay, seventy-five percent confident it will work," she says with a grin. "I was being hyperbolic."

Seventy-five percent is both more realistic and more concerning. But we have no reason not to try it.

Apart from it potentially doing something completely different from what we intend.

"Let's give it a go," I say, heading for the watchtower's balcony. "The others are waiting in the throne room."

"I'll stay here," Dizzi says. "Keep an eye on the circle. Also, I want to see what it looks like outside."

"Fair enough." I hop up on the railing. "Report back once the test is complete."

I Jet away from the watchtower and head back to the palace, making it back to the throne room in under a minute. Mirzayael, Nek, and Torim are waiting for me.

"We're all set," I tell them. "*Ollie, have you landed yet?*"

"*YEP,*" he says. "*I'M ON THE BLUE PAVILION. DO YOU THINK IT WILL LOOK COOL?*"

"*We're about to find out.*"

I gesture for Mirzayael to take a seat on the throne. "I'll keep an eye on the spell circles through the Dungeon Core to make sure everything goes smoothly. But it will be important for all present to know how to operate the spell network in case of an emergency."

Mirzayael awkwardly takes a seat, and the throne adjusts to her height, the stone visor sliding down over her eyes. She sucks in a breath, gripping the armrests.

"Are you alright?" Nek asks, hovering nervously nearby.

"Yes," she says. "It's just very strange. There are so many spells here to sort through. How are you able to handle all this at once?"

"I'm not," I admit. "The Dungeon Core does most of the heavy lifting. But for this, you only need to focus on the Watchtower spells. Can you find them?"

After a moment of tense quiet, Mirzayael says, "Yes. I think so."

"Alright then." I try not to betray my nerves. "Let's fire it up."

I watch the spell network through the Dungeon Core. The final tower, which Dizzi has dubbed the Control Tower, comes online, then Shield Tower and Eye Tower. We don't need Watchtower Three for this—at least, not today.

"It's working," Mirzayael reports. "Eye and Shield are feeding into the Control's architecture. It just requires input parameters now."

"Let's go with age again," I suggest. I've tried to get it to operate on Levels, but the magic didn't understand what I meant. It's not connected to the System, it seems.

I watch Mirzayael set the exclusion parameter to anyone over three hundred years old. Immediately, the Fortress's mana starts rapidly ticking down. Not enough to be concerning, given the amount of endless magic we have access to.

"Alright," she says. "I believe it's ready to turn on."

"Do it." My stomach flutters with anticipation.

The spell activates. I switch over to Ollie's senses, looking through his eyes as a dome of magic spreads across the sky. In a matter of seconds, the faint, orange shell has completely encompassed the Fortress.

"*OOOOOH*," Ollie thinks. "*PRETTY!*"

"It's up," I say, switching back to metaphorically peer over Mirzayael's shoulder. The spell is consuming an enormous amount of mana. Not enough to drain our supply today, but enough to wring us dry eventually. That's alright. We can start saving up now.

"Does it work?" Torim asks.

I check the spell network Mirzayael activated.

Control Tower contained a strange spell circle that took Dizzi and her crew significantly longer to puzzle out. It turns out its function was to combine the spells of the other watchtowers, creating new and interesting applications. Whatever was in Broken Tower has been destroyed, but the other three are already powerful enough on their own.

Shield Tower has the spell which creates a defensive dome over the city. Eye Tower contains the surveillance spell. When combined though the Control Tower, we're able to program certain conditions into the dome based on what is observed from the surveillance spell.

For instance, we can set the dome up such that anyone can pass through it—unless you're over three hundred years old.

In other words, it's an anti-god shield.

"There's no way to know for sure," I admit. And hopefully we won't have to test it anytime soon. "But the numbers look good."

"I think it will work," Mirzayael says. "I can... *feel* that it will do what we intended. This is a powerful asset."

Which itself is an understatement. I wonder if Fyreneth ever had the opportunity to use it, or if she was caught off guard before her designs were complete.

Either way, it will serve to protect her people. Across all this time, she's still finding ways to help us.

"Let's power it down for now," I say. "The longer we can keep this combination spell off, the more mana we'll have stored for when we need it. In the meantime, we still have the detection spell going; we'll be alerted if we need to activate the barrier."

"Fine by me," Nek says. He still appears nervous with Mirzayael operating the Fortress's magic.

I feel the spell circle deactivate, and then Mirzayael retracts the visor and stands up. "That was a fun experience." She looks at Nek. "Now you."

The felis looks significantly less excited to stick his head into the magic Fortress-controlling throne, but he makes it through the exercise anyway. Torim and Dizzi also take turns; no one has any trouble with the spells.

"Oh," I say, briefly startled as Dizzi is operating the spells with practiced ease.

Mirzayael tenses. "What is it?"

"My Role Range," I say. "With this spell on, my range is ten thousand kilometers."

"What?" Dizzi cries.

Mirzayael frowns. "What does that mean?"

"It means my range is nearly as big as the entire planet," I say, watching it in awe. Dizzi shuts off the circle, and my range decreases, but not as low as I would have thought. It would still cover over half the planet's surface. Just setting this spell circle up and linking it into the Fortress's spell network, ready to flip on at a moment's notice, has vastly increased my range. I bet when we create more combinations, that will add to the range, too.

Not to mention, simply landing the Fortress on the Drifting Isles was already a significant contribution.

Relief washes over me. If the range is a metric of how well protected the Fortress is, then this tells me my personal contribution to the city's safety is nearly obsolete. The Fyrethians will be able to protect themselves independent from myself and the Dungeon Core.

Good. This is exactly what I'd been hoping for. It's not complete security, but I suspect Fyreneth's Fortress just became the most protected city on the planet.

And I don't intend to stop here.

The other councilors retire as Mirzayael and I move to the red room. Its transformation from a war room to a cozy office has been remarkable. In fact, it's so comfortable, what with all the padded chairs and bookshelves quickly filling up with maps and scrolls, that I've actually started to relax in here even outside of our regular meeting times.

"Captain Marlowe sent a letter that he's garnering interest in our city in Valenia." Mirzayael gestures to the desk as she sinks into one of her arachnoid-designed chairs, rather like an oversized beanbag. "He'll likely return with new potential trade partners in the next few weeks."

I find the letter and glance over it myself. "I'm sure we'll have plenty of company before then." And still so much to do. There's been discussions about extending the Drifting Isles' base layer out beyond the cloud cover, so we will be more easily identifiable. We could also add airship docks out there.

The other option is to work with Attiru on controlling who has access to their tracking maps. They warned us that once it's known how accessible the Drifting Isles has become, we're likely to attract unscrupulous folk looking to plunder the Ruins. We'll have to keep a better eye on the rest of the Isles going forward. I'd rather not develop all the land in the Ruins, allowing as much of the local flora and fauna to continue to live undisturbed as possible. But we'll at least have to scout the land close to the city and set up some protection for the physical ruins themselves.

I chuckle, remembering when I'd thought we'd have some down-time after we finally landed the city. It was a nice thought, anyway.

The Greater Detection spell abruptly activates.

I stiffen, diving into the Dungeon Core in an effort to find where it was tripped. At the same time, my mind hovers over the god barrier—I hadn't anticipated we'd need to use it so soon.

"What is it?" Mirzayael asks, noticing the change in my demeanor.

"*The alarm tripped*," I think, keeping our conversation private. I have no idea where they are or how far their hearing might reach. "*It's a god or a champion.*"

Mirzayael stands up. Her hand brushes against the base of her spear, strapped across her back. "*Should we...*"

"Hello, Fyre."

Mirzayael snaps her spear from her back as a figure steps from the room's only doorway. I reach for my spells—then stop when I see who it is. I don't relax, exactly, but I am relieved.

Blair's gaze shifts over to Mirzayael. "I apologize for startling you. Though I doubt any entrance I could have made would have put you at ease."

Mirzayael withdraws from her fighting stance, but doesn't put her spear away.

"Blair," I say, deactivating the Greater Alarm Spell. I'll activate it again once she's gone so I don't have to have it buzzing in my head the entire time. "To what do we owe the pleasure?"

"*Displeasure*," Mirzayael mentally grumbles.

"I realize it's been a few months," Blair says, still standing at the doorway. "But I found someone I believe you would like to meet. Another Traveler."

I brighten. "Really? And you brought them to me?"

"I will not be making a habit of it," Blair replies, "but this is a special case. He also has a remnant. A rather strong one. He understands the risks of meeting you, and was quite insistent that I ensure you are aware of the risks as well. So this is me informing you: the encounter will likely be more tense than what you experienced with Sandro. Should you consent, I will bring him to meet you."

Mirzayael and I exchange a puzzled look. This is so abrupt. And what exactly does she mean by 'a rather strong' remnant? Like the Dungeon Core?

"*This sounds dangerous*," Mirzayael warns me, and I'm prone to agree.

But I'm the one who wants to take in more Travelers. This could be a good test of what I might experience without warning in the future.

Besides, I'm terribly curious to meet someone Blair describes as 'a special case.'

"Alright," I say. "I'd like to meet him. When should we set up a time?"

"I shall retrieve him now," Blair says, stepping back out of the doorframe.

Mirzayael and I are both raising objections when Blair simply vanishes, as if slipping beneath the surface of the water. The door is abruptly empty.

Mirzayael swears. "You should have led with 'let's establish a time and place first' before you told her you'd like to meet him."

"Sorry," I say, staring at the empty door. "I didn't realize she meant *now*. Well. I suppose there's nothing we can do about it at this stage. Be ready for anything."

"I always am," Mirzayael says.

Silence stretches. Longer than I would have expected. With each passing second, I can feel Mirzayael's tension winding ever tighter. Then, at least a minute later, Blair reappears, rippling back into existence. A man steps out behind her, also materializing in the doorway.

At least, I think he's a man.

He's wearing a charcoal-grey long coat which covers most of his body, but his hands almost appear to be made of crystal—and stranger yet, in place of his head is a floating, inverted, glass prism.

"*Okay,*" Mirzayael thinks. "*I wasn't ready for that.*"

"Fyre," Blair says, gesturing to the figure. "I'd like for you to meet Kanin."

COMING SOON...

Fyre will return in Book 3 of Fyre, *Wild Fyre*, in 2027
and Book 4 of Kanin, *Kanin Fyre*, in May 2026

SANDRO

THANK YOU!

This story never would have been possible without such incredible support from my beta readers and early fans. My Patreon supporters especially have been a huge source of motivation. I owe you the world.

If you enjoyed my book and would like to see more, <u>**a review is the best way you can help me out!**</u> I can't stress enough how important this is for indie authors, especially for a debut. It can make or break a career. Reviewing my book today helps ensure I can publish more tomorrow!

Also, if you'd like to read more short stories about NPSeeds characters, you can read all of them for FREE on **my newsletter.**

Once again, thank you so much for reading my book. It means more than I can say.

BOOKS IN THE NPSEEDS UNIVERSE

Glass Kanin

A Little Salty

Friendly Fyre

Nyte in Shining Armor

About the Author

Kia is the author of *Friendly Fyre* and *Glass Kanin*, and loves writing comedic, quirky, and queer fantasy. When not roller skating or sending people to the Moon, they can be found at home with a cup of tea working on any of their dozens of in-progress books.

You can find more about their projects on their website: www.KiaLeep.com